UNFINISHED BUSINESS

Beverly pulled into the cemetery. Since there was no headstone in place yet, she had to find Dave in relation to the trees and other markers. He was close to the road, in between two pine trees. You could still tell that his mound was fresh, even under the snow. Beverly reached into the back seat to get the flowers. She was not going to get Davey out because it was so cold. She was just going to leave the flowers.

"Fowers," said Davey. From his car seat, he had picked every blossom from the bouquet. Scattered in the back seat were rose petals, lilies and daisies and there remained only a vase full of stems and a couple of stems of ivy. "Fowers."

Beverly was livid. She scooped up some of the flowers from the floor of the car and retrieved a couple of rosebuds off the seat. She couldn't be angry at her son. He was too young to understand. She grabbed the vase and marched over to Dave's gravesite and took it out on him instead. She started throwing flower remains on his grave-- squashed roses, beheaded daisies and plucked carnations. She started yelling. "Happy anniversary! You're supposed to get *me* flowers on our anniversary! You're supposed to be alive! Sure, go die on me and leave me to take care of everything! What do you care if the car is making a funny noise?"

She dumped out the stems and the water and threw the vase into the trunk of the car. Beverly drove away, only she did not go home. After pulling into the Jensens' driveway, Beverly got Davey out of the car, carried him up the walk and rang the doorbell. Evelyn answered.

"Is this the Society to Prevent Child Abuse?" Beverly handed Davey to her. "Good! I'll be back in an hour or two."

"Beverly, are you okay?"

"No, I'm not okay. I'm losing it, big time." Evelyn handed Davey off to her teen-age daughter. "Alison, you're babysitting. I'm going with Beverly."

To Roxanne, Thanks for your support. Enjoy! SLC

Unfinished Business
by
Susan Law Corpany

[signature: Susan Law Corpany]

Hagoth Publishing Company

UNFINISHED BUSINESS

Published 2001
by Hagoth Publishing Company
P.O. Box 6384
Hilo, HI 96720

Printed in the United States of America
First Printing: 2001

ISBN: 0-9712915-0-0

Library of Congress Catalog Card Number: 2001094014

Cover photography: Dana Kehr
Cover design: Thom Curtis

Dedication

in memory of Paul M. Corpany
my "Diamond in the Rough"

and to Scott M. Corpany
who wiped away my tears

CHAPTER ONE
WHAT'S IN A NAME?

"David, it's time to get serious about naming this baby," Beverly groaned, as she laboriously hoisted herself up to a sitting position in her hospital bed. "The birth certificate lady has been around twice already. I promised her next time she came by we would have a name. I'm going home tomorrow."

"Okay, this time you pick the page and I'll pick how many down."

"I mean it!" She maneuvered herself onto her side, trying to find a position that was not painful. "If you open up that stupid baby name book one more time, I'm going to clobber you!"

"You don't look like you could clobber anyone at the moment."

"Then I'll call the nurse to come do it for me!"

"Not in front of little . . ."--he flipped open the book--". . . Bertram." The baby stirred in his glass hospital bassinet. "See, he likes it!"

"He woke up to protest," Beverly said. Soon his stirrings progressed to crying. "I told you so." Beverly reached to pull herself over to the side of the bed.

"Don't get up, honey." Dave jumped up before Beverly could even move to the side of the bed. "I'll change him. How hard can it be?" he asked nonchalantly, but despite his joking manner, his large hands fumbled as he cleaned and diapered his day-old son. Beverly watched, filled with love for the two men in her life. Dave picked up the baby, held him and gazed at him for a few moments before handing him to Beverly. "Here you go, Mama, all clean and ready for dinner. Did I do it right? The diaper's not falling off, is it? It was kind of tricky working around that belly button thing."

"The cord," Beverly corrected her husband, as she settled the baby in her arms and began to nurse him.

"That's a good name--'Cord.' We could name him after that guy in your old ward that liked your chocolate chip cookies--Cordell, and call him 'Cord' for short." Another thought occurred to him. "Or we could name him 'Umbilical' and call him 'Bill' for short."

Beverly laughed and then moaned. "David, stop making me laugh. It hurts! We have gone over every repugnant name in that book! You haven't made one serious suggestion from the time I found out I was pregnant until now. Why don't you like any of the names I've suggested?"

"Like which ones?"

"Clayton. My mother's maiden name."

"They'd call him 'Clay.' Sounds like a piece of dirt."

"Nathan."

"Sounds like an old sea captain."

"Matthew."

"They'd call him 'Matt.' Sounds like something you wipe your feet on."

"Okay then, you'd better make one *serious* attempt at naming this baby, or next time the birth certificate lady comes around, I'm going to name him Nathan David Crandall."

"I like that."

"Nathan? You just said . . ."

"Not Nathan. David. I think we should name him David Bradley Crandall, Jr."

"So that's what you've been holding out for--a junior. I should have known. And you've run every ridiculous name you could think of by me so I'd be sure to go for it!"

"The truth is I took one look at him when he was born, and I said to myself, 'No matter how much I love the name, he just doesn't look like an Elvis Englebert.'"

Beverly ignored him. After all, this had been going on for nine months. She sighed. "What about all the problems, you know, like asking people if they want 'Big Dave' or 'Little Dave?'"

"Well, if they ask for 'Big Dave,' I'll just tell them he's in his crib taking a nap," he said proudly.

Beverly shook her head. "I'm glad *you* are so proud of producing a 10-pound-plus baby. You might have considered *me* in the process," she said wearily. "And if we have anything to say about it, I don't think we should try for another August baby. Going through the third trimester and summer together was not a good plan."

Dave softened. "You've been through the war, that's for sure."

"I guess I had it coming. I never should have picked out all the wimpy-looking women in our childbirth classes who would probably deliver by C-Section. I just never thought--I mean, I'm strong and healthy and athletic. To have to go through all those hours of labor and breathing and everything without drugs trying to have a natural childbirth and then have to have an emergency C-Section--that was not what I had planned."

Dave looked at her affectionately. "Oh, Beverly, my little over-achiever. When are you going to learn to take life easy, like me? This is not some kind of a 10-K race. You're not a failure just because drugs were administered during childbirth."

"I asked the doctor, and he said that this doesn't necessarily mean that I have to have all the rest of our children by C-Section."

"See what I mean? Isn't it supposed to be the wife, hitting the husband with a frying pan when he starts talking about the next baby while his wife is still suffering from the pains of the first one? I'm sure you'll *do it right* the next time, honey, but if you ask me, I say we did just fine. He's healthy. You're alive . . ."

"Just barely."

"Don't you think we should name him after me?"

Beverly ignored him again. "I guess you're right. There's no way to train for this event. And then they give you the baby--like you know what to do because you put a diaper on a doll in some childbirth class. Do you really think they're going to let us take him home--a couple of rank amateurs? We don't know what we're doing."

"We'll probably have to sneak him out. But he won't be able to talk for a couple of years, so he can't tell anyone about all the mistakes we make."

Beverly laughed and then put her hand on her stomach and let out a deep breath.

"Whooaa! David, you're definitely going to have to stifle the sense of humor for a while."

"Stifle my sense of humor? How much more stifling can a man take?"

"Another six weeks' worth, at least."

The door opened. In came a nurse to check Beverly. She was followed by another lady with a chart. "Have you named the baby yet?"

Dave smiled at her, and said with a straight face, "Well, we were going to name her Twila Eleanor if she was a girl, and my wife wanted to name him Horatio DeWitt, but I talked her out of it." (Some things just can't be stifled.) He glanced back at Beverly, who had a tight-lipped smile, trying not to encourage him too much. "But we've decided to name him after a noble ancestor, instead. It's David Bradley Crandall . . ." He paused for a moment. ". . . Junior."

The birth certificate lady smiled. "Third junior I've done today. Tell me, is this a function of the male ego? How come there are no Susie Marie Juniors and Jennifer Ann Juniors?"

"Is this survey part of your job?" asked Dave pointedly.

"Well, no." She bent over her paper. "So that's the name, then? David Bradley Crandall, Jr. How are you spelling David?"

"How many ways *are* there to spell David?"

"You'd be surprised at the spellings I get for names I thought I knew how to spell. I always ask. That *is* part of my job."

Dave looked at Beverly. Beverly smiled. "I think you're taking advantage of my weakened condition." She looked down at the baby. "What do you think, Baby Davey?" Dave's face broke into a huge smile.

"So, it's okay?"

"Okay," Beverly said, resignedly. "It's a good name. When I thought of the name Alexander, I remembered my 5th grade teacher, Mr. Alexander, who used to yell a lot. When I thought of the name Ryan, I remembered Ryan Jacobs who always talked in this whiny, high-pitched voice. When I think of the name David, I think of the man that I love most in all the world. How can I *not* like the name David Bradley Crandall?"

That hurdle over, Beverly convalesced in the hospital for another day, and then it was time to go home and settle into the new routine of parenthood. As they pulled into their driveway, Beverly reflected on how good it was to be home. They went inside and put the baby down to rest in his new crib, which Dave had finally assembled.

"I'm glad to see you got the crib together."

"You knew I would."

"I didn't *know*. I had faith." She chided him. "The substance of things *hoped for*. The evidence of things *not seen*."

"Hey, I did a darn good job on this crib!"

She hugged him. "I can tell. But why, I wonder, did you talk me into buying a house that's a 'fixer-upper' when you aren't a Mr. Fix-It? Actually, you do okay, once you get going. That's the hard part, getting you started. Still, we've got the nursery looking pretty good. It's amazing what a little paint can do. And I think I did a pretty good job on the curtains. That's about the extent of my sewing ability. Hem the top, hem the bottom, turn it down an inch-and-a-half and make a casing for the rod to go through. Mom will be proud of me. She tried so hard to teach me to sew. I've been given a reprieve. We have a son. No prom dresses."

"Look at him there, sleeping so peacefully." Dave put his arm around Beverly's shoulders. "Can you believe that we made that little person? He's like our own private miracle." The two of them stood there for a long time as first-time moms and dads do, just staring at the little boy who had turned them into parents.

Beverly realized finally that she needed to sit down and rest. She shuffled slowly into the kitchen to get a drink of water.

"Dave, the house is so clean! Did you do this?"

"Well, I'd really like to take the credit. I did try to keep things up, but Sister Arletti . . ."

"Don't tell me. Sister Arletti and the 'Cleanliness is next to Godliness' crew came over."

"They also left four casseroles in the freezer."

"That woman is amazing!" said Beverly, sinking into the sofa they'd picked up for a song from the 'slightly damaged' room at the local furniture store. It was beige, plush, and it ran the entire length of one wall. Beverly examined it as she sat there. Something was different. "You fixed the sinkhole!" When they had purchased the sofa, it had a hole on one end where the springs had given way, as though a very fat person had sat in that same spot day after day until the springs had finally given up and pulled loose. Beverly had given up nagging David to try and fix it. She had finally tossed several throw pillows into the hole and made sure no one ever sat there. Even with the sinkhole, it seated four comfortably and was otherwise a very nice sofa.

"It wasn't that hard, really. I just turned it over, pulled the springs back into place and nailed them down."

"We're going to get this place fixed up yet! Come here. I want to give you a hug."

"Now Beverly," Dave shook a warning finger at her, "are you trying to seduce me?"

"In your dreams!"

"Well good, because I just don't feel up to it. Watching that childbirth really wore me out. In fact, I'm kind of hungry. What's for dinner, honey?"

"Very funny! You get in there and see what Sister Arletti brought over. I'm sure it will be better than anything you've been eating lately."

Soon David came out with two plates of delicious food, which they ate gratefully, while talking at length about the sweet sister who had provided it.

"Really? She cleaned down in the heat vents? The woman is obsessive! How embarrassing to have the ward superwoman come clean my house after nine months of bare-minimum housekeeping."

"She's not into housework any more than you're into jogging."

"But it's normal to be into jogging. Jogging is fun!"

"Not for everyone," Dave said, remembering Beverly's diligent efforts during their courtship to make him a jogging convert.

"Okay, so not everyone likes to jog. I know you were just trying to get into it because you liked me. I guess some people jog because they feel like they *have* to, to stay in shape, not because they enjoy it, the way most of us clean house because we *have* to, not because we enjoy it. *That's* what's wrong with Sister Arletti. She *likes* to clean house. She can't wait for someone to get sick so she can go clean their house."

"She had called and told me when she was coming, but I had forgotten. She came Saturday while I was working on the sofa and had it turned over."

"You mean she saw what was under the sofa?" Beverly moaned. "Do you know how long it's been since I vacuumed under the sofa? How *could* you let her look under there? That's probably what prompted her to clean out all the heat vents." Beverly looked like she was going to cry.

"Beverly, why can't you just be grateful that she did it? What's the big deal? It was a nice act of service. You were able to bring our new baby home to a house cleaner than I've ever seen it."

As soon as he uttered those words, he knew he'd said the wrong thing.

"Are you saying I don't keep our house clean? What do you want me to do, get down on my hands and knees and start scrubbing the floors a week after they have cut me open from sea to shining sea?"

Dave shook his head, bewildered. What had happened to his happy, secure wife? She had been replaced with this creature from the 'House of Hormones.' He had been warned about this, but somehow he hadn't thought Beverly was the type to go off about every little thing.

The next minute she was her old self again, composed and rational. "You're right. The house looks great. She did a great job. She likes to clean. She actually told me that it's what she does for enjoyment, so she must have had a blast here! You know, at homemaking meeting every month she does this little thing she calls 'Homemakers' Hints' where she will share some little-known fact about cleaning. Two months ago she had this whole presentation about the difference between different colors of shower mildew. I bet half the ladies in the ward went right home to their showers to see what kind they had. She is so perfect, she has most of the women in the ward on major guilt trips--everyone except Karen Donaldson. Karen is the polar opposite of Sister Arletti. She could stand a little guilt trip, but she sits there oblivious to it all at every homemaking meeting. I've heard some horror stories about *her* housekeeping." Beverly started in again on Dave. "Now they'll probably be telling stories about *me*. Did you *have* to let her look under the sofa? Were there any dead bugs?"

"Are you telling me that you think the ward homemaking leader would come over here to clean as an act of service and then go back to Relief Society and tell everyone what a mess the place was?"

"Yes," Beverly wailed. She was crying in earnest now. "That's how women are! It was Karen Donaldson's visiting teachers that told everyone all about her kitty litter box in the kitchen and . . ."

Dave put his arms around her. "Don't cry, Beverly. I never should have let her look under the sofa, but I'm sure she only found one variety of mildew in the shower, and I had all the dishes done before she came over."

Beverly pulled herself together. She wiped her eyes and blew her nose. "I'm okay now." She sniffled. "I just wanted everything to be perfect for the baby, and I'm glad the house is clean, but I didn't want anybody else to . . ."

"You didn't want anyone to find out that you weren't perfect. You wanted to give the house a once-over while you were in light labor, go down to the hospital, refuse all medication and pop that baby out 'au naturel,' convalesce for a couple of days and come home and get right back into your normal routine."

"Boy, I'm turning into one of *them*, aren't I? An obsessive female." She blew her nose again. "You know I refused to look in my shower after that homemaking night to see if Sister Arletti was right. I guess it's no better for ladies to come clean your house and talk about you afterwards than it is for me to make fun of Sister Arletti while I sit here in a house that she cleaned eating food that she prepared. *Men* don't do things like that. Women are weird."

A few weeks later, David, Beverly and the baby went for a drive up Little Cottonwood Canyon to see the autumn leaves. On the way back, they passed a billboard showcasing a shapely woman frolicking on the beach in a skimpy bathing suit. Beverly noticed Dave's eyes shift ever so slightly to the billboard and then back to the road.

"They could take that billboard down now. Nobody is still buying suntan lotion."

"I guess they could," Dave agreed.

"You know, as a paramedic, you really should complain about billboards like that on canyon roads. How many accidents are caused every year by men driving off the road while they are ogling some woman in an eighth of a yard of fabric?"

"I stayed on the road."

"Yes, but you looked."

"But I didn't *ogle*. I'll admit I looked, but I was only saying to myself, 'Hmmm, I bet that bathing suit would look great on Beverly.'"

It got very quiet in the car, and then Beverly burst into tears. "No, it wouldn't! I've got a great big ugly scar and I'm all fat and bloated. I have stretch marks all over my stomach, my ankles look like tree trunks and you don't think I'm attractive any more. You hardly ever come near me!"

"For crying out loud, Beverly, I've tried to be patient through this whole hormone thing, but I've had it! I've been trying to be the kind and considerate husband and let you tell me when you're feeling better. I've mustered every ounce of self-control that I have because you had such a hard time having the baby. Now because of a micro-second of a glance at a stupid billboard, you think I don't find you attractive? What is *wrong* with you?"

The rest of the drive home neither of them spoke--the only sound being Beverly's occasional sniffs. Soon the baby awoke and was crying along. When they pulled up to the house, Dave got out of the car and slammed the door.

"I'm going for a walk!"

Beverly took the baby inside and fed him, sitting in the middle of the sofa and crying the whole time. Dave walked around the block a couple of times and then decided to go home. When he came in, he saw his pretty dark-haired wife sitting on the sofa nursing their little baby, and to him she was prettier than a thousand shapely models in bikinis. He knelt down on the floor in front of her, and brushed back the hair from her blotchy, tear-stained face. "I love *you*. You're a real woman, not a picture on a billboard on the side of the road. I love your eyes and I love your smile, and I love your scar and I love your stretch marks, and I love your whatever-it-was that you said looked like a tree trunk. Did that woman on that billboard make this beautiful little baby? Sure, you've been in better shape, but give yourself time. No one expects you to bounce back from childbirth in just a few weeks--certainly not me. You'll get rid of those extra pounds eventually. I know you. But in the meantime, don't worry about it. I love you just the way you are."

Beverly was starting to smile. "You mean it?"

"Of course, I do. I think you're gorgeous!"

"You don't think I'm fat and ugly?" she asked, starting to be reassured.

As if on cue, one of the springs in the sofa where Beverly was sitting pulled loose. She sank down on one side. Next, another spring pulled loose and she sunk down on the other side. Dave looked at her warily. She was perched precariously on the edge of another crying jag. He watched helplessly as her brown eyes pooled up and the tears began running down her face.

"Here we go again."

CHAPTER TWO
FATHERS AND SONS' OUTING

"Dave, I'm going out to run some errands this afternoon when you get home, so I'll need you to babysit."

"I don't babysit."

"What are you talking about? You do it all the time."

"I'm his *father*, not some teen-ager that comes over here and watches him for money. I don't *babysit*."

"Sorry! Let me rephrase that. I've arranged for some 'male bonding' time for you and your son this afternoon while I go out and stimulate the economy. You know, you're right. There are too many dads out there who think they *are* babysitting--doing their wives some kind of a favor by staying with the kids."

"Well, I'm not one of them!"

After Dave left for work, Beverly pulled out Davey's baby book. He was six months old. It was time to make some entries. "I'm getting as bad as Dave, putting things off," she thought. She approximated the dates of the important events of his life so far--sitting up, rolling over, etc. What was important was that there were entries, she rationalized, not that you hit the exact date.

First Christmas. She thought back a couple of months. Dave had gotten her a jogging stroller. They'd bought Davey a little Christmas outfit and had taken him to Sears for the Christmas photo session. She hunted up the pictures and pasted one in. He looked so cute, she almost wanted to wake him up from his nap and play with him. She refrained, however, valuing this time to get something accomplished while he was asleep. She continued to approximate all of the "firsts" of his young life. She worked on it on and off throughout the day. Surrounded by pictures and mementos, Beverly did not realize how much of the day had already gone by.

She looked at her watch. Dave was due home soon. He was working the early shift, which meant that he would be home by mid-afternoon. She put down the baby book when Dave came in the door. Something in his face told her not to share the trivial details of her day. He had come into the house and had gone straight to the baby's room and picked him up from his nap. He came into the living room, hugging the now-awake baby boy tightly to his chest. There were tears in his eyes.

"Bad accident?"

"Yes, but I don't want to talk about it. I just needed to come home and hug my little boy." Beverly put her arms around him, and the three of them stood there for a long time in a family hug. Davey was pulling at his dad's hair and blowing spit bubbles. "Beverly, before you reformed me, I used to smoke two packs of cigarettes after a day like today, just to calm my nerves. Now it's as if I can't remember ever having that habit. I have you and 'Drooling Davey' to come home to, and that's all I need in the world."

They sat down on the sofa. Beverly put Davey in the sinkhole, and threw in a couple of toys. It was a built-in playpen there in the middle of the couch. Trying to lighten things up, she said, "Spit bubbles are kind of relaxing." She blew a couple of big ones. Dave joined in for a minute, then he started talking again. Beverly knew the routine well. He came home, upset, said he didn't want to talk about it, and then later, when they were through talking about it, he was back to normal.

"You know, sometimes I just don't know about this job. When you're able to save someone, you feel so great. Then there are the routine days that nothing much happens, and then days like today . . ." His voice broke. "One thing is for sure. This job insures that I'll never take my family for granted." He grabbed his little boy out of the hole in the sofa and started to kiss him all over his face and neck and tummy. Davey's squeals of laughter brought a smile back to Dave's face. "What did we ever do for entertainment before we had him?" he asked Beverly.

"Well, whatever it was, it wasn't as much fun."

Dave switched the conversation back. "Bev, you know how I told you that sometimes when we are working on someone and they seem to be slipping away, I talk to them. Because of what I've always believed about life after death, I figure that there's a chance that they might hear me. The other guys have gotten used to it by now. We were trying to revive this man today, and I was telling him to hang on, to come back. It was as if he answered me and told me that he didn't want to come back--I mean, I didn't hear anything. I just got this feeling--it's hard to explain--as if he talked to me without using words--talked to my spirit, communicated to my mind, like the Holy Ghost."

"That's not so hard to believe."

"We kept working on him, but I told the guys he wasn't coming back, and he didn't. His wife is in the hospital. She doesn't know yet. They probably want to stabilize her first. I'm glad I don't have that job--breaking that kind of news to somebody."

"You're lucky in some ways to have a job that constantly reminds you of your priorities. Today Sister Cirroni was here for a few minutes. They live in the big house next to the park, and you know that Italian restaurant, Cirroni's--they own that. She's my new visiting teacher. I had to warn her not to sit in the sinkhole in the couch, and so we got into a discussion about furniture. She spent more time talking about her new leather sofa than she did giving me the visiting teaching message. I asked her who her companion was. She said it was Karen Donaldson, but that she usually just goes out alone because their schedules don't match. I don't think she wants to go with Karen. But anyway, she invited me to be her guest next Tuesday at her health club--that new one on the corner across from the high school. They even have a nursery where I can leave Davey. I told her I would enjoy going but if it was one of those things where they try to sign you up, that we just couldn't afford it. She said that was too bad, because she could tell that I was the kind of lady who tried to keep in shape, not like some of the other women in our ward. Anyway, I told her that luckily you could exercise even if you were broke, and that with my new jogging stroller, I didn't even have to get a babysitter. She acted like she has no frame of reference for not being able to afford something. I don't think she has struggled much, but I shouldn't say that, because I don't even know her. Maybe that's the impression I've gotten from some of her lessons. She teaches Relief Society, and she seems to have this totally perfect family. She always uses them as examples of how things should be. Just between you and me--she seems to be swimming at the shallow end of the pool. But maybe it isn't fair for me to say that, since this was the first real conversation I've had with her."

"I think we all fall into that trap--some of us more than others--of thinking about what we have accumulated in this world, instead of focusing on our relationships. Like a lot of things, there's a fine line between what's appropriate and what's not. We are told by the prophets to keep up our yard and our homes--to give an appearance of cleanliness and to care about our surroundings. Then you can take it a step further, turning your home into a showplace with a satellite dish and a hot tub. Pretty soon you can be focusing more on those things than on your relationships with the people around you. You know what we need to do, as soon as we get a few more things fixed around here, is have a party, so we can get better acquainted with some of the people in this ward."

"Great idea! The incentive plan. We can have a party after every couple of things we fix. I think we should have a party two weeks from this Friday after you fix the faucet in the kitchen and the folding doors to the pantry."

"Am I being tricked?"

"Yes, honey. You've fixed all of the life-threatening things. Now we need to get down to the list of minor inconveniences. It takes forever to fill a baby bottle with that faucet trickling out a little bit of water at a time. This is not me speaking. This is direction from a prophet."

"Okay, so let's invite a plumber to the party."

"Now about that hot tub . . ."

After a few months, David and Beverly had several couples in the ward that they socialized with regularly. They had started a pot-luck dinner club that rotated from house to house. It consisted of other young couples, except for Fred and Edith. They had grown married children and grandchildren, but were young at heart--the kind of couple that livened up just about any gathering. As Edith put it, "You're only young once, but you can stay immature indefinitely." Each party had a little different mix of people, because whoever hosted it that month was in charge of inviting whomever they wanted. That kept it from becoming exclusive and gave them all a chance to get to know different people from time to time.

When it was the Crandall's turn to host the dinner, Edith cornered Dave as Beverly put the last few items on the dinner table. "I sat in front of you at church last Sunday. You've been hiding your light under a bushel. I had no idea you had such a wonderful singing voice. I reported you to Sister Woolston, and she's going to be after you to get into the choir."

"Good! I've been wanting to get into the Choir for several years now." Beverly walked by.

"He means the Tabernacle Choir, Edith. He's just waiting to turn the big 3-0 so he can try out."

"Are you really? Well, I don't doubt you'll make it, but you should really consider helping out the ward choir in the meantime."

"You know, maybe I will go next week. I wouldn't want the people in the ward, after I make it into the Tabernacle Choir, to think that I thought I was too good to sing in the ward choir. I would have already joined, but like all ward choirs, it's heavy on the 'Wobble-atos'--full of old ladies with wavering voices." Beverly elbowed him. He'd forgotten that Edith was in the choir.

Edith laughed. "So that's what you call us? Well, if we had a few more men in the choir, maybe it would help balance us out. Did you ever think of that?"

Dave's face turned red. "Oh, Edith, I didn't mean you."

"Like heck you didn't! Ain't anybody in the choir that can out-wobble me. You, Mr. Dave, are going to sing in our ward choir, or I'll tell all the other ladies what you have been calling us."

"Yes, ma'am. What time is practice?"

The following evening, Beverly had the television on in the family room, providing background noise while she made dinner. Dave came into the kitchen and pulled one of the bar stools up to the counter where Beverly was chopping radishes.

"This dinner party idea is great, especially when we get to keep the leftovers. It makes cooking dinner much easier." She slid the chopped radishes off the cutting board into the salad and held the board up for Dave to see. "Do you like this new cutting board?" It was clear, and it had a picture of a bunny painted on it. "We made these in Relief Society last month. They are supposed to be better than wooden cutting boards because . . ." Beverly's voice trailed away and she looked toward the TV, where all she saw was an advertisement for the Utah State Fair. Dave waved his hand in front of her face.

"Hey, where did you go? You look like a dog when it hears a high-pitched noise that no one else can hear. You can't leave me in suspense about how a cutting board with a bunny is better than a cutting board without one."

"Huh? Oh, that. No, it's not the bunny. Acrylic cutting boards don't trap bacteria. Ask Sister Potter. She's the expert on food poisoning."

"Now about the Fair--what was it about that commercial that got you so off-track."

"You're very observant today."

"I learned from the best."

" I thought I recognized the voice in the commercial, that's all."

"Let me guess."

"You're on a roll."

"He went to Utah State University, majoring in communications. He married his high school sweetheart, thereby breaking your heart and paving the way for me to come along and make you blissfully happy. It must be the golden-voiced Steve, now doing voice-overs for commercials in an attempt to make contact any way he can with the woman he gave up but never stopped loving." Dave looked very seriously at Beverly. "I can see that to save our marriage, we should get rid of our television and radio."

She threw a handful of radish remains at him. "Very funny! I'm sure a remote control with a mute button would probably suffice. Besides, I'm not sure it was him."

That night when they climbed into bed, Dave snuggled up next to Beverly and whispered seductively in her ear, "Twenty percent off our entire stock of ladies' handbags."

"I'll bet you say that to all the girls," Beverly whispered back.

"No, honest! You're the only one." He was quiet for a moment, and then in one of his rare truly serious moments, he asked, "Beverly, you haven't ever been sorry you married me instead of him, have you? He's obviously doing well for himself."

"Yes, for himself. Steve was always a little bit selfish, although I couldn't see it when I was madly in love with him. No, I've never regretted that he got away. He did me a favor marrying DeAnna. Steve never understood me the way you do. As for how well he's doing, I can't help it if the world values the services of people who make television commercials and tell people they can get into the fair free by saving bread wrappers more than they value the services of people like you who go out into the world every day and save lives. So what if he probably has a nice big house or whatever? I've got what I need to be happy. I've got you, and I've got Davey. I can't believe that he's walking already. It seems like only yesterday we were there in the hospital trying to figure out what to name him. I believe he has expanded his repertoire to five words now. Every day I spend my time with the people I love most in all the world. I hope Steve is happy, too, because I cared about him an awful lot, but I never have wanted, since I married you, for things to be any different than they are right now."

Over the next few weeks, Beverly became certain it was Steve's voice in the Fair commercial, and that he was also announcing several upcoming events at the Salt Palace. Dave teased her about it so much that soon Davey joined in--expanding his vocabulary by another two words--wobbling into the kitchen and telling his mother, whenever there was a commercial on the television, "It Steeb. It Steeb." He toddled around the house saying, "It Steeb. It Steeb." He liked the sound of it, although he had no idea what it meant or why he was saying it.

"Dave, you'd better be careful," Beverly warned him. "We named him after you, and he does everything you do."

"I know. What a great kid! By the way, did I mention that I want to take Davey on the Fathers and Sons' Outing coming up at the end of the month?"

"Don't you think he's a little young to go camping? Why are they having it so late this year?"

"Bruce was in charge, and he waited around too long to make reservations until this was the only weekend available. Believe me, he's heard about it from several people. And no, I don't think he's too little. They are having a special class on how to make a bedroll out of a security blanket and how to make baby food in a dutch oven."

"Dave, I don't like this. It could be cool at night and there's water and . . ."

"I *have* to."

"What do you mean you *have* to? He's just a baby."

"He's not a baby. He's a toddler."

"He started walking early."

"I'm a father. He's my son. We're going." The set of his jaw told her it was no use arguing.

Dave unloaded half the stuff Beverly tried to send with them. "We're roughing it. We only need one teddy bear." She looked at her little boy, all decked out in blue jeans and a plaid shirt that matched his daddy's. He had a plastic Fisher Price fishing pole, meant only for catching plastic fish. He had been carrying it around with him ever since Dave had bought it for him.

"Be careful with him." Beverly had never spent a night apart from her little one.

"I'm a paramedic, remember. We're going to be fine. We're going to catch a big fish for you to cook."

"Fishy," Davey echoed.

"Make sure he stays covered up at night."

"Yes, Mom."

"Don't feed him anything weird."

"Yes, Mom."

"Get out of here and have a good time."

"Yes, Mom."

CHAPTER THREE
TWO WORDS

"Beverly," Dave teased, "I never heard of anyone doing a test turkey."

"I can't have the whole family over next week for Thanksgiving and botch up the turkey. I have to make sure I can do it right first. Just think, when you come home from work today, you'll be greeted by the aroma of succulent roasting turkey."

"At last--a reason to come home."

"What I don't do to keep you hanging around."

"Are you kidding? There isn't anything you can do to get *rid* of me." He kissed her goodbye, and was still kissing her when his co-worker, Kurt, pulled up and honked.

It was an ordinary day--other than that she was cooking a turkey. She got Davey up and fed and bathed him. While he sat in the sinkhole watching Sesame Street, she prepared the stuffing. The turkey was still a little bit frozen, so she took Davey for a walk and then put him down for his nap. Upon returning to the kitchen, she stuffed the turkey, turned the oven on and cleaned up the kitchen. While waiting for the oven to preheat, she called her sister-in-law, Gayle, Randall's wife, to double check what she was bringing to the dinner.

"Hi Gayle. Just me, Beverly. I'm checking to find out for sure what you're bringing next week, so I know what we still need."

"I'm bringing a green salad and that potato side dish. You know, the one with the shredded potatoes and the corn flake crumbs on top. My mom used to call it Sour Cream Potato Bake, but lately everybody around here calls it 'Funeral Potatoes.'"

"It wouldn't be a Mormon funeral without them. A large pan of that, some lasagna, some dinner rolls, eleven Jello salads and you've got the grieving family covered." Beverly jotted Gayle's two items down on the list and looked it over. *"Okay, Gayle's bringing green salad and Funeral Potatoes. Mom's making the green bean casserole and the sweet potatoes with brown sugar and mini-marshmallows. Aunt Marlene will be bringing her wonderful pies. I wonder what we should have to drink."*

About that time, Davey woke up from his nap. She hurried and put the small turkey in the oven, checking the time. It was 1:10 in the afternoon. *"It should be done about the time Dave gets home from work, just like I said."* She lifted Davey out of his crib.

"What a big boy you're getting to be." She changed his diaper. "Now pick a book and Mama will read you a story." Beverly settled into the rocking chair and her little boy climbed onto her lap. Close by she heard the wail of a siren. Before she could say anything, as she often did, her little boy commented.

"Da Da." Little Davey had learned that the shrill noise of the big fast vehicles was somehow associated with his daddy. That said, he turned his attention back to the book. "Eh-phunt tory." Beverly opened the book and began to read. "Eh-phunt," said Davey, pointing to the cover where Horton sat perched on the nest. Grandma Marjorie and Grandpa Gordon had given him his very own small bookcase for his first birthday and stocked it with books. "Horton Hatches the Egg" was his latest favorite story, and he pointed out Horton in *every* picture.

" . . . I meant what I said and I said what I meant. An elephant's faithful one hundred percent." Davey pointed at the picture.

"Eh-phunt."

There was a knock at the door. Beverly set him down and got up to answer it. As she approached the door, she saw through the window that there was an ambulance in the driveway. Sometimes if Dave was in the area and not responding to a call, he would stop by for a brief hello. *"Why would he knock?"* she wondered, opening the door. On the doorstep stood an associate of Dave's, a fellow she remembered meeting at the summer picnic.

"Hello. Mrs. Crandall--Beverly." She nodded, impatiently. This kind of visit never brought good news. "James Perkins. We met this summer." He continued now that he had the pleasantries out of the way. "There's been an accident. Your husband is on the way to the hospital. I've been dispatched to bring you there."

There were accidents every day in Dave's line of work. He was always on the way to the hospital. It took a moment for her to realize what James was saying. *"Dave's* been in an accident?" Beverly stood motionless for a second, letting this news sink in. "How badly is he hurt? Is he going to be okay?"

"I'm sorry. I don't have many details. They dispatched me to your address, told me to transport you to St. Marks hospital as soon as possible. We can discuss it on the way."

"Yes, okay." She told herself, *"No use wasting time. Get to the hospital."* Beverly struggled to remain calm. She picked Davey up, grabbing her diaper bag, hoping the fact that it was heavy meant it contained necessities for a couple of hours. He was still holding the book as she ran him across the street to the neighbors.

"Eh-phunt, Mama."

"Not right now, Davey." She knocked on the door and greeted her neighbor as it opened. "Evelyn, Dave's been in an accident. I need you to call and have someone from the Elders' Quorum meet me at the hospital to administer to Dave." She motioned toward the ambulance in her driveway. "I'm going in the ambulance they sent." Evelyn took Davey and Beverly handed her the diaper bag. "I don't know what's in here. If there's anything else you need, I hope you've got it on hand."

"We'll get by," Evelyn assured her. "Which hospital? How badly is he hurt?"

"St. Marks. The emergency entrance. That's all I know." Evelyn stood there holding Davey as she watched her friend climb into the ambulance, which sped away, siren blaring. Davey pointed after it. "Da Da. Da Da."

Beverly sat with her head back against the seat, silently praying, when she was not cursing the traffic. *"He's okay. He's got to be okay. Please God, let him be okay!"* She switched gears. *"Get out of our way! We've got to get to the hospital. Now I understand why Dave gets so keyed up about people who don't pull over for emergency vehicles."* Her thoughts alternated between hope and faith and doubt and despair. She looked over at James. Neither of them had spoken since they started the trip. She was vaguely aware of another paramedic in the back. *"What isn't he telling me? Is it true that he doesn't know? I'm sure they prefer to tell you in person, someone who knows the details. Maybe he's got a broken leg, or some cuts that need stitches. It can't be that serious. He drives carefully. He always wears his seat belt. There would have been an air bag."* "Out of the way, people!" *"He wasn't driving our car today. He rode with Kurt. What if Kurt is injured, too? I wonder if Kurt's car has a passenger-side air bag. Dave might have taken the worst of the accident. It could have been one of those accidents where the driver walked away and the passenger was . . ."* She tried to stop the thought, but it came anyway. *". . . killed."* Beverly took a deep breath. She had to know.

"James, please tell me what you know. You have to know something." He turned his head slightly towards her. She saw that he was crying. He shook his head, meaning either he was unable to talk or that things were not hopeful. "It's bad, isn't it?"

Pursing his trembling lips together, he nodded. *"How do I tell her that the best we can hope for is that they'll be able to keep him alive until she gets there?"*

He pulled into the emergency entrance at the hospital and Beverly jumped out. She hurried in through the automatic double doors. What might have been a welcome sight under other circumstances, was a harbinger of the worst possible news to Beverly. Although she had always enjoyed seeing Dave's co-workers at the social gatherings, the group of paramedics and fire fighters were gathered there for an entirely different reason. Instinctively Beverly knew that the word would not have gone out and there would not have been this kind of response if Dave's injuries were minor. She felt herself and the world go into slow motion. She faced the sea of arms, received the hugs and handshakes. From what they were saying and from what they were not saying, her worst fears were confirmed.

"We're here for you."

"I'm so sorry."

Some averted their eyes, unable to look at her. Nobody said, "We're pulling for him." or "He's a fighter." The sea of arms parted and Beverly saw a more familiar face. Kurt Holland came towards her. She collapsed in his open arms. Like Dave, he was not a small man. He whispered two words, the hardest two words he had ever spoken.

"He's gone."

Kurt led her to a little room. Beverly sank gratefully down on the little sofa. She shook her head back and forth. "Not Dave. He can't be dead. He helps save other people. How can he be dead?" Kurt sat next to her, his arm around her shoulders.

"I've asked myself that same question, Bev, and I don't have the answer either. I wish to Heaven that I did."

"He was born here, you know. St. Marks. He was born and died at the same hospital. And there weren't enough years in between."

"The job brought him here regularly, too. The doctors and nurses were all pretty shook up, when they realized who they were working on."

Soon they were joined by a doctor.

"Are you Mrs. Crandall?" Beverly nodded.

"I worked on your husband, David. I'm so sorry for your loss. He was a familiar face around here. This has been a shock to us all. We never expect to see one of our own lying on a stretcher instead of carrying one." He continued with an explanation of Dave's injuries, of the treatment that had been tried, of the fact that for a few moments they had revived him only to have him slip away again. Beverly did not hear anything else he said. It wasn't just his use of medical jargon and unfamiliar terms, but the fact that there was not room in her mind for anything else to register. She listened numbly. His mouth was moving, but she had already shut off the sound. If it was true that Dave was dead, none of that really mattered at all. *If it was true . . .*

An officer came in from the highway patrol. More explanations. "Mrs. Crandall?" Beverly nodded her head. "I'm the investigating officer." He gave Beverly the details of the accident, showing her a small drawing illustrating the point of impact. The only thing that would remain in her memory from that conversation was the drawing he showed her with vehicles and a tiny stick figure drawn near the center of the road. It was unthinkable to her the horrible reality that drawing represented. It had been a bizarre accident. Dave had been working on an accident victim. They had been loading the accident victim into the ambulance when another car, driving too fast for the snowy conditions, attempting to slow down to go around the accident, slid out of control. Dave, standing at the back of the ambulance, had been hit and killed. "It was a hit and run, but they've got a lead on finding the driver."

Beverly remembered something that Dave had said once, and she thanked the highway patrolman. "I know this must be the hardest part of your job." He took her hand and squeezed it.

The doctor spoke again. "Mrs. Crandall, I don't want to burden you further, but we need someone to identify the body. Is there someone you would like to call or do you think . . .?"

Kurt stepped in. "Of course she can't . . ."

Beverly stopped him, suddenly matter-of-factly aware that this was something she needed to do. "Yes, I can. I need to. I won't believe it has really happened until I see him. I need to be able to plan a funeral. I can't do that if I don't believe this has really happened."

"His injuries are covered."

"I can't do it until my parents get here. I've got to call my parents."

The door opened and Evelyn Jensen came in followed by Brother Arletti and Brother Nichols. Beverly looked at her questioningly. "The older kids are home now watching Davey. He's fine. Brother Nichols called me."

"So you know?"

"Yes, we know," Brother Arletti answered. "We got here as quickly as we could. I'm sorry it wasn't . . ."

"So did I. I don't think there was anything anyone could have done."

Evelyn did the only thing she knew how to do at a time like this. She took her friend in her arms, her voice shaking.

"I'm so sorry, Beverly. So very sorry."

The doctor spoke again. "You probably have some phone calls you need to make. There's a phone here you can use. The phone book is in the drawer there. Take as long as you need." Kurt and the two brothers from the church stepped into the hall with the doctor, leaving Beverly and Evelyn alone in the room.

"I've got to call my parents," Beverly repeated. She dialed the phone. Her mother answered. Beverly's voice shook as she spoke. "Mother?"

"Beverly? What's wrong?"

"There's been an accident."

"Davey?" Naomi questioned, horrified.

"No, Dave. Dave's been in an accident and he's . . ." She couldn't say it. Wordlessly she handed the phone to her friend to continue. Evelyn took the phone.

"Mrs. . . ." she realized she didn't know Beverly's maiden name. "I'm Evelyn, from across the street." She forced the words out. "It was a fatal accident. He's dead." Evelyn fielded the questions the best she could. "I don't know. I just got here. They just told her. No, she wasn't alone. There is quite a contingent of firefighters and paramedics here, two brothers from the church are here now, and I got here as quickly as I was able. Davey is with my family." She paused. "St. Marks. Come in through the emergency entrance."

Somewhat composed again, Beverly motioned for her friend to hand the phone back. "Mom, they need me to identify his body. I can't do that without your help."

"Dad and I will be there as soon as we can."

"And Mother, how am I going to tell his parents? I can't do it over the telephone, but I have to do it soon. I can't let them see it on the news. Marjorie always watches the 6:00 news. You and Dad are going to have to help me tell them."

Beverly's father pulled into the parking lot. He headed for what looked like a vacant parking spot only to find it occupied by a motorcycle. "Damn!" Naomi Smithson had held on tight during the drive from their home in Rose Park, sure her husband's driving in his agitated state was going to land them both in the hospital, as well. He pulled forward to another parking spot and began to turn in, when he spotted the stenciling that said "Reserved - doctors only."

"Donald, it says . . ."

"I know what it says. I can read! Well, just let them bloody well tow me away!"

Naomi knew better than to say anything further, and held her tongue as her husband parked the car. "Our daughter's husband has died, and I'm not going to let any stupid parking lot regulations keep me from being by her side for one more minute! I feel helpless and useless enough as it is!"

Evelyn greeted them at the door and led them to the little room where Beverly was.

"Beverly, I can do this for you," her father offered. "There's no reason you should have to go through it.

"I'm going to do it, Dad. I have to." She followed the doctor, with her parents on either side of her. The doctor drew back the curtain where Dave lay, his body covered with a sheet, only his face visible.

"Yes, that's him." Beverly was holding up better than her parents. She began to talk to David. "So, you're dead. Is it different than you expected it would be?" Her mother and father exchanged troubled glances. She'd flipped out. She was talking to him as if it were any old conversation. "I told you to get a haircut last week. Now you're not going to look good for your funeral." She continued on, telling him how much she was going to miss him, promising to take good care of their son, as if he was going on a business trip. Then something happened as she stood there. She allowed herself to truly see the scene that was before her, not just that he needed a haircut, but that he was dead. *"It is true! He's dead. How am I ever going to erase this picture from my mind?"* Beverly was suddenly seized with an overwhelming desire to grab the sheet and rip it away--to see for herself his injuries, to find out what the paramedics would not tell her, what the doctor would tell her only in antiseptic phrases that meant nothing to her. Naomi noticed the change in her daughter's countenance, as though the reality of Dave's death had just hit her. She took Beverly's arm and led her away, out to the parking lot and drove her home.

Beverly unlocked the door and was met with the aroma of roasting turkey. It smelled as good as she had told Dave it would, and it made her sick to her stomach. Word went out that Beverly was home, and within minutes the Relief Society President and Bishop Parley were at her house.   She visited with them briefly, regurgitating as many of the details as she was able to remember. The bishop tentatively brought up the subject of Dave's funeral. She told them both, "I can't talk about anything else right now. It's after 5:00. We have to get to Dave's parents' home before the 6:00 news comes on."

Evelyn brought Davey back over. He was still clutching "Horton Hatches the Egg," not quite understanding why nobody that day had time to read him the "Eh-phunt" story. Beverly turned off the oven, got a few of Davey's things and asked to be driven to Dave's parents' home.

CHAPTER FOUR
THE FLOODGATES OPEN

Beverly lay in bed that night at her parents' home. She closed her eyes, but sleep did not come. Still she needed to rest her body, even if her mind would not shut off. *"I've got to plan a funeral. I need to find insurance papers. I've got to buy a casket and decide where to bury him. We need to order flowers and I need to write an obituary for the newspaper. I need to find a picture for the obituary. Did I turn off the turkey?"* She couldn't remember. *"Did I burn the house down? What if I did? Could I hurt any worse than I do right now?"* In lieu of sleep, Beverly had her thoughts. *"What about the driver of the car that hit Dave? Shouldn't I be angry and anxious to know if they have found the person? Maybe that will come later. I don't have room for any other emotions."* She just felt numb--like all her feelings were frozen. She wanted to thaw out, to feel something, but she couldn't. *"I have to handle things."* She wanted to cry, but she couldn't. When a person experiences a severe physical injury, they go into a state of shock. They can be missing a leg, and mercifully the pain will not register. The same thing happens with a severe emotional trauma.

The next morning, Beverly's parents gently tried to lead her through some of the planning. Her older brother, Randall, was there now also. "Beverly, do you have any ideas who you would like to have talk at Dave's funeral? Do you have any ideas for musical numbers? Mom said Aunt Marlene called and said she would be glad to sing."

Beverly's Aunt Marlene sang at all family events--sad or happy. Aunt Marlene was part of a musical group--four ladies called "The Lean Sisters." They were not sisters, and none of them were 'lean.' The group consisted of Marlene, Jolene, Colleen and Pauline. At every family reunion they would perform. Beverly and her brothers used to say, "It's not over until the fat ladies sing."

"Aunt Marlene can't sing, not at Dave's funeral!" Beverly announced emphatically.

Randall went into the other room to talk to his parents. "She's not making any sense. She said something about Aunt Marlene and that no 'Wobble-ato' is going to sing at Dave's funeral. What's a Wobble-ato?"

"I don't know, for sure, but I can guess, and it fits," Beverly's father stated. His wife gave him a stern look. "Admit it, Naomi. The years haven't been good to Marlene's singing voice. But all that aside, if Beverly doesn't want Marlene to sing, Marlene doesn't sing. Naomi, she's your sister. You'll need to make sure she knows that so that she doesn't show up here with some sheet music and start practicing. We all love Marlene, but you know how she can be." He shifted gears. "Sterling, I told you we are leaving the television set off until you hear differently-- *completely off.* You saw what was on the news yesterday. Your sister does not need to see that. In fact, when this is all over, I'm going to go down to that station and give somebody a piece of my mind!" He switched back. "Randall, did she say who she would like to have sing?"

"Yes, she wants the Mormon Tabernacle Choir."

"What?"

"You go talk to her then."

"Naomi, where is the phone number of the doctor that took out my gall bladder? He's in the Tabernacle Choir."

"Donald, you're not seriously going to call him?"

"Why not? If Beverly wants the Tabernacle Choir, I'm going to get her the Tabernacle Choir!"

"Get him the number, Mom. He looks like he means it."

Naomi rifled through her card file, waiting for her husband to come to his senses. She handed him a card with the doctor's phone number on it. He disappeared into the bedroom with the card. Naomi shook her head. He emerged from the bedroom a few minutes later, triumphant. "I did it!"

"The *Tabernacle Choir* is going to sing at Dave's funeral!?"

"Not the whole choir! For crying out loud, Naomi, give me some credit! It's going to be a male quartet. When I explained to Dr. Merrill about how Dave was trying out for the choir and how much this would mean to my daughter, he was glad to oblige. There are several quartets that perform, and he is giving one of them our number."

Beverly emerged from the bedroom, where she'd managed a short nap. She ran her fingers through her bedraggled hair and sat down on the sofa. Moments later, Davey was beside her, handing her his favorite "Eh-phunt" book. With her little boy sitting patiently beside her, she stared at the cover picture of the elephant ridiculously perched on the nest. *"I wonder how traumatic it would be for him if I 'lost' his favorite book?"* His patience finally wore thin.

"EH-PHUNT, MAMA!"

"Sterling, will you read this book to Davey, please? It's too hard for me."

"Oh come on, Bev," he said teasingly, hoping to cheer her up. "I bet you know most of the words." She didn't laugh.

"Just read it to him, okay?" she snapped.

The next day Beverly went to the mall with her mother. "I don't want a new dress, Mother. I'll wear the blue dress that was his favorite, and I don't really care if everybody thinks I should be wearing black. He'll know why I'm wearing it. Besides, this does not really put me in the shopping mood, like, 'oh boy, an excuse to buy a new dress.' I would just like to look in the children's section for something nice for Davey to wear--not a size 2 grey pin-striped suit or anything overdone--just something that looks dressy and . . ." Beverly stopped mid-stream. They were in the electronics department. Rows of television sets, all tuned to the same channel, were broadcasting the news at noon. Twenty television sets were blaring at Beverly, complete with pictures of the scene of the accident. There was a partially covered-up body, but she could see his feet. *"Local police have apprehended the driver who hit and killed a Salt Lake City paramedic Friday in a . . ."* Beverly turned and ran out of the store. Horrified, Naomi ran after her. She found Beverly hunched over on a bench in a shoe store. All of the tears that had yet to come poured out. Naomi sat down next to her daughter.

"Go ahead, cry. Get it out."

Beverly sobbed out the words. "How can they show it like that on television--like it's just another news story? They go in and take pictures as soon as they can get there and show as much as they can, as if people like to see smashed-up cars and people with sheets pulled up over their heads and somebody being loaded into an ambulance. That's my husband! That's Dave!" Beverly shook with sobs as she tried to get hold of herself, but the dam had been broken and there was no holding back the flood. Naomi sat and held her daughter in her arms and they cried together on a bench in a shoe store.

Nobody tried to sell them any shoes.

CHAPTER FIVE
GOODBYES

Beverly had refused the tranquilizer they had offered her at the hospital. The doctor had given the small bottle to her mother. "See if you can get her to take them."

As they pulled into the parking lot at the funeral home, Naomi opened her purse. "Honey, I know how you feel about these, but maybe it will help you just to get through tonight and tomorrow."

"Mother, thank you. I know you're worried about me, but I'm going to do this without any drugs. People get hooked on those things. Besides, all they do is bottle up your feelings and turn you into a robot. Maybe people don't expect you to be calm and relaxed and unemotional at your husband's funeral. There's another reason I don't want any drugs, Mother, so please don't offer them again."

"Are you pregnant, Beverly?" There was no putting anything over on Naomi.

"Pleeease, Mother. Don't say anything to anyone! I'm probably not, but I could be. You know what a hard time I had getting pregnant with Davey, so I'm probably not, but there's a chance. I'm really trying not to think about it until I know for sure. I'm overwhelmed enough at the thought of being a single parent of one. If word gets out that I even suspect I'm pregnant, it will be old news in ten minutes. You're the only one I've told. Now let's go inside. We don't have that long before everyone else starts coming."

"I'll give you a few minutes by yourself. Do you want me to take Davey?"

Beverly had hardly had any sleep since the news of Dave's accident, and her nerves were wearing thin. "No, I want Davey with me. He's all I have left right now, and I'm tired of people trying to take him away from me."

"They're only trying to help. People may say and do all the wrong things, but give them credit for having good intentions. They just want to help you with the burden of caring for him."

"Davey's not a *burden*! I overheard a lady the other day saying, 'That poor girl with a little baby to take care of all by herself.' Don't they understand how lucky I am to have him--to have someone to take care of and who needs me? What else would I have to live for right now? Would it be better if Dave had died and I had never had a chance to have a child with him? These are all the same people who bugged me for years about when I was going to have a child. Now they feel sorry for me because I *have* him?"

"Oh honey, don't add old pains in with the new ones that you're dealing with now." Naomi responded. "Of course he's not a burden--not in the sense that you're interpreting, but caring for him is a responsibility that you now carry alone. You've got to let people help you, Beverly. We're all worried about you. Have you gotten any sleep since this happened?"

"A couple of hours here and there--not really a whole night's worth. I lie in bed at night to rest my body, but I can't fall asleep." Beverly headed in the direction of the sign that said "Crandall." "I'm going in now. Would you tell the rest of the family to please give me a few minutes."

She entered the room where David was. As she walked toward him, the little boy in her arms lit up in recognition. "Da Da!" Davey reached out his arms.

Beverly began to shake with sobs--for herself, for the sweet, loving husband she had lost, for a little boy who was reaching out for a father who would never reach back, for a baby that she suspected she was carrying that would never even know its father.

Even in the midst of her tears, she was blessed with a feeling of peace as she looked upon him. The memory of the way she had last seen him at the hospital and the images from the news coverage had been haunting her thoughts. She felt those disturbing mind-pictures being replaced as she saw him lying at peace, dressed in the special burial clothes he had worked so hard to be worthy to wear.

She remembered how Dave had told her he would talk to people he worked on as a paramedic. She touched his hair. She could not bear to touch any other part of him, expecting warmth where there was warmth no longer. Her voice wavering, she began to talk. As she talked, she imagined him standing there looking at her looking at him. "I know you are here. I guess you know what it feels like to be dead now and have someone talking to you."

A communication came to her. *"It's better than being ignored. People ignore you when you're dead."* It was Dave! His spirit was communicating somehow to her mind.

"I'm going to miss you terribly, but I'll take good care of Davey and . . ." She stopped. If she was pregnant, he would know. She didn't have to tell him.

"I couldn't have left him in better hands." The communication seemed almost cheerful.

"Did you know? Did you know you were going to die?"

"I was just as surprised as you were. I would never leave you and Davey on purpose."

When Naomi Smithson and Marjorie and Gordon Crandall entered the room, they heard Beverly say, "I know you wouldn't. I know you wouldn't." It didn't strike Beverly as odd that she was carrying on what appeared to be a purely one-sided conversation with a dead man and it didn't concern her that in the back of the room, some of the other relatives had gathered and were whispering among themselves. Naomi hustled some of them out of the room. No one was going to intrude on her daughter's last few private moments with her husband. She took Marjorie's arm and, with Gordon on the other side, they approached Beverly, Davey and Dave.

Beverly heard footsteps behind her and turned around. Together they stood wordlessly and shared tears and unspoken memories, and then Beverly's mother took her hand and led her away, leaving some time for Dave's parents to have a few private moments with their only son. Soon they were joined by David's sister, Pamela, who had flown in from California. Beverly set Davey down on the floor. *"How would I feel if something ever happened to him? I wouldn't be able to stand it."* To lose a child would be to lose someone you were supposed to protect, someone you believed you would outlive. To lose a spouse was to have your life and future changed irreparably. Marjorie and Gordon had lost a child, and yet they had each other to lean on to get through it. The person she was supposed to lean on was gone--just like that.

Beverly stood back for a few minutes, and then she approached them both. She wanted to thank them, to tell them what a wonderful husband and father he had been, how much she had loved him, but mere words seemed inadequate to express those feelings, so she just put her arms around his mother and father and stood there with them and hoped her hugs said what her words could not. Pamela stood at the coffin, tears flowing. Beverly saw her slip something into the coffin. Gordon picked up Davey, who reached immediately for his glasses.

"I'm so glad we've got him, Beverly. He's a little part of Dave that he left behind." Gordon retrieved his glasses and wiped the little fingerprints from the lenses. Then he wiped his eyes. He spoke to Davey, "Now Davey, I hope you grow up to be a good man like your daddy, someone who helped people and cared about them. You may not remember him, but when you need to hear about him, you just come sit on your Grandad's lap, and I'll tell you stories about your daddy."

Pamela hugged Beverly, both of them crying.

"I hope you don't mind, Beverly. I put something in with David. I don't think anyone will see it. They wouldn't understand."

"What was it?"

"The Christmas right before Dave went on his mission, he gave me this cheap plastic waffle on a key chain for Christmas. I told him it was obvious he was saving all his money for his mission. I've carried it with me all these years, mostly because it was easy to reach into my purse and feel around for it to find my keys. In fact, Ross has always asked me why I kept it, and I couldn't really say, except that I don't think I could find my keys without it. A couple of years ago when you guys came out to see us, I had my keys sitting on the counter. Dave saw it and he said, 'I can't believe you still have that thing. You gave me such a bad time for getting you such a cheap gift. What else do you still have that you got for Christmas that year?' So I told him that I cherished it so much, I was going to be buried with it. I know if I had gone first, he would have made sure that happened, so I thought I'd give it back to him." Soon they were laughing through their tears.

Shortly more of the extended family gathered privately, before it was time to receive the other friends and family who had come to say goodbye to David Bradley Crandall, Sr. People filtered by, each doing their best to say something kind and comforting.

"Aren't you glad you've got him forever?"

"You're young. You'll marry again."

"If there is ever anything I can do . . ."

"Call me if you need to talk, anytime, night or day."

Beverly was gratified at the large number of Dave's professional colleagues who had turned out. The message was usually a variation on a theme.

"He was well-respected and will be sorely missed."

"He was a good friend. We're all going to miss him."

"I'm so sorry, Beverly."

Then two elderly ladies stopped to chat between themselves before they reached Beverly, but she was within earshot. "My, he looks so good!"

"Just like he's asleep."

"I'm really surprised. Why I'd heard that he had extensive head injuries but you can't even tell." Beverly winced at the thought of it. To them it was just a conversation. To her it was unbearable to think of--to be reminded of. Methodically, she thanked the women for coming, but she wanted to yell and scream at them and make them see the pain they were causing her.

Another person. "Remember, you've got the rest of your life ahead of you."
Beverly kept her thoughts to herself. *That's supposed to be comforting?"* Yes,
she had the rest of her life ahead yawning open like some black cavern full of who-
knows-what. She had lost her companion and now had to live the rest of her life
without him. *"What should I say to that,"* wondered Beverly. *"Yes, I'd been
looking for an opportunity to go back and finish my degree, and now I have it.
How fortuitous!"*

And then there it was again, the recurring theme. "You're young and pretty.
Why you'll be married again in no time." Beverly could not stand it any longer.
How could they brush off her loss like that? She turned to her mother.

"What am I supposed to say to that? 'Yes, thank you, and would you please
move along. I see a nice-looking single fellow down the line, and I'd really like to
get things moving so that I can get acquainted with him.' It's easy for them to all
tell me how easy it's going to be for me to get along without Dave. They've all got
their spouses."

Naomi understood that her daughter's anger came from the pain she was
feeling. *"Someday, Beverly, when you've lived a few more years, you'll discover
that there's more than one brand of sorrow. Someday having gone through all of
this will make you more compassionate to others but right now it's making you less
compassionate."*

"Beverly, you know they mean well even if it comes out awkwardly."

Another couple. The lady grasped her hand. "It was his time. The Lord must
have needed him more than you did."

Another friend. "There must be something the Lord wants you to learn from
this experience."

"We're really going to miss his voice in the choir."

"He's left a real void in our professional community. He gave his life in the
act of saving someone else. You can always be proud of the fine man that was your
husband."

"We're here if you need us. We've got an extra bedroom if you ever want to
come stay with us for awhile."

"I know how you feel."

*"Sure you do, because you once had to flush a goldfish down the toilet when
you were ten."*

"This will help prepare you for greater trials to come." Beverly turned to her
mother and rolled her eyes. This time even charitable Naomi agreed.

"You're right. You should have punched that one. Who was that?"

"Church person. Someone from the stake, I think."

One of Dave's co-workers told her, "Everyone that wanted to attend the funeral
can't, but those who have to work tomorrow are all going to turn on their ambulance sirens at 10:00 when the funeral starts and make a bunch of people pull off
the road in honor of Dave."

"He would have liked that."

"Look at all these people here, Beverly," Donald Smithson remarked. "It's
obvious Dave was very well-thought-of." Dave Crandall, in spirit, stood nearby,
doing his best to lighten things up, as always.

*"Nah. It's Monday night. They're all just trying to get out of planning a real
Family Home Evening."*

The next day a viewing was scheduled in the Relief Society Room at the church, an hour before the funeral was to start. Many of the people from the ward had waited to attend the viewing at the more convenient church building rather than going to the mortuary the night before. Therefore, as it was getting close to time for the funeral to start, the funeral director had to hurry the last few people through. Beverly was glad of that, because she was planning to punch the next person who told her that she was young and would marry again.

A tall young man walked by the casket. He had the beginnings of a moustache and looked about 17. Beverly didn't know him. He stood in front of her awkwardly, fumbling for the right words. "I'm sorry," he said.

Beverly reflected. *"Now that seems like the right thing to say. It's simple and can't be misinterpreted."* A woman who seemed to be with him grasped Beverly's hand. She did not say anything, but she had tears in her eyes. Beverly looked after them. *"Where do we know them from? He doesn't look familiar, and I don't recognize her, either."* She didn't have time to think about it, because they hurried the last several people through in an attempt to start the funeral on time.

Beverly took Davey back from her mother. Naomi commented. "He's being such a good boy today." It was true. He hadn't fussed or tried to get down and run around. Beverly and the family walked into the chapel. She was pleased to see the large number of people in attendance. Davey sat quietly on her lap. Beverly marvelled at that, because in church meetings he was always squirming to get down and play.

As the speakers gave their talks, Beverly felt Dave's spirit nearby. As the male quartet from the Tabernacle Choir stood up to sing, she instinctively knew that he was there with them. She heard it in her mind, *"Look, I'm singing with the Tabernacle Choir!"* She saw them part in the middle, leaving room for Dave--probably unaware that they had even done it, but Beverly knew he was there between them singing. Beverly pleaded to her Heavenly Father. *"I know he's there. Let me see him. Why can't I see him?"*

A quiet answer. *"To see him would be only to exercise your eyesight. To feel him is to exercise your spirit."*

She wanted him to be able to see that she knew where he was, so Beverly looked at the spot where she had such strong feelings that Dave was standing and smiled at him. Not many people noticed where Beverly's gaze was fixed, until the little boy in her arms cried out in recognition, "Da Da! Da Da!" The men were singing "I Believe." They were seasoned professional singers--knowing only that they were singing at the funeral of a man who had hoped someday to sing in the Choir, but one by one their voices faltered as they heard a tiny boy on the front row calling out to his "Da Da." Every Kleenex and hanky in the room was pressed into service as they finished the song. At least one of the quartet managed to keep singing at all times.

The service had been a beautiful tribute to Dave, all that Beverly had hoped it would be. She followed the casket out the side doors, carrying her little boy, enveloped with a feeling of peace. She left with a feeling that she had been married to a wonderful man who was well-loved and respected.

CHAPTER SIX
GOING HOME

It was cold and crisp at the cemetery. Beverly hugged Davey to her and shielded his little face from the cold. Almost instantly her mother was there with the blanket from his car seat. He hadn't napped all day and he had finally fallen asleep. Beverly warmed her hands under the blanket as she draped it over him. *"I think I'll die in the summer."* Under the weight of her slumbering child, Beverly gratefully sank down in one of the chairs set up in front of the gravesite. Marjorie sat on one side of her and her mother on the other. Pamela sat next to Marjorie. The men stood, having left the chairs for the female and elderly family members. Naomi reached out her arms, indicating her willingness to hold Davey, but Beverly silently shook her head. Even as heavy as he was when he was sleeping, Beverly clung fiercely to her little boy that day. Gordon Crandall dedicated his son's grave, and Beverly watched numbly as they lowered Dave's casket into the ground. She stood shivering at his gravesite, a tiny child asleep on her shoulder, as everyone filed away. It was then that she realized this was the end of the process.

He was dead and buried.

It was over.

It was time to go. She watched people leave, knowing they could now go back to their normal lives. *"If only there was a way I could go home and find everything as it had been. They do it on television, in the movies, in cartoons. But this isn't a movie. It's my life. I can't fire the writers and go for a new ending."* The sleeping child in her arms had become unbearably heavy. Finally, she turned and handed him to her mother, who had known that although Beverly's will to have her child with her would not give out, eventually her arms would. "Can you take him, Mother? He's been so good today. He was quiet during the funeral. He hasn't fussed. I wish I could see the angels that are around us today, because I'm sure several have been attending to Davey." She tightened her coat around her. "He's been so mellow, considering what a disruption all this has been to his normal routine." Bone weary, Beverly trudged through the snow to the waiting vehicle. *"I wish I could just fall asleep in someone's arms and they would carry me off and put me to bed."*

After the ceremony at the cemetery, the family all gathered back at the church in the cultural hall for the luncheon put on by the Relief Society. Beverly gently removed Davey's snowsuit and left him sleeping in his carseat, which she set on the floor near the tables. She tried to eat a little, but she honestly had no interest in food. It seemed too incongruous to come from just burying your husband and then to ask Sister Russon for the recipe to her Chicken and Broccoli Casserole.

Beverly addressed her family. "I guess no one is still planning on Thanksgiving at our house day after tomorrow."

"We'll just move it to our house. That's the last thing I've been worried about with all this going on," Naomi assured her. Beverly listened as her family reaffirmed the assignments they had been given for the upcoming holiday.

"I'm bringing pies--apple and pumpkin," Marlene reported. "Do you still need the extra tablecloths?"

"That would be great, Marlene, and would you bring your folding table, if you still have it."

"I was bringing a green salad, and um, a potato side dish. I think I might bring Twice-Baked Potatoes," Gayle added, embarrassed.

"Oh, go ahead. You can say it, Gayle." Beverly picked up a spoonful of the potato side dish that was on her plate. "We all call them that. Gayle was going to bring 'Funeral Potatoes.' How was she to know we would be having our fill of those a couple of days beforehand?"

Sister Thompson, the Relief Society President, sat down across from Beverly. "You know, Beverly, I can't help but to have heard several of your relatives offering for you to come stay with them for a few days or a few weeks, and it's certainly up to you, but sometime you've got to go home and face the fact that he's not there. You could probably bounce around from relative to relative for quite some time, but the longer you put it off, the harder it will be."

Beverly did not respond, but the words rang true.

"Also, I'm sending the leftover food to your house. I know that you don't feel like eating right now, but sooner or later, your body is going to notice that it's hungry."

As Beverly sat talking to Sister Thompson, she overheard Sister Cooper and Sister McAffee at the serving table.

"I saw on the news that they caught the hit-and-run driver, a young fellow. Did you know that his mother had the nerve to call the bishop to see if it was okay if he came to the funeral? Can you imagine?"

As she overheard this, suddenly she was overcome with a tremendous feeling of peace and love, as if Heavenly Father had just put his arms around her. There was no room for anger or hate or unpleasantness. She knew, without having to be told, that the boy and his mother had been at the funeral--the young man and his mother she had been unable to place. She remembered the anguish she had seen in the woman's eyes and understood now the reason why. Beverly stood up and went over to Sister Cooper and Sister McAffee. She disregarded the unkind judgmental words she had heard. "He *was* there."

Sister Cooper's mouth dropped open.

"I met him. His mother, too. He told me he was sorry."

"You're going to press charges, aren't you?"

"It's not up to me. Leaving the scene of an accident is very serious, even without an injury involved. It's up to the police how they proceed. I don't know to what extent it will involve me, but I can't add hate on top of all the other emotions I feel right now. He's young, inexperienced. He was driving too fast for the weather conditions. He panicked and made wrong choices, and there will be consequences. He will live the rest of his life knowing that his actions resulted in someone's death. I hope they're not too hard on him, and if there's anything I can do in his defense, I'll do it."

"Maybe you wouldn't feel so forgiving if it had been a drunk driver or . . ."

"Maybe not, but it wasn't." Beverly struggled to help her understand. She was able to forgive because she had seen this young man through Heavenly Father's eyes and not her own. She had seen what was in his heart. She had felt of the unspoken emotions behind the awkward "I'm sorry."

Beverly had seen and felt the mother's love for her son, just as if she, herself, had been standing by a 17-year-old Davey who had made a terrible terrible mistake. A new comprehension flooded Beverly's soul. *"Heavenly Father really does love each of us and knows what's in our hearts."* His love was made known to her, not only for her and for Davey, but for this young man who had caused and then run from this tragic accident. It wasn't something she could explain adequately, or at all for that matter. She felt comforted and loved and assured that Dave was all right--and beyond all right, he was happy.

"She's probably still on tranquilizers," explained Sister Cooper to Sister McAffee.

Davey had not stirred since she had set him down in his carseat. Postponing the inevitable for as long as she could, she waited around until the luncheon was completely cleared and Sister Thompson was ready with the keys to lock the building. She bundled Davey back into his snowsuit. He stirred but did not awaken. Beverly announced to her family, the only ones still there, patiently waiting to see what the day would bring next. "I'm taking Davey now, and we are going to go home."

"But don't you think you should . . ."

Beverly caught Sister Thompson's eye. "I'm going home. I have to go home. This little guy needs to sleep in his crib for a change, not in his carseat or on someone's couch." She took her mother aside. "Mom, I hope you can understand this. I don't think I'm going to be there on Thursday for Thanksgiving."

"Beverly . . ." Naomi began.

"It's too hard, Mom. We were so excited about having Thanksgiving at our house this year. We worked so hard getting the house in good shape . . ."

"But we need you there. I'm already missing one of my children with Reggie on his mission in Texas . . ."

"Try to understand, Mom. For me, it will be like this funeral luncheon all over again. I can't do it."

It began to snow. The day had been clear, but cold. She buckled Davey in his car seat, even just to go the three blocks to their home. There would never be a time when she would take chances with his safety. The house looked dark and empty, but Beverly unlocked the door, swallowed hard and went inside. She remembered the turkey--the test turkey. Someone, probably her mother or Evelyn or one of the Three Nephites, had removed it from the oven. *"Thank Heavens it hasn't been in the oven since Friday."* She took it out of the refrigerator and threw it in the garbage.

"I never want to see another turkey as long as I live!"

CHAPTER SEVEN
GREEN JELLO

Davey was still asleep from earlier in the day. She had tried to wake him up and feed him, but he was out. He didn't stir as she changed him into a warm sleeper and covered him up for the night. Suddenly she realized how very tired she was.

She put on a nightgown and climbed into bed. The sheets were cold. She got up and turned up the heat and got back into bed. The sheets were still cold. Dave used to go to bed earlier than she did because he had to get up early for work, and he used to sleep on her side of the bed until she came to bed--to warm it up for her. Now she realized that he would not be there as a buffer between her and the cold sheets ever again, so she moved her arms and legs back and forth under the covers to warm things up. It surprised her that she barely had enough energy to do it. Finally, she fell asleep, curled up in one position, careful not to move outside the small area warmed by her body heat, lest a stray arm or foot should be assaulted by the cold and awaken the rest of her.

Her days became a blur of simple tasks repeatedly performed. One day seemed pretty much like the next. Get up. Shower. Dress. Eat breakfast. Feed Davey. Bathe Davey. Dress Davey. Put Davey down for a nap. Lay down. Feed Davey lunch. Watch Sesame Street. Put Davey down for afternoon nap. Open mail. Do laundry. Feed Davey dinner. Eat. Read bedtime story--anything but the "Eh-phunt story," which had been stashed somewhere on a shelf in Beverly's closet. Put Davey to bed. Put herself to bed.

It was the beginning of re-establishing a routine in her life, but she rarely got past the first two or three tasks before someone would come calling, and then she would fit her routine around her unannounced visitors. At least she was getting several hours of sleep a night, although some nights were better than others. Those were the nights she was somehow able to shut off the thought processes and let sleep overtake her. On other nights she was alone with her memories and fears until the wee hours.

Morning came quickly. Beverly got up, wrapped her robe around her and went into the bathroom. She opened the medicine cabinet. There was Dave's toothbrush, his shaving cream, and his razors, just like they had been every other morning. As she brushed her teeth, she contemplated what to do with Dave's personal things. *"Some of this stuff might still be useful to someone. Maybe one of my brothers can use the shaving cream and the razors. I hate to throw away perfectly good stuff. On the other hand nobody wants . . ."* She picked up Dave's toothbrush and threw it in the garbage, fighting back tears.

The doorbell rang. Hurrying down the hall, she stubbed her toe on Davey's folding stroller, which had fallen from where it had been propped up against the wall. She kicked it, which didn't make her foot feel any better, said a word she hoped Davey would not add to his growing vocabulary, and continued on to the door, as the bell rang insistently a second time. Beverly opened the door to find Sister Prescott on her doorstep and invited her in out of the cold. Roberta Prescott surveyed Beverly standing there in her bathrobe. Beverly ran her fingers through her hair, apologizing for her appearance. "I guess I slept in. Sometimes it takes me a long time to get to sleep, so when I finally do, I sleep as long as I can or until the little guy wakes up and needs me. I'm afraid I've got his rhythms all mixed up, too." She managed a weak smile.

"I'm sorry to bother you. I just came to get back my bowl from the luncheon." Beverly looked toward the counter where she had a stack of at least 15 assorted pans, bowls and casserole dishes that needed to be returned to their rightful owners.

"Which one is it?" Beverly asked.

Sister Prescott smiled and answered. "It was the one with the green Jello."

Beverly motioned wearily toward the counter. "Why don't you see if you can find it?" While Sister Prescott searched for her container, Beverly bent over and examined her toe, realizing she had nearly torn her toenail off. Sister Prescott found her bowl, and she was off, with a few encouraging words.

"Remember, when life gives you lemons, make lemonade."

After she was out the door, Beverly muttered to herself, "Lemonade and green Jello--the cure to all of life's ills."

Before she had a chance to get a bandage for her toe, Davey began to call for her. He had also slept late but was now awake and had noticed he was hungry. As she settled Davey into his high chair, she heard another knock on the door.

"Maybe if I don't answer it, they'll go away. But my car is in the driveway. If I don't answer it, they'll panic and think I'm not okay."

She pulled her bathrobe around her yet another time and answered the door. It was Brother and Sister Anderson. Beverly surmised that it must be Saturday, otherwise Brother Anderson would have been at work. She invited them into the kitchen to visit with her while she fed Davey. Beverly knew that the onslaught of visitors she had each day was an indication that people cared about her, but there was nothing left of a normal routine to her life or Davey's.

Brother Anderson was giving Beverly financial advice--unasked for financial advice. In between spooning bites of cereal into Davey's mouth, she answered him politely. When the bowl was empty, she poured a bunch more Cheerios on the high chair tray for Davey, along with a cut-up banana, and tried to turn her attention to Brother Anderson. Her toe was throbbing.

"Yes, I appreciate that, Brother Anderson, but I *do* know how to balance a checkbook. I've got all our accounts on my computer. And you're right, putting the entire proceeds of an insurance policy into a regular savings account would not be good money management."

"Are you aware that you can file for Social Security for you and your boy?"

"Yes, Brother Anderson. I filled out all the papers last week."

"Well, good. And what are your plans for the future?"

"Plans for the future? Well, I'm thinking of doctoring the toenail I almost ripped off this morning, and I would really like to take a shower and get dressed sometime today." Sister Anderson elbowed her husband.

"Maybe Beverly needs a little time to herself and we can talk about this later." Marion Anderson stopped at the door after her husband had gone out.

"I'm sorry, Beverly, if we upset you or came at a bad time. Jim just wants to help, and I'm afraid he thinks you're like me. He's always handled all of our financial affairs, and I would not know *anything* if he died." Beverly shook her head. So he would come to teach *her* how to survive, but would most likely neglect to leave his wife with any survival skills if *he* died. That made a lot of sense. She put Davey on the floor with his blocks, put a Bandaid on her toe, and was preparing to climb into the shower when the doorbell rang again. She pulled her robe back on. It was Toni Cirroni, her visiting teacher.

"I was just about to get in the shower . . ." she told Toni.

"I just came to give you the visiting teaching message. I won't take long." Beverly opened the door and Toni came in. "You're not looking so good, Beverly." Toni looked her over. Beverly's cheeks were sunken in. She looked old and tired. It was too bad. "You're a pretty woman. You need to get hold of yourself, girl. Here it is, 1:30 in the afternoon and you're not even dressed yet." Toni switched gears. "Come to think of it, you're probably a visiting teacher, right, so you have a copy of the message, don't you? I don't want to bore you by giving it to you if you've already been out. It's something about learning to love people by serving them--a couple of 'feel good' stories and a scripture. Anyway, you can read it in the Ensign. Also, I want to invite you to a Mary Kay party I'm having next Saturday. You can come have a free facial. It might be just what you need."

Beverly was too tired even to get angry. "Yes, I'm sure that's what's missing in my life."

Toni looked hurt. "Well, I think it would do you good to get out. At least think about it. It's a shame about your husband and all, but if you let yourself go, you're never going to find another one."

"I've got to start writing these down. No one will believe me, otherwise."

Just as Toni was leaving, another car pulled into the driveway. Aunt Marlene and Beverly's cousin, Jenny, got out and came to the door. Beverly let them in as she let Toni out. Aunt Marlene bustled into the house. Beverly gave her a hug.

"Honey, you look like something the cat dragged in."

"Thank you, Aunt Marlene. That was the spiritual message my visiting teacher just delivered, too." Marlene picked up Davey.

"I'm sorry to come by without calling first."

"Why not? Everyone else does. I've been trying all day just to get into the shower."

"So don't let me stop you. Don't let them stop you, either. If they're rude enough to come by without calling, you should just leave them sitting out here on your couch and go get in the shower, myself included. Go on! Go take a shower." She handed Davey to Jenny. "Jenny, entertain this little kiddo."

When Beverly got out of the shower, Marlene had a load of laundry washing and had made the bed. She had done the dishes and was dusting the furniture when Beverly emerged from her bedroom, feeling better just by virtue of being clean. Jenny was on the floor building block towers with Davey.

"We're going Christmas shopping. Jenny is going to babysit. Show her what you need to show her and go get in the car."

Aunt Marlene was a take-charge kind of woman. Beverly briefed her cousin on babysitting duties, and she and Aunt Marlene headed to town.

"We're going to do up the ZCMI Center and the Crossroads Mall." Marlene softened. "I know this won't bring him back, but when I'm depressed, I shop, so you should be up to a major shopping spree. Christmas is coming. I know you're not in the mood, but it's coming anyway. I've got my Mastercard and Visa. Your Uncle Roger will have a fit, of course, but I'll take care of him. He expects it this time of year."

"I can't let you pay. I've got money," Beverly said.

"You put your money away. This one's on me."

"Aunt Marlene, I can't . . ."

"Oh knock it off, Beverly. This is me. We're kindred spirits. You can and you will. Women always say, 'Oh, no, no, no, I can't let you do that,' even though they are going to, but they have to protest two or three times before they give in, so that it goes on the record. You've always had a little bit of me in you, you know. I've never been able to beat around the bush and be sweet and sugary like other women. Maybe you're not quite an old battle-ax like your Aunt Marlene, but I know you. You may not see it now, but you've got the strength to get through this. The first thing you've got to do is take charge of your own life. Your mother is right, that people have good intentions, but you've got to look to your own needs and that little guy's needs. If I were you, I'd go down to that hotel you used to work at and ask them for one of those 'Do Not Disturb' signs they put on the doors. I'd put it out in the morning until you've had a shower, are dressed and have bathed and fed your little one. Then I'd accept visitors."

"That's a good idea. I guess I hadn't realized how much I'm letting people, however well-meaning, walk all over me. I've never had so much unsolicited advice. People are asking me personal questions about my income and our insurance. I would never ask them how much money they made or how they were handling it. Don't they think I'm intelligent enough to seek out advice from the right sources? The things Brother Anderson was talking about were so basic, I wanted to tell him that I had lost my husband, not my mind. I find myself wishing that someone else in the ward would have a crisis so that everyone would stop paying so much attention to me. I have so many visitors every day, my routine, what there is left of it, is totally disrupted."

"Oh, Beverly, some people can't help but treat you like a helpless female. They don't know you like I do. Women like us just have to be who we are and find men that will accept us for what we are. I even read 'Fascinating Womanhood' once after this friend of mine convinced me how much it had helped her marriage. After I'd been 'fascinating' for about two weeks, Roger told me, 'Marlene, I don't know what you're doing, but for Heaven's sakes, *cut it out!*' Besides, all the advice you get won't be useless. You just have to do what I do--listen to everyone, pretend their advice is good so that they feel helpful, then go ahead and do what *you* think is right. Only you have the big picture. If people give you advice based on part of the facts, feel free to take only part of the advice."

"Basically, they either tell me how well I'm doing, because once a week I get dressed up and go sit in church and try to put on a happy face or they come over and treat me like an idiot. They don't know what it's like lying awake at night, wanting to sleep, but not being able to, or hearing the wrong song on the radio and bursting into tears, no matter where I am."

"How would you like people to treat you?"

"It sounds like I don't even know. I complain if they come over too much, but I also complain if they don't come at all. I would like them to treat me like I'm competent and strong enough to get through this, like you said, but not to treat me like it isn't hard for me or as hard for me as it would be for them. Someone said to me, 'How do you even get out of bed in the morning? I wouldn't have been able to come home. I would be at my parents' home. I could never handle it like you do.' Then the next person comes along and tells me that the Lord has something He wants me to learn from all this or that the Lord doesn't give us more than we can handle. I get angry at myself for being strong and able to handle things. I wonder if those women who could never handle something like this will never have to and if I'm strong, the Lord will just give me even more trials."

"People just try to make sense of things like this. They don't have the answers. You don't have the answers. I certainly don't. I'm just an old Wobble-ato, after all."

"You know about Wobble-atos?"

"I overheard Dave talking once about your ward choir. I wasn't born yesterday. I told the girls about it, and we had a great laugh. We're not as young as we once were, I know. When we called ourselves 'The Lean Sisters' because of our names, who knew that we would all turn out to be women of substance? We were joking about changing our name to 'The Four Wobble-atos.' That would cover our voices and our figures." She laughed heartily. "We used to perform quite a bit back in our younger days, you know. We were in demand. We were babes, I tell you. You kids never heard us in our heyday. We do it now for fun. Mother Nature takes away our youthful good looks, our abilities, our mental capacity as we get older. The one thing I get better at is having fun." She returned to the subject from earlier in the conversation. "I know Dave is gone, but don't drive yourself nuts trying to figure it all out. When people say they could never handle it, maybe they think God has some angel taking notes for future reference. Maybe they're not trying to make you feel better. They might be trying to reassure themselves. They're trying to convince themselves it won't ever happen to them because they couldn't deal with it. People are uncomfortable around you because you're a reminder of what could happen to them. Some stuff just happens. Either your husband died because it was his time or because the road was slippery and there was an inexperienced driver behind the wheel. It makes us all feel better if we can come up with some explanation."

"But it doesn't make me feel better."

"Let them know. Take out the garbage. Don't let it pile up. That's my philosophy. Sure, I'm known for my big mouth, but I don't go around festering for years like some people who don't have the courage to stand up for themselves. You don't see me tankin' up on the Maalox. When Stanley Burton was supposed to head the clean-up crew for the ward Halloween party, and he didn't show up, I called him at home, and I told him to get his behind down there and start cleaning up. I sure wasn't going to stick around until 11:00 at night carrying pumpkins out to the dumpster. I don't know what he was doing, or why he wasn't at the party, but he came right over. Sure, that story went around the ward, but when I assign a clean-up crew now for one of our parties, they show up! If you're hurting, let people know. If you put on a front, they'll think you're doing better than you really are and pretty soon they think you're all better when you're not."

"I'm going to remember that. Taking out the garbage. Like those two old ladies that stood over Dave's casket and talked about his injuries. I should have said something to them."

"What would you have said?"

"How about this? 'You know, the mortuary goes to great lengths to make a deceased person look as good as possible to bring a feeling of peace to their loved ones, and to hear you discussing Dave's injuries takes away that feeling of peace.'"

"Sure, Beverly, if you've got time to write up a script. I'd have told the old biddies that if they didn't shut up, they would have their own injuries to talk about!"

Beverly laughed, surprised that she still possessed the capacity to laugh. "Aunt Marlene, you're the first person who has really made me feel better since Dave died."

"Think of it this way--if you don't take out the garbage, it will sit and get rotten and stink up the house. Even garbage can be put to good use. You can make an emotional compost heap. Somewhere in all that crap there may be something useful that can be used for your growth." Marlene paused for a minute. "Are you angry at God?" Beverly did not answer at first.

"Aunt Marlene, right after Dave's funeral, I kept having all of these wonderful feelings as if God was almost physically with me. I was on a spiritual high, understanding and accepting all of this and knowing the reasons why things are the way they are. It was like life is a test and I got a look at the answers. I thought I would automatically pass, but now I still have to go back and take the test. I'm angry at almost everybody. I'm angry at people with husbands that tell me nice little cliches about how to get through this. I'm angry at Dave for dying. And yes, I'm angry at God! There are plenty of women married to jerks who would have gladly been rid of their husbands. Why couldn't He have taken one of them and done some poor woman a favor? Why did He have to take Dave, when we were just starting out and we were so happy? It stinks!"

"Is it important that you know for sure whether or not it was Dave's time, why he was taken?"

"Well it would be comforting . . ."

"So you would feel better if you got some message that it was his time, that there was some reason he died November whatever-day-it-was? Suppose it wasn't his time? Suppose you found out he was supposed to live a long life and you were supposed to have more children and grow old together--wouldn't he still be dead? He may have cut in line, Beverly, but the bottom line is he's had his ticket punched. Sorry if that sounds as blunt as a brick wall, but I'm afraid that's the way I am. Let me ask you this. Looking back, would you give up the happiness you had with David, give up ever having known him, give up the possibility of being together forever, not to be going through what you are now?"

"No."

"Would you give up your son, to be spared years of being a single parent?"

"No, of course not."

"Do you think it's worth going through all this now to have had what you had together and to have this little boy to love?"

"Yes. I would have to say it's worth it."

"Maybe that's the only answer you need right now."

Beverly unloaded her packages into the house and hugged Marlene and Jenny goodbye. Davey sat in the middle of the living room still playing with his blocks. Beverly built a few towers with him, and he squealed with delight when they fell over. *"If only I could be so easily entertained,"* she thought. Thirsty, she went into the kitchen to get a drink of water. When she came back into the living room, she noticed that Davey had lost interest in his blocks. Down on all fours, something under the sofa had caught his attention. He crawled over, stopped in front of the sofa and reached his hand underneath. It came up empty. Beverly got down on the floor so she could see the object of his attention, but she couldn't see anything. Davey adjusted his position, his little bottom sticking up and his head turned to one side and pressed to the carpet. Whatever it was, he was willing to work for it. He reached under the sofa again, but still his hand came up empty. He moved down and reached under the sofa once more. In his hand he triumphantly held a dusty Cheerio, which was headed right into his mouth.

Beverly swooped down and snatched it away from him before he could eat it. Davey began to howl with despair. Beverly empathized. He had worked hard for that Cheerio, and just when he had finally obtained it, she had taken it away. It wasn't fair. It wasn't nice. She sat and held him and they cried together. *"It isn't fair, Heavenly Father. I had just found him, and You took him away."* Davey cried for his Cheerio and Beverly cried for Dave, and she didn't understand why Dave was gone anymore than Davey understood why the Cheerio was gone. She understood her reasons, of course, for not letting her son eat an old dusty Cheerio, and she supposed God had His reasons, but they didn't seem as clear as they had. She didn't know what they were, and, like Davey, she didn't care what they were! Whatever they were, they weren't good enough, because she couldn't have what she wanted.

CHAPTER EIGHT
TAKING OUT THE GARBAGE

Beverly arranged a lunch date with one of her former co-workers from the hotel. There were only a couple of people still there who remembered her, but Holly had been glad to see her and had gladly donated a "Do Not Disturb" sign to the cause.

Beverly met her in the lobby at the appointed time.

"Boy this place brings back old memories!"

"I guess it would. You and Dave had your courtship here."

"We spent our wedding night here, too. After all, this hotel is where we met, when he used to come in here with his co-workers on their breaks."

"I'm sorry. Maybe I should have met you at the restaurant. I didn't mean to stir up old memories."

"They're good memories. I don't want to forget. In fact, do you mind if we just stay here and eat at the coffee shop?"

"Well, I guess I can try out the restaurant at that new Sheraton some other time."

They went into the coffee shop and were seated in a booth. Beverly was somehow comforted by being in a place that held so many memories of the early days of her acquaintance with Dave, the wayward returned missionary and paramedic.

"Remember the time he decked that co-worker of his and broke his nose after he made an off-color remark about you? I'll never forget how Cora came running out of the gift shop, saw some blood and yelled *'Call the paramedics.'*"

"I'll never forget that one, either. I'm going to have some stories to tell Davey when he gets older," Beverly laughed. "Dave was trying to quit smoking around that time. He was kind of moody there for a while. And he lived in fear that while he was trying to get back on the straight and narrow path, some other guy was going to come along and flash a temple recommend at me and I'd be gone." Beverly switched gears. "Is Cora still here?"

"Yes, she's the only one that's been here longer than I have. You should go say hello to her. She lost her husband recently also. Of course, she's at the time of life where you expect that to happen."

"I doubt it's easy at that age, either, especially if you've spent a life together. In some ways, I can probably snap back easier than she can."

"Would you come tell our Young Women's group your story? I'm Young Women's President now. I think it would be good for them to hear how you held out for a temple marriage, especially now, with what has happened."

"Sure, set it up and give me a call. It would probably be good for me, too, to have a chance to talk about it, and to feel that my experiences were helping someone else. Lots of people seem uncomfortable now when I talk about Dave. They change the subject or just give body language that it's an uneasy subject. I'm glad to be around someone who doesn't mind letting me talk about him. I'm not always going to run from the room crying."

"Remember the gum?"

"The gum! I'd forgotten all about that."

"I'm not sure you ever clued me in on that one. I remember you saying he was so hard to get along with while he was trying to quit, that you were tempted to go buy him a pack of cigarettes. There we were working the desk, and he plopped that paper with that big old wad of gum stuck on it down on the desk and asked you if you'd enjoyed your date."

"I'd gone to lunch with an old friend from college, a guy friend. Dave came in just as we were leaving, and saw us together. He thought I was testing him to see if he could keep from smoking under stress, so he chewed all that gum while I was out and gave me the evidence that he hadn't smoked and then stormed out. So much of our early history took place right here in this hotel." Beverly's voice took on a note of melancholy. "I miss him so much."

"I'm sorry I wasn't able to make it to the funeral," Holly apologized. "I heard about the accident on the news, and when I realized it was your husband, I tried to get the day off, but we have a new manager. If Erik had still been the manager, I know he would have remembered you and given me the time off. Anyway, I meant to get hold of you . . . I haven't been a very good friend. I wasn't exactly there for you."

"Hey, the whole ward was there for me. Now they're back to their regular lives, for the most part. You're here now and we're having lunch. You're someone who remembers my courtship with Dave, even some of the parts I'd rather not remember. Who else can fill that bill? I appreciate that you thought about me and that you tried to get there. It didn't even occur to me that any of my former co-workers would hear about it. My family did a good job of shielding me from the news coverage, so I never really realized how extensively it was publicized, because of the hit-and-run thing."

"They found the person, right?"

"Yes, they found him, he came forward, but I don't really want to talk about that now. I was really just enjoying the pleasant memories." Beverly changed the subject. "It's mostly new faces here. Whatever happened to Linda? We used to work the night shift together. She was a lot of fun. She's a little younger than I am, but we used to have a good time. I wouldn't mind looking her up."

"She just got back from a mission. I believe she's living with her parents for now. Yeah, you get to know someone reasonably well when you work the front desk together. You spent most of my last pregnancy with me. I remember reading a book that said that your baby comes to know familiar voices even before it's born. I told my husband our new baby was going to look around and say to itself, 'Where's Beverly?'"

The "Do Not Disturb" sign did the trick. Although Beverly had a hard time sleeping, she managed to get a few hours of sleep each night and visitors were not interrupting her morning activities quite so often. Beginning to establish a routine again during the day, she was forcing herself to eat, even though she had no interest in food, because she was even more certain now that she was pregnant.

She had made an appointment with the doctor. So far, her mother was the only one that she had told about her suspicions. A pregnancy would give her all the more reason to take charge of her life. The visitors had slacked off, so had the sympathy cards. For a while, each day when she went to the mailbox, there had been a handful of cards from out-of-town friends and relatives or people who had been unable to come to the funeral. Some of them contained checks, for which she was grateful. The people in the ward had also come forth with donations, which had paid her house payment for that first month before she got the insurance check. She was so grateful that Dave had worked in a profession that dealt with life and death issues, because for that reason he had not been lax in carrying life insurance on himself. She was also grateful for caring friends. At the same time, however, some of them made her life more difficult, blurring the fine line between discussing someone in a concerned way and sharing publicly things that should have been private. Too many people knew her every move, which was the main reason Beverly had told only her mother about her pregnancy.

Christmas season was in full swing, and Beverly knew she needed to do something to celebrate. Thanks to Aunt Marlene forcing her to go shopping, she had a few gifts for Davey. She was doing her best to ignore everything else. Mom and Dad and the brothers came by one evening with pizza and a small Christmas tree, which they helped her decorate. She put it in the family room, because Dave's co-workers and their families had already brought them a large tree, which she had in the living room. There were so many gifts for Davey under it that she had accused them of robbing from the Toys for Tots program that the firefighters and paramedics sponsored every year.

"Well, Mom, everyone has pretty much slowed down on the sympathy cards. Now I'm getting Christmas cards and funeral junk mail--advertisements for places you can purchase a headstone and pre-planning packages from every mortuary in town. Now that Dave has died, I guess I'm supposed to just go pick out a nice coffin for myself, prepay my funeral expenses and wait it out, huh? Also I get tons of mail from financial planners and brochures for investment opportunities. Most of these are probably legitimate investment opportunities, companies that have been around forever, but some of them are kind of questionable." Beverly showed a brochure to her father. "This one should have a swarm of vultures circling a dead cow as part of the logo."

"The sad thing is, Beverly, many widows fall for this stuff, invest without investigating. I read somewhere the other day that no matter what the settlement, most widows go through it all in two years."

"I'm glad you told me that. It seems like so much money that I can see how a woman must feel that it's inexhaustible. The way I see it, I need to plan for the worst and hope for the best. I need to handle this money so that if I never marry again, I can provide for Davey and myself for the rest of our lives. When Davey starts school, I'll go back and finish my degree, but I just want to be home with him for now."

"Have you decided where you're going to purchase a headstone?" Beverly picked up the Yellow Pages. Turning to the appropriate section, she showed him that she had checked off every company that had sent her a brochure.

"I'll get one from whatever company does not send me some stupid 'Gone but not Forgotten' flyer in the mail."

"How about this?" Sterling said. "Tombstones R Us."

"Sterling!" Naomi said sternly, not wanting to make light of this delicate subject.

Beverly laughed. "I think he's onto something. Maybe they should just advertise like everyone else does, or combine their business with something else to make it more palatable."

Evan was next. "McMortuary--have your loved-one laid out in the drive-through window--pay your last respects and get a burger on the way out." Now Beverly was really laughing.

"Dave would have loved that one!"

Sterling continued, speaking in a deep voice. "Good afternoon, I was in the neighborhood delivering a coffin to your neighbors, and I just happened to have several coffins leftover . . ."

Beverly was laughing out loud now. "They came last week--the meat guys."

". . . so little lady, I think we can talk turkey. I'll have to clear this great deal I'm offering with my manager, of course, but I think we can do business. Name your price. What'll it take to put you in this coffin today?"

Naomi shook her head. She had wanted to bring a smile back to Beverly's face, but this was not what she'd had in mind. "Which side of the family did they get this from?" Naomi asked her husband.

"You know what I want it to say on my headstone?" Sterling asked. "Here lies Sterling. He is dead. Leave the flowers and go."

"It figures you would find a way to be anti-social even after you were dead," Randall observed.

Laughing with her brothers was the most fun Beverly had during the holiday season. It relieved some of the weight that was always on her shoulders. She wondered how long it would be before she would awaken without this terrible ache in her heart--an emotional hurt that she felt so strongly it was almost physical. Each morning she faced a bathroom with only one toothbrush, and each night she faced an empty bed. She missed kneeling with Dave at night by their bed, saying prayers. She missed their late-night conversations and cuddling, missed making love, being close emotionally and physically.

The doctor had confirmed her pregnancy. Dr. Richards took a little extra time with her, admonishing her to take especially good care of herself and to avoid what stress she could. "Losing your husband has you at the top of the stress charts already. Don't lift Davey more than you need to. Get lots of rest. Do you have some help?"

"My family is close by. Don't worry, Doctor. Carrying this baby is my top priority right now. I won't overdo it. I've even been eating."

"Let's hope so."

In bed that night, Beverly wondered who this little spirit was, growing inside of her. Overwhelmed, she also felt excited. Experiencing the anticipation of a new life was comforting. Arrivals were so much better than departures. She thought of this baby as Dave's parting gift to her. Yes, it would be hard to go through the pregnancy without David, and to raise two children by herself. Still, she told herself that years later she would look back on this time, and how difficult it had been and look at the child she loved and not be able to imagine not having and loving that child. She knew that just as Aunt Marlene had said she would conclude that it had all been worth it. Maybe it would be a little sister for Davey. She had always hoped for a sister, but Mother had never cooperated, although she wouldn't trade any of her brothers for a sister. She reasoned it would be good to have one of each, since she might never have any more children. On the other hand, if it was a boy, then he and Davey could be best buddies and play together and entertain each other. She did know more about boys than she did about girls, and she was outfitted for a boy. She tried not to think too far ahead--to labor and delivery. She knew that her mom and sister-in-law Gayle would be there with her. Instead she imagined Dave in Heaven spending time with this baby before he or she came to earth, a comforting thought, and Beverly's last as she drifted off to sleep.

Before the news of Beverly's pregnancy had even been announced to the entire family, she found herself at the doctor's office again. Dr. Richards was replaced by the doctor on call. He came into the office where Beverly was weeping quietly.

"Don't feel bad," he said. "About 10 to 15% of all pregnancies end in miscarriage. It was very routine, actually. You weren't really very far along."

Beverly exploded. "Don't feel bad? I think I have every right to feel bad! What a stupid thing to say! Maybe it was routine for you, doctor, but it wasn't routine for me! So what if I wasn't very far along? I was pregnant! I was hoping and planning! This might have been my last chance to have a baby!"

"I see no reason you can't get pregnant again. You're young, healthy and . . ."

"Oh yes there is a reason! My husband died last month! But don't worry about it, Doctor, because I understand that 100% of the people who are born, die! statistics are so comforting, aren't they?"

"Now Mrs. Crandall, I know you're upset about losing this baby, but you're young. Maybe this was a blessing in disguise. It would have been awfully difficult for you to go through a pregnancy alone. You've got your whole life ahead of you. You'll probably marry again and have several more children."

Beverly sat back down on the examining table. Through clenched teeth, she said, "If one more person tells me that I'm young and will marry again, I am going to scream! Don't they teach you in medical school how to deal with people's pain, instead of adding to it? Isn't that part of your training? A blessing in disguise? Why don't you tell me that the Lord wanted me to learn something from this experience or that He needed that spirit more than I did? What did He do, change His mind halfway through? How about a blessing that's *not* in disguise?"

He looked at his clipboard. "Mrs. Crandall, I have someone else I need to see now. I'm sorry about your baby." He was gone. And her baby was gone, too.

Numbly, Beverly continued to go through the motions of the season. She took Davey to the ward Christmas party, so that he could sit on Santa's lap. He was wearing a little red sweatshirt that said, "I've Been a Good Boy." As the line moved closer to Santa, Sister Dayton walked in with her new baby--a little girl with lots of curly dark hair. Beverly began to cry. She left Davey standing in line with Evelyn's children and decided to go hide out in the bathroom for a few minutes. Cutting through the buffet line, she attempted her getaway into the bathroom. Sister Barnes noticed her expression.

"Beverly, are you okay?"

"I'll be fine," she lied, to nearly the entire ward, who all now seemed to be looking at her as they stood in line for the food. Then she remembered Aunt

Marlene talking to her about taking out the garbage, and Beverly had been saving up. She backed up the dump truck, and pulled the lever.

"No, I'm not okay! I was pregnant, and I had a miscarriage." Conversations were abruptly halted. Everyone was listening. "The doctor brushed it off like it was nothing. He told me I was young and that I would get married again, and I could have other children, just like I've heard 5 kazillion times from all of you! Sure, maybe I will, but that doesn't erase the pain I feel right now! If someone is driving down the street and there has been an avalanche of rocks in front of their car, you don't drive by and tell them that there are clear roads up ahead! You get out of the car and help them move some of the rocks! Brother Anderson, do you really think I'd put all the insurance money into a savings account? Do I look that stupid to you? While you're at it, why don't you teach *your wife* how to balance a checkbook instead of keeping her dependent on you for everything?"

Despite the fact that the buffet table was well-laden with turkeys, hams, festive side dishes and holiday desserts, the food line had not budged an inch since Beverly started her tirade.

"Sister Hansen, yes, I'm glad I have my husband for eternity, but you've got your husband for eternity *and you've got him now, too!* By the way, how much money did you make last year, Brother Cooper? I wouldn't pry into your financial situation the way you pried into mine, and if I did come over with the intention of helping you and was privileged to some information, I would certainly not share it with Sister Cooper, who has the biggest mouth in the whole ward! Brother Arletti, how do you know it was Dave's 'time?' Did you fast and pray about that? What is it that the Lord wants me to learn from all of this--how to turn on a lawn mower, how to use jumper cables? How do you know what the Lord had in mind? Did you ask Him? Do you have some kind of inside information? About my plans for the future--I'm sorry if I don't have everything all mapped out nicely since it has been almost a month. Do you have any idea how many papers I've had to fill out, how many insurance forms I've had to process, running on three or four hours of sleep a night? Do you know what it feels like to have to go to the hospital, hoping against hope that your husband is alive, and be asked to go in and identify his body?! How long do you think it takes to recover from something like that--two, maybe three weeks? And you have the nerve to ask me about my *plans!* It's all I can do to get out of bed every morning, get dressed and take care of Davey. Sister Litton, why should I go get a job to 'take my mind off of this.' Could you take your mind off of it if it happened to you? There's *nothing* that can take my mind off of it. I don't have an on/off switch on my brain, and I'm in no shape to take a job, if I wanted to, and at the moment, I don't. Davey has lost one parent. He doesn't need to lose the other one to the workplace. It was acceptable for me to be an at-home mom when Dave was alive. Why am I supposed to all of a sudden become a career woman, just because he died? Why should I have to tell you of my financial situation inside and out before you're convinced that I don't need to work right now? Can't you trust me to make the decisions that are right for me at the time that's right for me? And Sister Prescott, my husband died a month ago! *Do you really think I would remember which bowl the green Jello came in?"*

Beverly collected Davey and left the party, embarrassed that she had said all that she had said, but at the same time, feeling better somehow that she had said it.

The buffet line at the church began to move, slowly and quietly and people began to talk among themselves. The next week at church nobody told Beverly how well she was doing and how strong she was.

CHAPTER NINE
HAPPY ANNIVERSARY

Winter dragged on interminably. January was cold and dreary. Stagnant air hung over the valley. She hadn't paid attention when she heard it on the news-- some weather pattern. She just knew that it was dank and depressing. Having made it through Christmas, January now seemed to go by a minute at a time. She changed diapers, read stories, watched Sesame Street, did laundry, fixed meals, often feeling like a robot--going through the motions of life, but with the joy taken out of it.

The phone rang. It was Lori, one of her old friends from high school. She had just been to visit Lori and her husband a couple of nights before.

"Oh, I'm okay, I guess. This weather is so depressing, but thanks for inviting me over the other night. It was good to see you guys. I hope I didn't keep you up too late." She knew that she had stayed too late, but it was so hard going back home to an empty house. In fact, on the way home with Davey asleep in the car, and driving through a windy snowstorm, Beverly had wondered what would happen if she drove off the road late at night. There was no one at home to report them missing. She had expressed this thought the next day to Lori as they talked on the phone. "Or if something happened to me at home, how long before anyone would wonder where I was."

The next night around ten o'clock, the phone rang. It was Lori. "Just checking to make sure you're home. Everything okay?" After that, Lori called every night about the same time. If she did not find Beverly home, she called the next morning. "Are you alive and well?" It was a small thing, but it meant a lot to Beverly, to know that someone sensed a need and filled it.

January melted into February. One day as Beverly returned from a visit to her parents, she drove by an industrial area and noticed a small shop with three or four headstones out front. She pulled in and unloaded Davey from his car seat. Inside the shop, she found a stocky older man with a thick German accent. "I need a headstone," she told him. "I've never heard of you. Do you advertise?"

"My verk is my advertisement," he said gruffly.

"Well, I like your work. Can I tell you a little bit about what I had in mind?"

Dave and Beverly's wedding anniversary was late in February. She decided to get a nice flower arrangement and take it to the cemetery. The headstone would not be ready for several months, and could not be put in place anyway until spring. She had called the florist and ordered a rather expensive bouquet of flowers, something similar to the flowers from their wedding. She picked them up and put them in the back seat next to Davey's car seat. On the drive to the cemetery, she noticed the car was making a funny noise. "What now?" She began to talk to herself. "My life is just one thing after another." She looked heavenward. "Do You think You could take it easy on me for a while? I'm doing the best I can! Do You think I need car troubles now, too?"

She turned on the radio to drown out the car noise. They were playing an old Elvis tune--the song that David had sung to her when he had proposed. Tears came to her eyes. A little voice from the back seat said, "Okay, Mama?"

"Yes honey, Mama's okay. Just a little bit sad today." She looked in the rearview mirror. She kept him situated in the middle of the back seat where she could look at him occasionally. Also, she had read that the back seat was the safest place to put a child in a car seat. She pulled into the cemetery. Since there was no headstone in place yet, she had to find Dave in relation to the trees and the other markers. He was close to the road, in between two pine trees and down from "Winnifred Johnston, Beloved Wife and Mother." You could still tell that his mound was fresh, even under the snow. Beverly reached into the back seat to get the flowers. She was not going to get Davey out, because it was so cold. She was just going to leave the flowers.

"Fowers," said Davey. From his car seat, he had picked every blossom from the bouquet. Scattered on the seat were plucked rose petals, limp lilies and decapitated daisies. There remained a vase full of stems and some ivy. "Fowers."

Beverly was livid. She scooped up some of the flowers from the floor of the car and retrieved a couple of rosebuds off the seat. She couldn't take her anger out on her son. He was too young to understand. She grabbed the vase, and marched over to Dave's gravesite and took it out on him instead. She started throwing flower remains on his grave--squashed roses, beheaded lilies and plucked daisies. She started yelling. "Happy Anniversary! You're supposed to buy *me* flowers on our anniversary! You're supposed to be *alive*! Sure, go die on me and leave me to take care of everything! What do you care if the car is making a funny noise?" She dumped out the stems and the water and threw the plastic vase into the trunk of the car. Angrily, Beverly headed towards home, only she did not go home. Instead, she pulled into the Jensen's driveway, got Davey out of the car, carried him up the walk and rang the doorbell. Evelyn answered the door. Beverly handed Davey to her.

"Is this the Society to Prevent Child Abuse? Good. I'll be back in an hour or two."

"Beverly, what's wrong? Are you okay?"

"No, I'm not okay. I'm losing it, big time." Evelyn Jensen handed Davey off to her teen-age daughter.

"Alison, you're babysitting. I'm going with Beverly."

Half an hour later, they ended up at Cirroni's restaurant. Evelyn showed Beverly a picture from the dessert menu. "This looks like something a depressed woman would order." Beverly eyed the picture of the chocolate cake with a scoop of vanilla ice cream, smothered in hot fudge, topped with whipped cream and covered with chocolate curls.

"It looks like you should have a designated driver if you eat one of those."

"No chance. If you get one, I'm getting one. Damn the diet."

Alex Cirroni had seen them come in and came over to their table. "Good evening, ladies. Is this the Ev and Bev show? What'll it be?"

"Hi Alex. I'll tell you what--we're here to violate our obedience to the Word of Wisdom the only way we know how. We'd like two of these 'moderation in all things' Chocolate Triple Plays."

Beverly recounted her trip to the cemetery to Evelyn, only somehow under the influence of chocolate, it seemed more funny than anything else. "I was throwing the flowers on the ground and yelling at him."

"It probably felt good--I mean to get it out."

"Sometimes I get really mad at him because he doesn't have to deal with this stupid earth life anymore. He's somewhere peaceful and restful. I'm here struggling and trying to cope. It stinks!"

"You know we're always here if you need a break from Davey. I know you're not ready to date or start back to school or anything full time, but maybe you should take a night class or join a bowling league or do something that will get you out of the house on a regular basis. I remember those years with three pre-schoolers at home. There were days. Of course, teen-agers make you long for those days. How do you convince a 14-year-old girl that a pimple on the side of her nose does not signal the end of the world as we know it? How do you help mend a 17-year-old's broken heart when you're doing cartwheels because this boy you have never felt good about is dating someone else and has lost interest in your daughter?"

"I've got a while before I start worrying about the dating years. My goal is to be married again before Davey's a Cub Scout, so I don't have to figure out how to make a Pinewood Derby car."

Evelyn laughed. "And as much as I can, I understand somewhat how you feel. Warren is a great dad, but when it comes to some things, we *all* might as well be single mothers. My dad was very handy, and I guess I thought all guys were that way. Warren does the best he can. I don't let him attempt the handyman repairs anymore. It got more expensive calling a professional to fix what he'd started. Drew's first Pinewood Derby car did not even make it to the finish line. Even gravity couldn't get it down the incline. Warren didn't know that the weights on the bottom were supposed to be recessed, and it dragged on the track. After a while, I noticed that Drew had disappeared, and I started looking around the church building for him. When I couldn't find him anywhere inside, I started looking outside. I saw two police cars over by the field on the other side of the parking lot. I went running over. He was sitting there crying on that big rock near the road, and a passing policeman had seen him and come over to see if everything was okay. He told them, no, that everything was not okay--that his Pinewood Derby car was a loser. That's when he said the other police car got there. I could just imagine the first guys calling for a back-up. 'Depressed Cub Scout at Oakwood and 7th East. Beware. He is armed and dangerous. He has a pocketknife.'"

Beverly laughed. "It's funny now, but to him, he was probably so devastated at the time that he didn't think anything of the fact that four policemen were tied up trying to make him feel better."

"Didn't cross his mind."

"Speaking of making people feel better, I think this chocolate is starting to take effect. Thanks for bringing me here. Thanks for knowing what I needed--some adult company, some perspective."

"Beverly, that works both ways. I was a little stressed-out tonight, too. Perhaps we can do this again. You know, your crisis or mine?"

"Sounds like a plan." Beverly took another bite of the delectable chocolate creation. "Hey, Evelyn, how well do you know Brother Higginbotham?"

"They've been in the ward about as long as we have. I know him pretty well. Why?"

"Well . . ."

"Go ahead. You can say it. It's just between us. It's about Brother H., isn't it?"

"Okay, so I'm not the only one who thinks he's somewhat obnoxious?"

"He's got a good heart, but yes, he's got his idiosyncrasies."

"It's about his calling as ward mission leader. You know what great neighbors Jeff and Juanita are. He 'assigned' Dave and I to be friends with them, when we first moved in. We found that somewhat amusing, because we were already friends by then. They live next door, after all. We babysat a couple of times for their baby, Sarah, before we had Davey. They told us we needed to find out what babies were all about before we decided to have one. Anyway, every time he sees me, he asks, 'How is your friendship with Jeff and Juanita going?' I know that since there are only two families in the ward that aren't members of the church, he has to zero in, but I'm worried that one of these days they'll find out somehow that we are on *assignment* to be their friends. Brother Higginbotham doesn't always think before he speaks. I know he swings by there from time to time. Last time we talked he wanted to know if I'd ever had any religious discussions with them. I told him that Juanita had asked me if we were counseled not to make friends with members of other wards. Their older daughter, Amanda, had been invited to a birthday party for a friend from school. Juanita had asked Leigh Watters if she knew these people from church, to find out if she knew where their house was, because their daughter was also invited to the party. Leigh didn't stop to think about who she was talking to and responded kind of impatiently, told Juanita that she didn't know, that they lived in the other ward. She was so snippy that Juanita thinks we have some kind of moratorium on being friends with people outside the ward boundaries."

Evelyn put down her glass of water. "Don't tell me stories like that while I'm drinking. Yes, didn't you hear that letter they read from the first presidency last week? Good grief! The sad thing is, to observe some people--Leigh Watters for example--you would really think that's true."

"Brother Higginbotham drops by there occasionally."

"Yes, I've seen him."

"Okay, here is the question. Sorry it's taking me so long to get around to it. How do I tactfully tell Brother Higginbotham that he and some other people are doing more harm than good? Jeff and Juanita are our friends. Or I guess I should say 'my friends' now. It's hard to get out of the habit of thinking I'm still part of a couple. Anyway, our friendship with them is not based on whether or not they're interested in the church. It's genuine and not as a result of some 'assignment.' When Dave died they were very upset. They were very touched by his funeral service and had a lot of questions. I was able to explain to them about eternal marriage, and the plan of salvation, and they explained some of their beliefs to me. It was a good opportunity for sharing. We've had other conversations where Juanita has told me how it feels to be transferred in from Boston and try and fit in here in Salt Lake City, somewhere where when you meet people, they say, 'Oh, you're the non-members who bought the Millers' home.' I told her that if anyone else refers to her as a non-member, she should pull out her Costco card and show it to them. Anyway, she says sometimes when Brother Higginbotham stops in for a chat, he asks them about how many children they are planning on having, stuff like that. You know how he is, missing that little filter between his brain and his mouth."

"So you feel that whatever progress you make someone else comes along and undoes it?"

"That about sums it up. Whether or not they are interested in the church, I think it's important that we don't give them the impression that Mormons are too weird, living in our little microcosm, having 25 children each, exchanging Jello recipes and ganging up on the unbelievers in our midst. Since I've been on the Activities Committee, I've invited them to a couple of ward parties, and they haven't come yet, but if they do, I don't want them to be mobbed and led off to the baptismal font by Brother H."

"Well, I don't think Brother Higginbotham will ever change. If your friendship with them is close enough, I would just tell them to take him with a grain of salt."

CHAPTER TEN
THEM

When Beverly saw the first birds of spring, she felt like Noah welcoming the returning dove with a twig in its beak. Little green buds began to pop out on tree branches. Dressing Davey was not such an ordeal every time they wanted to go outside. Her mood began to improve. She became a regular sight in the mornings running through the neighborhood with Davey in the jogging stroller. Despite the constant loneliness, she began to feel more in control of her life. She began to feel as if she had a future as well as a past--but that didn't mean she was ready for *them!*

They came up her walk one Sunday afternoon after church--Randy Postlethwaite and Charlene Morgan, the Stake Single Adult representatives. Beverly's first impulse was to hit the floor and pretend that she wasn't home. Their social activities were fine for other people. She did not want to be one of *them.* Not that there was anything wrong with *them*, but she did not want to be reminded anymore than absolutely necessary, that she was a *single.* Charlene was very pleasant, and what one might euphemistically call "chubby." Randy was very businesslike. Neither had ever been married. They detailed some of the activities and programs the Single Adult program sponsored, including their Singles' Family Home Evenings and firesides. Right before they left, Randy mentioned something else.

"I don't know if you're interested, but they also have a dance somewhere in the valley every Friday night. You can call the Hotline and find out the location." He handed her a card. "Here's the Hotline number. It has a recording so you can call it anytime day or night."

"Isn't that convenient? When I can't sleep, I can call this Hotline in the middle of the night to see where the next singles' dance is. Somebody tell me this isn't my life." Beverly spoke. "There's a Hotline? Is it a toll call?"

"Oh no, no charge. You can call it as often as you want."

"Okay good, I'd hate to be racking up a big phone bill trying to find out where the dances are," she said sarcastically. Charlene smiled, not sure how to interpret Beverly's tone.

After they left, Beverly tossed the card with the number on it into the garbage, put Davey to bed and sat down in front of the television for the seventh and last installment of the Esther Williams Film Festival. She had watched them all so far-- Monday through Saturday. The movie was just starting. In this show, Esther Williams was in the army. *"I wonder how they are going to work the water ballet into this one."* She propped a pillow up under her head *"I have a full and exciting life. I don't need those stupid singles' parties."*

Beverly turned the page on the calendar. *"Spring's over. Well, good! Spring is just a bunch of stupid people going around falling in love. The Single Adults probably come around on purpose in the spring just to get people signed up when they are under the influence of the season."* She was strong. She hadn't surrendered. Beverly was glad to see summer.

The grass had started to grow. One afternoon Beverly looked out her window and saw Brother Hopkins who lived down the street mowing her lawn. She waved at him and later took him out a glass of lemonade. About once a week he came over and mowed the lawn. Beverly and Davey sometimes made chocolate chip cookies for him.

One day as Beverly rounded the curve and drove by the Hopkin's house, she saw that their lawn was being mowed--by Sister Hopkins.

As she pulled into the garage, she saw Dave's lawn mower--hers now. She pulled it out of the garage, realizing she didn't even know how to turn it on. With four brothers, she had escaped ever having to mow a lawn. She went next door and knocked on the door. "Jeff, can you show me how to start my lawn mower?"

"I can mow your lawn for you. Don't worry about it. We'll take care of you if you need help. I've seen that fellow from your church doing it a lot, but I can certainly mow it for you if it needs it."

"Thanks, but it was just mowed. What I would really like is to learn how to operate my lawn mower so that I don't always have to rely on other people."

"Sure, I'll come over in a few minutes." Jeff came over, true to his word, and showed Beverly how to start the lawn mower. After a few tries, she had it down. "Do you want to learn how to change the oil, too?"

"Oil? I'm not sure my ambitions extend that far."

"I'll tell you what. When I change the oil in my lawn mower, I'll come over and change the oil in yours, too, that way you can mow your own lawn, but you don't have to do oil changes."

"That sounds like a plan I can live with."

Brother Hopkins noticed the next week when he drove by Beverly's house that someone else had cut her grass. Beverly found out it was harder than it looked, but it was good exercise and a great stress reliever. She would wait until she was upset about something and take the negative energy out on her lawn. She could talk to herself or pretend she was telling someone off and never be heard above the roar of the lawn mower. She always felt better afterwards. Besides, she liked the feeling she got when she took care of what she could herself. There were many areas where she would have to ask for help occasionally. At least she was doing what she could to keep from being the ward service project.

Beverly and Davey often went for bike rides to the park that summer. She had a child seat on the back of her bike. She would pack a snack and something to feed to the birds. Davey threw crumbs and chased birds around the park and she pushed him in the swings. Some days they filled up his wading pool and she sat with him in the back yard under the big tree. One afternoon she looked up at the tree. *"I bet if Dave were here he would build Davey a tree house in that tree. He's a little young for that yet, but hey, I learned how to run a lawn mower. Maybe I can build a tree house."*

Unlike spring, Beverly hated to see summer end. She threw a small party for Davey's second birthday, inviting all the relatives. For Beverly, Davey's birthday always marked the end of summer. The dreaded fall would come, and she would be forced to remember things that she was doing her best not to think about. She blew up the inflatable wading pool for the last time. Davey didn't seem to notice that it was getting cooler, but summer was definitely on its way out.

CHAPTER ELEVEN
UPS AND DOWNS

"Toilet Training in Less Than a Day?" Beverly shook her head. *"What they don't tell you is that it takes six months of trying before you get to the day."* Beverly sighed. *"It's pretty pathetic when the high point of your day is your child's bowel movement."* Davey stood up from his potty chair.

He stood proudly over his offering. "Look Mama, the letter 'S.'" Beverly looked. Okay, if you used your imagination, it was an 'S.' *"I should never have tried to teach him his alphabet and toilet train him at the same time."* She was tired of diapers. She was tired of the ABC song. She was tired of reading "The Monster at the End of the Book"--his new favorite story since Horton and his egg had mysteriously disappeared. She looked at the clock. Jenny was supposed to be there to babysit so Beverly could go to the ward party.

She went in the other room to get a nighttime diaper for Davey. As she came back, she heard the screen door close. She dropped the diaper and ran to the door. Davey had escaped from the house and was already to the end of their sidewalk. Wearing only a shirt, he was running as fast as he could. By the time Beverly got to the end of their sidewalk, he was two houses away. He looked back. He could tell she was gaining on him. She looked pretty mad. Ducking into the neighbor's yard, he crouched down behind their fence. The flaw in his logic--it was a chain-link fence. Beverly slowed down a bit, now that Davey was "hiding." As she approached the fence, her thoughts were of the little bare behind that was going to get a swat. As she looked at a half-dressed little boy crouched down in full view who imagined that his mother could not see him, the humor of it hit her.

She wished Dave were there and could see Davey hiding out in plain sight, and together they could laugh about it. One of the things she missed most was laughing with Dave. They'd had a lot of private jokes. You couldn't clue someone else in to your private jokes. It wasn't the same. Nobody else knew what a "Wobble-ato" was. Well, maybe a few other people did now, thanks to Dave's efforts over the years, but none of them were around when she needed them. Nobody else knew the Hawaiian word Dave had picked up from his mission that he had used to describe Davey's pungent diapers--*"pilau."* Nobody else would ever call her "Honolulu Lulu." Dave had always wanted to take her to Hawaii, show her his mission field and introduce her to the people there who had meant the most to him. She had been more than enthusiastic about the idea and they had planned to start a Hawaii Fund as soon as they got a few more things fixed up on their house. *"It would have been nice if he had lived at least that long."*

A realization hit her. *"I wonder if Dave feels sad sometimes missing out on being able to watch Davey grow up. What if I had died and had left this little boy behind and couldn't be part of his life, and what if I looked down and saw Dave going through life like it was a drudge and not enjoying him--like I often do, just bathing, feeding, cleaning up--when I would give anything just to be with him and play with him and enjoy him?"* She made a resolution there beside the fence that she was going to enjoy her little boy more--enjoy life more. Beverly reached the fence. She crouched down on the opposite side of the fence. "Can you see me, Davey?" He nodded his head. "Do you think I can see you?"

"Mama can't see me. I hiding."

"Then how come I know where to talk to you at?" She stood up, walked around the fence, picked up her little boy and started for home. "You have been very naughty going out of the house when you shouldn't have. I ought to spank you, Davey. I ought to spank your bare little bottom. You know you're not supposed to go out of the house without me or another big person. I was all alone, and I missed you. You're too little and I don't want you to do that again. You could get lost. You could get hurt. Next time you *will* get a spanking."

"Don't spank me, Mama." She put him down, and he ran into the house with both hands covering his little behind.

"Now, since you wanted to go outside, when Jenny gets here, you can go for a ride in your wagon. We'll get it out so that it will be ready. Bring me your jacket, not to mention we need to get some pants on you, young man. I'm going to a party at the church, and maybe you and Jenny can walk down to the church with me." Beverly thought for a minute. "No, I need to take the car. I'll give Jenny some cookie money. Would you and Jenny like to take a walk to the Seven-Eleven and get a cookie? You'll have to be ready to go right when she gets here so you can get back before it gets dark."

Davey was sitting in his wagon when Jenny got there, and he did not scream and carry on when Beverly left for the Elders' Quorum volleyball party. She hugged Jenny, kissed Davey and headed off to the party. She could tell that everyone had been reminded in a meeting to make sure to invite her to the Elders' Quorum party, because she had received way too many invitations and phone calls reminding her about the party. Actually she had made other plans with a friend of hers, just back from a mission. She and Linda were going to meet at 7:30 for dinner. Beverly planned to stay at the ward party for about 45 minutes so that everyone who had invited her would feel successful and then sneak out and meet Linda at the restaurant.

They had the volleyball net set up inside the cultural hall. Beverly put her pot-luck dish on the table and joined one of the teams that was forming. After a couple of enjoyable games, she was amazed at how much the physical exercise boosted her spirits. She looked around her at the people in her ward. *"They all care about me. They're nice people. I'm glad I came. I'm having fun. I really hate to leave, but I'd better sneak out now before they start another game."*

Jerri Klegg was eyeing her athletic husband through the net. She announced, "Next game is *husbands* against *wives!*"

"Okay! We can beat them, can't we, Kathy?"

Two men began to chant, "Power in the Priesthood!"

Sister Plodgett pointed to her short overweight husband. "None of that 'unrighteous dominion' stuff. We know your weak spot!"

As the two teams began to form, Beverly went over to the side of the stage, picked up her jacket and put it on, planning to slip quietly out the side door. As she turned to say goodbye, everyone froze. *"Why is everyone looking at me?"* she wondered.

Sister Klegg ran over to her. "I didn't mean *husbands* against *wives!* I meant *men* against *women*, *brothers* against *sisters* . . ." She was followed by all the other ladies. They crowded around her.

"Don't leave, Beverly. We need you on our team!"

Brother Arletti spoke up. "No, *we* want Beverly."

Sister Plodgett put a motherly arm around Beverly's shoulders. "You can't *have* her. She's our strongest server."

They were all trying so hard not to hurt her feelings, it just reminded her that she was alone, and she began to cry. Jerri was then certain she really *had* offended Beverly.

"Look everyone, I'm not leaving because you're playing men against women. I'm leaving because I have plans with a friend."

She saw Sister Cooper's ears perk up. "I appreciate your invitations and making sure I feel wanted, but please, if you could, just try to treat me like you used to. Beverly, fellow ward member, not Beverly the widow. I really would not get offended that easily, I promise. You don't have to pretend that you don't have husbands for my sake, okay? But I really do need to go. I had a good time. Thanks for inviting me."

At the restaurant she explained to Linda, "I got mobbed on my way out of the ward party. I'm trying to move out of my spot as the ward service project, but I unloaded on everybody at the ward Christmas party, and now nobody dares say anything to me." She looked over the menu. "So tell me about your mission. You've been home now for a while. Have you met anybody *special*? Sorry, I was compelled to ask that. It's in the bishop's handbook that you have to ask, especially female returned missionaries."

"Boy, it's the same everywhere, isn't it? At least you were married and have that 'somebody wanted me' Good Housekeeping Seal of Approval stamped on your forehead."

"Maybe, but if I ever want to play church volleyball again, I'm going to need to find a counterpart for the men's team." They laughed and enjoyed their dinner together. Beverly was glad that Linda was home. They had really enjoyed working together. Even though she was younger than Beverly by quite a few years, it was good to have someone to get out with.

"How's your steak?" Beverly asked Linda.

"It's great, thank you. How's the chicken?"

"It's good. Okay, now aren't you glad somebody asked? A while ago I went out to dinner with a group of couples after Stake Temple Day, and I got emotional-- just one of those things that hit me wrong. I hate that. I was having a reasonably enjoyable time, and then Brother Arletti asked Sister Arletti how her dinner was and she gave him a bite off her plate. Then she asked him how his dinner was. It seemed that all the other couples did the same exchange when their dinners were served. I started crying. I felt so stupid. Someone asked me what was wrong, and I said, 'It's nothing. It's just one of those stupid things.' Finally I confessed that I was crying because Dave was not there to ask me if my food was good. So then they all asked me, and I asked Sister Rogerson if it was okay if I gave her husband a bite of my steak, just so I wouldn't feel left out. It's hard to be the fifth wheel, but I still would rather be out with married people than go to singles' functions. It's fun being out with you, with one other single person, but I'm not ready for all that other stuff--dating and going to dances. I had enough of that the first time around. We need to do this more often. I forget to make plans to get out with adults. I think it probably makes me a better mother when I get away for a while. You won't believe how big Davey is now."

"Oh, didn't I tell you? I'm starting at the 'Y' in September."

"You're going to BYU? Linda . . ." Beverly fixed her with a disapproving stare.

"I know, say what you want. I'm going there looking for a husband. His name is Elder, I mean Ron, Welch. He was in my mission. I guess I let that influence my choice of a school. What can I say? We got acquainted as well as you can on a mission without breaking any rules. I have good feelings about getting to know him better, and hey, I'm not getting any younger."

"Oh, okay. You can go to BYU, but I want you to have pangs of guilt now and then about me all alone back here in Salt Lake City with the Single Adults nipping at my heels. You know I'll get lonely enough I'll start going to those things. You'd better call me and come up for a weekend now and then."

As Beverly increased her social activities, Davey began to notice an increase in the number of times his mother left him home with any one of several young girls-- most of whom he recognized by now as babysitters. The arrival of one of them would signal to him that his mother was leaving. This, in turn, led to him clinging to his mother and crying.

One particular afternoon, Davey was especially upset at the prospect of his mother leaving. She looked down at her barefoot boy and said, "You don't have any shoes on." He ran into his bedroom to get his shoes, believing that putting on his shoes meant he could go with Mom. Meanwhile, Mom took that opportunity to sneak out of the house. Immediately Beverly felt bad for tricking Davey. As she backed out of the driveway, the curtains parted and she saw a tear-streaked little face looking over the top of the couch. He was holding his shoes. She pulled the car back into the driveway and went back in the house. *"What kind of mother am I?"* He had understood what 'go get your shoes' meant and other commands long before he had been able to talk. Maybe there were other things he was capable of comprehending.

She sat down and held him on her lap. "Honey, you know that Mommy likes to be with you and play with you and build blocks with you, but sometimes mommies need to spend some time with other big people without their kids, and it helps them to be better mommies. I'm not going anywhere that would be fun for a little boy, so I'm letting you stay here where you have toys to play with and fun things to do. Soon I'll come back and take the babysitter home, and it will be just me and you again, okay?" Much to her surprise, he got up off her lap and went into his room to play. Astounded, she recalled all the times she had tried to distract him and sneak out. Perhaps he had not understood everything she had said, but he understood what he needed to know--she was coming back.

Another series of events about to affect Beverly's life were shaping up. First, the Single Adult chain of command relayed the information that Sister Crandall seemed resistant to joining their ranks. Brother Higginbotham had cornered Beverly again in the foyer after church and admonished her that she needed to do her duty and get married again, or at least start looking. She had flippantly asked him, mainly just to shut him up, "How do you know there is *not* a man in my life?"

Sister Cooper was still trying to find out about Beverly's mystery friend that she had met up with after the volleyball game. Then, Sister Hughes had shown Beverly the new closet shelves that Sam Jeffries had built in her bedroom closet. Sam was nearly 19, preparing to go on a mission. He'd been working with his father in his contracting business the last couple of years and had become a skilled carpenter in his own right. Sister Hughes told Beverly that he was doing odd jobs to earn money for his mission. Beverly had approached him about the possibility of building a tree house for Davey in the big tree in her back yard. Sam had come over a couple of times to look at the tree and to plan with Beverly just how the project would end up. They had gone shopping together for the lumber, and Beverly had Kelsey McAffee come over to babysit Davey.

Kelsey told her mother that Beverly had gone out with Sam. Of course, Kelsey did not intend her mother to take it the way she did. She knew that Beverly and Sam were working on something and that they had come back with boards and supplies. Her mother had asked her where Beverly had gone and "out" had seemed to cover all possibilities. As Sam worked on the tree house, Beverly noticed that he was developing a great camaraderie with Davey. When Linda came into town a couple of times for the weekend and she and Beverly went out, Beverly asked Sam to babysit. While Beverly was out for a round of dinner and late-night bowling with Linda, Sam's distinctive, beat-up car was observed in her driveway until the wee hours. She hadn't thought about this being grist for the rumor mill. If anyone had bothered to ask, they would have been informed that Sam was babysitting. Sister Cooper was unusually restrained and waited until she had seen his car at her house late in the evening a *second* time. Quietly she hinted to select sisters that Beverly was "involved" with someone in the ward. Sam's car was seen at Beverly's house with increasing frequency. Beverly had signed up for a community school night class. Sam was earning money for his mission babysitting and playing superheros with Davey.

One day after church, Sister Cooper overheard Beverly talking to Sister Jeffries. "I'm so glad to have found Sam. He's such a blessing in my life." Sister Cooper nearly hit the floor. *Sister Jeffries approved!?* Why according to her calculations, Beverly was six or seven years older than Sam! Beverly and Sister Jeffries continued their conversation.

"He's so good with Davey. He plays with him and does things that the teen-age girls who babysit all the time don't do. We're really going to miss him when he goes on his mission."

"You've contributed a lot more toward his mission than you realize, Beverly."

"The other day when I paid him for babysitting, he gave five dollars back to Davey and told him it was for the start of *his* missionary savings. That was such a sweet thing to do. I need to introduce him to my cousin, Jenny. She's still a little young, yet. Maybe I'll wait until he's back from his mission. But anyway, he did a great job putting my rain gutter back up. He has really fixed a lot of things around my house. He's like a substitute husband. And the tree house is really coming along. I thought about trying to do it myself, but I want it to be done by someone who knows what he's doing so that it will be safe. He's a nice kid. I'm glad he's about done with it. The weather is turning cool awfully fast."

Another snatch from that conversation was picked up by Sister McAffee as she walked past. *"Substitute husband! That's what she said! I heard it with my*

own two ears!" She ran out of the church to see if she could catch up to Sister
Cooper in the parking lot. "Lorraine! Lorraine!"

Soon the rumors had escalated, placing Sam's mission and Beverly's temple
recommend both in peril. Finally the story reached Evelyn Jensen at homemaking
meeting. She laughed out loud. "Beverly and *Sam?* He's been *babysitting* for
Davey and doing odd jobs around her house. Really ladies! You've been watching
too much daytime TV."

Annette Jeffries was not so amused, camping out the following Sunday in front
of the bishop's office. She wanted Sister Cooper brought to task! The bishop
passed the rumor control chore to the Relief Society President, and eventually the
truth quietly spread--although not nearly as quickly as the rumors had. Sister
Jeffries confronted Sister Cooper.

"I believe that you owe both my son and Sister Crandall an apology, Lorraine
Cooper!"

"I only reported what I saw. I'll admit that appearances might have been
deceiving, Annette, but we *are* counseled to avoid the very appearance of evil," she
said sanctimoniously.

"The appearance of evil? That must be what we get whenever *you* show up.
My son is a good boy. He was earning money for his mission, building a tree house
for the little Crandall boy--you know, 'pure religion--to visit the widows and the
fatherless.' I don't think you realize the damage that's done by your gossip,
Lorraine Cooper. Anytime a false story goes around the ward, there's a trail that
leads right back to your wagging tongue! I hope you enjoy your movie!"

"What movie? What are you talking about?"

"The movie of your life that you get to watch on the judgment day. If I were
you, I'd get in there while there's still time and do some editing."

CHAPTER TWELVE
GOBBLE GOBBLE WOOF WOOF

The Sam incident had blown over. He was safely off on a mission to Brazil, and Beverly and Davey sent him a letter occasionally. By now she knew which people she could count on to be there for her and which people she could count on for nice cliches about life. She had also figured out which people to steer clear of as much as possible in her local Mormon congregation. Beverly was flabbergasted that some people really had believed that she had tried to romance someone fresh out of high school, and less than a year after Dave's death. She supposed she really was going to have to break down one of these days and join the singles group, if only for the sake of her reputation. *"Maybe I'll do it next year, after I've gotten through the holidays."*

As Beverly dressed Davey in his Halloween costume--tiger pajamas complete with tiger-ear slipcovers that went over top of the ears on his Mickey Mouse hat-- she contemplated the approaching holiday season with dread. First, right before Thanksgiving would be the first anniversary of Dave's death. Then would come Thanksgiving, Christmas and New Year's Day. January would be awful because it was January. Their wedding anniversary was in February, along with Valentine's Day, and then she would be done with the onslaught of holidays. *"Why was I so set against being a June bride?"* All these occasions were coming at her at the time of year when graying skies encouraged depression. *"What I need is a calendar with no holidays,"* she thought to herself.

She surveyed her little boy and tried to channel her thoughts in a different direction. He growled at her and moved his backside to wag his tiger tail around. Beverly had made his costume from tiger-striped flannel, so that after the ears and tail came off, it became a pair of pajamas. After all, sewing did not come easily to Beverly, and if she was going to spend time sewing something it was going to be for more than one night. She took Davey around to a few houses close by, meeting up with the Baldwins, a new couple in the ward with a little baby. They were dressed as "The Three Bears." Sister Baldwin could *really* sew. Baby Bear was asleep in her stroller and oblivious to the holiday going on around her. Davey didn't fully understand, either. He was dressed up like an animal and people were giving him candy. A good time!

Beverly was fighting a down mood, trick or treating with the Baldwins. So it had never been one of her fantasies to sit at her sewing machine for hours making Fred and Wilma Flintstone costumes for herself and Dave. It was her fantasy now! Davey could have been BamBam. Never mind that she had always taken the path of least resistance when it came to Halloween costumes before. Like last year, when they were getting ready to go to the ward Halloween party, she had Dave wear a ski mask and she had taped three empty mangled breakfast cereal boxes to his body-- Cheerios, Wheat Chex and Fruit Loops.

"What am I?" he had asked.

"You're a 'Cereal Killer.'"

But it was different now. "If I had it to do over again . . ." She caught herself. *"How stupid can I be? As if Dave is off somewhere in Heaven wishing we*

*had once dressed up as Boris and Natasha. As if when I die, they are going to ask
me: 'Were you a good person? Were you charitable to your fellow man? Were
you honest and faithful? Did you make whole wheat bread? Did you sew homemade Halloween costumes for your family? Did they follow a theme?'"*

When someone dies, everything turns into an opportunity for regret. When
you're alone, the world is full of couples. Everywhere she looked, she saw some
happy couple--a husband with his arm around his wife in Sacrament Meeting, a
man holding the door open for his wife at the department store, a couple laughing
in the car next to hers at the red light. From Beverly's perspective, the ward
Halloween party had been full of Tweedledums and Tweedledees. Papa Bear,
Mama Bear and Baby Bear. She watched them enviously. Later that night, Mama
Bear could say, "Someone's been sleeping in *my* bed." Papa Bear, that's who.
Beverly was tired of going home to a house without Dave in it, to a bed without
Dave in it. She'd bought herself an electric blanket, and it kept her warm but it
didn't keep her company.

Beverly decided it was time to take Davey home. She said goodnight to the
Baldwins, picked up her little tiger and carried him the rest of the way home. By
the time they arrived, he was asleep in her arms. She worked his arms out of his
coat without waking him, unpinned his tiger tail, took off his hat. A trip to the
bathroom, a nighttime diaper, and he was ready for bed. Pulling the covers over her
little tiger-boy, she stood there surveying him for a moment. His light hair fell
softly over his forehead and his cheeks were rosy from the cold. She leaned over
and kissed his cheek. "Goodnight, tiger. I love you." Someone else was also there
observing--someone who stole away from Heaven every once in a while to quickly
look in on his little family. Quietly, a voice spoke into her mind. *"Looks to me like
you're doing a great job."* A warm feeling came over Beverly, like an invisible
hug. Then he was gone.

Beverly let Davey eat some of the candy and threw out the rest. Working on an
anti-depression plan for the holidays, she was trying to reduce sweets and eat right
so that her body would not be depleted of stress-fighting vitamins. She had decided
not to face anything that was too hard to face. She was going to be kind to herself.
She was going to keep her sense of humor intact. She was going to survive!

A few days after Halloween, she answered the door to find Sister Howard
and Sister Layton, from the Young Women's presidency. Beverly invited them in,
and they made a little small talk. Then Sister Howard came to the point, or rather,
tried to come to the point.

"Beverly, I want you to know that I've debated long and hard whether or not to
extend this invitation to you." Sister Layton nodded her head in agreement. "We
didn't know if you would be offended to be invited or if we would offend you by not
inviting you."

Beverly smiled, having no idea what Sister Howard was talking about. "It's
always possible I'll be offended either way," she said jokingly, trying to put Sister
Howard at ease. "So did you come here to invite me or to tell me that you're not
going to invite me?" Despite Beverly's attempt at humor, Sister Howard started
to cry, reinforcing her standing as the leaky faucet of the ward. Sister Howard
could not come within ten feet of the podium without crying. She began again.

"Every year the Young Men and Young Women put on a special Thanksgiving dinner in November for all the widows and widowers in the ward. I tried to imagine how I would feel if I were you, and I had decided not to invite you--at least not this year. Then we had a meeting yesterday with the Laurel President and found out that the girls have planned a special menu for your little boy, so I told them I would invite you. Believe me, we'll understand if you decide not to come." She tried to gain control of her emotions, fishing in her purse for a Kleenex. "I'm sorry for crying. I'm just such an emotional person."

"It's okay," said Beverly. "It helps more when people can cry with me than when they tell me to get on with life and don't try to understand my feelings. Thanksgiving isn't my favorite holiday, as you can understand. I'm not sure if I can come to the dinner, but I'll try to work up the courage."

"Courage." Sister Layton put in. "It's interesting to hear you say it that way. I guess it does take a lot of courage to go on with life sometimes. I wouldn't have thought that it takes courage to go to a dinner party, but in this case . . ."

"I know this sounds totally stupid, but I was cooking a turkey when I got the news about Dave's accident, and I haven't been able to make or eat turkey since."

"We're serving ham."

"Well, I don't have any hang-ups about ham. Turkey's not the only thing. I can't read 'Horton Hatches the Egg' either. That's the story I was reading to Davey when I got the news. It was his favorite book. I put it in the back of the closet and eventually he forgot about it. But everyone else is not that easy to fool. They still insist on celebrating Thanksgiving every year."

"The dinner is on Saturday, the 9th. We just wanted you to know that you are invited, and that even if you decide not to come, we are thinking about you." Sister Howard's voice began wavering again.

"And I appreciate that. Really, I do," said Beverly, trying to help Sister Howard out. "Hey, would you like to see the rocking horse I bought Davey for Christmas? It's wooden, and I'm painting it myself at night after he's in bed. It's kind of therapeutic for me."

Beverly debated whether or not to go to the dinner. She didn't really *want* to go, but she was touched by the love and caring of the young women, many of them Davey's babysitters, who were making special considerations for her little boy, and by the caring of ladies who had taken the time to worry about inviting her. They had probably discussed it in their meetings, wondering what to do. She decided to go. *"Maybe soon there will be a ward meeting where my name doesn't come up."*

November 9th arrived way too quickly. Beverly bundled Davey up in his snowsuit and loaded him into the car. *"Why am I doing this?"* As she pushed him in his stroller down the hallway at church that led to the gym, two smiling young women came down the hall to greet them.

"We're supposed to seat you."

Beverly looked into the gym. There was no one there that appeared to be under 60, definitely no one else pushing a toddler in a stroller. She reached into her pocket and pulled out a dollar bill and gave it to one of the girls. Under her breath, she said, "Seat me with the bachelors." It was her only defense. If she did not

make light of this, she was going to burst into tears and run from the building.
They seated her at a table with Brother Samuelson and Brother Morton, who were
having a lively discussion about the recent changes to Medicare. Beverly busied
herself playing with Davey. Soon two elderly sisters joined them--Sister Murray
and Sister Ingram. She didn't know either of them well, but she recognized their
faces from Relief Society. Sister Murray leaned over and patted Beverly's hand.

"It's good to see you here."

Beverly was not sure how to respond to that. It wasn't good to be there--to be
under thirty years old and a widow, having dinner with all the old folks, supposedly
the people with whom she now had something in common. She looked around her.
*"Are any of them plagued by their hormones? How many of them remember what a
hormone is?"* She smiled and said, "Thank you, Sister Murray."

Sister Murray continued to pat her hand. "Just remember--endure to the end."

Sister Ingram came alive. "Pshaw, Edna!" she expectorated. "That requires a
little more commitment from Beverly than it does from you!"

"Well, I was only trying to help, Lucille."

As the two little ladies discussed Beverly's plight in life, dinner was served--
Thanksgiving dinner with all the fixings. Two young girls came out carrying a
special platter they had made up for Davey. They had a booster seat so he could sit
up to the table by himself. They set him up in front of his meal--a hot dog, cut up
in little pieces, Tater Tots, baby carrots, a cut-up banana, and a glass of juice. One
of the girls beamed. "It's a *turkey* dog. That was *my* idea."

Beverly heard the word "turkey" and was transported back, nearly a year ago.
The knock on the door. The drive to the hospital. The news. The end of life as she
knew it. She fought back the tears that those memories brought forth. Thank
goodness for other associations. Davey heard the words "turkey" and "dog" and
said, "Gobble Gobble Woof Woof." Beverly came back to the present. The
girls laughed and ran back to the kitchen to tell the others. Soon all the young
women were surrounding their table. "Turkey dog, Turkey dog," they chanted.
Davey responded each time, "Gobble gobble woof woof." In the midst of that, it
was difficult for Beverly to be depressed.

Beverly had survived the Thanksgiving dinner at the church, but she was not
sure she could make it through another one. She called her mother.

"Davey and I are not going to be there for Thanksgiving this year."

"Not again!?"

"We're going to Disneyland. I decided yesterday. I've already got the tickets.
We're going to stay in San Diego with Robyn and Craig and then Robyn and I will
go to Disneyland with the kids. I need to get out of town over the 16th and Thanksgiving."

"We'll miss you, but I guess I can understand."

"I know it looks like I'm being an escapist, but I've faced things the best I
could up to now. If I go somewhere warm, maybe I can forget it's Thanksgiving. If
I'm here at home on the 16th, I'll just rehearse to myself the events of last year at
this time. We'll be back on the 28th."

CHAPTER THIRTEEN
ONE TEAR AT A TIME

On vacation, Beverly tried not to pay attention to what day it was, and thus she passed the 16th day of November, the anniversary date of Dave's death, without really being sure what day it was. Were they at the San Diego Zoo or Disneyland that day? She couldn't say for sure. Beverly made it through Thanksgiving with the help of Goofy, Donald, Mickey, Minnie, Robyn, Craig and Lindsay. Nobody at Disneyland tried to make her eat turkey. She and Davey had corn dogs and Mickey Mouse ice cream bars for Thanksgiving dinner. Beverly and Robyn worked out the details of an arranged marriage between Davey and Lindsay and took scores of pictures of them together on the rides. Robyn was pregnant, so she couldn't go on many of the rides, but with the little kids along, they wouldn't have gone on those rides anyway. For Beverly it was just good to be with Robyn. They had been best friends and roommates in college, but Craig's computer job had taken the family to the west coast. They only got to see each other when Robyn came for a visit to her family in Utah.

By the time Beverly and Davey got back from California, the Christmas season was in full swing. They had been back for a couple of days before Beverly un-packed her suitcases. She had found a place in Davey's room for the giant stuffed Pinocchio and Jiminy Cricket she had bought for him at Disneyland. They were so big, the flight attendant on the plane had joked about finding an empty seat for them. With a twinge, Beverly realized that she had bought them somehow to make up to Davey for losing his father. *"I've got to stop doing that,"* she told herself.

She hung her clothes back in the closet. All of Dave's things were still there. She went over to his suit and pressed her face to it. It still smelled very faintly of his favorite cologne. She closed her eyes and tried to imagine that he was there, but the smell was too faint. Tears came to her eyes. *"It's just a stupid suit! It's a stupid suit that he's never going to wear again."* She grabbed another handful of her clothes and forcefully hung them up, angry at the world, angry at Dave for dying. Out loud she said, "Heavenly Father, how am I supposed to get through this?" The closet rod came loose from the wall and all the clothes slid to the floor. "Oh, thanks a lot! That's what I get for praying!" She had lifted that line from "It's A Wonderful Life," which she had watched the night before on channel 5. "Me and George Bailey! Where are all of my friends to come to my rescue?" Just as she said that, her doorbell rang.

Beverly went to the door. It was Sister Richter, from down the block. She was such a nice person. Beverly repented of her anger at her Heavenly Father. He had sent Sister Richter just when she really needed someone to talk to. "Come in, Barbara."

"Oh, I don't have time to come in." She handed Beverly a plate of fudge. "I've been making candy all day, and I want to get this delivered while it's fresh."

"Don't you want to come in for a minute and get warm? I could really use some . . ."

"Oh, you're my first delivery. I'm not really cold, yet. I wanted to deliver to you first, because I know what a hard time the holidays must be for you. Merry Christmas, Beverly."

"Are you sure you won't come in for a minute?"

"Oh thanks for asking, but I really must be off."

Sister Richter was on the fudge delivery circuit. *"Neither hail nor snow nor dead of night--the fudge must be delivered."* Beverly set the plate of fudge down on the table. "Thanks for asking," she muttered under her breath. "I wasn't asking for you, I was asking for *me!"*

Davey came in with his Muppet Babies puzzle, which they put together for what seemed like the millionth time. Beverly began to cry as she put together the picture of Kermit the Frog and Miss Piggy. *"Even fat bossy Miss Piggy has a man in her life! Now I'm really losing it. I'm jealous of a Muppet!"* Little Davey saw that his mother was crying. He climbed down off his chair and ran as fast as he could on his short little legs off to the bathroom. He returned with a minuscule piece of toilet paper, sufficient in size to blot one tear, maybe two, if used efficiently. Beverly leaned over and her little boy stuck the small piece of tissue on her cheek, catching a teardrop. Then he spotted a tear on her other cheek. Time after time her sweet young son ran back to the bathroom for another piece until all her tears were dried. She held Davey on her lap.

"What would I do without you, Davey? You're not even three yet, and *you* know what I need." She carried him to his room and got him ready for bed. In his prayers, he said, "Bess Mama not cry," which, of course, started her crying again. She quickly wiped her eyes on the shirt she had just taken off of him, tucked him in and gave him a kiss on the forehead. Then she went back to the kitchen table, sat down and ate the entire plate of fudge. Staring back at her from the empty paper plate was a little elf, and the words "Merry Christmas."

"Yeah, sure." Beverly talked to the paper plate. "That's easy for *you* to say!" Eating all these sweets did not help with her anti-depression plan. She turned on the TV and watched whatever was on until she fell asleep on the couch, covered by the afghan Great Aunt Winnie had crocheted and given them as a wedding present.

CHAPTER FOURTEEN
HAPPY HOLIDAYS

In the morning Beverly awoke, still dressed, still on the couch. The television was still on. She got up, turned it off, took a swipe at her hair, and debated whether to get dressed in a different jogging suit or just wear the same one she still had on. *"Who's going to notice? Who cares? Is anybody going to look at me today?"* She poured herself a bowl of cereal and looked out the window. It had snowed all last night, and it was still snowing. Someone was outside shoveling her sidewalks. Beverly went to the window. It was two of the young men on her block, Andy and Tony Barnes. She grabbed her coat and pulled on her boots as if she was a fireman getting ready for active duty. Opening the garage door, she came out with a snow shovel and started shoveling snow and yelling at the boys.

"I know what you're doing! Don't try to hide it! You're shoveling sidewalks for all the widows! I've been to those welfare meetings! I know what they talk about! You're probably singing Christmas Carols tonight at the nursing home!" She was throwing snow with all her might. "Look at me! I'm not 85! I can shovel snow! You should be doing this for Edna Murray and Lucille Ingram and Doris Holloway, not for me! I'm tired of being the ward service project!" She put down her snow shovel and picked up a handful of snow. She packed it hard and sent it flying. It hit one of the boys in the side of the head. Andy stood there, stunned. He looked at Tony for some idea of what to do. A snowball hit Tony in the chest. She was creaming them. They couldn't take this from a woman! He picked up some snow and lobbed a snowball back at Beverly. Andy followed suit. As the bishop drove by on his way to work, he was shocked to see two young men from the ward pelting snowballs at Sister Crandall, who, with one arm guarding her face, was shooting them right back as fast as she could. The sidewalk was not being shoveled. He stopped his car and rolled down the window.

"Boys, what is the meaning of this?" he asked sternly.

Beverly shot a snowball into his car. "You stay out of this, Bishop! This is the most fun I've had all season!" He drove off, shaking his head. *"Time to see the stake president about a new assignment."*

That evening Beverly bundled Davey up and decided to walk over to the bishop's house and apologize. His house was only a couple of blocks away. The stroller wouldn't go through the snow, so she piggy-backed Davey on her back. As they rounded the corner, singing "Jingle Bells" and in reasonably good spirits, Beverly heard laughter and voices. "So now is the main course at Fred and Edith's or are they dessert?" Several more couples emerged from the Dobson's home. It was the old dinner club--the one that she and Dave had organized! They were having a progressive dinner, and she had not been invited.

Beverly quickly ducked behind a huge pine tree in the corner lot. She couldn't bear for them to see her. They would be embarrassed. She would start crying, and then she would have a bunch of people standing there feeling sorry for her. She just wanted to be normal. She didn't want people feeling sorry for her. Then someone would insist she join the party and they would pretend like they couldn't figure out how she had been excluded. It wasn't that they were mean or unkind people or that they had called a special meeting and blackballed her.

It was plain and simple.

They were couples.

She was a single.

She didn't fit anymore. People used to say that she and Dave were the life of the party. "One of us is *still* alive," Beverly said quietly. Thankfully, the party headed in the opposite direction. When the voices died down, Beverly came out from behind the tree, and headed back home. *"We would probably just be inter-rupting some family activity at the bishop's home, anyway,"* she told herself.

"Jingo bells, Mama."

Beverly tried to sing again, but the jingle had gone out of her bells.

The next day she decided to attend church at one of the singles' wards she had heard about. She still hadn't apologized to the bishop, and she didn't want to see any of the friends from the dinner club. She was afraid all the feelings of the previous night would come rushing back. An old high school friend was in the bishopric of a singles' ward, and had called a while back to invite her to come visit his ward. Brian and Beverly had been in the same Seminary class their junior and senior years and had worked together on the Seminary Council. They were buddies. She found herself looking forward to seeing Brian. She still felt unready for singles' functions, but it would be nice to talk to a man--someone who was not her dad or brother or home teacher. Brian came and sat by her during Sunday School. He bounced Davey on his knee. They sang from the same hymn book. She missed having somebody to share a hymn book with. Beverly remembered how comfort-able she had always felt with Brian. After the meeting, she had an idea.

"Brian, do you still have your pick-up truck?"

"Not the same one."

"How would you like to help me pick up a Christmas tree and come over and decorate it? I've just got this little car and . . ." Beverly was envisioning this as a social event. She wouldn't have asked him if she didn't know him well. It could be fun. She would put on Christmas music and make some fudge.

Brian's bishopric training kicked in. People needed to go through the proper channels. "Why don't you call your home teachers?"

"Yeah, I guess I could." Beverly ducked into the nearest classroom, tears stinging her eyes. She closed the door and began to talk to herself. "I meant it as a social invitation, not a service project, you idiot! Sure, call my home teachers! And they will help me get a tree, and put it in the stand and then they'll go home because they have families and because it's not appropriate to stay and help me decorate the tree because that would be too much fun to have with a *single* sister who might pose a threat to somebody's marriage. But my family will help me again." Davey looked at her quizzically. *"I guess Brian has plenty of women after him, being in this singles' ward, and now he thinks I'm one of them. All I wanted was a friend, a little male company, some pleasant conversation, maybe a platonic hug."*

She stayed in the room for a few minutes and composed herself and then went into Sacrament Meeting where Brian was conducting. After completing the ward business, he said, "Now at this time of year when we celebrate the holidays, let's try to remember to take time to visit those who are in need, people who are lonely and have no one to spend the holidays with. If each of us just did one small thing for someone, think of the lives we could brighten." Beverly sat there in disbelief. She wanted to jump to her feet, stand up on the pew and yell, "Put your money where your mouth is!" She had asked for his help and he had brushed her off like so much dandruff! She listened to the talks, sang the hymns and went home, writing off Brian and his singles' ward.

Jim Dayton was searching in his camera bag for the flash attachment to his camera so that he would be ready for Christmas day. In his bag were the pictures he had taken last year at the Fathers and Sons' Outing. He had a funny feeling that he should get those pictures out and look at them, but he dismissed it. He was too busy. That was ages ago. The feeling came again.

"Look at the pictures."

"Why?" he asked himself. He did, however, take the pictures out of the bag and gave them to his wife to put in the family album. Despite the numerous other tasks at hand, she had a nagging feeling she should put those pictures in the family album that day. She dismissed it. That was the kind of thing you did when you had nothing else to do. But the feeling would not leave, so she turned the job over to two of her kids, on holiday from school.

"Boy, nobody listens to you when you're dead!" Dave would not give up. Maybe he would have better luck with the kids. Ten-year-old Jeremy came to his mother a few minutes later with a picture.

"Do you think Sister Crandall would like to have this picture, Mom?"

Dave waved his hands. *"No, not just a snapshot! You can do better than that. Think what it would mean to them."*

Christmas Day, Beverly was awakened by her doorbell ringing. When she got to the door, no one was there, but there was a gift sitting on the doorstep. It was rectangular and flat, and the label said it was for Davey. She picked it up, examined it and put it under the tree. Looking at the clock, she decided to get Davey up to see what Santa had brought him. She hadn't bothered to wrap anything, because he didn't quite get the hang of opening things yet, and she still struggled to have the Christmas spirit. Davey was too busy playing with his Christmas toys to be interested in the mystery present, so Beverly began to unwrap it. As she got some of the paper off, she saw what it was and she began to cry. Someone in the ward had taken a picture of Dave and Davey at the Fathers and Sons' Outing and had it enlarged and framed. Dave was holding a fish he had caught. Standing in front of him was Davey, in his matching plaid shirt, holding a plastic fish in each hand. Beverly wished she knew who it was from so that she could thank them. Dave stood nearby, *"Well, it's from me, of course! I had to tear myself away from my harp class. I almost had to go AWOL. That stands for 'Angel Without Leave.' Gosh Bev, you used to laugh at my jokes. Come on, cheer up. You look so sad all the time. I worked hard to get you guys this present. Believe me, it's not easy to get people to cooperate. Smile, Beverly. Come on, it's not that bad. You've got that beautiful little boy. He's getting so big. Sure, I'm dead, but we'll be together soon."*

"Look, Davey! Somebody sent us a picture of you and Daddy. See, Daddy caught a fishy and you caught two fishies." She smiled.
"Good! She smiled. I can go now."

Later, the whole family got together for dinner at Mom and Dad's. Beverly took the picture along. "You know, when he wanted to take Davey on the Fathers and Sons' Outing, I told him I thought Davey was too young, but he told me 'I *have* to take him.' It was as if he knew that was his only chance, but yet I don't think he knew he was going to die, he just knew somehow this was something he had to do. It makes me feel better, as if he was being prepared somehow--like maybe it *was* his time to go. I've struggled with that for a long time. Somehow this picture helped."

Beverly unveiled her platter of fudge, popcorn balls, peanut brittle, Christmas cookies, Rice Krispie Treats, pecan logs and divinity.
"Beverly, you must have been cooking and baking for days!"
"Not me, everybody in my ward."
"They must love you a lot."
"Yes, but are they going to love me when I tip the scales at 200 pounds? But I know they mean well."

After dinner, they all sat down to watch another Jimmy Stewart movie called "Mr. Krueger's Christmas." It was produced by the Church, and it was about a lonely old man who was befriended by a little girl during the holidays. In one scene Mr. Krueger tried to lure some Christmas carolers inside. *"I'll make some hot chocolate."* It reminded Beverly of Sister Richter and the fudge. Soon Davey was off in Grandma's bathroom getting pint-size pieces of toilet paper for his Mama's tears.
Beverly tried to pull herself together and went in one of the bedrooms for a while. Soon she was joined by her sister-in-law, Gayle. Gayle and Beverly had been friends long before Gayle and Randall had married, and they were very close.
"I don't know how you do it, Beverly. I could never be as strong as you."
"I don't know why everyone always thinks I'm doing such a good job of it. You do what you have to do, and this is what I have to do. If you had to do it, you would do it, too."
"I don't even like to think about it."
"Nobody does. People don't like me to talk about Dave, don't want to be reminded of what could happen to them. They don't want to invite me to parties. They just want me to go to those stupid singles' dances and find someone and get married again--get on with life and act like he never existed."
"I'm sorry. Maybe I'm not helping much."
"If I sound angry, I'm not angry at you. You're trying to understand, only I wish people wouldn't tell me how well I'm doing, and how they could never do it. It makes me think they feel like I just bounced back from losing my husband, but they never could, as if it's less of a loss to me because I'm able to keep going. They don't see me in the middle of the night when I can't sleep. They don't see me hiding behind a tree so they won't know that I know I didn't get invited to their stupid party. When I put on my happy face and go out to face the world, that's

when they see me. Then they all tell each other how well I'm doing so that they don't feel guilty for not being there for me. Most of the time, I'm either angry or depressed or jealous of people who have partners. I was even jealous of Kermit and Miss Piggy the other day. Is that stupid, or what? I can't even put together a puzzle with my son without feeling sorry for myself. That's how well I'm doing. I can't even go to a family party without being a downer. I'm jealous because Randall bought you one of those little rubber rings that goes in the bottom of your blender."

"Well, I wouldn't have thought that a gift from the Under a Dollar Store would make anyone jealous . . ."

"It's the fact that he went out and looked for it, on purpose, because he knew you needed it. It's because you have someone who is in touch with you."

"Well, Beverly, there are a lot of women who don't have that, even though they are married."

"Yeah, I guess I should remember that. I get real irritated when I hear women complain about their husbands. Insensitivity can work both ways, I guess, but I even miss the things I didn't like about Dave. I hate being able to balance my checkbook so easily and not to have to get after him to give me all the slips from the cash machine."

"Would it make you feel better if I came to your house once a week and threw dirty socks all over your bedroom floor?"

Beverly smiled a little bit. "Speaking of laundry, the other day I dumped a load of unfolded towels on my bed. I went to bed without folding them and just shoved them over to the other side of the bed. In the night, I turned over and bumped into them, and it was like he was there. I slept with those towels for a week, pretending they were Dave. Pretty pathetic, isn't it?"

"No, something similar happened to me. I slept with Randall all last week before I discovered he *wasn't* a pile of towels. He's been working so much lately, I hardly ever see him."

"And then his one day of freedom, and I had to make him come over and fix my closet rod," Beverly apologized. "He's a good guy. You got one of the good ones."

"You did, too."

"Yeah, and now all I have to do is like Sister Murray said--endure to the end." Beverly pulled a face. "Maybe we should go be part of the family before they send out a 'search and rescue.'"

There was a large item in the corner with a blanket draped over it with Beverly's name on it. When she uncovered it, she found that her parents had gotten her a cedar chest. She knew it must have cost them a lot. Beverly was surprised.

"What's this, Mom, another hope chest, so I can store up dishtowels and pillowcases for the next time I get married?" Her mother did not respond, and Beverly immediately felt sorry for her sarcastic remark. "I'm sorry, Mother. Maybe I should have gone to Disneyland for Christmas, too. It's beautiful, it really is. Sorry to be so touchy. Last week Brother Higginbotham cornered me after church in the lobby and asked me again why I wasn't working harder on finding a new husband. He told me that I was letting my prime child-bearing years go to waste. They are expecting their ninth child, and I don't think he thinks I'm doing my part to multiply and replenish the earth by remaining single. I had a nightmare that night that his wife died in childbirth and that he proposed to me, since I was young and hardy."

"What did you tell him?"

"In my dream or in real life?"

"In real life."

"Oh, I was polite in real life. I told him I would take it under advisement. But do you want to hear what I told him in my dream?"

Later when they were alone, Naomi told her daughter. "I thought maybe you could use the cedar chest to store the things of Dave's that you want to keep." The intent was the same as what other people had said, "Why do you still have his things? Haven't you gone through the closets yet?" But it was different. It acknowledged that there might be some things that she did want to save. It was a nudge, but a gentle one. "Time to go through his things." But Naomi did not say, "Beverly, don't you think it's about time . . .?" She knew Beverly would do what needed to be done--when she was ready.

That evening Beverly took Davey over to see Dave's parents. Gordon got out his camera and shot an entire roll of film of Davey opening his gifts from Grandma and Grandpa. He made quite a haul. Everybody was trying to make up to him for the loss of his dad. He stood there with his arms full of a stuffed Big Bird, Cookie Monster, Bert and Ernie and Oscar the Grouch. After Grandpa Gordon took several pictures, Davey asked, "Where's my Snuffleuphagus?"

CHAPTER FIFTEEN
GROUP THERAPY

Beverly's dad brought her new cedar chest over the next day. It had a padded top, and she decided to put it in Davey's room at the foot of his new big-boy bed. Several months ago, Beverly had discovered that Davey had been getting out of his crib through a series of Houdini-like maneuvers, which she had finally witnessed as she lay in the hall outside his bedroom—out of the crib, over the dresser and down the toy shelves. She had decided it was time to get him a bed before he hurt himself. She talked to him about his dad as she folded up the things of Dave's that she had decided to save. Little by little, things had been distributed or disposed of except the things that had the most sentimental value. It was that last cut that was the difficult one. Now they would be saved, but not on display, and no one would feel that she was not getting on with life.

Perhaps it was the fact that she had finally stored away Dave's things, or perhaps it was the fact that it had been over a year since he died, or perhaps it was the fact that she had a new necklace and earrings that she needed to wear. It may have been the fact that she did not want to spend New Year's Eve watching the festivities in Times Square on television that made Beverly decide that she was ready for a Single Adult function. They were having a valley-wide dance on New Year's Eve. Beverly picked out a nice dress and got dressed up for the evening. She thought about calling another single sister in the stake who was going and riding with her, but she did not want to be without means of escape if the experience was too intense. She had arranged for a neighbor down the street to babysit Davey, because by the time she had finally decided to go, all the babysitters were already booked. Joyce came to the door in a worn-out old bathrobe, holding her new baby. Beverly took Davey's coat off. Already dressed in his pajamas, he ran into the other room to play with Matt—or more accurately, to play with Matt's toys. Beverly sat and chatted with Joyce for a minute. Joyce began to nurse her baby. "You sure look nice," she said wistfully. "I bet you'll get asked to dance a lot. Is that a new dress?"

"No, I just never have anywhere to wear it."

Joyce looked enviously at Beverly. *How would it be to get all dressed up and go out on New Year's Eve and have exciting new men ask you to dance and be interested in what you had to say instead of trying to compete with the television for your husband's attention?* Beverly looked enviously at Joyce. *How nice to be dressed in a comfortable bathrobe and curled up on a couch nursing a new baby, and then snuggle up in bed next to your husband while all the Single Adults of the world try to match up with somebody at some dumb dance.* Beverly voiced it.

"Wanna change places?"

"Just for a night," sighed Joyce.

"So do I."

The first person Beverly recognized at the dance was Cordell Hill. Cordell was from Beverly's home ward in the neighborhood where she had grown up. He had been in the singles' program for as long as she could remember. He was tall and skinny, with blond hair and a pronounced Adam's Apple. Beverly had always thought he looked like Ichabod Crane. Cordell had always liked Beverly. They had even been on a date years ago when he had bought her lunch at the stake Young Adult auction and they had eaten together. She made a mean chocolate chip cookie! She had even made some for him once—his own personal batch. He remembered that day well. He might have had a chance with Beverly if that Dave guy hadn't come along when he did. Cordell made a beeline for the refreshment table and cut her off at the vegetable dip.

"Well, I never thought I'd see you at one of these again! How long have you been divorced?" It served her right for marrying someone else when he had been there ready, willing and able all along. He wasn't surprised it hadn't worked out.

"I'm not divorced." Beverly thought everybody from the old ward would have known, but then she remembered her mother saying that Cordell's parents had sold their home, booted Cordell out, and had gone on a mission to New Zealand.

Cordell was concerned. "You're not supposed to come to these unless your divorce is *final*. They're really strict about that. Of course, I won't tell on you this time, but it's right there on the sign when you come in. *'All divorces must be final.'* Didn't you see it?"

"Yes, I saw it." So, she didn't care. Cordell was shocked.

"Well, Beverly, this surprises me. I mean, I know that guy you married was not that great. I remember he smoked . . ." he said bravely, because, after all, if she had left him, she must feel the same. He, Cordell Hill, would now be there to pick up the pieces. ". . . but I thought you would manage to keep *your* standards high."

"I'm not divorced, because I'm a w . . ." She couldn't say it. "Because my husband died."

Cordell had blown it. No use asking her to dance now.

"Oh. Uh, Beverly," Cordell stammered, "can I get you some refreshments? Some Hawaiian punch? Some cheese and crackers? Vegetables and dip?"

A nice-looking dark-haired fellow appeared almost out of nowhere with two glasses of punch. He handed one to Beverly. He addressed Cordell. "Why don't you just chew on the foot that's in your mouth for a minute, and I'll take care of this young lady." On second glance, Beverly discovered he was not actually that good-looking, but he was dressed to perfection, his hair perfectly styled, and he had an air of self-confidence that made the bumbling Cordell look even more awkward. To Beverly, he said, "So did I overhear you say that you were a widow?"

"If you were eavesdropping, I guess you must have."

"That's too bad." He shook his head sympathetically. "You're so young to be alone and so . . ." He looked Beverly over admiringly. "Such a waste. Do you have children?"

"I have one little boy."

Beverly listened incredulously to his mock sympathy.

"I hope he didn't leave you without insurance—with your little boy to provide for and all."

"I hope so, too," Beverly said, not giving out any information. His interest was heightened by this evasion. She must be in pretty good shape.

"Beverly, is it? I want to get better acquainted with you. In fact, this dance is kind of boring. I prefer smaller more intimate gatherings. What do you say we go back to your place and order a pizza and get a movie?"

"Oh sure, just like that."

"Why not?"

"I don't know you. I don't invite strange guys that I've known for ten minutes over to my house at 11:00 at night."

"I'm a nice guy." He pulled out his wallet. "See, these are my kids. Aren't they cute? I'm a registered voter, Republican. Here is my temple recommend, good until July. Did I mention that I'm a returned missionary?"

"So what."

"So what? I'm a nice guy. What do I have to do to convince you?"

"Okay, let's say I believe you. You can come over after the dance."

He smiled. That wasn't so hard. He knew his way around women.

"What about directions to your house, and I don't know your last name." He pulled a small business planner out of his pocket.

Beverly took it, closed it, and put it back in his pocket. "Oh that. I figured you're so spiritual you could just get there by following the promptings of the Holy Ghost." She walked away.

Cordell appeared. "I heard you tell that guy he could come over to your house later," he said accusingly.

"Does everybody around here listen in on everyone else's conversations?"

"Well, if you're going to be *that* friendly to someone you barely know . . . I mean, you know I've always liked you, Beverly. I've got my own place now. It's real nice, not the Taj Mahal or anything, but I'd really like to have you over sometime."

Cordell's place was a three-room basement apartment rented out by an elderly couple for a little extra income. Mrs. Jenkins had ingress and egress through Cordell's living room to get to her fruit room. This basically kept Cordell on the straight and narrow path, that and his limited social skills. He hadn't really entertained any hot dates there yet because of the possibility that Mrs. Jenkins would come down for a jar of plum preserves when he was in the company of a young lady.

"So do you want to come over sometime? I've got a microwave and a VCR. We could pop some popcorn and watch a movie. I've got this real comfortable Naugahyde couch the Jenkins let me have."

"No, I don't think so, Cordell."

"Why not?"

"I'm against Naugahyde couches. I'm a member of 'Save the Naugas.'" He gave her a blank look. Another great comeback wasted on Cordell. "Look Cordell, if I'd wanted a date with Orville Redenbacher and my TV set, I would have stayed home. What is it with this 'my place or yours' stuff anyway? Don't people go out on dates to public establishments anymore? I'm not sure I'm ready for any of this yet, anyway. I just want to be friends, okay Cordell?"

"But what about that other guy?"

"You can ask him if he'd like to come over. I don't mind." Beverly left Cordell standing there trying to figure that one out.

Beverly looked around and made an assessment. Many of the people at the dance seemed to be quite a bit younger than she was, but there were a few people closer to her age. She spotted a table of older-looking women over in the corner who seemed to be really having a good time, most of them appeared to be in their thirties. Maybe she would go over and get acquainted. She approached the table, noting the one seat left.

"Mind if I join this party? You all seem to be having more fun than most of the people here."

"We're an exclusive group. Out on the town. You're single obviously, or you wouldn't be here. Tell me, did your husband leave you?"

"In a manner of speaking."

"Well then, pull up a chair!" Beverly sat down. The spokeswoman introduced herself. "I'm Jean. My husband ran off with his secretary. That's Marilyn. Her husband just ran off. That's Maureen. Her husband outgrew her. That's Shelly. Her husband was going through a mid-life crisis or male menopause or something. Nobody knows. He doesn't know. He just didn't want to be married anymore, but he said it was nothing personal, didn't he Shelly?" They all laughed. Shelly nodded her head. Jean continued, "And this is Laura. Her husband is a doctor. He ran off with his nurse, just like on General Hospital." They all laughed some more.

"So this is like group therapy in a social setting—killing two birds with one stone. My name is Beverly. I could use some group therapy."

"So Beverly, did you keep the house?"

"I kept everything."

"All right! We're all great 'house keepers' in this group!" They all laughed. again. "So, how did your husband leave you?"

"He died."

Stone silence. Beverly looked around the table. "Don't kick me out of the group—please! I fit in here better than I did at the ward dinner for the widows, believe me. Otherwise, I'll have to go out there and dance with guys that I probably babysat when I was in high school. I promise not to tell you how wonderful he was or anything that will spoil your fun. I get mad at him sometimes, too, for turning me into a Single Adult, the ward service project and basically a social misfit."

Jean turned to the rest of the group. "We'll have to take a vote. Should we accept Beverly into this group, based on the premise that she promises not to reminisce too much about Dear Departed—what's his name?"

"Dave."

"Dear Departed Dave." She continued. "Anybody have any comments?"

"Well, she did say she was a social misfit."

"Okay, all those in favor of letting Beverly join our group based on her status as a social misfit, raise your hand." They all raised their hands. "You're in! Welcome to the Island of Misfit Toys," Jean said jovially. "Have a seat!"

When Beverly picked up Davey, Joyce asked her if she'd had a good time. "Did you meet any interesting men?"

"I met a fun group of women."

"You got all dressed up like that to go meet women?"

On New Year's Day, Beverly was awakened by the sound of kids in her yard. The noise was coming from the backyard. She looked out and saw a sign stuck on a post in the snow that said 'Happy New Year.' Since the snow shoveling incident, Beverly had been discussed again in the welfare meeting. It was another service project. Snowfall had been unseasonably heavy that year. The youth, led by Andy and Tony, were making a snow fort for Davey in the backyard. They had planned it on paper, so everyone knew what they were supposed to do. Some of them were in charge of making an arsenal of snowballs, which they were storing in one of the Barnes' plastic laundry baskets—one which Sister Barnes was not aware had been 'borrowed.' They had brought old blankets to line the bottom. They worked on it in shifts. Sister Howard arrived with a vat of hot chocolate. An noon they were still working away. Beverly ordered pizza for the whole crew, and Davey watched with excitement—his little face pressed against the window.

"I guess this is because I yelled at the boys when they tried to shovel my sidewalks, isn't it?"

Sister Howard stirred the Crockpot of hot chocolate. "Beverly, some people have a hard time learning how to serve and some of us have a time letting people serve us. A few years ago, my husband and I started a business. It went well for a while, but then we made some wrong decisions and the business went under. We almost lost our home. That was one of the hardest times for me, because I had to learn to accept help. All of a sudden I was the person who couldn't drive the girls to camp because I couldn't afford the gas, and I had to admit that and accept money from people. It was very hard for me, because we had never been in that situation before."

"Well, I guess I should tell the boys that they can shovel my walks. We've had enough snow lately, I'm getting tired of doing it myself. It's really hard work! Since I've been doing it, I've been thinking of getting a snow blower. I guess the hard part about having them shovel my walks is that it reminded me I was a—you know, how they always tell you to shovel the sidewalks for the widows. I just can't bring myself to use that word to describe myself."

"If it's any consolation, it really livened up the welfare meeting, hearing how you threw a snowball at the bishop and told him to mind his own business."

"So, let's see. I need to apologize to Andy and Tony, the bishop . . . Is there anybody else I'm leaving out?"

"I don't know about the bishop but Andy and Tony think you're really cool now. None of the other widows would come out and have a snowball fight with them."

The following Sunday, Davey acted up in Sacrament Meeting. Brother Barnes was giving the opening prayer. "We come before Thee this day with great *thanks-giving* in our hearts." Davey heard the word 'thanksgiving' and some connection was made in his memory. Throughout the reverent chapel the words reverberated. *"Gobble gobble woof woof."* There were titters from several young women. Beverly quieted him as she reflected. *"If only that was the connection I made with Thanksgiving, we'd be in good shape."* Then a realization hit her. *"I made it through. I made it through Thanksgiving, and I made it through that first year!"*

January dragged on. Davey and Beverly played for short periods of time in his snow fort, after she insulated him in several layers of clothing, but she was tired of winter. She knew, though, that Davey was not going to understand when his snow fort melted. What did they call that kind of situation where something positive was paired with something negative? She remembered back to psychology class. Approach avoidance. That was it.

The next time she got together with the ladies from the New Year's party, she explained this concept to them. "Approach approach is when you have your choice between two equally-inviting choices—two men ask you for a date for the same night, and you would like to go out with both of them. Approach avoidance is when something good is paired inseparably with something bad. A guy asks you out to a sold-out concert that you've been wanting to go to and you want to go to the concert, but you don't want to go out with him. Avoidance avoidance is when you have to choose between two equally bad choices, for example, you can swerve to miss your neighbor's cat, but in order to do so, you have to plow down their mailbox." They sat around in Jean's family room eating Chinese food and thinking up stupid examples, mostly that had to do with their ex-husbands.

The five ladies were all from the same stake, and they were all trying to survive their failed marriages. None of them wanted the title 'divorcee' anymore than Beverly wanted to be called a widow. However, Beverly silently noted, there was an element of choice in their situations. Every once in a while, one of them would say something, and she would wonder what the other side of the story was. Shelly was struggling to collect child support and just seemed to be trying to survive. Laura, a beautiful lady, was full of bitterness and out to take the doctor for all he was worth. Jean was laughing on the outside and crying on the inside. Maureen was struggling to maintain feelings of self-worth. Marilyn seemed to have a good working relationship with her ex-husband, even a friendship. They were her friends. She needed women friends. But the more she came to their gatherings, the more she felt like she did not quite belong there, either.

CHAPTER SIXTEEN
BACK TO SCHOOL

"No, Davey, you can't go in the water. This is just a 'look at' fountain, not a swimming pool," Beverly said, as they sat by the fountain on the University of Utah campus. "So what do you think of my school? Do you see that big 'U' up on the mountain? That stands for the University of Utah. I'm all registered and as soon as you start going to your pre-school, I'll start going to my school. All of these buildings are part of my school."

"Is there a big letter 'P' on the mountain behind my school?"

"No, I don't think so. But there's not a great big box of toys at my school."

"No toys? Not in any of these buildings?"

"No, and you can't even go wading in the fountains."

"I like my school better."

Beth Myers stood at the door and greeted each of the children warmly as they went down into her basement, which had been transformed into the "Ready, Set, Go Pre-school." She placed a color-coded name tag on each child and told him or her to go find the coordinating chair downstairs. Davey raced downstairs to find the green chair.

"I'm so glad you decided to do this. It's so convenient."

"Well, teaching full-time had just gotten to be too much, and if we are really careful, we should be able to get along without my salary. I had twelve more people who wanted to sign up than what I could take, so there are people interested."

"Well, I'd better let you go, and I need to get on my way. My class goes from 9:30 to 11:30, so I should be able to pick him up at noon or soon afterwards."

"Don't worry about it. He can play with Benjamin until you get here, if you're late. Were you able to get the classes you wanted?"

"Yes. I only signed up for two classes--this one that I'll be taking on Mondays, Wednesdays and Fridays, and a Tuesday and Thursday night class. That way I take one while Davey is in pre-school and I'll drop him off at my brother's on Tuesday and Thursday evenings. Most of my credits transferred, but I have to take a couple of general education classes to satisfy the different requirements, so I'm taking one psychology class and an expository writing class to teach me how to write term papers. I'm in no big rush, and I don't want to overload myself. It's been a while."

"Well, you're welcome to join us for a refresher course anytime."

That night at dinner, Davey asked her about her school.

"What color chair did you get, Mom?"

"The chairs are all the same at my school. And I've already got a paper to do."

He jumped down from his chair. "I did a paper today, too." He reached into the little backpack his teacher had given him. He unfolded and straightened the picture. "This is my picture of what 'Ready Set Go' means." It was a picture of several young children being shot out of cannons toward a ring of many-colored chairs. "That one is me. I'm being aimed at the green chair."

"That's really a good picture. You have a good imagination. It looks more like 'Ready, Aim, Fire' than 'Ready, Set, Go.'"

"Let's see your paper, Mom."

"My paper isn't done yet."

"Did you forget your crayons?"

Beverly laughed. "You know what? You're getting to be pretty good company. Maybe we're not like every other family, but it's good to sit down at the end of the day and discuss our school work with each other." She listened to her son. *"He really thinks he's my peer,"* she thought. *"But then again, who else is ever around? He's my child and my main companion at the same time. That makes for a unique relationship. I wonder if it's wrong--or just different? I wonder if there's anyone I could ask about this kind of thing?"*

A few days later, at the end of Beverly's psychology class, Nancy, the teaching assistant made an announcement. "I'd like to introduce Kelly Cameron. Kelly is a grad student from the psychology department."

Kelly stood up. "As part of my Masters program in counseling, I'm supposed to provide supervised counseling for several people, for at least 8 sessions, free of charge. By supervised I mean that I would counsel with you one on one, the sessions would be taped, and a licensed therapist would evaluate my counseling sessions from the tapes and my notes. Interested parties please see me after class." As Beverly went forward to sign up, she heard a couple of fellow students talking. She recognized one of them as Kyle, an intimidating fellow who always had all of the answers in class.

He remarked so all could hear, "Let's see who signs up, so we'll see who thinks they need a shrink." A couple of people who were heading toward Kelly turned self-consciously and walked out the door. Beverly continued forward, ignoring Kyle's arrogant glance. She sensed somehow that the people behind her would follow her lead--either to sign up or to keep going. It was like a buffet table at a baby shower. No one wanted to be first, but as soon as someone broke the ice, everyone else would follow. Had she ever been embarrassed to step up and fill her plate if everyone was sitting around waiting for someone to go first? No! That was stupid! Some women would starve to death before they would be first in line. She signed the paper.

Then she said, equally as loudly, in response to Kyle's statement. "This class is full of people who hope someday to be psychologists and yet some of them don't see the value of seeking counseling. Does a medical doctor distrust medicine? If so, why would he want to become a doctor? Or would he perhaps just take out his own appendix, since he knew everything already? I'm sure that one of the biggest hurdles in counseling is overcoming people's stigma about seeking professional counseling, but if counselors themselves have that same stigma, it's like admitting they don't see the worth of their own profession. I'm a single parent and there are plenty of things I could use some counseling about. It's free. I think we ought to stand back and see who is stupid enough *not* to sign up." She signed the paper, walked back to her desk to get her purse, past Kyle Pace and the girl who found him so amusing, and out the door.

Beverly picked Davey up from his pre-school. He looked unhappy. "Megan is a bully. She pushed me off my green chair. She said I have to have the yellow chair."

"What did your teacher say?"

"She told Megan I get the green chair, and she has to have the yellow chair, but Megan kept pushing me when the teacher wasn't looking."

"Well, guess what, Davey? Our schools *are* a little bit alike. There's a bully in one of my classes, too."

Beverly sat next to Beth Myers in Relief Society a few weeks later.

She leaned over and whispered, "How are Davey and Megan getting along?"

"They're doing a little better."

"Last week when I tried to put his brown pants on him, he told me that he couldn't wear them anymore because Megan didn't like them."

"I missed that one."

"So I was wondering if he couldn't wear them because he didn't want to *displease* her or if he's starting to like her and wants to *please* her."

"Maybe their Primary teacher can give you some additional insight."

"I guess we'd better shut up. They're getting ready to start."

The following Monday Beverly found herself assigned to work on a project with Kyle Pace. After a few uncommunicative hours at the library, Kyle asked her, as they walked toward the parking lot, "So when are we going out?"

"We're not."

"Admit it, Beverly. You want me."

"In your dreams! Besides, I'm way older than you."

"Okay, let's explore the psychological hang-ups that lead society to believe that the man must be older and taller than the woman--over dinner. Or perhaps you could ask your shrink about it," he teased her.

"I don't have to. It's a control issue. Man feels that he must always have the advantage. Age and size are obvious ways for him to be superior. The only reason I'm interesting to you is that you know that I can't stand you and that, therefore, makes me a challenge. I know your type--the professional bachelor. You have women falling at your feet, baking you cookies, inviting you over for dinner--and you take the cookies and the dinners and the attention and give just a little bit back, enough to encourage their hope, but you never really build a relationship with anyone but yourself. A few of the girls will eventually give up, but there are always some new ones there to take their place. If I was interested in you, you wouldn't give me a second glance, but since I'm not, you find me interesting and challenging. When the Indians killed buffalos, they did it for a reason. They made use of all the parts. When the white man killed a buffalo, it was so that he could pound on his chest and proclaim, 'I killed a buffalo.' You're not interested in me for real. I'm just another buffalo. You have probably left a trail of rotting buffalo carcasses behind you. I don't like you. You're a big know-it-all."

"I'm not any more opinionated than you are."

"I beg your pardon?"

"Do you always evaluate people this quickly?"

"Yes, as a matter of fact, I do. In high school I had a nickname. My friends called me 'Wanda One-Date' because that was all it took, either way. They knew after one date whether or not they wanted to spend more time with me, and I knew after one date if I liked them or not. As an adult, I've learned that I can trust those instincts. There have been times that I've ignored them, and in the final analysis, when I go back to my first impressions of people, I've usually been right on the money."

"Scared them off after one date, huh?"

"If that's the way you want to look at it. I prefer to think I have good instincts. I observe people."

"Oh, I get it. You're observant and I'm opinionated. Well what would you say if I told you that I made that remark in class that day because Kelly asked me to so that only the people who were *really* interested in counseling would sign up?"

"She did?"

"No, but if she had, wouldn't it change that judgment of me?"

"Maybe, but she didn't, so it doesn't."

"But it makes it possible for you to admit that your judgment could be based on incomplete evidence or faulty perceptions. So why won't you go out with me?" He followed her to her car.

"Because I don't like you, and that's *not* based on faulty perceptions. You think you are the apotheosis of eligible men."

"Ooooh! Apotheosis! An SAT word." He leaned up against her car. "I think it's because you *are* like me. What is it that you're scared of?"

"I'm not afraid of anything. I'm here to get an education, not dates." She reached into her purse and retrieved her keys.

"Okay, have it your way. You aren't worried about being a buffalo carcass rotting in the sun. You're worried about letting someone get close to you who is as curious about people as you are. Why did you tell everyone that you're a single parent but you didn't say that you're a widow?"

"That's none of anybody's business, certainly not yours."

"So you *are* a widow. I knew you weren't divorced."

"That was a cheap trick!"

"It worked."

"How did you know?"

"Every woman I've met who is divorced complains about the 'ex' sooner or later. You talk about your little boy, but you never mention his father."

"You're very nosy and obnoxious! I'm going home now. I'll type up my half of the paper. You type up your half."

"Good idea! And one of these days we'll have to go on half a date. You can go see the first half of the movie and I'll see the second half, and then we can get together and compare notes. See you Wednesday, Beverly. See you Friday. See you every Monday, Wednesday and Friday until you decide to go out with me."

"I don't date."

"You don't date? Oh, I get it. You're going to live out the rest of your life as a monument to your one true love and be alone until you die. How touching!"

"That would certainly be preferable to putting up with the likes of you," she retorted. "You have no any idea if I've been widowed for two years or two days. I don't have to put up with your intrusive questioning. When I want to go on a date with someone, I will. I can guarantee it isn't going to be with *you!*"

"You *are* scared. That's what *my* instincts tell me about you. You are scared to death--pardon my choice of words--to get involved with anyone for fear of losing someone again."

Beverly did not respond, but he saw by the look on her face that he had hit close to home. She fumbled with her keys as she struggled to get her car door open and escape. Kyle continued.

"So you're not even going to give me the requisite one date? Just call me 'Walter One-Date.' And I'll call you 'The Widow Crandall.' It would help if you would dress appropriately so red-blooded American males such as myself would have a clear sign that you are still in mourning, maybe one of those black hats with the little veil . . ."

Beverly got her car door open, finally, and got in, slamming the door behind her and drove off, angrily. *"How much longer am I going to have to put up with that jerk hanging around pushing my buttons?"*

"How was school, Davey?"

"We learned about phones today. We made a book with everyone's phone number in it." Before he could get it to show her, the phone rang. A very young female voice asked for Davey.

"It's for you." She handed the phone to Davey.

"Hello," he said. "Uh huh. Uh uh." He shook his head. "Oh, okay." Long period of silence. Davey hung up the phone. A couple of minutes went by. The phone rang again.

"Is Davey there? He got cut off while he was talking to my Cabbage Patch doll, Marisa Daphne."

Davey picked up the phone. "I don't want to talk to your Cabbage Patch doll and you can't have the green chair!" He hung up. Megan called back several more times, until Beverly finally had to tell her that Davey didn't want to talk to her anymore that night. Marisa Daphne was very disappointed.

CHAPTER SEVENTEEN
CHIPS AHOY

"Phoenix, Arizona? Do you know anybody that lives there?"

"We're staying at Howard's."

"Howard? Who is Howard?"

"Howard Johnson, Mother, you know--the hotel. That was a joke."

"Beverly, this is not a joke. We want you to be with the family on Thanksgiving. Won't you even think about it? Are you going to spend the rest of your life avoiding Thanksgiving?"

"I might."

"How did you come up with Phoenix?"

"There was a special airfare between here and there. I can't be gone too long. I have to be back for classes, so I decided we'd fly instead of drive. I just went on-line looking for bargains. The airfare was cheap. I've never been there. It's probably warmer than here. We can eat enchiladas and bean dip for Thanksgiving dinner. I know the family thinks I'm being weird, and I know it has been long enough that everyone thinks I should have dealt with this, but I've faced everything else. You all are going to have to understand that I can't face Thanksgiving."

"But the thought of you and Davey all alone in a hotel room . . ."

"Mother, we'll be together. Davey and I are a family, a little one, maybe, but we'll have a good time. We'll pay $10.00 for some Fruit Loops from room service, watch a few cartoons, go visit some Indian ruins or whatever there is to see in the area."

Beverly and Davey flew back into town the weekend after Thanksgiving and resumed their schooling. The following Friday, after her last class, Beverly got the travel bug again. She loaded Davey and a few necessities into the car and headed out of town. She had no specific destination in mind. They ended up in Evanston, Wyoming. Beverly turned onto one of the main streets, looking for an inexpensive place to stay. *"Motel 6, Super 8. Well, the numbers are going up."* Then she spotted one that looked just right. *"This sounds like us."* She pulled into the Vagabond Motel.

"Good thing you didn't come next week. We'd've been all booked up. The ice fishing festival is pretty big around here, you know."

"I saw the signs coming into town. Maybe we'll come back for that, when my son is a little older."

"They have it every year about this time."

Soon she and Davey were settled inside a room. Upon a recommendation from Hal at the front desk, they dined at the Country River Restaurant down the street. Then they went back to their room and turned in for the night. The next day they found a place on the outskirts of town where you could chop down your own Christmas tree.

Beverly pulled into her parents' driveway late Saturday afternoon and honked the horn. Her parents came out. Beverly had a small straggly Christmas tree strapped to the top of her car. "We cut down our own Christmas tree, up in Wyoming. What do you think?"

Tactfully her father said, "Well, you can never judge a Christmas tree until you see it standing up."

Beverly said truthfully, "Oh, it doesn't look great. I already know that. I didn't pick it because it was a nice-looking tree. I picked it because it had a skinny trunk and I thought it would be the easiest one to chop down."

He turned to Davey. "Is this true? Did your mom really chop down this tree?"

"Yup. I watched. From real far away."

"Dad, can you come over and help me put it in the stand before it gets dried out?"

Naomi had to admit that Beverly was in good spirits. Maybe she did know what she could deal with and what she couldn't. The family would just have to deal with the wanderlust that came over Beverly every year around Thanksgiving.

Christmas that year was not too bad. Beverly gave Davey some money and Aunt Gayle took him shopping for a present for his mother. Gayle reported back. "I gave him husband lessons. I asked him your favorite color and whether he thought you were small, medium or large. I asked him what kind of things you liked to do for fun and was there anything broken around the house that you needed a new one of or anything that you complained about."

"How did he do?"

"You'll just have to wait and see."

Christmas morning Davey watched as she opened her gifts from him--a cookie cookbook, an extra-large green bath towel, a jigsaw puzzle, and a book bag. He filled her in. "The cookbook is because you like to make cookies, and that big towel is because of that one day when I came in your room after you got out of the tub and you said you wished they made a bath towel that would cover you all the way around, and it's green--your favorite color. The puzzle is for when you need something to do that doesn't take another person, and that bag is for you to carry your books in when you go to school."

Beverly looked at him proudly. "I'm doing okay. We're doing okay."

January, as usual, dragged on. Beverly put together her puzzle. February arrived. Jean called and she and Marilyn dragged Beverly out to a singles' Valentine's dance. She was doing okay, not having a great time, necessarily, but surviving. "Would you like to dance?" Beverly looked up to see an older man smiling at her. She gave him her hand and followed him onto the dance floor. The music began. It was a song that had memories from her life with Dave. She had closed her eyes and tried to imagine that it was Dave she was dancing with. She knew that wasn't fair, but she did it anyway. It was close to their wedding anniversary, and she couldn't help but think about him. To everyone around her it appeared she really liked the man she was dancing with, and to him as well. Lost in her memories, she had herself so convinced it was Dave, that when she opened her eyes and saw the stranger smiling at her, she excused herself and ran out of the building. He had no idea what he had done. She had been so cuddly to dance with. She stood out back crying behind the air conditioner and didn't go back in until the dance was over. *"I can't do this anymore. No more dances. If Dave can't hold me in his arms, I don't want anyone else to, just because he asked me to dance. This is too hard after you've been happily married. It would be different if it was someone that you would like to be held by. Why, when I was doing so well and feeling so optimistic and up, would I be stupid enough to come to one of these and get myself all depressed? No more dances. Maybe I'll go to the firesides, but I'd rather be home with my little boy than at one of these dances. Heavenly Father, did you hear that? If there's someone else out there that You would like to get me together with, You're going to have to put him behind me in line at the grocery store or in one of my classes at school, but not at one of these dances."*

True to her word, she stopped going to the dances, but she did attend an occasional fireside. They usually had good speakers, and the only time you had to be social was over the punch and cookies. She was mingling at the refreshment table with the other singles one Sunday evening in April after a valley-wide fireside. As she watched people line up to shake hands with the General Authority who had spoken, she contemplated getting in line. *"I could ask him if it's in the official church rule book that they have to serve store-bought cookies and red Hawaiian punch at every singles' gathering. Maybe the church has stock in Chips Ahoy."* She had discovered that they came in handy when dodging advancing men, however. She had perfected the art of taking a swallow of punch or a bite of a cookie just when it looked like a man was making an approach, so that she was unable to talk.

She spotted the fellow she had told he could get to her house by following the promptings of the Holy Ghost. He was headed her way. Taking a couple of quick bites from a cookie, she spotted somebody else she knew. It was her dentist, Dr. Evans! *"He's single? He's a Mormon?"* A piece of a chocolate chip cookie went down the wrong pipe. Unable to breathe, she began to cough to try to dislodge it. The next thing she knew, Dr. Evans was behind her and had his arms around her waist. He made a fist and brought it in and up--the Heimlich maneuver. The piece of cookie was dislodged and Beverly could breathe again.

"Are you okay now, Mrs. Crandall?"

"You can call me Beverly, Dr. Evans, since you had your arms around me." Beverly realized that for the first time since Dave had died, she was flirting with someone. She had talked to men, but this was the first time she had flirted.

He laughed. "Only if you'll call me David. I try to lose the 'doctor' stuff at these singles' functions. Otherwise, I tend to attract a following of women who think I'm a brain surgeon or something."

"It could be good for business."

"Sure, that's why I'm here, to find up new patients. If only. Speaking of business, aren't you overdo for a check-up?"

"Yes, I guess I am. I'll have to make an appointment." Beverly could still remember how it felt to have his arms around her, and his name was *David!* But while she was daydreaming about how she could get a date with Dr. David Evans, he had started talking about dental floss. Disappointed, Beverly promised to floss faithfully before her next appointment. She thanked him again for the Heimlich maneuver. He extended his hand and she shook it. Dr. Evans' wife had passed away about three months ago, and whenever he found himself attracted to a woman, he talked about dentistry. It shut things down every time. He just wasn't ready for socializing.

A couple of months later, Beverly ran into Dr. Evans again, this time at Trolley Square. She and Davey were having an outing. She had bought him his first ice cream cone, and he was a terrible mess. They were sitting on a bench out front. She had already used up all the napkins she had grabbed on the way out, so she had just decided to let him make a mess and then take him home and clean him up. Chocolate ice cream was dripping from his chin. His hands and face were covered with sticky chocolate.

"Here Davey, let Mom lick some of the drips." She took the cone away from him to try and lick off the melted parts. She handed it back to him. Now *her* hands were covered with chocolate, and she had a big drip of chocolate sliding slowly down the front of her t-shirt. As she scooped it up and into her mouth, she looked up. Coming up the walkway was Dr. Evans, looking as handsome as ever. He smiled a nice white dentist's smile.

"Beverly, we meet again." He extended his hand in greeting. No doubt about it, he was a Mormon through and through. Embarrassed, Beverly held up her chocolate-covered hands. He withdrew his hand, amused. He surveyed the two of them. They looked so happy sitting there enjoying an ice cream cone together. Beverly was an attractive woman, even with chocolate smeared on her chin. "This must be your little boy." Beverly took a swipe at her chin with the back of her hand.

"So you noticed the family resemblance?" she said, trying to make a joke about the two of them sitting there covered with chocolate.

"Does he eat a lot of sugar? You know, you need to be very careful about cavities, even in baby teeth."

"This is his first ice cream cone. That's why I let him make such a mess with it." Beverly felt a need to defend herself. "I feed him right, really I do. I gave him strained vegetables before . . ."

"How old is he? You know, children should have their first check-up around age three."

"He'll be four in August. I guess we're overdue. I'll make an appointment soon. I promise we'll bring all of his cavities to you." She backtracked. "Not that he's going to *have* any cavities. I mean everyone gets one or two, but he's not going to be one of those kids that . . ." *"Why do I feel so uncomfortable around this man?"*

"He's a fine boy." He tousled Davey's hair. His hand came back covered with chocolate ice cream. Beverly reached to hand him a napkin, but all she had was a bunch of wadded up chocolate-covered napkins.

"I'm sorry, Dr. Evans. I mean, David. We're out of--we've used up all of our napkins."

"It's okay. I'll just run my hand under the drinking fountain over there. It was good to see you." He walked off, shaking his head. Twice he'd blown a perfectly good opportunity to get better-acquainted with Beverly. He wanted to and yet he didn't want to. *"Why do I get so nervous around this woman?"*

She saw him walking away, shaking his head. *"I blew it. He thinks I don't floss and that I feed Davey a constant diet of sugar."* She went home and bathed Davey and spent another lonely evening at home.

A few weeks later, Meredith Zollinger caught Beverly on the way out of church. "I have someone I want you to meet. He's one of my husband's friends. He's here visiting from California. He's very nice-looking, and he's into physical fitness like you are. I'd like to set you up with him."

"Well . . . okay," Beverly said, hesitantly. "I guess next Friday or Saturday would be okay."

He called her to make the date. "We're going sailing on Utah Lake. A friend of mine has a catamaran."

"That sounds fun. Will we be out into the evening? It might get cool on the lake. What do you think I should wear?"

A deep male voice said, "As little as possible."

"In your dreams. I just wanted to know if I needed a sweater."

Saturday afternoon, Beverly was briefing her baby-sitter on Davey's schedule, when she heard a car drive up. Angela ran to the window.

"Beverly, he's a '10!'"

Beverly looked out the window. All she could see so far was his car.

"Angie, your idea of a '10' is a '2' in a Corvette. Maybe I should stay home and you can go out with him."

When Beverly opened the door, there stood a tan, muscle-bound fellow, with close-cropped blond hair. His red Corvette was parked in front of the house. He was about five inches shorter than Beverly, but what he lacked in height, he made up for in biceps.

Several hours later Beverly reported back to her friend, Lori, who still checked in every once in a while to see if Beverly was alive and well. "I just got back from a date with a California beach bum. All he talked about were his 'delts' and 'pecs' and how he takes bee pollen to improve his virility. He was half a foot shorter than me and so over-developed that he looked like 'Mighty Mouse.' My babysitter was drooling over him. I think she's closer to his age than I am. We went sailing with some friends of his. I was the senior citizen of the group. I guess Sister Zollinger thinks I'm younger than I am."

"Oh Beverly, I'm so glad I don't have to do that all over again. It must be awful!"

"Are you kidding? This was one of the better blind dates I've been on. Brother Arletti set me up with one of his co-workers, a fellow named Jason. I've never met anybody so cheap! He told me that we were going out to dinner and to the movies, so I got dressed up, thinking we were going to a nice restaurant. I mean, there's nothing wrong with saving money, but he was so obvious about it. He brought one of those coupon books. He had told me that he had made reservations at La Caille, so I got all dressed up. Then he pulled out the coupon book and showed me that if we just got something at the food court at the mall, we could make the earlier show, which he had a two-for-one coupon for. We didn't pick the show according to what we wanted to see, but which theater the discount was at. So we went to the mall, and then he gave me my choice of the three things that he had discount coupons for. I had a corn dog and a small frozen yogurt. I was afraid to ask for topping because that wasn't on the coupon. It's not that I expect to be taken to the most expensive restaurant in town, just maybe somewhere that I could eat sitting down with real silverware instead of a plastic knife and fork at a lunch counter. If he works at the same company as Brother Arletti, he must make enough money to pay full price at the movies."

"Could you imagine being *married* to someone like that? If people threw rice at the wedding, he'd probably pick it up and add it to the food storage."

"Other than that, though, he was real nice, so when he called to ask me out again, I accepted. Being cheap is not the same as being a serial killer, after all. We actually went out to eat somewhere nice that time, but I doubt he'll ask me out again."

"Why not? You still doing the 'Wanda One-Date' thing? He's already over-quota."

"Wanda sized him up. He's cheap but harmless. He can hold a decent conversation. He's okay company. I'm afraid my warped sense of humor did it this time."

"I'm listening."

"Well, he told me was taking me to a new restaurant in Deer Valley. When we got there, I thought he was trying to make up for the last date, because we were at a really nice restaurant. Then he confessed that it was one of those time-share presentations where they give you a free dinner for two if you listen to their sales pitch for condominiums and asked me if I wouldn't mind pretending like I was his wife."

"What did you do?"

"What could I do? We'd already started eating. I did just what he asked me to. After the dinner, when they did the presentation, he was really downplaying his job, told them a time-share condo really wasn't something we could afford right now. Then he turned to me and said, 'Right, honey?'"

"So I said, 'Well not unless we use some of the money you just got from Uncle Harold's estate.' He gave me a dirty look for saying that, couldn't think of a quick comeback. After that, the salesman was all over him. We would never have gotten out of there if I hadn't had that attack of morning sickness. Anyway, I think that's the end of him. At least he couldn't treat me like I owed him something. There was this other guy--the Higginbothams introduced me to him at a dinner party, which, I suspect was thrown in order to get the two of us together--and he asked me out, with some urging from the Higginbothams, I'm sure. All he had was a motorcycle, so I suggested that we could take my car. He offered to buy some gas, so I told him he could put a few dollars' worth in if he wanted. He filled the whole tank. Then he asked me how many miles I got to the gallon and informed me that I was *his* for the next 320 miles and that I'd better not park with anyone else on his tank of gas."

"What did you say?"

"I told him that in the first place, parking didn't use any gas, and in the second place, not only was I not going to park with anyone else on his tank of gas, I wasn't going to park with him, either."

"What did he say?"

"He asked me if had a siphon. You know, Lori, when people are having trouble in their marriages, I think they should be sentenced to spend an evening together at the singles' dance. It would get them back together real soon. Anyway, then Brother Higginbotham wanted a report of my date with this guy. Apparently he had told Brother H. that I was a cold fish or something to that effect, because he gave me this big lecture Sunday after church about not comparing everyone to Dave and that sooner or later I had to let go and stop expecting 'Mr. Perfect' to happen along. Some guys don't need to be compared to *anybody* to look bad. I just told him that I didn't hit it off with his friend, but he kept pushing and pushing. Finally I told him that I had to fight him off at the door and that I wouldn't have even considered inviting him in for a few minutes, and I was not interested in seeing him again. Then he says, 'I've never known him to be like that,' like I was making it up or something, so I told him, 'Well, maybe he doesn't find *you* attractive, Brother Higginbotham.' He told me I should give him another chance. I was as nice as I could be, but I can't abide the thought of kissing somebody I don't want to kiss. I would genuinely rather spend the evening at home with Davey than be out with someone I don't really want to be with. I don't want to waste his time or mine. This obnoxious guy in one of my classes keeps trying to get me to go out with him. He keeps asking me why I won't go out with him. I've told him several times that I don't like him. I don't need any other reason. I don't know if I'll ever get rid of him. He's in psychology, too. He'll probably keep showing up in all of my classes. Now if there was someone I was interested in, it would be a different story."

CHAPTER EIGHTEEN
KNOCK KNOCK

Beverly's check-up with Dr. Evans revealed a cavity. He cleaned her teeth and made a follow-up appointment with her to fill her cavity. He was very businesslike with her, so she was very businesslike in return. She had pretty much given up any hopes she might have had about getting to know him better.

She dropped Davey off with her mother. "I've got a hot date with my dentist. We're going to discuss the merits of waxed versus unwaxed dental floss over a glass of Listerine."

"Now Beverly, didn't you tell me that your friend who knows him said his wife died only recently?" Beverly had been checking around about Dr. Evans and had discovered that he was in Jean's stake. "Don't you remember how that first year or so was for you? Maybe he just needs friends right now."

"You're probably right. You're always right."

"How are you feeling now?" the nurse asked Beverly, to see if the gas had taken effect yet.

Beverly giggled. "I just thought of a good 'knock knock' joke."

"Okay, let's hear it."

"Knock knock."

"Who's there?"

"Dentist."

"Dentist who?"

"Dentist the Menace."

"Doctor, I think she's ready." Smiling, Dr. Evans came into the room from the hallway, where he'd heard the end of Beverly's 'knock knock' joke.

"How are you feeling, Beverly?"

She stuck her arm out. "Why don't you find out for yourself?" She giggled again. Dr. Evans began to work on her tooth. She babbled away incoherently while he scraped and dug at the cavity, even trying to talk while he was drilling. Finished, he put the drill down.

"Now what were you trying to say?"

"I just wanted to tell you what nice strong hands you have, Doctor, and how nice it is having you work on my teeth."

He smiled. "You won't feel that way in a few hours."

"Yes, I will, honest! I would even choke on a cookie if you would put your arms around me again." Dr. Evans blushed. He looked around frantically for a dental tool.

Beverly went to collect Davey from her mother. "How did it go?"

"Well, let's put it this way, Mother. You see these nice clean shiny white teeth? Take a good look, because this is the last time they'll look this good. I can never go to the dentist again. I flirted with Dr. Evans today while I was under gas. I can't even remember everything that I said, but trust me, what I *can* remember is bad enough!"

David Evans was on his third time down her street. He had a bunch of daisies, a package of Chips Ahoy chocolate chip cookies and sweaty palms. He had located the house. Her car was there. The lights were on. *"What am I doing driving up and down the street like an idiot? I feel like I'm seventeen years old. What am I afraid of? Her father is not going to come out and chase me away. I'm just an adult calling on another adult."* Aside from a couple of firesides he had attended, this was the first time he had attempted socializing since his wife, Diane, had died. Both his teen-agers had gone out for the evening, and he had been jealous and lonely. Another evening at home alone with the cat was more than he could stand. Before he gave himself time to think about what he was doing, he looked up Beverly's address, and now he was driving up and down her street trying to figure out what to do next, every bit as nervous as he had been on his first date 20 years ago. He pulled into the driveway.

Beverly heard the doorbell ring. She wasn't expecting anybody. She turned off the television and went to the door.

"Who's there?" she asked, making a note to get a peephole installed in her door.

"Dentist the Menace." Surprised, Beverly opened the door. "I, uh, came by to check and make sure you didn't have any problems with your filling." He handed her the flowers.

"Do you make housecalls for all your patients?"

"Just you." He smiled. "This is very awkward for me. I've never done this before. Can't you tell? I know it's not very professional of me. I don't really want to think about how unprofessional and presumptuous it is for me to just show up unannounced on your doorstep." He held up the bag of Chips Ahoy cookies. "I brought cookies, your favorite." He continued. "Our mutual friend, Jean, told me that your husband had died. I didn't know that. Sometimes it would just be nice to have someone to talk to who understands. Or just someone human, for that matter. Tonight is one of those times. I couldn't face another evening at home with Paganini."

"Paganini?"

"My cat."

"I wasn't really doing much tonight either. Come in. Have a seat." Beverly gestured towards the sofa. "I'm going to put these flowers in some water." David Evans surveyed the picture on the wall of Beverly, David and Davey before he sat down on her sofa.

"Be careful of the hole in the middle. I guess I could get it fixed, but I'm a little bit sentimental about it. It reminds me of--well, it's hard to explain. I was feeling down because I was pregnant and popped the springs and my husband said all the right things to make me feel better."

"I think I do understand. I find myself being sentimental over strange things, too."

"You do? Like what?" Beverly came over with a plate of the cookies, and she sat down near him on the couch, on the same side of the sinkhole, but with the plate of cookies between them. They talked about their respective dear-departed spouses, how hard it was to be a single adult, ate cookies and fought against their attraction to each other. After they had polished off all the cookies, Dr. Evans moved the plate out of the way and closed the gap between him and Beverly. He took his hands and began to rub the back of her neck. Closing her eyes, she felt herself relax. Just as she was relaxing and snuggling up to him, Dr. Evans stood up, rather abruptly.

"I really should go." He helped her up and leaned over, intending only to give her a quick brush of a kiss on the cheek, and be off into the night--but he missed and somehow got her lips instead. Beverly had forgotten what it felt like to be kissed and old feelings surfaced like a diver coming up for air. She had become so skilled at dodging men's advances, she had forgotten what it felt like not to want to dodge. Dr. Evans held her close against his chest, and she could hear his heart beating. She was sure he could hear hers, too--that the neighbors could hear it, that the bishop could hear it--and it was saying, "Don't go. Don't go." He stroked her hair and thought about how good it felt to hold and be held again. Tentatively she said his name, knowing that there in the dim light it would be easy to confuse just which David this was. And yet, she told herself, she was genuinely attracted to him--this other David. He kissed her forehead, and held her close, and soon they were back on the couch and kissing again.

No clock rang out to signal the passing of time, but Beverly was vaguely aware that it was quite late and that the smaller portion of the evening had been devoted to conversation and cookies, the greater part to cuddling and kissing. *One of us needs to have some self-control. I really should ask him to leave. On the other hand, it's probably his turn. I resisted the guy with the delts and the pecs, despite the bee pollen, and I resisted the guy who bought the gas. I would have resisted Jason if I'd needed to, but he was a perfect gentleman, even if he was cheap.* She silently prayed for strength. She imagined herself sitting in front of her bishop explaining how she had been carried away on a wave of passion after sharing a bag of Chips Ahoy cookies with her dentist--not even anything she could call a bona fide date. She imagined David watching her kissing another man. Even that didn't work. *"That's what you get for dying!"*

David Evans whispered softly in her ear, "Diane." Immediately, they both froze. "I'm sorry," he apologized. "I don't know how that slipped out." Beverly sat up and moved to the other side of the sinkhole.

"It's okay. When I call you David, the line kind of blurs for me, too. It's been a lot longer for me, but if I was being honest, maybe I wasn't always sure which one of you I was kissing, either, but I think it was you most of the time." She smoothed out her hair. "Actually, it's probably good that you said that. I was running short on self-control. That brought me back to my senses. It's not right for me to be pretending I'm with Dave and you to be pretending you're with Diane. Our church does a lot of things by proxy, but I don't think this is supposed to be one of them."

He looked at her, and his eyes filled with tears. "I'm sorry, Beverly. I never should have come over here tonight. I'm being unfair to you. You're a very nice person, and I like you a lot, but I just miss her so much. I closed my eyes and it seemed for a few minutes there like I had her back again. I'm so sorry."

"That happened to me once, at a dance. You don't have to apologize. I understand. I should apologize, too. I should know that we are at different stages in the grieving process. I flirted with you when I should have known better."

"You were under the influence."

"My subconscious should have known better."

"Do you know how much that brightened my day? The rest of the afternoon everyone kept asking me what I was smiling about."

"I didn't know what to think when I saw you standing on my doorstep with those flowers. Do you think the 'Friday Night Movie of the Week' stood a chance after that?"

"I came over for moral support, not immoral support, honest!"

"I believe you. I do. You really were planning to leave. I *wanted* you to kiss me. I should have . . . Maybe we can step back and pretend we never had this-- this romantic evening. Why don't we start by just being friends. Next time you get lonely and need to talk to someone, give me a call. Next time I have an awful blind date and need to tell someone about it, I'll call you."

"Okay, let's do that. I could really use a friend like that. But I have to tell you, Beverly, this was the best date I never had!" They hugged and Dr. David Evans went out to his car and drove home.

CHAPTER NINETEEN
WALK A MILE IN MY SHOES

The following Sunday, Beverly contemplated going in to talk to her bishop. *"And tell him what? That I was tempted? That I discovered I could feel something for someone besides Dave? That I'm confused? If I tried to discuss this with him, he would probably think I was there to confess something serious. He would think that 'I was kissing my dentist on the couch' was the lead-in. Spiritual leader or not, I don't think anyone quite understands something like this if they don't have a frame of reference."* He would counsel her to have self-control. She could counsel *herself* to have self-control. In the light of day, sitting in church with a little boy on her lap eating Cheerios, self-control didn't seem that unattainable.

As Beverly walked out of the chapel and into the foyer, Brother Mangum, the high council representative over the singles' program, approached her.

"Beverly, can I speak with you for a minute?" He extended his hand. He was a pleasant-looking fellow, tall with prematurely gray hair, and a smile that put people at ease. He sat down on the sofa and Beverly joined him. She handed Davey a couple of picture books and a couple of toys out of her bag and he sat down on the floor.

"What can I do for you?"

"I just got this assignment over the older singles, and I *really* want to understand what it's like to be an older single in the church. I'm concerned that we are losing a lot of our single members. The rate of inactivity among the single adults is high. I thought I would talk to some of you and see what insights you can give me." Beverly studied his face. *"He's going to the source. That's a good idea. He does seem genuinely interested."* Beverly settled back against the sofa. She looked around. The foyer had pretty much cleared out. Actually, she was glad to have someone who really wanted to know and she decided to tell it like it is.

"You always hear the obvious things--how difficult it is being a single in a family-oriented church. Personally, I don't necessarily feel singled out . . ." Beverly smiled. "Poor choice of words--because Davey and I *are* a family, we're just missing someone. What I mean to say is that I'm not offended when they talk about families, because those are my values, too, but I don't think people realize how lonely single parents get for adult company. Several people in the ward are bent on finding me a new companion, but I get so tired of going to singles' parties trying to meet someone. I get together with some of my friends I grew up with every once in a while, but they have their own lives and activities and husbands and children to take care of. Those are the times I feel most loved and accepted, though, because they've known me for so long. I'm just Beverly to them, not a 'single.' Single people need to be loved and accepted the way they are. Sometimes it feels like being single is like being unemployed. It's considered an undesirable circumstance and you're expected to rectify the situation as soon as possible. I get tired of people asking me if I've met anyone special. I know married people don't think about it or do it on purpose, but they throw Noah's Ark parties--two by two. I'd much rather have been at the Hall's New Year's Eve party last year with people I know and am comfortable with than at a singles' function trying to meet people, but guess what? I wasn't invited. I don't even get invited anymore to parties thrown by a dinner club that Dave and I started. Do you know what that feels like? I would like to see singles included more in things like that than just socializing together, all in pursuit of a mate. In that atmosphere, you always have to try to look gorgeous, be witty and well-informed and interesting lest you should be passed over like the bean dip that's been sitting out too long next to the cheesecake somebody just brought in. It's no fun. It's pressure. You're not with people you know and feel comfortable with. You're constantly breaking ground with new people. I crave adult company after spending all day with Davey, but it does not always have to be an 'SWM.'"

"SWM?"

"That's the personal ad abbreviation for Single White Male."

He looked shocked. "Personal ads? The internet? Don't you think those are dangerous? That's not a very good way for people to meet other quality people."

Beverly looked him in the eyes. "We're getting off-track here. I didn't say that I would ever place a personal ad. I would never advertise myself like some sort of used car--clean, one-owner, low mileage--come kick my tires and check under my hood." He smiled. Beverly continued, "Of course, I do know people in the church who have been lonely enough that they placed personal ads."

"I just don't think it's proper," he said. "There are church programs for the singles that . . ."

Beverly continued for him, ". . . that can introduce you to as many strange people as you would ever meet through a single's ad. And I have friends who are meeting nice people on the internet."

"There are lots of creeps are out there. How do you know who you're talking to, if they're being honest? What about traditional ways of meeting people, like going to school?"

"Have you considered that in a few years using the internet will *be* one of the *traditional* ways of meeting people? I'm going to college. The professors are closer to my age than most of the students."

"I'm sorry, but I don't approve of this internet stuff."

"It's a tool. A hammer can be used to build a house or to injure someone. It's all in the way we use it. If your wife died, and you had children to take care of when you got home from work, homework to supervise, clothes to wash, meals to prepare, groceries to buy, when would you have time to go out and try to meet someone? And how long do you think you would last trying to do it all yourself? Checking your e-mail at 6:00 in the morning and dashing off a quick answer to someone you're getting acquainted with might just be the best fit in a circumstance like that. Yes, there are people out there on the internet who are up to no good. If you're chatting with someone on the internet and they cross a line, you can click a button and make them disappear. You can block them from contacting you. There are lots of things you can do. I've wished I had that capability with a couple of blind dates I've been on."

"Who set you up?"

"People from church. That doesn't always make a lot of difference because guess what, Brother Mangum, working with someone doesn't mean you know everything about them, either. There are sites specifically for LDS Singles. Did you know that? You can request to exchange e-mails only with active temple-worthy people. Yes, you have to take their word for it, at first, but you have to take people's word for things in person, too. Although I haven't tried it, I have friends who have, and I don't think you should be so judgmental. If a brother in my ward wanted to line me up with someone and I said, 'Give me a short biography of him and give the guy my phone number. Let me talk to him 10 or 15 times on the phone, and then I'll decide if I want to go out with him.' He would say, 'Who do you think you are?' But that's what you can do on the internet, send a few e-mails back and forth, chat a few times, get a feel for who the person is. Do your own screening process. I understand the jerks tip their hand, usually sooner than later. I know some ladies who are meeting high-quality professional people that way, active serving members of the church."

"I still think it's dangerous to meet someone that way."

"We're talking about adults with judgment, not twelve-year-olds, running off to meet someone at the mall because he said he could tell by your picture on-line that you could be a model. But you're right. It's dangerous. Being single is dangerous. Living alone with only a four-year-old for protection is dangerous, too. The internet is no more dangerous than a blind date--getting in the car with a perfect stranger based on someone else's recommendation. Sometimes they may know the person well, sometimes they may not. And the church singles' functions, there could be any number of predatory creeps at those things, too."

"I can't believe that. The singles' program is inspired and . . ."

"Brother Mangum, the church is *true*, okay, but the singles' program is not the only program of the church that doesn't always run according to the ideal. Come on, do everyone's needs get met through the home teaching program? Do people who have no interest in or commitment to the church ever get help through the welfare program by posing for a few weeks as active members? I thought you wanted me to tell it like it is. Anyone can call the singles' hotline that tells where the dances are. It's listed in the phone book. They find out what's going on, and they have a whole bunch of sweet trusting lonely Mormon singles to prey on. Do you know how lonely you have to get to do any of this stuff trying to meet someone? What's the loneliest you've ever been, Brother Mangum? How long have you been married?"

"Twenty-seven years."

"You said you wanted to know what it was like to be a single adult, and I'm trying to tell you, but you're not listening because you're too busy judging! Do you know what it feels like to be so lonely that you develop a crush on your dentist because of how nice it feels to have a man touch your face? That's lonely! Frankly, Brother Mangum, there's a high rate of inactivity among the singles because there are moral problems."

"Too many people living it up?"

"A divorced woman who feels abandoned and let down by her husband is vulnerable to attention wherever she may find it. A man who has lost his wife and is struggling to raise kids alone may have an affair with a woman at the office because she listens to him. It's an emotional thing, more than a physical one. I'm not talking about people with no morals. I'm talking about people who find themselves in situations they can't handle, not through pre-meditation, not 'I'm-going-to-throw-all-my-standards-and-everything-I've-been-taught-all-my-life-down-the-tubes,' not 'I'm-going-to-break-every-covenant-I've-ever-made-and-alienate-myself-from-all-my-friends-and-my-family,' but through loneliness, something you can't figure out because you haven't lived it. People stay away from church when they are struggling. They feel guilty. Then they don't get the strength that helps them withstand temptation. Never-marrieds simply stop coming because they are tired of having people suggest to them that life has passed them by if they haven't found a mate. Even if they are managing to keep the commandments, singles often feel like they just don't fit."

"We can't expect the church to meet all our needs or solve all of our problems."

"No, but it should be a place where people can go and feel that they are understood and not judged. That if they stumble or are different, there will be love and acceptance, not a bunch of married people looking down their pious little noses at them! They need to be able to come to church and feel better about themselves, not to leave feeling worse because they came!" Beverly stood up. "I've been a widow now for going on two years--two years without the emotional and physical closeness of a mate. I'm 28 years old, and I'm lonely!" She reached down and pulled off one and then the other of her high-heeled shoes. "You say you want to understand, Brother Mangum? Here you go!" She dropped the shoes in his lap, right on top of his scriptures. "Walk a mile in my shoes! Why don't you try abstaining from talking to and touching and being touched by your wife for a month or two. *You* might find yourself making out on the couch with your dentist!" Beverly knew she was not making any sense, and beyond that, saying things she would be embarrassed about later, but she was on a roll. "I thought you wanted to try to understand, but you couldn't stop judging long enough to listen to what I'm saying!" She walked out of the building in her stocking feet, leaving behind a shell-shocked Brother Mangum.

Later that evening, William Mangum sat stupefied on the sofa in his living room as his wife questioned him about a pair of high-heeled shoes she had found in their bedroom. Lucky for him, his wife trusted him and was not as quick to judge as he was. "I'm sure there's a logical explanation for these. I have no idea what it's going to be, but I'm sure it will be interesting."

After the explanation of his conversation with Beverly and how he came to acquire a pair of navy-blue high-heeled shoes, Sister Mangum told him, "I think we should return these shoes to Beverly, don't you?"

"Oh honey, I would really appreciate it if you would."

"I said 'we.' You know how when you owe me an apology about something, sometimes you'll put up some shelves or do some other chore that I've been nagging you about, in lieu of apologizing. I call those 'physical apologies' for times when you can't seem to find the words. I think you owe Beverly an apology. You can do it with words, although you don't seem to have done that well with words, or you can give her one of your famous physical apologies."

"Isn't it kind of late?"

"Wouldn't you rather do this under cover of darkness?"

When a horn honked in her driveway, Beverly looked out the window and turned on the porch light. She saw Brother and Sister Mangum coming up the front walk. Brother Mangum was hobbling awkwardly in a pair of high-heeled shoes. Sister Mangum was grinning from ear to ear. When he reached the door, she opened it, and he handed her the shoes. "I'm sorry, Beverly. It's hard for old married people to imagine what it's like to be single. Kind of how I've always wondered how you women walk in these shoes, but now I *really* know."

"It helps if they're the right size," she offered, taking back her shoes. "I'm sorry I got angry like that. I was impressed you wanted to know what it was like to be a single in the church, and then I got frustrated when it seemed like you didn't understand." She switched gears. "Would you like to come in for a few minutes? Davey's in bed, and I'm putting together a jigsaw puzzle." A new insight came to Brother Mangum as he imagined sitting alone late in the evening trying to piece together a jigsaw puzzle.

"Well, it's kind of late . . ." said Sister Mangum, not wanting to impose.

Brother Mangum broke in, ". . . so we can only stay for a little while, right, dear, and help Beverly put together some pieces of the puzzle."

CHAPTER TWENTY
DO YOU WANT TO GO TO HEAVEN?

Davey was giving his first talk in Primary, a talk Beverly had written for him. She hadn't intended for him to memorize it, but as she had helped him become familiar with it by having him repeat every few lines after her, he had insisted on starting over every time he got a word wrong. Despite her misgivings that he had the dreaded Smithson perfectionist tendencies, she was proud of his efforts to learn his talk. She stood beside him, ready to prompt, knowing that a key word here or there would be all he needed. He held up his crayon drawing, lopsided, and gave his talk with just a little help from his mother.

"This is Norman Mormon.
Wiggly Wendy is his friend.
They make noise in church
from the beginning to the end.

We should be 'active in the church'
Norman had heard his mother say,
so he wiggled and giggled and tickled
and thought it was time to play.

At the drinking fountain
he splashed all around.
He scratched his nails on the chalkboard
to make that awful sound.

He tipped in his chair
and tormented his teacher.
In short, Norman was quite
an irreverant creature.

He whispered to Wendy
and made her laugh out loud.
He looked all around when
his head should have been bowed.

His Primary leaders
called his mother and dad.
'Come help us with Norman.'
This made them very sad.

They told him something,
and we all can try it.
'You can be 'active in the church'
and can still be quiet.'"

Beverly was not the only proud parent there that day. Dave stood nearby while Davey gave his talk, then he moved closer to Beverly.

"Bev, you're doing such a great job with him. What a great kid! Smart, too! Of course, he comes by that naturally, with us as parents." Beverly smiled. *"You know I'm here, don't you? Sometimes I can tell when you can feel me here. Hey, I'd love to stick around for singing time, but I've got my own singing time. They recruited me to sing in a Heavenly choir. It's great! We go to temple dedications all over the world, but the best part is--no Wobble-atos. I stand next to Moses. Okay, so not THAT Moses. It was a popular name a while back. We've got a lot of them up here. Well, it's been fun. Gotta go."*

Beverly hugged her little boy and he went back to his seat with his class. Sister Jackie Meltzer was his teacher. She was a sweet eighteen-year-old fresh out of the Young Women's program. She loved her four-year-olds and they all loved her. She smiled graciously the day Ricky Samuels brought her an offering of flowers that he had picked from the church flowerbed. He had plopped the petunia in her lap, dirt still clinging to its roots, and she had given him a hug and thanked him. Davey always tried to sing well for Sister Meltzer, because she was pretty and nice and so he would get picked to be a helper and make her proud of him.

Sister Osborne, the Primary President, was doing Sharing Time. She was talking to the boys and girls about being good and keeping the commandments.

In her best Primary voice, she asked them, "Now, boys and girls, we always want to choose the right and keep the commandments because we want to make good choices so that we can all go back to live with Heavenly Father. How many of you want to go to Heaven?" Hands flew up. Davey looked down at his feet. He was thinking about this. Last time she asked them how many of them wanted to color, she had handed out crayons and papers right then and there to everyone who raised their hand. Maybe she wouldn't notice if he didn't raise his hand. Maybe if he didn't say anything, she wouldn't make him go. Would Sister Meltzer be disappointed in him if he didn't raise his hand? She was such a nice teacher and he wanted her to like him. Still, he couldn't do it.

Megan blurted out, "Davey's not raising his hand!"

Sister Osborne noticed Davey looking down. "Don't you want to go to Heaven?"

In a small, scared voice, he told her, "No, I don't wanna go."

Sister Osborne was surprised. "Why ever not, honey?"

"Because my dad went to Heaven already, and it made my mom sad, and if I go, she'll be all alone."

Sister Osborne's voice choked up. "We're not getting up a trip right now, Davey. You can stay here and take care of your mother." She turned to the chorister. "Sister Shands, how about a couple of songs?"

Beverly took Davey home and he changed into his play clothes. She hugged him extra tight because of something that the Primary President had shared with her after church.

"Hey, Buddy, why don't we go outside for a few minutes and meet our new neighbors. Let's get your shoes on." She had noticed Warren Jensen outside talking to the new couple who had moved in across the street.

"Do you think they have any kids, Mom?"

Beverly took Davey's hand and walked over in front of the next-door-neighbor's house where everyone was standing. She let go of his hand to shake hands with the new neighbors, the Paddocks. The little Jensen boy across the street came out of his house. He had a Slinky that he held up for Davey to see. "Look Davey."

Davey followed his first impulse, which was to get a better look, and he immediately ran into the street, right in the path of an oncoming car. Beverly turned and everything went into slow motion. She tried to scream at him, but no sound came out. Frozen, she saw her son in the street in front of a car and was helpless to do anything but brace for the impact. For several excruciating seconds, she stood there in indescribable terror, listening to the screeching of the brakes. The next thing she knew, the car had stopped and Davey was on the sidewalk on the other side of the street. There had been no impact, no accident. Davey was okay! The blue car had pulled over and the driver had jumped out.

"I didn't hit him? He was right there! He just ran out in front of me! How did I miss him?" Beverly ran across the street.

"Davey, are you okay?" She picked him up and held him tighter than she ever had and carried him back across the street. The driver, shaken, but secure that Davey was not hurt, headed on his way. After making sure that Davey was truly okay, Beverly turned him over her knee there on the grass and gave him a spanking. He turned his tear-stained face to his mother.

"Why would you spank a kid for not getting run over by a car?"

"I'm spanking you for running out into the street without looking. Do you understand that? You did something very naughty and you could have been hurt very badly or even killed." She sat him up. "I only spank you if you do something that's naughty enough to deserve it, or unless you do something that's dangerous and I need you to remember. Now do you think you have been spanked enough to remember?"

"Yeah, I'll remember, but don't worry, Mom. If any more cars are coming at me, I'll just go into 'warp speed' again." Beverly marched him into the house. She opened the refrigerator and took out six eggs and put them in a bowl. Outside they went. When the coast was clear, Beverly set down all six eggs several feet apart in the road in front of their house. She sat Davey down on the curb and sat down beside him. Soon a car came along and ran over one of the eggs. Davey watched with interest. Another car came along and ran over two more. When there were six flattened eggs in the road, Beverly turned to her little boy.

"Did you see what happened to those eggs?" she asked sternly.

"Yes."

"Did you know that cars can do that to people, too? Now let me explain something to you, Davey. I don't know exactly how you escaped being hit by that car today. It must have been your guardian angel. You're not a superhero. You can't go into warp speed. You never go into the street without me and never without looking. Do you understand?"

"Yes, but Mom . . .?"

"What?"

". . . now what are we going to eat for breakfast tomorrow?"

CHAPTER TWENTY-ONE
IT STEEB!

Beverly had stopped in at Jean's house one Saturday morning. She had been in the area and so she stopped by. Okay, so she didn't just *happen* by. She had gone there on purpose to pick Jean's brains about Dr. Evans, who was in Jean's stake. Beverly had taken a chance that Jean would probably be there, because she was kind of a homebody. Jean ran up from the family room when the doorbell rang.

"I'm sorry I didn't call. I just came by to visit."

"Come in. You can keep me company while I fold clothes." She followed Jean downstairs. Beverly sat down near a pile of towels. Davey ran off to find her kids in the backyard. Jean had a little basket where she was collecting all of the mateless socks. She pulled a shirt and pair of shorts from the pile of clothes. "I can't believe Tyler did this again. He unloaded his gym clothes from the 'Bog of Eternal Stench' into my clean basket of laundry. I tell you Beverly, once the hormones kick in, the brain cells are gone." Jean removed the wadded-up bundle of clothes, shook her head and continued folding. "So what's new with you?"

"I had another date for the record books last night."

"Anybody I know?" Jean smiled. Beverly looked at her closely.

"She hasn't heard about my evening with Dr. Evans, has she? No, he wouldn't have said anything. I sure haven't newsed that one around. I'm imagining things. She knows I'm interested in him, though. Who do I think I'm kidding?" Beverly picked up a towel and folded it. "I was introduced to this guy by one of my old friends. She told me he was newly divorced and . . ."

"Huh?"

"I said, he was newly divorced."

"Oh, I thought you said *nearly,*" Jean laughed. "Sorry, go ahead."

"Anyway, we went for pizza and then to a movie, and for the first time in recent history I was really having fun on a blind date. He was easy to talk to, had a good sense of humor, nice-looking. So when he took me home, I asked him if he would like to come in for a bowl of ice cream, so he did, but then he got really weird on me. He gave me a critique of our date. I was sitting there eating my ice cream, and he says, 'Beverly, I had a really good time tonight. I just wanted to let you know that just because I'm not going to ask you out again, it doesn't mean I didn't have a good time. You're a really nice girl, and you're fun to be with, but you're a little younger than I am, and I know that you probably want to have more children, right?' So, I said, 'Do we need to decide on our first date if we're going to have any children together?' He laughed, told me how much fun I was and said, 'I've been divorced now for almost three months, and I've been out with 22 different women. You're number 23. Like I said, I wouldn't mind seeing you again, but I've already got four children, and I don't want any more, so there's no use getting involved with someone who wants more children.' I asked him if maybe he could work me in as a comic relief date every ten women or so. The guy was on some kind of dating marathon. I imagine he's chalked up several more dates since he took me out. Is he trying to prove to the world how desirable he is?"

"Maybe he's trying to prove it to himself. More likely to his ex-wife. She might have remarried right after the divorce. It sounds like he's looking for a suitable wife, has his criteria all mapped out, and is not going to be deterred from the search just because he finds someone he likes. He has to show her that he can do it, too."

"People wouldn't get divorced for such stupid reasons if they didn't get married for stupid reasons."

"With all due respect, Beverly, your husband died, he didn't divorce you. At least you know he loves you. You have never experienced the rejection that comes when the person who probably knows you better than anyone else in the whole world decides he doesn't want to be with you anymore. Try not to judge the guy. Then it goes beyond plain and simple rejection, which is bad enough, because when you try to work out the divorce settlement, before long you're both saying the most unkind, mean and hateful things about each other in court and every other place, church included. Church especially, because that's where you feel the most defensive. The judge sees divorcing couples all day long. He doesn't know you from Adam. It's no big deal to him, but at church you feel you have to justify to yourself and others how you let your eternal marriage go down the toilet. Talk about an exercise in how to achieve low self-esteem. You feel so devastated and like such a failure, and the only way to save face is to try to show that *he* was the bad guy, and he's doing the same thing--trying to make you the bad guy. It gets ugly real fast. 'He had an affair. He went out with another woman. I was wronged.' Then he will tell someone that if a man is getting fed steak at home, he doesn't go out to a restaurant for dinner. What do people get from that? That we had no sex life? That I'm not as attractive as I used to be? That life had become humdrum? There are shades of meaning, and you don't know what interpretation people are putting on things. Pretty soon, you're constantly on the defensive. You see other women who have had several children and who are not looking as youthful and in-shape as they used to be, and their husbands still love them. You feel resentful. You sit on the back row in Relief Society lessons about marriage and listen to Sister Covington tell how she kneels in fervent prayer each night with her husband and how the sun has never set on an angry word between them and you want to go up there and stuff those silk flowers on the table down her throat to make her shut up. You slump down in your chair and hope the class will end soon."

Beverly nodded. "Yeah, I guess I didn't stop to think about things like that. I was just so frustrated to have found a nice man that I had fun with and disappointed to have him tell me that he wasn't going to call again. We all have the baggage, don't we? I'm going to write a book someday--a psychology book called, 'Why Don't the Airlines Ever Lose My Emotional Baggage?'"

"I'll buy several copies. I've tried to get rid of mine. There's always that one bag that just keeps going around and around the carousel--the one that keeps coming back."

Jean pulled over the basket of loose socks. She pulled one or two out. "I keep these in here in hopes that I'll find mates for them. Every once in a while, a match does turn up, but it seems more often that each time I do laundry I add a few more singles." A thought occurred to her. She dumped out the basket of mis-matched socks. "This is us--the singles." She pulled out a used-to-be-white sock with a hole in the heel. "This is your blind date for next Friday night. Or how about this one?" She pulled out a long skinny stretched-out tube sock. Greg put a tennis ball in the toe of this sock and swung it around for a few weeks just for fun. Now it goes up to his waist. "It's your chocolate-chip cookie friend."

"Amazing resemblance."

"Let's face it, Beverly. Nothing against the singles' program, but you can see why some of these socks don't have mates." Jean pulled on the edge of the bundle of gym clothes until it opened up, and she pulled out a smelly gym sock. She held it up and plugged her nose. "I know I danced with this one at the last singles' dance I attended." She started putting the socks back in the basket. "So I ask myself--*'Why do I keep them? Why not just throw out the whole lot of them?'* I'll throw away the ones that are in really bad shape, but I can't help thinking that maybe in the next wash . . ."

"That must be what keeps us going to those singles' functions. We think that maybe next time we'll meet someone nice."

"Not me. I'm giving it up. I have my children. I have good friends. I don't need to spend my precious time out looking for Mr. Right, part II."

"Speaking of men, what happened to Dr. Evans' wife? You knew her, right?"

"It hasn't been too long. She was ill for a long time beforehand."

"Ovarian cancer," Beverly added.

"He took care of her for a long time before she died. They fought it every way they could. He's had it real rough."

"What was she like?"

"I didn't know her well. Before she got sick, she was the Stake Cultural Arts Specialist--very musical, and I hear she was sort of a gourmet cook. He has two kids, teen-agers, good kids--a girl and a boy."

"Alisa and Kendall."

"How interested *are* you, Beverly? You seem to know more about him than I do. I hear there are a lot of single ladies in the stake taking casseroles over to the good dentist and none of them are getting anywhere."

"Interested? I'm not *interested*--really. I mean, we had one sort of date, but it didn't go very well. I might be more interested if he was ready to date, but he really isn't. We found that out." Beverly's thoughts wandered off. *"He's a great kisser, though."* Back to the conversation at hand. "I've got this friend at the university. She's looking for people to study for a project--people with certain types of losses--people who had terminally-ill spouses. I thought she might want to talk with Dr. Evans."

A few days later, Jean called Beverly to ask her if she wanted to go to the BYU Singles' Conference in Provo. "This is the deal. We are going to meet at my house and go in Laura's van on Saturday. There are classes during the day and a dance that night."

"I thought you were giving this up."

"I am, right after this, but people from all over the country come to this conference. There are classes on Thursday and Friday and a dance on Friday and Saturday nights, and a fireside on Sunday. Do you want to go up, just me and you, on Friday?"

"Let's stick to Saturday. I've got classes on Friday."

On the way up in the van, Jean informed everyone. "Okay, ladies, we are here for spiritual enrichment. We are not desperate women in search of male companionship. Anyone striking up any kind of lasting relationship with a man this weekend, will be subject to a $5 fine, payable to each of us."

"I can't afford that," said Marilyn.

"You'd shell out $25.00 to find a nice man," said Jean. "Think of it as reverse psychology. If you try hard enough not to meet someone, maybe you will."

"They say that men come to this conference from all over the country," said Carrie. Carrie was Marilyn's younger sister, and she had just recently been divorced.

Beverly picked up on Carrie's statement. "I thought we just said we weren't going to this function to meet men. We have to accept ourselves as single people-- not necessarily as 'singles,' but just as worthwhile women who have a lot to offer with or without a husband. Then we don't come across as needy. I hate being needy."

"But what if I *am* needy?" Carrie wanted some answers.

"Then don't act needy, or you might fall into a relationship for the wrong reasons, and if someone finds you attractive when you're needy, he might be even needier than you, and the last thing you need is someone needy."

"But if I pretend not to be needy, what if I just meet another person pretending not to be needy, and we really are both needy?"

"Needy is a state of mind, not a state of affairs. Think of it like pretending not to be afraid of a dog so that he won't bite you. If you pretend long enough, one day you'll find that you really are not afraid anymore. And even if you're afraid, what purpose is served by letting the dog know that?"

"That's easy for you to say. Your husband left you with insurance. You don't have to struggle like I do. You only have one child."

Beverly met Carrie head on. "But you can't just go out there looking for financial security. Don't you think I've ever felt needy? Women who are financially secure can still feel needy. Sometimes they use their financial security as bait because they are so lonely. But everybody--whether they are male or female-- deserves to be loved for who they are and not for what they have. You have to make the best of your situation, whatever it is--and not be always looking for someone to rescue you from it. Those kind of relationships are on shaky ground. How long have you been divorced anyway?"

"Two months."

"Then you shouldn't try to meet anyone yet, like Jean said. It's too soon. You're lonely, and you would rather replace your missing husband than come to terms with the fact that he's gone and face the reasons why. Sooner or later, you have to deal with all your unfinished business."

Jean broke in. "We're going to have to start paying Beverly soon for her advice. She's going to finish up her psychology degree before you know it. Get it now while it's free, Carrie."

Carrie smiled at Beverly. "Oh, you're a psychologist. I just thought you were a know-it-all."

"A little of both. I've learned from my own experience and from the classes I take. Besides, I'm a long way from actually being a psychologist. I'm sorry if I came on a little strong, but I've been in this singles' environment for quite a while now and I observe people. I've been doing it all my life. I've driven my parents, brothers and several roommates around the bend. I've started back to college to finish my degree. I have a plan for the future, so maybe I'm not quite so needy as I was. I had a blind date recently and I really liked him, and when he told me he wasn't going to take me out again, I tried to talk him into it, as much as my pride would allow. We all go back and forth between trying to be okay and taking care of ourselves, trying to believe that it's okay to be alone and then turning around and trying to figure out if the guy behind us in line at the dry cleaners is single. There's room in my plan for a man, but the plan does not revolve around finding a husband. Often people look for something or someone that will make the pain go away, without even realizing that's what they're doing."

By the time they got to Provo, Beverly had taken Carrie under her wing. They sat together in a couple of the classes, and she had guaranteed Carrie that they would be wallflowers together at the dance. As they entered the dance, Beverly said, "You can always tell the singles because they are the ones in church the next day who were not quite able to erase the stamp of the yellow smiley face from their hands." As they mingled around the refreshment table, Beverly spotted her old roommate, Wendy, at the punch bowl. She still wore her red hair in the same little-girl hairdo, looking just the same as Beverly remembered her from their college days.

"Beverly, I thought you got married!"

"I did. There was an accident. He died." Beverly had learned to get the explanation over with as quickly as possible.

"Oh, I'm sorry. I didn't know." Wendy began to apologize profusely, as if she was personally responsible for Beverly's loss of a husband. She was still the same old Wendy.

To stop her from apologizing five times for having asked, Beverly broke in. "I have a little boy. He just turned four." She pulled out a picture. "His name is Davey."

"Oh, isn't he cute?"

"He's a lot of fun. He gets me through. What have you been doing since college?"

"I teach Kindergarten in Honeyville. I still live at home, you know, with Mom and Dad. I haven't really done much." Wendy was still just as lacking in confidence as she had been in college. "I came here with the singles from the Honeyville Stake."

"Whatever happened to that guy you were writing to on his mission--Dale?"

"Oh, he got married to some girl he met in the mission field."

"Why don't you come sit by us? We're starting a wallflower section." Wendy followed them over to the row of chairs where the other ladies were sitting. Soon a tall, skinny, stretched-out-gym-sock of a fellow made a beeline for Beverly. Wendy poked her.

"Here comes a hunk in your direction!"

Beverly looked up. It was no *hunk*. It was *Cordell*. In all the years Beverly had been in the singles' program, Cordell's 'Beverly radar' had never failed. He was always able to detect her entrance and be the first there asking her to dance, in hopes of someday kindling a relationship, and securing for himself a lifelong supply of her homemade chocolate chip cookies.

"Hi Beverly. Wanna dance?"

Beverly reached down and began rubbing one of her feet. "I'm not feeling up to it right now, Cordell." She smiled, and turned to Wendy. "Would you mind filling in for me? Cordell, this is Wendy. She's one of my old roommates from college. Wendy, this is Cordell. We grew up in the same ward." She smiled to herself as Wendy and Cordell went out onto the dance floor.

Jean observed, "That was pretty slick."

"She thought he was a 'hunk.' What else could I do? I couldn't handle Cordell right now. I'm not up to a 'close encounter of the nerd kind' tonight. Are they talking?" Beverly observed Wendy and Cordell. It was a fast dance, so they couldn't really get acquainted, except for stealing some shy eye contact with each other. Then the band started playing a slow song.

Jean observed, "Don't you love this part? First, the girl goes to put her arms around his neck for the 'bear hug' and . . ."

"Wendy would never be that bold," said Beverly.

"Oh yeah, look."

Beverly was amazed. "Wendy?" She had put her arms around Cordell's neck. "Yeah, but Cordell is standing there with his arms out for standard dance position like he learned in 7th grade gym class."

"Oh yeah, look."

Cordell had taken Wendy's cue, and had readjusted his position and put his arms around her. Wendy and Cordell were doing the 'bear hug!' Wendy had a dreamy look in her eyes, and Beverly observed that they were conversing--something *she* had never been able to do with Cordell.

"Looks like I started something."

"Yeah, they would flunk the old Book of Mormon test for sure."

"What?"

"Didn't your Young Women's leaders ever tell you that when you danced a slow dance they should be able to get a Book of Mormon in between you? Those two don't even have room for the Pearl of Great Price. So how does it feel to have possibly started a romance?"

"Well, knowing them both the way I do, I think I did pretty well. Maybe that's all I can hope for from this conference, that Cordell will give up on trying to ask *me* out. All I need to do now is slip Wendy the recipe for the cookies. She teaches Kindergarten, so she should be able to handle Cordell."

On and off the rest of the ladies danced and sat out the dances. Beverly had been wandering the dance floor for a while, and decided it was time to roost again. She sat down next to Shelly.

"Where is everyone else?"

"Jean's getting refreshments. Laura has been dancing all evening, as usual, and Carrie is dancing with a real nice-looking fellow."

"Good. I hope she has a good time."

When the song was done, Carrie's dance partner led her back to the area where she had been sitting. Beverly was paying attention to her conversation with

Shelly, when she heard a distinctive deep voice say, "Thank you very much, Carrie. Maybe we'll see you . . ." Beverly looked up, surprised, and cut him off.

"*Steve!*"

He was equally surprised. *"Beverly?!"*

"What are you doing here? You're married."

"Not any more, I'm not. And you?"

"Obviously, I'm at a singles' conference, aren't I?"

Carrie scowled as Beverly got up to dance with Steve, and she continued to sulk as Beverly danced the rest of the evening with Steve.

They danced for quite a while without updating each other on their situations, not wanting to spoil the mood by discussing unpleasant things. Finally, Beverly asked, "What happened to your marriage, Steve?"

"DeAnna left me--left the kids, too. I've got three little girls I'm taking care of by myself. She's off finding herself."

"I'm sorry."

Steve's usually pleasant voice took on a bitter edge. "Don't be. We're better off without her. Maybe I'm getting a chance to correct the mistake I made when I chose her instead of you, a chance to make things the way they always should have been."

Beverly greeted this remark with mixed feelings. Steve was assuming they could just pick up where they had left off and ride off into the sunset together. A part of her was elated to be with Steve, and to know that he wanted to be with her. Compared to many of the other men in the singles' program, Steve was a catch. He was college-educated, had a good job with a future, was good-looking and pleasant, and a good strong member of the church. Against the backdrop of so-so men, Steve looked awfully good. Steve continued. "I don't know what went wrong with your marriage, but running into you here like this makes me believe in second chances. It looks like maybe you married the wrong person, too."

"I didn't make a mistake, Steve. I married a great guy, and we were very happy together. I'm not divorced. I'm a widow."

Steve pulled away from her. "I just assumed . . ."

"Everybody does. Widows are supposed to be 70 years old."

"How did it happen?"

"Do you remember a couple of years ago that accident where a paramedic was hit as he worked on an accident victim. It was in the winter. That was my husband."

"Yes, I remember that. It was on the news. Did you--do you have any children?"

"I have a little boy. He's four years old."

"Beverly, this seems so strange, after all these years, and as close as we were, sitting here talking about our children. I'm sorry about your husband, but I'm not sorry I found you again."

"No, I'm not sorry either, Steve. Tell me, several times I thought I'd heard your voice on television . . ."

"Oh, the commercials. Yes, KSL's been good to me, and it's opened a few doors. Being sales manager is a little more lucrative than narrating the Christmas story for the ward party. I've done some church-related stuff, too--some videos. I've done the voices for Laban and Moroni."

"It's that voice. I remember how all the girls in our Sunday School class would swoon when you read from the scriptures. Do you remember that time you filled in at my ward Christmas party when I took you home to meet my family? You even got a write-up in the ward newspaper."

"It's been such a long time, Beverly. I always had so much fun with you. It would be nice just to sit and visit for a while about old times. Can I give you a ride home?"

"Well, I'll have to let the ladies I came with know." Beverly's good judgment tried to win through. *"Is it such a good idea to let Steve take me home? But if I ride with the ladies, Carrie is sure to be mad at me. Here she thought she'd found a great guy who was about to ask her out, and I took him away. Besides that, I would be interrogated by all of them, and they will probably even make me give them each $5.00. Who am I kidding? I want to be with Steve. This is an obvious choice. Sorry, ladies!"*

On her front porch, she had another debate. *"Invite him in. No, don't. Oh, come on! You know you want to. Be sensible. Don't rush things."* She fumbled for her key. "Steve, you don't know how much I want to invite you in, but it feels like we might be rushing things, but I do have a babysitter to take home. Having you come in is certainly easier than me having to get Davey up and take him along, like I usually have to."

"Well, then I should at least come in while you take the babysitter home."

"Yeah, I guess so, but then I think you should go."

"Same old Bev. Remember how I used to tell you not to think so much. I'm not thinking. I'm feeling, and I like how I feel. Take the babysitter home and we'll talk."

When she got back from taking the babysitter home, she found Steve looking at the family picture on the wall. "You know I could swear I've seen him before."

"You have."

"When?"

"He was there at the coffee shop at the hotel the day you told me you were going to marry DeAnna. Do you remember a guy at the table behind us who was smoking and blowing all the smoke in your direction?" Beverly laughed at the memory of it. "That was Dave. We were dating at the time, and I was trying to help him quit smoking, and he knew about you. You probably don't remember how hard I tried to get you to go to a different restaurant than there at the hotel where I knew he would be coming in on his break. When he came in and saw us together, he thought we were getting back together and that you had come to tell me that you had finally broken up with DeAnna, so he lit up and . . . "

"I tried, Beverly. I really did try to talk to her, but everyone seemed so intent on pushing us together. There was really no way out."

"I wonder, Steve, if maybe she felt the same way, and that's why she wanted out now."

"At this point, I don't really care how she felt or why she did anything." He looked at the picture again. "Did he quit smoking? Did you get married in the temple then?"

"Yes, we did."

"I was afraid of that."

"You'd rather date somebody that had run off to Vegas?"

"So, you're sealed to him."

"Yes, I am. We were married in the Salt Lake Temple. It may be bad news to *you*, but knowing that we'll be together. . ."

"Well, I guess there's nothing I can do about that."

"Steve, my goodness, we only ran into each other a few hours ago. We have both been married. We can't be talking like this already."

"Yes, but it's not as if we just met. Face it, Beverly. Fate has intervened. We are meant to be together."

"How long have you been divorced?"

"What difference does that make?"

"You have to have time to adjust, to come to terms with . . ."

Steve moved closer to Beverly. He touched her hair, then brushed his hand against her cheek. He looked into her eyes. She tried very hard to remember what she was trying to say. ". . . your loss." Then he was kissing her, and she was kissing him, and all her psychology and common sense went and hid in a faraway corner of her mind.

CHAPTER TWENTY-TWO
JUST LIKE OLD TIMES

The next day Steve sent her a dozen roses.

"I think he likes ya, Mom," Davey exclaimed when the flowers came. Beverly sat down and opened the card.

"Boy, life sure does take some interesting twists."

"You mean like the ice cream cones at McDonalds?"

Beverly laughed. "Well, not exactly, but . . ." She opened the card. It said, "To the woman I love." It was not in his handwriting. That meant he had ordered them over the phone, not that there was anything wrong with that, but she wondered if it was embarrassing to tell some sales clerk a mushy message to put on the card rather than do it in person and preserve your privacy. *"Why do I notice stupid things like that?"* she asked herself. She put the vase of flowers in the middle of her dining room table and straightened up the house a little.

Later she called Steve to thank him for the flowers.

"Are we still on for Friday night?"

"I've got my babysitter all lined up. Where are we going?"

"We're having dinner at Park City."

"That sounds fun."

The doorbell rang. Beverly was ready to go. She had never learned how to play girl games, like keeping her date waiting. "Steve, this is my cousin, Jenny. She's babysitting tonight. And this is Davey."

Davey looked him over. "Are you the one that gave my mom those flowers?"

"Yes, that was me."

"You wanna marry her, don't ya?"

"Do you have a problem with that, Davey?" Steve asked.

"Why don't the two of you talk it over and let me know what you come up with," Beverly said sarcastically. "Davey, you know the rules."

"I know, Mom. Don't ask 'barrassing questions to your dates."

"Does your mom have a lot of dates, Davey?"

"Yup. 'Specially 'cause Brother Higginbotham keeps sending these blind guys over here to marry my mom before she gets so she can't stand kids anymore."

Steve laughed. "I don't think your mom needs a blind guy. She's much too pretty for a blind guy. Anyway, from now on, she will only be going on dates with me."

Out in the car, Beverly resumed the conversation. "Pretty sure of yourself, aren't you, Steve?"

"Any reason I shouldn't be? Never mind. Don't answer that. I think Davey can give me any information I need. What a great kid!"

She switched gears. "You like Davey. I'm glad, but I would really prefer if you don't try to get too close to him, at least right now. Adults understand the comings and goings of romantic relationships. Kids don't."

"Anything else you'd like to spell out for me?"

"I'm sorry. I didn't mean to sound so . . . "

"Uptight?"

She gave him a dirty look. "What I meant to say is that Davey has his grand-pas and his uncles that are around to stay, and if he gets attached to someone I date and the relationship fizzles, he's hurt, and I don't want that to happen."

"You aren't really very sure of me, are you?"

"Well, let's just say that we do have a history in that area."

"Beverly, I'm really sorry. I know that I hurt you very badly when I married DeAnna and . . ."

"Steve, I don't want you to think I'm still hanging on to that after all these years. Maybe that's a little part of it, but it's more than that. Maybe it's that I don't know what I can count on. I thought I could count on Dave living past the age of 30, too. It's nothing personal. It's my baggage. It feels like everything here is temporal and temporary and anything and anybody can disappear out of my life. But I'm sure you must have things like that, you know, as a result of your divorce."

"Not really." He shook his head. "She's gone. I'm free."

"The Reader's Digest condensed version?"

"There's nothing to condense." He continued. "I'm not going anywhere, Beverly. Are you dating someone else?"

"Not really, but just for the record, I consider myself free to date other men, and you're free to date other women. In fact, you should. You're getting off way too easy, running into me like this, while the ink is still drying on your divorce papers."

"I thought it was 'before the body is cold.'"

"No, that would be for me. I've got that covered. I seduced an 18-year-old in my ward right after Dave's funeral. See, I can tell we need to spend some more time getting reacquainted."

"I've found what I want. I want to get to know your little boy, Beverly, and I want you to get to know my girls, because I have a feeling we are all going to be a family someday."

"So tell me about your daughters, Steve."

"Monica is 7, Erica is 5, Annalisa is 3. They're all blond."

"How about some adjectives? Don't you remember that set of dating questions I made up once when we were in college, to help people really get acquainted?"

"Oh, yeah. I do faintly remember you asking me a bunch of questions about diapers and The Ten Commandments and Elvis Presley."

"No, it wasn't The Ten Commandments. It was the Sermon on the Mount."

"How many guys did you use them on?"

"I have a good memory about stuff like that. I remember that you didn't know anything about diapers. You've had three kids. Know anything now?"

"They stink." He looked at her. "Okay, I can see the wheels turning. You're working on another set of questions, aren't you?"

"I'll start. I'm going to think of four adjectives that describe Davey. He's precocious, imaginative, funny and loving. Now tell me about your girls."

"Well Monica is smart, um, a little bit bossy, neat and she asks a lot of questions. Erica is sensitive. She gets her feelings hurt easily. Beverly, this is easier for moms. They're with their kids more."

"Well, you're with them now."

"Yeah, okay. She's neat."

"You already said that about Monica."

"They are all neat, okay. DeAnna was like that, made them learn to pick up and be careful about things. Erica loves animals. She is shy. Monica is more outgoing."

"A firstborn trait."

"Annie is just cute. She's very affectionate."

"Now see, I have a much clearer picture. I look forward to meeting them."

"Well, I don't know if I can have you around being a bad influence on them."

"That's not what I said about Davey, Steve. Like it or not, you've got a lot of things to work out with DeAnna, and I think I should be in the background."

Steve parked the car. He reached over and kissed Beverly. "Well, I'd rather be alone with you, anyway."

Beverly and Steve had been dating for a couple of months before she decided it was time to take him to church. Heads turned as Beverly, widowed for over two years now, walked into church with Steve beside her. Brother Higginbotham caught them on the way out. "So, Beverly, I see you took my advice and found yourself a fellow."

"Calm down, Brother H. We're just dating, not procreating."

"What was that all about?" Steve said.

"Oh, Brother Higginbotham feels personally responsible . . ."

"Is he the one who keeps lining you up blind dates?"

"Oh, yes. Davey mentioned him, didn't he? Yes, he feels responsible to match me up with someone before my certified child-bearing years have passed into oblivion. Good grief! I'm not even thirty yet. We've got to get out of here. We'll be mobbed."

"Don't you want to introduce me to your friends?"

"Well, yes, but not en masse. We'll catch a couple of people out in the parking lot. Here comes Sister Cooper. We need to leave her guessing. I can't give her the satisfaction of having the scoop on this one, besides it will be more interesting to see what she makes up. You've met the Jensens and my next-door neighbors, Briant and Cindy." She steered him toward the car. Davey stooped down to pick up an interesting stick. "Grab him, Steve, before he gets his church clothes dirty. Thanks."

Toni Cirroni was loading her family into their new van. She turned and her face lit up in recognition. "Steve! What are *you* doing here? You're with Beverly? Where did you two meet?" she gushed. Beverly suddenly had the feeling it was Toni who had known Steve for years and that *she* was the casual acquaintance. After Steve explained how he and Beverly had become reacquainted, Toni remarked, "It's a small world."

Beverly finally got a word in. "Where do you and Toni know each other from?"

"Oh, they do the commercials for their restaurant at the same agency where I do the voice-overs." One of Toni's children came out of the van.

"I'm tired. I want to go home."

"Corina, honey," Toni said, giving the keys to her oldest daughter, "turn on the van and put in a video for him, would you? Thanks." She turned back to Beverly and Steve. "This new van is *such* a lifesaver! I told Alex we didn't need the loaded model with the VCR and television, but I have to admit he was right. We can play

educational videos on the road for the children, so we are like a traveling field trip--
Cami and Marcus are both being tested for the gifted program this year--and we
have the entire set of animated Book of Mormon tapes. Even little Alex knows the
Nephi song and . . ."

Steve smiled. "Did you recognize Laban's voice?"

"You're Laban! Well, Steve, another feather in your cap." Toni grabbed his
arm and giggled. "Of course, you haven't been the voice of the Almighty yet."

Beverly walked over to the van and looked inside at Toni's perfect children in
their perfect van. They weren't watching Nephi and Lehi. They were watching the
Roadrunner and Coyote. It made Beverly feel a little bit better. When she got back
to Toni and Steve, they had already arranged for a double date. "See you next
Saturday, then," Toni said. She waved to them as she pulled out of the parking lot.

"I hope you don't mind, Beverly. Toni and I thought it would be fun for the
four of us to go on a double date."

"Oh, sure. Toni and Alex. That'll be fun."

"You don't sound so sure."

"I just don't know them very well, that's all. What are we going to do?"

"We're going to have dinner with them at their country club."

"Oooooh."

"I bet David never took you to the Fort Douglas Hidden Valley Country Club."

"I can't believe he died without doing that. I guess he had to go to one of the
lesser kingdoms as a result." She looked at Steve. "Are we setting up some kind of
a competition here? Dave only lived to be 30, so you're bound to outpace him in
several areas."

"I'm sorry. I was just excited about taking you to a nice place, but what right
do I have to take credit? I don't have a membership."

"And I don't care. I like to go to nice restaurants, and all that, but hey, I can
have a good time if we go for a picnic up the canyon."

Steve changed the subject. "Beverly, why did you hurry me out of church so
fast? Didn't you want to introduce me to your friends?"

"I don't know. I don't like having to meet large groups of people all at the
same time. I guess I just assumed you felt that way too."

"I don't mind the attention."

"No, you like attention, I think."

"Do you need to turn this into some kind of a character flaw, Beverly?"

"I didn't mean it that way. I guess I was just thinking about it as another one
of the ways that we think very differently. I mean, how compatible are we really,
Steve? It didn't work out the first time. What makes us think it will work out
now?" They pulled into Beverly's driveway. She jumped out and opened the door
to get Davey out.

"Beverly, you're supposed to wait for me to come around and get the door for
you."

"Oh, Steve, I'm really out of the habit of that. I'm just used to getting Davey
out and . . ." He gave her a stern look. She sighed and got back in the car and let
Steve come open the door for her.

"Maybe we can do like Dave and I did. If I was in a dress, he would open the
door for me. That way I knew when to wait."

"Oh, if he did it that way, I'm supposed to do it that way, too, is that it? I bet Toni Cirroni lets Alex Senior open the car door for her."

"I bet Toni Cirroni--by the way, she likes to be called Toni Leigh so that her name doesn't rhyme--does a lot of things I don't do. And there are a lot of things she doesn't do. She told me once that she doesn't even know how to pump gas."

"Somehow I can believe that."

"Well, I'm no Toni Cirroni, if that's what you're looking for."

They went in the house. Beverly made some soup and sandwiches and then put Davey down for a nap. She and Steve sat on the sofa. She snuggled up close to him and he put his arm around her.

Steve picked back up on the conversation. "No, Beverly, Toni is not what I'm looking for. I love you. I think we should get married. I wasn't planning on doing this today, and I promise to do it up right later with a ring and all, but I thought you would like to help pick it out. Will you marry me, Beverly?"

"I love you, too, Steve. But I've been wondering--is that enough? Marriage-- that's such a life-changing decision. Don't you look at it a little bit more cautiously having already been married and knowing what it takes and what can go wrong? Is this feeling of love really enough to get us through?"

"It's supposed to be, isn't it? It's supposed to be the most powerful force in the world."

"Is it? Then why do so many people who start out loving each other end up hating each other? There needs to be a back-up generator that kicks in when the power goes out that keeps people together through their problems. Is love what gets people through their problems? Maybe commitment is a better word. I believe people have an obligation to explore some of the issues of life that might come along and how they might handle them and explore their compatibility." Beverly moved away from him so she could talk to him face-to-face. "I know you can't map out a marriage like making a business plan, preparing for every contingency, so that some third party can tell you if it has a chance for success. You can't know what lies ahead. Marriage is always an act of faith. You put your life in the hands of another person and you hope that they will act from then on not only on what's best for them, but what's best for you. Then you add in the kids, or in our case, the kids are already here, most of them, anyway, and that situation has got to be full of extra challenges. In a step-family, your relationship with your children has a longer history than your relationship with your new spouse. Isn't it kind of oversimplify- ing things to just say, 'We love each other, therefore we're getting married.' What does it mean, exactly, when you say you love me?"

"I love you, Beverly. Don't ask me to analyze it. I love you now and I always will. Isn't that all you need to know?"

"It sounds good."

She sat back and stretched her arms. "Okay, think about this. Parents love their kids, but you don't fall in love with your kids. You don't stand at the nursery window and pick one. You give birth. They clean them up and hand 'em to you. You don't know him or her. Love is a choice you make. I'm going to love this little person, no matter what. If he's handsome or ugly or sweet or mean or whatever. Love is a verb, not a noun. It's not a state of being that happens to you, like 'I'm in love' or 'I'm in a coma' or 'I'm in Idaho.' No. You meet someone you like. You choose to love them. When people say that they stopped loving someone, .

it means they chose to give up, to stop caring, maybe based on that person's actions, but they make the decision. It begins and ends with us. It's *our* choice. People can become difficult, even impossible to love, but you're the one who has to decide to stop loving and caring. Because you *pick* someone to marry, you have both an advantage and a disadvantage, because you have the choice of some things--funny or serious, tall or short, but some other things will always come as a surprise later when you start to live together. You also have a disadvantage, because you chose that person, it implies that you have the right to un-choose them by getting divorced, if there turn out to be problems.

What do parents do when their relationship with a child doesn't work? There may come a time when they say, 'If you can't live by the rules of this house, go find another place to live.' But do they stop loving them? Maybe some people do, but I believe that most people love their children *no matter what.* Let's say that marriage is like adopting a child. It's a choice, but if there are problems, you don't just un-adopt them. You love them. You keep trying. If there's a question of your ability to commit entirely to an adopted child, then you shouldn't adopt one. Commitment to your spouse should be the same. If people can't commit fully to each other, then they should not get married. Maybe that's what I'm afraid of is our ability to commit."

"Are you saying I'm damaged goods because of my divorce?"

"You won't talk to me about it, so I have no idea how hard you tried to save your marriage, whether you tried at all. All I see is the anger. But I'm not just talking about you. Dave is dead and part of my past, but I'm sealed to him, so he's also part of my future. I'm left to fill up the present, but my commitment to you or any other man would only be for this life. Right there, that's less of a commitment to whomever I marry than what I had with Dave. Have you thought about that, Steve, really thought about it? I won't change it or cancel it in 20 or 30 years. Believe me, I've heard about people's opinions on the subject. 'Someday you'll marry again and then what will you do when you've spent 40 years and had several more children with your second husband and you had so few years with Dave and you decide that you want to be sealed to your second husband?' I won't marry anyone if they think that I'm someday going to change that. You don't marry someone for eternity but only if they don't die prematurely. The whole purpose of the ceremony is to transcend the bonds of death. Dave didn't choose to die. The bishop says--I asked him once because people were telling me things that were totally off the wall, so I wanted to clarify--that even if I wanted to, I couldn't cancel my sealing to Dave unless I could show that he was unworthy, because he has rights that are protected and should be protected. Love is not measured by how many years people are together, although I'm sure that it takes a great deal of love and commitment to stay together 40 and 50 years, but hey, at the rate I'm going, I'll probably die of old age before I get to have a golden wedding anniversary with anybody. Maybe if I hurry I can make silver, but anyway, my commitment to Dave is still there. Sometimes I wonder whether my commitment to another man would be as strong. There would not be the eternal perspective when there were problems. That's got to be one of the things that keeps people in the church together and working on their marriages. I would only be financially dependent on you to a point, too, hey, and let's face it--that keeps a lot of women in marriages that they might otherwise leave. Somehow I feel like I have to make up for the liabilities by making extra sure that I'll be as committed as I want to be, as I should be--as much as it's possible to be. Steve, we've only been together again for a couple of months. Do we just go ahead and get married and see what happens? It seems a little like Russian Roulette, doesn't it? And if the time comes that there are really and truly unresolvable differences, you live apart, you divorce--but is it right to hate? If you have unconditional love, wouldn't you still love them, even if you couldn't live with them? Wouldn't you still want them to have a good life and be happy?"

"Sure, Beverly, but if they had the capacity to do that, they would probably have had the capacity to work out their problems and stay together. It's not as easy as you make it sound."

"Well, yeah. I don't really know, since I haven't been divorced. But I don't ever want to be. There are major kinds of things that are hard on marriages, like money problems, in-laws, differences on raising kids, etc. We need to talk about a lot of that stuff. People need to match up values, I think. Often people let their attraction for each other overshadow their common sense, even if they do detect major areas of difference. How about dating activities that help you *really* get acquainted? Instead of dinner and a movie, say, we get together and balance our checkbooks and then go grocery shopping."

"Are you worried that because DeAnna and I got divorced, you and I will, too?"

"Let's just say that the odds aren't in our favor. You have a lot of anger towards her. You need to deal with all that before you get too involved with me. I have this group of divorced ladies that I socialize with sometimes, and it seems to me that in divorces people use intimate information against each other. Like the one lady--she's very beautiful--and her ex-husband is a doctor. She's always bragging about how much she took him for and how she's making him pay. Then there's another one who, at first, I thought was very strange, because she talks about her ex-husband like he's her friend and they even go out sometimes. They go together to their kids' school functions. How many people are really able to do that? Not very many. The anger and animosity are what I see trailing along behind you. I bring my own baggage, too. I know that, but I can't just pretend I don't have concerns about this. I see people messing up their kids--children that they say they love--and yet they can't or don't put aside their own desires to do what's best for their kids. I'm not sure you're doing what's best for your kids. My friend Jean has tried to clue me in to the real world of divorce. See, but you never really talk about your divorce that much, so I don't know what's going on. I worry about making a decision to marry based on loneliness or hormones and having it not work and then having to experience the death of a spouse and the death of a marriage. Do you know what the statistics are for second marriages? They are pretty lousy. First marriages have a high enough divorce rate. It's even higher for second marriages. Third marriages--I wonder if anyone has ever studied those? It would seem to me that by then you would either have learned from your mistakes and get it right or you would think of marriage as a disposable contract and be ready for number four and number five, if it worked out that way. A part of me--a big part of me--would love to just ride off into the sunset with you, Steve, but you've had one kind of loss, and I've had another. We've both got a lot of unfinished business."

"Beverly, when I asked you to marry me, I didn't make one thing clear. It was a 'yes' or 'no' question, not an essay question."

She grabbed a pillow off the sofa and began pummeling him in the head.

"Make fun, then, Steve. I know. I need to work up a whole new set of questions for people about to get married who have been married before."

"You're really worried about all of this?"

"Not just for me. I see so many people, even in the church, making choices and ending up apart, and that's scary. I remember the emphasis being put on just getting married. We need more classes on how to be a good marriage partner or how to make a good decision on who we marry. That Family Relations Class that they teach sometimes in Sunday School? Why isn't that going at all times in every ward, rotating people in and out of it?"

"That's not what it's called anymore. They've got a new one now."

"First they change homemaking meeting and now this? I hope it's something easier to remember than Home, Family and Personal Enrichment Meeting. What are they calling it? Parenting, Marriage, Relationship Development Class?"

"If they are, I think you've got those in reverse order," Steve observed. "I know at least that much, even though I have a failed marriage. It's supposed to be a good class. I forgot what they're calling it. I'm surprised you haven't been called to teach it, you're such an expert on the subject."

"I hear the first lesson is called 'Building Relationships through the use of Sarcasm,'" she retorted. "I'm going to ask my bishop if it's being taught now."

"You're going to volunteer to teach it?"

"No, give me some credit, Steve. I don't aspire to callings. Besides, I like the one I have now. I'd like to attend it."

"Sure, heckle the teacher, teach it from the congregation. I know the type." He hesitated. "Maybe I should attend that class, too. I want to be sure to marry the right person this time."

"It's not just the choice of who you marry that affects the outcome, but the accumulation of all the little choices you make every day from then on."

Steve leaned back and rolled his eyes. Beverly continued. "In fact I think those might almost be more important. The *how* is more important that the *who*. Do people who divorce--did they make the wrong choice in *who* they chose, or was it the little choices over the course of the relationship by either or both that add up to a failed marriage? 'Do I show up at the ward ball game to cheer my husband on, or do I stay home and watch a miniseries on television?' 'Do I come home from the office for lunch with my wife since I know that I'll be working late tonight?' Somehow we forget that all the little decisions add up to the big ones. We have to take a good hard look at the priorities and habits of the person we are considering marrying. Observe the choices they make and figure out how you feel about them before you make the commitment. Listen for things that reveal attitudes. See if they seem to have learned from their mistakes or do they just repeat them. Get them to talk about themselves."

"Excuse me, Beverly, did you say in a successful relationship, I should be able to get you to talk? Then I'd say we have a successful relationship." She picked up the pillow again. He grabbed her and kissed her.

"Don't try to distract me now, Steve. I'm on a roll." She kicked her shoes off. "Let's say I meet some guy. I feel sorry for him because of some supposedly outside circumstance in his life, and so I'm sympathetic, but if I was smart, I would look and see if maybe there was a pattern in his own behavior that led to that circumstance. One of my brothers was dating this girl who was really selfish. Everyone in the family could see it except him. She would be sitting at a family dinner next to a couple of the little kids who needed help and not even see it or help them. She always referred to the guys she used to date by telling us what kind of car they drove instead of who they were. Luckily, they had a big fight and broke up--that and I don't think he had a cool enough car. People cause a lot of their own problems, especially the chronic ones. When we are dating we always want to be sympathetic to whatever people's circumstances are. They may just be suffering the consequences of their own actions. There are always consequences. We may repent, but God always leaves us the consequences. A person may smoke all his life and finally quit, but he may still die of lung cancer. Too many people want to do what they want to do and have no consequences."

"Beverly, I didn't expect this overflow of analysis." He got down on his knees in front of the couch and did his best puppy dog eyes. "I just want to marry you. Isn't that okay?"

"No, it's not okay. I can't marry you. I can't marry anybody."

"Why not? I mean why not me, not why not anybody?"

Beverly started to cry. "I don't know, Steve. Maybe it won't work. Maybe we'll be a statistic."

"Maybe it will."

"It would be too hard on the kids to adjust."

"Kids adjust better than adults."

"Maybe you won't like my cooking."

"I liked the sandwich."

"I can't marry you, Steve, because maybe you'll die."

There she had said it--admitted something that she hadn't even admitted to herself. It was easier to go on a bunch of blind dates with men that she was not remotely interested in than to have a serious relationship with someone she cared about. To love again was to be vulnerable to loss again, and it was scary. She wanted to run to him and away from him at the same time.

"I guess there's nothing I can say to set your mind at ease there, Beverly. The men in my family have good hearts. I'm in good health. Is this going on your list, too? Check his medical records. Check his credit report. Check his church attendance."

"I'm sorry, Steve. I just want to be sure I know what I'm doing. You know, loneliness, hormones, increased financial security, wanting a father for Davey--all of those things influence me. Finding you again was too good to be true. I've always wondered how you were. I mean, not always, but when I heard your voice on those commercials, I thought about you and hoped you were happy. When you decided to marry DeAnna, I hoped at first that someday you would hurt like I hurt then. Eventually, of course, I let go of that and got on with my life. When I ran into you again and found out that you *had* been hurt, I wasn't glad. A part of me has always cared about you and always will, but I don't know if I can marry you, Steve. I don't know if I can marry anybody."

"You need time. I've got time, Beverly. I hate to have to go right now, because my parents will be at my house with the girls soon. It's good that we talked about all this. There's a lot to think about. Are you going to have a new list of questions ready for me next time I come over, because I want to study up on Elvis and the Ten Commandments."

"You're making fun of me now."

"Maybe, just a little. Oh, before I go, there was one other thing I wanted to ask you about. I want to introduce you to the family--my kids, Mom, Dad, sisters and their families--the whole bunch. Everybody is getting together up in Newton on Thanksgiving. Will you come with me?"

"Thanksgiving?!"

Beverly wrapped her coat around her as they walked from the car to the house. "Where did you get that dress? You looked so good tonight. There wasn't a better-looking lady in the whole country club." They went inside.

"Thanks. You look pretty good yourself. I bought this dress for a New Year's Eve party a few years ago. I'm glad you like it." Steve helped her off with her coat, and she hung it up. "It's kind of a funny story, actually." She thought back to the event. She and Dave had decided to go to the stake New Year's Eve party, but neither of them had paid much attention to the announcements or flyers. They had just noted the date and that it was a dance and had assumed it was a dress-up affair. Beverly had splurged on a new dress for the occasion. Walking into the cultural hall dressed to the hilt, ready for a romantic evening of dancing, they had discovered that it was a western-themed party with square dancing--The "Hoe-down Countdown." There was a big banner that read "Harvest the Old, Plant the New" and people were sitting around on bales of hay drinking apple cider and eating donuts. Realizing they were overdressed, Beverly and Dave had gone home, turned on the stereo and had their own romantic evening of dancing and romancing.

"What are you smiling about?"

Beverly blushed, fearing Steve could somehow read her mind and know of the memories she was rehearsing. She and Dave weren't dancing anymore. "Oh, it's just that story--about the dress. You probably wouldn't think it was funny. I bought it for a party that turned out to be casual and I walked in decked out like the Queen of England, compared to everybody else."

"Well, I was glad to be your escort tonight, Your Highness."

"Oh, knock it off, Steve." She headed for her room. "I'll be right out. I'm going to change. I've got to get out of this dress and get more comfortable."

"No, keep it on. I like it. We can put some music on the stereo and dance."

Beverly was in her room before he finished the request. "No, I'm going to change. I might get it dirty," she shouted down the hall. "I'll be right back." Beverly hung the dress in the back of the closet and came back dressed in an old jogging suit.

Steve was upset. "Hey, what happened to the Queen of England?"

"She was dethroned. I'm now a scullery maid." She got a couple of plates out of the cupboard. "I made a Blueberry Cheesecake. You want some?"

"Sure." He sat down. "You never told me yet if you're coming on Thanksgiving."

"Steve, I don't think . . ."

"Your family can get along without you for one year."

"My family is used to getting along without me on Thanksgiving."

"Well then it's settled. We'll leave early Thursday morning."

"No, it's *not* settled, Steve."

"Beverly, you're confusing me. If your family doesn't care, what other plans could you have that could be more important? Are you booked up at the ward dinner for the widows?" Steve remarked, unaware of the memories that dredged up.

"Don't even go there, Steve," Beverly warned. "I just can't face Thanksgiving. It would be really hard for me because . . ." Beverly tried to explain to Steve about the accident and the turkey and her past couple of efforts at avoiding Thanksgiving.

Steve's agitation showed. "That's the stupidest thing I've ever heard! What do you mean you don't like Thanksgiving? Everybody likes Thanksgiving!"

"You don't understand, Steve, and don't yell at me."

"I'm not yelling!" he yelled.

"I was trying to explain to you about it and you just got mad at me! Dave died right before Thanksgiving, and the day he died I was cooking a. . ."

"So what? Does that mean you have to boycott a perfectly good holiday for the rest of your life?"

"So what? Is that all you care about my feelings? If you'd let me finish, maybe you'd understand. You've interrupted me three times!"

"Look, Beverly. He's dead!" He stood up from the table and got his jacket off the back of the chair and put it on. "He's been dead for years! It's about time you got on with your life!"

"Oh, sure, by going into denial, like you? 'What divorce? What problems? Reader's Digest version? There's nothing to condense. She's gone. I'm here. I've got the kids. She doesn't.' I work through things as best I can. I didn't *say* I wasn't going to come. I've been thinking about it. I was trying to explain so you would understand. I don't want to meet your whole family at a time when I might get emotional about things. I know I need to face Thanksgiving sometime, but maybe this doesn't seem like the right time. You don't know what kind of memories it brings back."

"Well fine, you've got your memories." He opened the door. "I hope they'll be enough for you!"

She went to the door and yelled out after him, "I *am* getting on with my life, and you can be sure *you* won't be a part of it." She slammed the door, plopped down in the sinkhole in the sofa and cried.

Beverly and Davey went to West Yellowstone snowmobiling for Thanksgiving. They had chili and chips and root beer for Thanksgiving dinner, bought a couple of souvenir moose mugs and headed back home. *"I'm improving,"* she told herself. *"This time we were only gone 4 days."* She talked back to herself. *"Of course, that has as much to do with having to be back for school as anything. Oh well, it's progress, for whatever reason."*

She got used to explaining simply to people in the family and at church about Steve. "We broke up." She had a way of saying it that didn't invite further inquiry, but at Christmas time her mother asked her about it.

"What happened between you and Steve, Beverly?"

"We had a big fight, and I told him to get lost and he did."

"What did you fight about?"

"Oh, it was one of those stupid fights that isn't really about what it's about. He asked me to marry him and so I went into this whole dissection of the institution of marriage as if it was a frog in Biology class, instead of telling him what he wanted to hear. Then he tried to make me eat turkey."

Naomi laughed. Beverly joined her. "I guess that sounded pretty stupid, didn't it."

"And you haven't heard from him since? It sounds like pride that's keeping him from calling. Beverly, women who wait for proud men to make the first move back, often end up alone. Only you know how you feel about Steve and if you want to patch things up, but if you do, don't wait for him to do it."

CHAPTER TWENTY-THREE
GO FLY A KITE

Beverly spent a lonely January and February. In March, when she saw the beginnings of spring, she realized how much she missed Steve. When she read in the newspaper that there was going to be a kite-flying contest, she mailed him a note.

"Dear Steve,

Remember last November when I told you to "go fly a kite?" If you want to see me, meet me at noon at Sugarhouse Park on March 14. Bring a kite.

Love,
Beverly

P.S. I'm sorry about Thanksgiving.

She enclosed the newspaper flier about the contest.

As she and Davey held their kite aloft, Beverly scanned the crowds for Steve. He hadn't come. She reeled in the kite, and they broke for lunch. She ordered two chili dogs at the snack cart. From a distance, Steve had been watching her look for him for quite some time. A voice behind her said, "Make that three." She turned around. The voice--always the beautiful deep voice. It was so good to see Steve!
She tried to be nonchalant. "And I suppose you want me to pay for it, too."
"You're the one who invited *me*."
"You're a cheap date. You want a drink, too?"
"Cheap for you maybe. I spent $45 on a trick kite."
"What did you do that for?"
"To impress you. Not that it will, of course, because I can't get it off the ground. Kind of like our relationship."
"Really? I bought a $2.95 plastic K-Mart special, but it flies."
"It's a dragon," said Davey.
"Does it breathe fire--like your mother did last time I saw her?" Steve asked. Beverly gave Steve a dirty look. They collected their food and walked to a picnic table.
"I probably will after I eat this chili dog, too, so look out."
"I was surprised to hear from you, Beverly."
"Pleasantly?"
"I'm here, aren't I?"
"You are. I didn't think you were coming."
They ate their chili dogs and then walked over to the playground and sat down on some logs and finished their drinks.
"My offer still stands, Beverly."
"That sounds like a line from one of your commercials."

"You want a commercial? Offer good through June 30. Limit, one to a customer. Visa and Mastercard accepted."

"That was not bad."

"If it was you, you'd do an infomercial." He turned to Davey. "Have you ever noticed that your mother talks a lot?"

Davey giggled.

"It would depend on what I was trying to sell. Some products need an infomercial. You don't need an infomercial, but can I get you cheaper if I save bread wrappers?"

"Do we have a taker?"

"I know it's supposed to be a 'yes' or 'no' question, Steve. Will you accept a 'maybe,' like we can explore the possibility?"

"Maybe."

"Maybe?"

"Give a 'maybe' get a 'maybe.'"

"That's fair. I can live with that. I'd like to meet your girls, Steve. I thought maybe you'd like to all come over to my house for Easter dinner."

He smiled. "You want to meet my girls? Aren't you worried about the long-term psychological effects this could have on them if you're not around later?"

"Maybe I will be."

CHAPTER TWENTY-FOUR
THE EASTER EGG HUNT

Steve and his little girls were coming over for Easter dinner. Beverly picked up Davey from his Primary class and hurried home to frost the Easter cake that she had made. She poured the two cups of coconut into her largest mixing bowl--the huge Tupperware bowl that was standard issue for every Mormon woman who occasionally had to make an industrial-size potato salad. She put in a few drops of green food coloring and put Davey on the job, standing him on a chair so he could reach the counter. In this case, she reasoned that the smaller the child, the larger the bowl should be, and there would be less chance of fallout.

"This is a magic trick. You're going to stir and turn this coconut into green Easter grass. Let's put on your cookie apron that Grandma made you." Davey loved his cookie apron. It had Cookie Monster on it, and it said, "Me Want Cookie!"

"Like this, Mama?" He began to stir and was fascinated as he saw the coconut turn green. Beverly began frosting the cake. Even with the huge bowl, Davey managed to spill a little coconut out the sides, but he did manage to turn it all green. Beverly sprinkled the Easter grass onto the cake and then she and Davey placed "M & M" Easter eggs around in the grass.

Beverly had four colorful Easter buckets with shovels that she had filled with chocolate Easter candies, knowing that either Steve or DeAnna had probably already gotten the girls Easter baskets. She had hidden eggs all over the yard for them to find and had made a special "Easter Bunny nest" that contained Easter grass and little surprises inside of colorful plastic eggs--one for each of them.

Steve arrived as quickly as he could get there after his church meetings let out. Beverly watched as three beautiful little blond girls in frilly pink, yellow and green pastel Easter dresses daintily got out of the car. Beverly had only seen the picture of DeAnna years ago on the wedding invitation, but she remembered her as blond and petite and feminine. She could see that these were her children. Steve introduced them.

"This is Monica, Erica and Annalisa." They went inside and sat gently on the living room sofa--the one that Davey was always removing the cushions from to make a fort--and smoothed their dresses. Mentally Beverly took note. *"Monica-pink. MONica. Monday. Wash day. Don't put a red sock in the wash or you'll turn the whites pink. Erica-green. ERICa. 'Eric the Red.' Red and green--Christmas colors. Annalisa-yellow."* Beverly couldn't make any connection between Annalisa and yellow. *"Annalisa--the other one."*

They had a nice dinner and then Beverly announced, "Okay everybody, it's Easter Egg hunting time!" She turned to Steve. "Did you bring them any play clothes?" Whenever Beverly went somewhere straight after church, she always took play clothes for Davey, and for that matter, for herself. Dave's sister, Pamela, had given Davey an adorable little outfit for church--a pair of pants and a vest marked "Dry Clean Only." Beverly knew that any line of clothes for children that said "Dry Clean Only" was designed by someone who owned a dry cleaning conglomerate.

"No, I didn't even think about it."

"We'll figure something out."

"Like what?"

"I don't know, but they can't hunt Easter eggs out in the yard in those nice dresses. Where did you buy them? They are adorable."

Erica said shyly, "Our mother made them for us." Steve frowned.

"Well, your mother is a very good seamstress. She must love you a lot to make you pretty dresses like that." Erica smiled. Beverly was nice.

Beverly had an idea. "Come in here. I have something you can wear to keep your dresses pretty." They hesitated. "You don't want Davey to get all the eggs, do you?" Monica shook her head. The other two followed suit. "Okay, let's go!" In her room Beverly pulled three of Dave's old shirts out of the closet. She had kept them for Davey to use as painting shirts. She put one on each of the little girls, backwards, buttoned up the back and rolled up the sleeves. They looked at themselves in the mirror and giggled. "Off with the shoes. I guess you can go barefoot. The lawn is greening up. Just stay on the grass and it should be okay. I wouldn't want you to scuff your shoes." They took off their shoes and socks and lined up the three little pairs of white patent leather shoes on the side of the wall, with their frilly little ankle socks tucked neatly into each pair of shoes. Beverly marvelled at the neatness of these little girls. "If I marry Steve, *they* will clean up after *me.*"

In keeping with their newfound freedom, they hurried down the hall in a blur, each grabbed a bucket, and the four of them ran outside and began scrambling to find the hidden eggs.

"What are they wearing?" Steve asked.

"Just some of Dave's old shirts that I kept for . . ."

"My daughters are running around outside wearing a *dead man's* shirts?" Steve was appalled.

"Steve, don't be so morbid. Honestly! He was alive when he wore the shirts. If it was *the* shirt he died in, okay, I could see you having a problem with it."

"Beverly! How can you just talk about it like that?"

"I'm just glad you didn't say that in front of the girls so they could tell everybody they came to my house and hunted Easter eggs dressed in a dead man's clothes. Look Steve, like it or not, death is a part of life--not the most pleasant part, from our point of view--but definitely a part. I can't just pretend like Dave never existed, like you seem to think you can do with DeAnna. At least I'm trying to face up to my situation."

"Yeah, well, if you're trying to face up to it, why do you still have all his old shirts, anyway? Is he going to come back and wear them?" He started to sit down on the sofa.

"Don't sit there!" Beverly shrieked. Steve jerked to his feet before he hit the sofa.

"What's wrong?!" he asked, looking back at the couch warily.

"A *dead man* once sat on that couch!" Steve gave Beverly a dirty look and sat down. "And what was that comment about why do I still have his shirts? You know, Steve, that's not really any of your business--or anybody else's for that matter--what I keep and don't keep and when and where and how and why I keep it or don't keep it, just for the record."

"Okay," said Steve, and then proceeded to ask, "And what about all of these pictures around here? I find it kind of intimidating to come to your house and see him looking at me from every wall."

"Every wall? I have *one* picture of the three of us in the family room. Didn't you hear what I just said, Steve? I'm allowed to have a picture of my 'family' in my 'family room.' The rest of my pictures are in my bedroom, which is not a room where I entertain, just for the record. But if we get married, I plan to have a life-sized picture of him hanging over the bed. Give me a little credit, Steve! Just because you're full of negative feelings about your ex-wife and are trying to wipe every trace of her existence from your life, doesn't mean I should do the same with Dave."

"Speaking of minding your own business, I didn't appreciate that remark about the girls' dresses."

"What remark?"

He mimicked her. *"Your mother must really love you to make you such pretty dresses."*

"Steve, there's nothing wrong with letting three little girls know that their mother loves them. She's divorced from you, not from them."

"Not if I can help it. I've got custody and I intend to keep it. She abandoned them. My attorney says . . ."

"Is that what's important to you--getting revenge? What about what's best for the girls? They come from DeAnna. I can't believe that she doesn't love them. I know what it takes to make a ruffly little dress like that. I was a bridesmaid eight times. It almost killed me making those dresses! Their sense of self-worth is tied to where they come from. DeAnna is part of where they come from, yet you constantly convey to them that she left them, therefore she does not love them. If you tell them or imply to them that she's not a nice person, that she doesn't love them, how are they supposed to have any sense of security?"

Steve sat silently, then he said, "I never thought about that."

"Maybe it's about time you did. The whole idea of this gathering today was to get our kids acquainted with each other so that we could begin to build a future together, and . . ."

Steve and Beverly's conversation was cut short by the sound of crying. In limped a sobbing Annalisa. "I got stinged by a bumblebee!" Beverly sprung into action.

"Davey, take your bucket and get some dirt." He dumped out his Easter eggs onto the floor and ran out with his shovel to the flowerbed. She took the little girl and sat her down and examined her foot. Davey came in with a bucket of dirt. "Now get me a glass of water." He grabbed a little plastic glass out of the bottom cupboard where Beverly kept a few things for him to be able to learn to meet his own needs. She poured a little of the water into the dirt. "Now stir in the water and make some mud." Davey got a spoon. This was fun! Annalisa sat on the floor sniffling quietly. Beverly took the bucket from Davey. She stirred it just a little bit more. The spoon hit something hard on the bottom. Davey had left his chocolate Easter eggs in the bucket when he filled it up with dirt. She turned to Annalisa, and said, "This should make it feel better. My mom always did this for me when I got a bee sting. We are just going to put a little mud on your foot." Annalisa let out a wail. "Does it hurt a lot, honey?" said Beverly tenderly. But that wasn't what was wrong.

"*Mud?* You're going to put *mud* on my foot?" she wailed.

Annalisa had never been dirty in her life.

CHAPTER TWENTY-FIVE
FAMILY DATES

Steve pulled into Beverly's driveway. Davey ran outside to meet him.

"Chuck E. Cheese! Chuck E. Cheese!" He ran around and around the car chanting it over and over.

Beverly came out. "I love these family dates. Should we take two cars?"

"No, Davey can just crowd into the back seat with the girls, and you can sit in the front."

"I want Davey to be in a seat belt."

"So put him in the front with you and share one."

"I think we'd better take two cars."

"If you wanted to take your car, Beverly, why didn't you just say so, instead of asking my opinion."

"I'm sorry. It's just that I don't want anything to happen to him."

"Chuck E. Cheese is only three miles away, Beverly. Don't you think you're being a little over-protective?"

"Okay, I'll see if I can fit Davey and Annie into one seat belt."

Beverly buckled Davey in with Annalisa and climbed into the front of the car. Steve reached over and took her hand. "If you're a good girl, I'll buy you a balloon." She gave him a frozen smile. "See," he said, "you don't always have to be in the driver's seat."

"This was not about me being in the driver's seat."

"You have to admit you're a little bit independent."

"Why does that bother you so much? Is it because you can't control me? This wasn't about my independence. It was about Davey being in a seat belt. Besides which, it's the law. I hope you don't go driving around without the girls in seat belts."

"Of course I don't. They know they are supposed to buckle up. And they know that 'Monica the Monitor' will tell on them if they don't."

"Well, that's good to know." She switched gears. "About the independence thing, I have to be. I have to take care of myself and Davey."

"I'll take care of you, Beverly. You've been taking care of yourself too long."

"Really, Steve? Will you kill my spiders and change my light bulbs?"

"Are you making fun of me, Beverly?"

"I want our relationship to work, Steve, but for the right reasons, not because I could move into a bigger house or have you around to open mayonnaise jars."

"So which do you think has more pull--the house or me opening the mayonnaise jars?"

"Well, it's a really nice house, Steve, and I do like the idea that if I hear a noise in the night, I can roll over and ask you to go downstairs and see what it is."

"Among other things we could do in the middle of the night."

"Like what, Dad?" Monica piped up from the back seat.

Beverly turned around. "Like open mayonnaise jars."

"What for?"

"For a midnight snack," Steve added.

"Oh."

Beverly turned to Steve. "Really, Steve, we *are* on a *family* date."

"Sorry, I forgot."

"Imagine--making innuendos on the way to Chuck E. Cheese."

"Do you know how long it has been since I've *had* a midnight snack?"

"Don't think about it, Steve. It only makes it worse."

"How can I not think about it, with you around?"

"Isn't that part of the reason we're going on more of these family dates? Besides, we can't sit here acting like a couple of lovestruck teen-agers. We both have children to consider. We have to be responsible adults."

"But we can't ignore our own needs in favor of the children, either."

"We can't? We're going to Chuck E. Cheese, aren't we?"

"Well, you do have a point there."

In the distance, Beverly heard a siren. She reached over and turned off the radio.

"Hey, I like that song."

"Sshhh. There's a siren. Pull over, Steve."

"Let's wait and see where it is."

"Why wait? I think you should pull over."

"I'm driving, remember. I'll pull over when I see if I need to. Besides, Chuck E. Cheese is in the next block."

By the time Steve could see the ambulance in his rearview mirror, the next lane was too crowded for him to pull over to the right. The ambulance was three cars back, lights flashing and sirens blaring, and Beverly was just slightly less audible. "You should have pulled over when I told you to. Then maybe some of these other people would have pulled over!" The ambulance pulled out to the left of the cars, with two wheels on the median strip until it came to a left-turn lane. It turned left and was gone. Beverly's anger was not. "You think it's more important to get to Chuck E. Cheese fast than to pull over for emergency vehicles? Tell me, has anyone you love ever ridden in an ambulance? If that was someone you know being rushed to the hospital, do you think you would have pulled over?"

He didn't answer her. "Calm down, Beverly." Steve pulled into the parking lot for Chuck E. Cheese and got the kids out of the car. Some of the fun of going to Chuck E. Cheese had just worn off. Beverly wouldn't get out of the car. "I'm taking the kids in. You can come in when you're ready."

Beverly finally went into the restaurant where she and Steve ate pizza in silence and were entertained by an animated moose and his friends rather than talk to each other. Steve brought her a balloon as a peace offering.

"Steve, sometimes you treat me like a kid."

"Beverly, I get just a little tired of you analyzing everything I do. Do you want the balloon or don't you?"

"Okay, I'll take the balloon, but I wanted yellow."

On the drive home, Beverly summoned all her self-control and did not once remark to Steve how unsafe it was driving a car with five jumbo helium-filled Chuck E. Cheese balloons blocking his view from the rearview mirror. He didn't understand how it felt to have lost someone the way she had lost Dave. He just didn't understand.

Later that evening after Steve was gone, Beverly called Dr. David Evans. He had called her a few times recently when he was feeling down, and she knew he would understand about the situation with the ambulance and how she had felt. They talked for a while, and Beverly felt better just to talk to someone who understood. Then she called and smoothed things over with Steve, and by the time they finished talking, they were in love again.

She helped Davey with his prayers and tucked him in bed. "Davey, do you like Steve and his girls?"

"I like Steve, but doesn't he have any boys?"

"No, but how would you feel about being his boy? Would you like it if I married Steve and he could be your new dad?"

"Could we still live here?"

"No, we would go live at Steve's house."

"With all those girls?"

"Well, think about Steve over there all alone with all those girls. He needs another boy around to keep him company."

"Yeah, poor Steve."

"So you'll be okay with this?"

"Well Mom, I need a dad so that if you die, I won't be like Little Orphan Annie."

"I knew I shouldn't have rented that movie."

"If you marry Steve, and you died, would I still live with Steve or would I go live with Uncle Randall and Aunt Gayle like you said?"

"Well honey, that's one you've thought about more than I have. You'd probably stay with Steve and the girls." Beverly kissed him goodnight and went to the living room to be alone with her thoughts. *"Would I be comfortable changing Steve over to be Davey's guardian right away? And if I'm not, what am I doing considering marrying him?"*

CHAPTER TWENTY-SIX
MEMORIAL DAY

Beverly took an arrangement of flowers to the cemetery for Memorial Day. Davey was running around nearby chasing a bird. As she clipped the grass from around the stone and brushed the collected debris out of the crevices, she began to converse with Dave. "Dave, I'm getting married again. I hope this won't make you turn over in your grave, but . . ." At that moment, a lawn mower in a nearby yard started.

Dave was there. He whispered in Beverly's ear. *"Did you hear that? That was the sound of me turning over in my grave. It was the best I could do on such short notice."* He sat down on the grass, right next to Beverly. He had learned that it was useless to try to wave his arms and jump around to get people's attention. *"Get close by and let them feel you."* Sometimes it worked. Sometimes it didn't. Even though she was talking to him, it seemed her thoughts were more on Steve and she couldn't sense his presence. *"Beverly, I always knew that you would get married again. I don't want you to be alone, but be careful. You don't have the big picture, but it's okay. I've actually got permission to get you through this one, to get you the information you need, to help you let go of me and of whatever else you need to let go of."*

She continued talking. ". . . I'm going to marry Steve. We have some problems, but we're working on them. He's got these three adorable little girls, and he's good with Davey. I guess I'll have to sell the house, but I'll never forget all the happy memories we had there and . . ." Beverly stopped talking, suddenly self-conscious as a couple walked past and looked her way. *"I suppose I look like I'm sitting here talking to the grass."* She voiced it. "Can you hear me? I like to think you can, that I'm not just some crazy woman sitting here talking to the grass. I can't help but wonder sometimes if this is just something I do that brings me comfort. There have been times I've felt you nearby, and I don't think I just imagined it. It would be nice to know. Last week at church I said something about you checking in on us and Brother Cooper told me that he thought spirits in the spirit world were too busy to worry about what we were doing down here. I told him that if they didn't let you know how we were doing, they wouldn't get any work out of you. Anyway, I guess there isn't any way for you to answer that one, is there? I'll just put it on the list of things I want to ask about when I get there."

Davey interrupted her reverie. "Mom, how come it's so hard to catch a bird? I've been trying to catch a bird for a whole year!" He sat down in disgust. Dave laughed. Beverly had a warm feeling come over her. She hugged her little boy.

"Here, there's a hug from me and one from Daddy." She didn't realize how true her words were. She got up to go to the car and took her little boy by the hand. "I don't know, Davey. There are a lot of things I don't know, and how to catch a bird is one of them. I wish it was the only one."

Beverly started the car. She reached over and popped out the tape she had been listening to, realizing that she had been driving around with that same tape playing for several days. She pushed a button on the radio.

"Nope. Wrong station." Dave talked to her from the back seat of the car. *"You want the station that plays the oldies."* A new song came on. *"You don't like this song."*

"I don't like this song," Beverly said, as she pushed the button for another station.

"One more button. Come on. Work with me here."

That radio station was airing a commercial. Beverly pushed the next button in line. She heard the first strains of a song she didn't recognize.

"There's your answer, Bev. Don't mind me. I'll just sing along from here in the back seat."

After a couple of lines, Beverly was crying so hard she pulled the car off the road and listened to the rest of the song, marvelling that somehow Dave had found a way to answer her questions.

> There is someone walking behind you.
> Turn around, look at me.
> There is someone watching your footsteps.
> Turn around, look at me.
> There is someone who really loves you.
> Here's my heart in my hand.
> Turn around, look at me.
> Understand. Understand,
> That there's someone to stand beside you.
> Turn around, look at me.
> There is someone to love and guide you.
> Turn around, look at me.
> I've waited, and I'll wait forever for you to come to me.
> Look at someone who really loves you.
> Turn around, look at me.

CHAPTER TWENTY-SEVEN
CHOICES

"Steve, I told you I didn't need an engagement ring. A wedding band would have been fine."

"Go ahead. Open it." She sat in the middle of Steve's living room, in the beautiful house that they soon would share. Their four children were lined up against the stair railing looking down.

"I think we are being spied on."

"I told them they could watch."

"Why do I feel that I'm the only one who is not in on this?"

Beverly opened the jewelry box, and Steve put the ring on her finger. It was official. They were engaged.

"It's beautiful, Steve." She motioned to the children. "Well, come down and see."

The girls crowded around Beverly's hand. "It's really pretty," said Monica. "How much did it cost, Dad?"

"Monica!" Steve took Beverly's hand. "Beverly is going to be your new mother. In just a few months we'll all be a family."

Annalisa climbed onto Beverly's lap and gave her a hug. "Do I get to play with some of Davey's toys when you move here?"

Davey cocked his head to one side. "Does she, Mom?"

"Well, Davey, you're going to have to get used to having three sisters and learning to share," Steve said. Beverly took him aside.

"You know, Steve, my counselor said that during this transition time it's important that Davey has a sense of ownership of his things. He's losing his territory. We're moving into your home. I'm not saying that he doesn't need to learn to share, and I think that will come naturally once he realizes that his territory is not threatened, but we both need to confirm to Davey right now that his things are his."

Steve was silent. Beverly interpreted that to mean that he agreed with her, so she explained to Davey, "Your toys belong to you and they always will, but maybe when you would like someone to play with, you can invite Annalisa to play superheros with you." He looked at Annalisa.

"You can be Wonder Woman. She cooks dinner for Batman and Superman." Steve smiled.

Beverly shook her head. "The male ego. It's standard issue, just something you guys come with--like a gall bladder, isn't it? As a single mother I've raised this child free from attitudes like that. Where did it come from?"

"Aren't you going to cook dinner for me, Beverly?"

"Of course I'm going to cook dinner for you, Steve, and do the laundry and clean the house. I just don't want you to think that's all it takes for a woman to have a full and complete life. I have talents and interests and abilities, too. That's all. If all she's going to do is cook, why does Wonder Woman have any superpowers, anyway?"

"This is one of the stupider fights we have had."

"We are not having a fight. We just got engaged. We can't be having a fight. We're having a discussion."

"So now we are going to fight about whether or not we are having a fight?"

"No, we are going to discuss our discussion."

"I never realized you were such a women's libber."

"Why? Because I'm going to school? The church emphasizes the importance of education for a woman. Home and family issues are addressed differently by different women in different situations. You can't just set an exact standard and expect no deviations. We have the ideal and we try to get as close to it as we can within the confines of our situation. I know what my priorities are, and I feel good about them. I stayed home with Davey when he was tiny, and I still work my class schedule around his school schedule. And if you die, I've got something to fall back on."

"I'm not planning to die."

"Well, you *do* have your ego in place. I'm dating one of the Three Nephites? Are you going to be translated or are you going to live forever? Or are you a superhero?"

"Sorry. I didn't mean that you shouldn't go to school, but it's when women go outside their homes to the workplace--well, that's when they have affairs and . . ."

"We're playing 'your baggage or mine' again, Steve. Okay, so you're not going to die next week, and I'm not going to go off and have an affair with one of my professors. Every woman that works doesn't have an affair. A woman needs to find some sort of outlet for her talents or her interests outside her home. I really believe that. I don't think it needs to be a job, but I don't presume to tell someone else that it shouldn't be a job. If she has children, she will be responsible for the choices she makes regarding them and she will experience the consequences if her priorities are not right. The ideal is the mother in the home with the children, the father gainfully employed. There are a lot of variations on that theme. Let's say I never become a psychologist. I like to think that somewhere along the way I've used the things I've learned."

"All the time." Steve rolled his eyes.

"I didn't like the tone of that. And that eyeball thing. You can have that surgically corrected, you know, so that your eyes don't roll back in your head that way. They stitch them to your eyelids. It's an outpatient procedure. Insurance usually doesn't cover it, unless, like in your case, it's a necessity."

"Beverly, every time I turn around, you're quoting some counselor or spouting some theory or telling me the appropriate way to handle some situation. I get kind of tired of it."

"You know, Steve, we shouldn't be discussing these things in front of the children. It's not good."

"See, there you go again. *I'm* messing them up. What about tonight when I try to put Annie to bed and she asks me about that eyeball thing. Did you think about that, huh? Did ya, huh?"

She turned to the kids. "Grown-ups have problems like learning to share and work together, too."

Steve changed the subject. "Why don't we go have some cake in the kitchen?" He got the plates down out of the cupboard and set them on the counter. Beverly observed.

"He's not as helpless as all that. Maybe I overreacted. Besides, it's good for us to discuss these things so we know how we each feel."

Beverly noticed that Erica was being very quiet and withdrawn. She ate her cake with her head down and didn't join in the conversation with the others. She had been quiet all day, in fact. As they cleared up the dishes, Beverly remarked to Steve. "Have you noticed that Erica has been awfully quiet today?"

"Yes, she's been like that a lot lately. She's real moody and she cries a lot. It must be one of those female things."

"Female things? She's only six years old, Steve, a long way off from female mood swings." She whacked him with a dishtowel. "You need to learn that not all female moods are caused by PMS. Sometimes it's just *life.*"

He grabbed her and kissed her. "Okay, so why don't you go talk to her, Wonder Woman?"

She found Erica sitting on the floor in her room holding a doll on her lap. "Who is this?"

"Her name is Aurora Camillia."

"Don't you have a dress like that, too?"

"My mom--my other mom--made me and my doll matching dresses."

"That makes it special, doesn't it?" Erica began to cry. Beverly sat down next to her. "Erica, you can talk to me. I know that you're not happy today, and I want to help you, if I can."

Erica sniffed a couple of times. "I like you and Davey, and I know that you're going to marry my dad and be my new mom, but what about my old mommy? When I try to ask Daddy about her, he just gets mad. I miss her."

"You haven't seen her for a long time."

"Dad says she left us and that she wouldn't do that if she cared about us."

"She cares about you, honey. There are a lot of things going on--grown-up things, that make it hard for your mommy to see you. Maybe later when your dad is not so angry, he will work things out better with your mommy. I'm trying to help him see that being angry is not a good choice. I want you to understand one thing for sure, and that is that just because I'm marrying your dad and am going to be what they call your stepmother, doesn't mean that you can't love your other mother. You *should* love her. She loves you. She made that pretty dress for your doll, didn't she? She made you and your sisters those pretty Easter dresses. When you say your prayers at night, maybe you can remember to ask Heavenly Father to help your mom and dad to work out their problems, so that you can see your mommy and I'll try to do what I can to help, too."

Beverly went back downstairs. Steve was still in the kitchen putting the cake away. "I was wrong. It *is* PMS--'Pigheaded Male Stubbornness.' The girls need to see their mother, Steve. Erica is very confused. She wants to accept me, but she feels torn because she misses her mother. She says you get angry when she asks about DeAnna." They sat down at the kitchen table.

"Beverly, I know you mean well, but there are things you don't know about the situation. DeAnna has flipped out. She's not stable. There's another man involved--Jerry. I suspect she's having an affair with him, and some of the outfits she models--well, let's just say that it's obvious to me that she has abandoned all her morals--and then some. I don't have any intention of letting my sweet little girls go visit her in some den of iniquity."

"Couldn't she come here to see them?"

"I don't want to have to see her."

"This isn't about *you* seeing her. It's about the girls seeing her. Steve, maybe us getting married is not right--at least not right now. Maybe we should wait. You need more time. How can you marry me if you haven't even gotten over the pain of seeing DeAnna?"

"Beverly, I need you. The girls need you. Don't you leave me, too. You can help us all get through this."

Beverly unconsciously twisted the ring on her finger. "But Steve, you won't let me help. You won't listen to me."

"I'll talk to her, okay. I don't promise anything, but I'll talk to her."

Their conversation was interrupted by Annalisa. She had a book in her hand and gave a little tug on Beverly's sleeve.

"Will you read me a story, Beverly?"

"Sure, honey." She looked down and caught a glimpse of the cover. There he was, Horton the "eh-phunt" sitting on the tree. She looked at Steve. "Or maybe your dad would like to read it to you."

"Let's see, I've read 'Green Eggs and Ham' 457 times, 'Hop on Pop' 232 times. Between all three kids, I've read that one 869 times. I'll let you read it. What's the matter. Don't you like Dr. Suess?"

"Nothing. Nothing's the matter. I love Dr. Suess. He's the best." She turned to Annalisa. "Let's go in to the sofa and I'll read you the story there." Beverly fought the mind pictures that came as she started to read the book. The picture that tugged at her heart strings was of a little toddler, too young to understand what was going on, wondering why none of the people who loved him had time to read him his favorite story that day. She remembered how Davey had still been clutching the book when she had picked him up from the Jensen's and his simple one-word plea that she had ignored. *"Eh-phunt."* Annalisa looked at Beverly questioningly. Giving no explanation for her emotions, she continued with the story. *"He was so little. It's so unfair to have to show your child who his father is by pointing to pictures. At least I have memories of Dave."* Beverly continued reading. Soon she was relating to the elephant who came to sit on the nest in the absence of the mother bird who had flown off to Palm Beach to relax and party. And there was part of her that couldn't help but feel sorry for the mother bird when she found she had come back too late to claim her offspring. Finally she came to the end of the book.

"Why did that story make you cry, Beverly?"

"It just does." A few minutes later, she returned to the kitchen, hoping the water she had splashed on her face had done the trick.

It hadn't. "What's wrong, Beverly? I don't remember 'Horton Hatches the Egg' being a tearjerker."

"Not for you, maybe. It's all about someone taking over for a mother who has flown the coop. Maybe I was just relating to it a little too much." She consoled herself. *"That wasn't entirely untrue. Besides, Steve wouldn't understand. I know he wouldn't, especially when I just got through lecturing him about **his** baggage.*

He will never understand how one little thing like that can take me right back to that day."

"Hey, good idea. Maybe I'll pass that along to my lawyer. The 'Horton Hatches the Egg' defense."

"Gosh Steve, does everything come down to that court hearing now? When you talked the other day about those cards the girls had given you and how you were going to be sure and save them, I thought you meant because they had sentimental value, but you couldn't wait to give them to your lawyer as evidence."

"Well, when he gives them back to me, I'll still save them."

"But it wasn't the messages that cheered you up, it was the fact that you could use them as evidence that seemed to give you pleasure. Forgive me for saying this, but sometimes this hearing seems to be more about you winning at any cost than about your children's well-being."

Beverly collected Davey and drove home. She doubted that she felt exactly how a newly-engaged person was supposed to feel. Still, she told herself, it was not easy to put two families together. Was she going to back down from the challenge? She was the Superglue that was going to hold this family together. On the other hand, if you were not careful with Superglue, you could end up gluing all the wrong things together and they were stuck for good.

CHAPTER TWENTY-EIGHT
MAN OVERBOARD

Beverly was still counseling with Kelly. It was a different semester with different classes, but she and Kelly had carried their counseling relationship beyond the hours Kelly had needed for her Masters program.

"I feel like I'm taking advantage of you, Kelly, getting all this free counseling."

"No, I think I'm the one taking advantage of you. Just think of all the issues we have covered with just one person's problems. I'll be ready for just about anything. Last time we met we were talking about you and Steve."

"Speaking of Steve, we're officially engaged." Beverly held out her hand to display the ring.

"Congratulations. I wish you every happiness."

"You don't sound so sure."

"I'm very sure that I wish you happiness."

"But . . . ?"

"If you're on the shore and you see a person drowning, what do you do?"

"You throw them a life preserver, if there is one, or a board or something else that floats, I guess."

"Do you jump in and try and save the person yourself, if you're not a trained lifeguard?"

"No."

"Why not?"

"Because they might pull you under with them. But that's not me and Steve. I mean, maybe it might look that way, but couldn't I be considered like a trained lifeguard. The stages of loss through a divorce are the same ones you go through with grief--denial, anger, guilt, depression, and hopefully eventually acceptance."

"Where do you think Steve is?"

"Anger."

"Where do you think you are?"

"Well, maybe acceptance with occasional side trips back to anger and depression."

"Interesting comment. So you can revisit some of those earlier stages."

"Yes, but I don't stay as long as I used to."

"Beverly, I'm not here to tell you what to do, only to help you explore the choices you make. Everything in your relationship with Steve should be feedback toward those choices. People sometimes get stuck in a phase of the cycle and never move on. Sometimes they grab onto a new relationship to save themselves from, for example, having to face the part they may have played in the deterioration of their marriage."

"This happened very suddenly. *She* left him. He tries really hard to be a good father to his little girls."

"Are you trying to convince me, or are you trying to convince yourself? Beverly, I know you care about him, but remember that you have to be honest with yourself. Take things slowly--look for progress, not perfection, but remember, you have a right to expect progress."

"I love Steve, and I love his little girls. I know it's not going to be easy. I'm not expecting it to be easy. When I had the miscarriage after Dave died, I wondered if I would ever be able to have any more children. I didn't have an easy time with Davey. I love my son, but growing up with brothers, I always wanted a little sister. When my last brother was born, my mother told me that even though I had another brother, that maybe someday I would have a little daughter of my own. Now I'm going to have three. I love those little girls."

"I can tell. And I have every confidence that you'll do what's best for them. Just don't let your desire to mother them cloud the issues that you and Steve have. They'll grow up and leave. Your relationship with him is the primary relationship you need to focus on."

CHAPTER TWENTY-NINE
DIRTY LAUNDRY

Beverly opened the door for Steve. In his hand was a bouquet of mixed flowers. On the porch were three bags full of dirty laundry. He handed her the flowers.

"For me? How sweet!" She looked down. "And what's this?"

"That's for you, too." Steve looked sheepish. "I had a busy week. I was hoping that maybe you would help me out and . . . ."

Beverly smiled at him. "I'd really love to, Steve," she said, picking up one of the bags and handing it to him, "but laundry is like sex--not until after we're married. I'll go put these flowers in some water while you load that back into the car."

As Steve loaded the dirty laundry into the trunk, he muttered under his breath, "If laundry was like sex, I wouldn't be trying to get someone else to do it for me."

Beverly came back out of the house as though nothing had happened and let herself into the car, since Steve didn't get out and open the door for her. "Are you mad at me because I wouldn't do your laundry?"

"Why should I be?"

"I didn't ask you if you should be. I asked you if you were."

"Well, I didn't think it would hurt to ask."

"Well, you asked. Did it hurt you? It didn't hurt *me.*"

"It didn't hurt you to say 'no.'"

"Come on, Steve. I don't expect you to come over here every week and mow my lawn."

"But I stay here late at night sometimes to protect you."

"Perhaps I should kick you out sooner so that you have time to do your laundry. Now are we going to spend our entire evening together talking about your laundry? Where are we going to eat?"

"Cirroni's. I ran into Toni and Alex today at the ad agency and they invited us to a party they are throwing for one of their kids at the restaurant."

"Are we supposed to bring a gift?"

"I'm sure we'll be okay."

When they got there, the entire restaurant was decorated in pink. It was Cecily Cirroni's Sweet Sixteen birthday party. There were about 300 people there, and they had rented a dance band for the evening and had cleared the floor for dancing.

Beverly commented to Steve. "Isn't this a bit much? I've seen wedding receptions that were less well-attended and probably cost less, too."

"This is a big deal to them."

"I don't see anyone else here from the ward."

"You don't like the Cirronis, do you Beverly?"

"I just feel a little out of my league."

"Maybe this is your league and you just don't know it."

"Steve, I just don't get into this country club atmosphere. These people don't seem to be real friends with anyone. They just schmooze their way around the room. Why are most of the guests adults? This party isn't for Cecily. It's for Toni

and Alex and *their* friends. For my 16th birthday, I went roller skating with a
bunch of friends. What happened to that guy from Newton I used to know? Yes,
it's fun getting dressed up and mingling with high society. Sure I enjoy an
occasional double date with Toni and Alex, but I guess I get the feeling that you're
more into this whole country club scene than I am."

Steve's answer was to take her onto the dance floor where he held her close and
whispered in her ear. "I love you, Beverly. I never stopped loving you." Those are
the things that every woman wants to hear, yet somehow it troubled Beverly. If he
had never stopped loving her, did that mean that he had never fully committed to
his wife and his relationship with her? What had been missing in their relationship
that she would just up and leave? Or did he not mean it literally but just as a nice
thing to say that he thought she probably wanted to hear.

"Steve, don't you ever worry that it won't work out?"

"Why should I?"

"Well, there are a lot of issues we haven't even touched on."

"We'll deal with them when they come up."

It wasn't too long before one of them came up. They were at Sugarhouse Park.
It was one of the last warm days of summer, and so they'd taken the kids on a
picnic. The kids were at the playground, and Steve and Beverly were sitting on the
grass nearby.

"I got an offer on the house, Steve, but it wasn't a very good one."

"I think you should take it anyway."

"But we are not planning to get married until next spring. I don't think I need
to take the very first offer someone makes."

"You bought it as a fixer-upper, so you can't expect to get a real high price for
it. You'd be making money on it, right?"

"But Steve, Dave did a lot of the fixing up--maybe not all of it--but I shouldn't
have to sell it at a ridiculous price. Sure, I'd make a little money, but this offer is
way below what the realtor thinks I should be able to easily get." Beverly thought
back to the early days in the house with Dave, how they had moved in and put all
their furniture in the family room, and one-by-one had painted and moved the
furniture into each room until all that was left in the family room was their old
couch with the sinkhole in the middle and their television set. Dave had told her,
"It's furnished just like a model home--one or two pieces of furniture in each
room." It would seem like a betrayal to sell the house they had shared together for
less than a fair price, as if she were devaluing Dave and the work he had done to fix
it up and the happy times they had shared in that little house. She was jarred back
to the present.

"We don't need the money."

"This is not about the money. I'm planning to put the proceeds into Davey's
mission and college fund, anyway, like we had discussed. Maybe it's just the
principle of the thing--that I want a fair price for the house."

"I think you should take the offer, be satisfied with a modest profit, and I think
we should get married as soon as you close."

"That could be as soon as a month."

"So why not? We're going to get married. We aren't having some big
reception that we have to plan and organize. We can easily move it up. We can go

to the temple, get married, have a nice dinner at a restaurant for all of the family and a few close friends, and it's all over with."

"I didn't realize you were so anxious to 'get it all over with.'"

"Think about it, Beverly. We both have temple recommends. We could elope."

"Elope to the temple? Can you do that?"

"I don't see why not."

"Oh sure, just grab somebody in the hall, and say, by the way, while we're here, is there somebody that can marry us?"

"Okay, so you have to call and make an appointment. It would have to be a little premeditated. We could just ask for the next available time. How hard is that? If nobody else was there, they would just assume we were the only members in our family."

"Steve, you can't be serious."

"I could marry you tomorrow, Beverly."

"Well, you aren't the one that's being uprooted. I think we have already rushed things, as it is, and I still think we should get married in April or May like we planned, to give you time to have things worked out with DeAnna."

Steve leaned over and whispered in her ear. "Marry me now, Beverly."

"Has the laundry piled up that much?" She threw a handful of grass on him, got up, and ran over to the swings where the children were playing together. Monica and Erica were on the slippery slide. Davey and Annalisa were on the swings, trying to see who could swing the highest.

Beverly's heart welled up within her, watching the children play together. She loved those three little girls. It felt like a family, and Beverly really wanted a family. Soon Steve was behind her with his arms around her waist. She hadn't been so happy in a long time.

"Don't make me wait, Beverly. Let's do it now."

"Okay, Steve, we can get married soon--whenever you want. I'll take the offer on the house."

Beverly countered the offer that had been made on the house, because even though she intended to sell it, she knew they were starting low and expected her to try to get them to come up. They began negotiations to arrive at a price. Since Steve could see all of this beginning to happen, he confessed to Beverly, over pizza, this time at his house. "I've got a hearing coming up, a custody hearing, at the end of next month. My lawyer says that I can probably make the abandonment thing stick, and that with the research that he's done, I stand a real good chance of being able to get full custody of the girls."

"Are you sure . . . ?"

"You can never be sure," Steve interrupted, "but he also says that it will help a lot if we are married by then, because I can provide a more stable home life for the girls, and that should help our case."

"*What?* In the first place, what I was starting to say before you so rudely interrupted me was to ask you if you're sure that trying to get full custody of the girls is right. In the second place, this is why you have been so anxious to get married sooner, isn't it?! In the third place, this is not *our* case, it's *your* case! You never listen to me or my opinions about what's right or best for the girls. I've tried to tell you, Steve, that you can't just plant me in the hole that was left by

DeAnna and tell them that they have a new mother and that the old one doesn't exist anymore! This is so crazy! Here, I thought waiting until spring would give enough time for you and DeAnna to work things out, have all these proceedings out of the way and for things to stabilize. Why aren't we ever on the same page, Steve? She left, true. I don't know why she did what she did, but I know that she didn't abuse the kids and that she's not an unfit mother. She's confused, maybe, and has made some wrong choices, but you can't tell me that she doesn't love the girls! It just doesn't fit, Steve."

"Why do you always take her side?"

"This is not about *sides*, Steve. How many times do I have to tell you I'm neutral in this war. I'm Switzerland. This is about your children. But if we are drawing up sides, and you have your side and she has hers, someone has to be on the side of the girls--that's which *side* I am on. How can you involve me in their lives and let me grow to love them, and then expect me to stand by and watch you mess them up? I'm not going to marry you and take up your bitterness and anger and help you spend the rest of your life fighting with your ex-wife. Get over it, Steve. Let her go on with her life and you go on with yours. If you try to punish her using the kids, they are the ones who will suffer. Is that what you want? Good grief! Don't you want any peace in your life?"

"Well, what about you? You just don't want to sell your house because of all the old memories of you and Dave. You can't give it up. You say you're negotiating, but you haven't settled on anything."

"That's not fair! I told you the buyers were having trouble with their financing."

"And what about that depressed dentist that's always calling you. If you told him you're getting married, how come he keeps calling?"

"Oh, good, Steve! Smoke screen! Let's bring up all *my* hang-ups! Sure, I might have a difficult time leaving my house, but *gosh,* it would certainly be worth it if we could get married sooner so that we have a better chance of looking like the All-American Family in the courtroom! And Dr. Evans is my friend. He needs somebody to talk to."

"How close can you be if you still call him 'doctor?'"

"Okay, his name is David."

"Well, isn't that convenient?"

"His wife died, and he's doing better than you. He's all the way to 'depression' and you're still stuck in 'anger,' and *you* got a head start."

"What are you talking about now, Beverly?"

"The stages of grief and loss."

"Trust *you* to carry around some little checklist! So does he know that you're getting married?"

"Yes, I told him. He was very happy for me."

"How could he be happy? He's depressed, remember?"

"Look, Steve, he's my *friend.* Just like Jean is my friend."

"Well, fine!"

"Fine!"

"You think you're doing so well. What woman in her right mind would turn down the possibility of a honeymoon in Hawaii?"

"I didn't turn it down. I just asked if we could skip the island where Dave served most of his mission, so I wouldn't be thinking about him and things he has told me and making associations. How could I be there and not look up the Matsumori family? Do you want that on *our* honeymoon?"

"Oh come on, Beverly. You don't go to Hawaii and skip Honolulu. Admit it, you don't want to go to Hawaii with *me*. You wanted to go with *Dave.*"

"Oh Steve, what's the use?"

CHAPTER THIRTY
DEANNA

DeAnna Winston shivered and pulled the short, clingy dress down as far as she could get it. She was not used to wearing clothes like this. She breathed a sigh of relief when they turned off the fan and her spot was over for the time being. She sat down on a stool and threw a towel across her legs, partly for warmth, but mostly for modesty. As short as the skirt was when she was standing, it almost disappeared when she sat down. She wanted to cry, but she just felt kind of numb inside. She was going downhill and picking up speed. She wanted out. This was not what she wanted from life. But now Steve had charged her with abandonment, and she had no other support but what she was making modeling, so how could she quit? Her parents would take her in, give her a place to live, although they hadn't approved of her recent choices, but then they would just try to control her life and treat her like a child--especially since she had blown it. And how would all of the sheltered people in Newton, Utah, treat her--like some kind of a floozie, worldly and fallen. But she hadn't been unfaithful to Steve, not in the way he had accused her of. She had never had an affair with Jerry. She had just let him control her, talk her into leaving Steve to embark on a modeling career. He had promised her big things, but what she was doing was mostly catalog shoots. He had told her that Steve was trying to control her, but now she realized that she had just traded in Steve's control for Jerry's control. How had all this happened?

She reflected back to when she had started working at the ad agency. She had told Steve that she wanted to get some kind of part-time job, just to have a little spending money of her own. He hadn't understood.

"DeAnna, all you have to do if you need some money is ask me. You don't need to work."

"I just want to do something on my own. I won't work full-time. I won't neglect the girls. I just need to feel like I'm accomplishing something." It had started because of the "help-wanted" sign she had seen at World of Fabrics. It was close to home, and it was something she knew a lot about--sewing and fashion. She had wanted to tell him what she wanted to do, but she didn't know how Steve would feel about her working at what he would probably consider a menial job that would reflect on his abilities as a breadwinner, so she had referred to her ambitions rather vaguely. "I was thinking about something in the fashion industry." Well, maybe that wasn't how lots of people thought of World of Fabrics, but sometimes when she shopped there, she realized that she knew more about fabrics and sewing than the ladies waiting on her. When Steve had finally agreed to let her work, he had come home and announced to her that he had talked with one of his associates at the ad agency where he'd done some commercial work. They had a part-time opening, and he had arranged an interview for her. She landed the job before she had decided if she really wanted it. Working in the mail room hadn't exactly been what she had in mind, but she did enjoy seeing the goings-on at the company as she made her rounds, and though she was shy, she had made lots of nice friends.

How could she have known the day she went into Mr. Kirby's office that delivering that package would change her life so drastically? There they were, several executives sitting around the office, talking in heated tones. She had knocked and come unobtrusively into the office with the package and forms for his signature. Mr. Kirby had been on the phone. "We've got the whole shoot set up. We are losing money every second that we delay. I have 80 people on the payroll, sitting around. Where are we supposed to find a size 6 blond for the jeans commercial? No, that won't do. She has to be 5'4". This is a stair-step line-up and it goes blond, brunette, redhead. We are missing our size 6, 5'4" blond. This commercial is for the jeans that fit every woman, every size." He paused to take a package from the size 6, 5'4" pretty blond girl from the mail room. And the rest is history.

Now she sat on the stool, as sad and unhappy on the inside as she was made-up and beautiful on the outside, and DeAnna Matthews Winston made up her mind to take charge of her own life.

Jerry was incredulous when she told him she was leaving. "We have a contract. I can sue you."

DeAnna cast her eyes down and began to cry. "I've already lost everything of real value to me--my family. If there's anything else you think you can take from me, go ahead. I'll be working for World of Fabrics, if your lawyers need to contact me. Steve is suing me, too, so you might as well get in line."

He couldn't bear to see her crying. She was so pretty and fragile. He put his arms around her. "DeAnna, you're upset. You're not thinking straight. Why don't you go home and think about this and we can talk in the morning."

She pulled away from him and looked him straight in the eye--something which DeAnna just didn't do--and told him, "No, I'm thinking straight for the first time in my life. It may be too late for my relationship with my husband, but I can still fight for my children."

CHAPTER THIRTY-ONE
MAY I HELP YOU?

Beverly had looked all through the Halloween section of the pattern book. There were patterns for pirate costumes, but none of them included a wooden leg. Davey wanted to be a pirate--nothing else. She had figured out how to make a patch over his eye and tie a handkerchief around his head pirate-style and she could handle the little vest, but above all, he wanted to have a wooden leg. She was going to have to explain to him that she just couldn't figure out how to do it.

She picked out a pattern and went to the cutting table with the black cloth for the vest and pants. A petite blond lady asked her how much fabric she needed. Beverly handed her the pattern. "I'm not sure. I can never remember how to figure it out."

Looking at the pattern, she informed Beverly, "You know, if you make the vest out of black felt, there won't be nearly as much sewing involved, just the seams, and you can use some of the felt to make an eye patch."

"Really? I'm for anything that cuts out the sewing. I only do Halloween costumes because nobody expects them to be perfect."

"What are your other children going as?"

"I only have one. He wants to be a pirate, which I think I can handle. I don't sew very well. But get this--he wants me to figure out how to make him a wooden leg."

The sales lady studied the pattern for a minute and then she informed Beverly, "If you were to make the pants out of black and gather them to a cuff or let it balloon, then you could make a peg leg out of brown fabric that hugged his leg from the knee down, and it would look like a wooden leg."

"How would I do that? Can you put it in simple terms for a remedial sewer who flunked home ec?" The sales lady grabbed a piece of paper and sketched a pattern for a pair of pants showing Beverly how to measure for a cuff and how to attach the peg leg. "What fabric would you use?"

"Well, I would use a heavy felt for the peg leg and attach it with Velcro. Regular fabric would work for the pants, the one you've got here is fine. You could put a brown sock on his foot, maybe over a couple of other socks, and a shoe on the other foot. He would hobble automatically, and it would help to camouflage his foot."

"Wow! Thank you! You have been very helpful--above and beyond the call of duty. I bet you never flunked out of home ec."

"Some people would think it must be really boring to work at World of Fabrics, but I really like it. My mother started teaching me to sew when I was seven. Did you see the display window on the way in? Those are the costumes for my daughters. They will be on display until a couple of days before Halloween. Just last week they put me in charge of window displays for two stores. For Thanksgiving I'm going to . . ."

At the mention of Thanksgiving, Beverly cut her off. "Well, I really need to be going now. Thanks a lot for your extra help. If I'm down this way, I'll bring it in to show you when I get it done." As she walked out, she admired again the three filmy fairy princess dresses in the window--adorned with sequins and complete with magic wands--one pink, one green and one yellow.

Beverly stitched the pieces of Velcro to the brown felt. "Okay, Davey, time for the last try-on." It was not done flawlessly, but the important thing was that it worked for Davey.

"Oh boy, it's my wooden leg! Ahoy, matey! I'm going to make you walk the plank!" He brandished his tin-foil-covered cardboard sword.

"That's what I get for making you this good Halloween costume?"

"Okay, you don't have to walk the plank until after Trick or Treating."

"Thank you, um, what's your pirate name?"

"Captain Hook."

"Thank you for sparing my life, Captain Hook. Now we have to hurry and eat dinner because Steve and the girls will be here soon to go Trick or Treating."

Beverly was just finishing her last couple of bites of dinner when she looked out the window and saw Steve coming up the walk followed by three little fairy princesses, Monica in pink, Erica in green and Annalisa in yellow--their signature colors. She opened the door, her mouth gaping open, as the realization hit her. The sweet helpful woman at the fabric store was *DeAnna*--the worldly fashion model from the den of iniquity?!

"Why are you staring at the girls like that?" asked Steve. "Can we come in?"

"Just admiring your Halloween costumes," she said to the little girls.

"Yeah, guess where they came from," said Steve sarcastically.

"I don't have to," said Beverly. "I can't believe this. I was at World of Fabrics getting fabric for Davey's Halloween costume and . . ."

Davey appeared from behind the door. "I'm Captain Hook! Walk the plank!" He batted Annalisa's magic wand to the ground with his sword. Beverly knelt down so she could talk to him at eye level--at least in his one remaining eye.

"All right, Cap'n Hook. These are magic fairies. Do you want to be turned into a rock? Give Annalisa back her magic wand and apologize to her. And keep that sword under control or it will disappear, got it?"

"Sorry." He handed the wand back to Annalisa. "What are you going to turn me into?" This sounded fun.

Annalisa looked thoughtful. "A brother."

"A brother?" Davey looked at his mother. "Girls have dumb imaginations!"

"What do you want to be, Davey?" Erica asked. "I'll turn you into something."

"A werewolf."

"I don't know how to do a werewolf. I'm a good fairy," she said solemnly. "I only do nice magic. I can turn you into a flower."

"Oooh, yuck! A flower?"

Steve and Beverly stood back on the sidewalk as the kids collected candy. "You're awfully quiet tonight."

"I'm thinking."

"About what?"

"Halloween costumes. Did she bring them over? Did you let her see the girls?"

"I picked them up. And don't start on this again, Beverly. They are *my* girls and I'll do what I think is best for them."

"Steve, if I'm going to be your wife, I need to have some indication that we are going to be able to work out our problems and that my opinion counts for something. Like I started to say, the other day at World of Fabrics . . ."

"World of Fabrics, what a happening place." He grimaced. "I'm the Priesthood holder. Just follow my lead."

"I believe I'm supposed to follow you in righteousness, not in stupidity and pigheadedness. Why don't you admit it, if not to me, at least to yourself? You're using the kids to punish DeAnna for leaving you." They continued the conversation as they wound from house to house through the neighborhood.

"It's none of your business," Steve said sullenly. "I'll handle it. You don't know everything that I know about DeAnna."

"I know more than you think, but you don't want to hear what I know or what I think. It's none of my business? Am I not involved with these girls, about to be their stepmother? How can you say it doesn't concern me? How can you ask me to love the girls and be a mother to them and expect me to stand idly by and watch you mess them up? I can't do that, Steve. If you want some woman with no opinions about anything, then go find one--a nice compliant woman who will never question your judgment or your motives. I'm sorry, but I just can't do things that go against my system of values."

Steve placated her in his smooth television voice. "Look Beverly, as soon as custody is decided, I'll try to take all this into consideration. There's a lot of stress on everyone involved. Just help me get through the hearing and then we can sit down and have a nice long talk about what's best for the girls. I want the best for them, I do, and I think that what's best is having them with you and me and Davey and being a family. I'm just doing what I can to make that happen. You're a woman, and a wonderful mother, and I know it's hard for you to imagine how any woman could just up and leave her children. Because you would never do that, you naturally sympathize with her because you imagine that she has those same feelings, but she doesn't."

The following Sunday, Beverly sat in Sunday School class as the Gospel Doctrine teacher talked about Samuel the Prophet. He told about how his mother had promised God that if she was able to have a child, she would give him up to serve in the temple. Keeping her word, she took young Samuel to the temple, only able to return to see him once a year. Every year she would sew a coat to take to her son in the temple. The teacher talked about the love and tenderness that must have gone into every stitch, and with her woman's heart, Beverly thought of DeAnna sewing Easter dresses and Halloween costumes for the little girls she was not allowed to see. She told herself that there was a reason she had found Steve again. In the atmosphere of Gospel Doctrine class, where everything seems to be divinely inspired, she reasoned that Heavenly Father had sent her to Steve to help him to see that he needed to forgive DeAnna and let three little girls have a relationship with their mother.

Perhaps He did send Beverly to Steve to help him through this, but He had also given Steve agency, so that he was free to accept or reject the help that came. A couple of days later when Beverly tried to tell Steve about Samuel's mother and the little coat she made every year, he was hard put to see the connection. "Beverly, you always could pull things out of the scriptures and put interesting interpretations on them."

"Steve, the world is full of people who are full of anger and hate. If you can keep DeAnna from being involved in the girls' lives, will that make you happy? What will you feel? Triumph, maybe? Power? Can you honestly tell me that you think DeAnna doesn't care about her daughters?"

"She made choices that brought her to this point."

"You didn't answer my question."

"Okay, maybe she cares."

On the way home from Steve's house a few nights later, Beverly passed a theater that was showing a Disney film. They could use some light-hearted entertainment. She turned in and checked the show times and found a parking place. There was a 7:15 show. If they hurried, they could get a burger across the parking lot and run back over just in time. She jumped out of the car. "Come on, Davey. We're going to see a movie." She knelt down so that he could ride piggy-back and ran over to the fast-food drive-up intercom.

"We're not in a car, Mom."

"Make some car noises. They won't know until we get around to the window. Nobody is behind us to run us over." Beverly hurriedly gave their order. They 'drove' up to the window and picked it up, with Davey making car noises. The lady smiled at them as she handed them their burgers. They were having a good time-- such a good time that Beverly walked right past her car without noticing she had left the lights on.

Two hours later she came out of the theater, trying to remember where she had parked the car. It was easy to spot. It was the one with the lights on--just barely on. She looked around for someone that might be able to give her a jump. You could trust people who would go see 101 Dalmations on a Tuesday night, she hoped, but that wasn't very many people. There was an elderly couple and a mother with five children in tow. She approached the elderly man. "Do you have some jumper cables? I might need you to jump my car. Do you mind waiting while I try it?" She got in the car. Maybe it would start. The parking lot was nearly empty. "Davey, we are going to say a prayer that our car will start. Do you want to say it?"

"Okay. Dear Heavenly Father. Please help our car to start because my mom forgot to turn out the lights and because it's past my bedtime and we need to go home. Amen." He paused. "Mom, if it doesn't start, can I watch that old man try to jump our car, like you said? But how will that make the car start and what if he gets hurt?"

She turned the key. The engine came to life. She mouthed a "thank you" and waved the man on his way. "What a good battery!" She repented. "I mean, thank you, Heavenly Father! Well, Davey, it looks like your car prayer worked."

"It did!" He beamed.

Beverly reflected. *"So why do You answer the car prayers and not my prayers about Steve?"*

A thought came into her mind like a silent caption coming across the bottom of the TV screen. *"It's easier to answer car prayers because I didn't give cars free agency."*

The next morning Beverly asked Davey to give the blessing on their breakfast. "I only do car prayers now."

"Oh? Why is that?"

"Because my car prayers work. Nothing ever happens to the food."

"And nothing happens to us when we eat it, now pray. You can't stop praying just because you don't see anything happen."

So Davey continued to give both food and car prayers, and Beverly kept praying for Steve, Monica, Erica and Annalisa and now for DeAnna.

CHAPTER THIRTY-TWO
PLEASE APPROACH THE BENCH

Beverly steered Steve into another department. "I don't need a new dress," she said. "What I really need is a new purse."

"Well, I want to buy you a new dress," said Steve.

"What for?"

"What's wrong with you, Beverly? Doesn't every woman jump at the chance for a new dress?"

"Okay, I'll let you buy me a new dress! I usually only buy a new dress if there is some sort of occasion."

"Well, actually there is an occasion."

"There is?"

"Well, the hearing is coming up and . . ."

"The hearing? Who cares if I have a new dress for that? Is there dancing afterwards?"

"Beverly, be serious. My attorney gave me some guidelines for how I should have you dress."

"He did? I didn't realize that I played so prominently in all of this. You told me that the judge would probably just want to ask me how I feel about the girls and how I get along with them and stuff like that, right? Now your attorney wants to dress me just so?"

"Look Beverly, it's an image thing. If, like you say, you're only going to be talking very briefly, the only other statement you make about who you are is by what you wear, and we need to be sure that we send the right message."

"Well, yes, I guess I can see that."

Steve went to a rack of dresses. He pulled out a conservative navy blue dress with a white lace collar. "What do you think?"

"It's not me."

"It's perfect."

"I say 'it's not me,' and you say 'it's perfect?' I guess that means that I'm not perfect."

"Beverly, you're not cooperating."

"I thought you were going to let me pick."

"You need to make a good impression on the judge. Judge Rhinehart is very conservative."

"Okay, how does this sound? 'Yes, your honor, even though I'm not capable of dressing myself suitably without help, I am sure that I should be the mother of choice for these little girls.'"

"Okay, so you don't like that one. How about this?"

Steve showed her another outfit--a pink two-piece dress."

"Steve, in all the many years you have known me, have you *ever* seen me in a dress like that? Did the attorney specify a little white collar? I hate those things." She grabbed herself around the throat and did a choking noise. "Let's find something with a v-neck."

"No v-necks."

"Are you serious? Did I say I was looking for something with a plunging neckline? I just want to be able to breathe." She pounded an imaginary gavel. "'Would you please approach the bench. You there, in the v-neck, would you approach the bench a little closer?'"

"Beverly, what am I going to do with you?"

"I'll tell you what you're going to do. You're going to take me home, and we are going to pick something for me to wear from my own closet, something that I've chosen to buy that reflects who I am and my taste in clothes. If we can find absolutely nothing in my present wardrobe that's suitable for me to wear in court, then you'll have no choice but to conclude that I, myself, am unsuitable as a potential mother for your girls and as a potential companion for you. I'll put my best foot forward for you, Steve, but I won't be phony. There's a big difference." She paused as they approached the exit from the store. "You wanna buy me a new purse?"

CHAPTER THIRTY-THREE
THE HEARING

Beverly wore a forest green top with a scoop neck and matching mid-calf forest-green pleated skirt, navy blue heels, a navy blue belt and a navy blue and forest green scarf. The judge wore black. Steve was wearing a white shirt and a power tie. DeAnna was wearing a pink and white dress with a little white lace collar.

Steve leaned over to Beverly. "See, she comes in here dressed all conservatively, after she works all week modeling mini-skirts and skimpy bathing suits." Beverly had tried a couple of times to tell Steve of her encounter with DeAnna at World of Fabrics, but she'd finally given up and decided it wouldn't make much difference to him anyway. Surely DeAnna would get a chance to tell her side of the story--whatever it was. Beverly considered herself as one with a neutral stance. She was there only to tell the judge that she would try to be a good stepmother to Erica, Monica and Annalisa. While she didn't agree with what Steve was doing, she would answer the questions she was asked as honestly as she could and do her best to show that she would be a good stepmother. The judge would have to weigh out all the other factors and decide how to arrange things between Steve and DeAnna and the girls.

"See, good thing I didn't let you buy me that pink dress. Don't you think the judges are onto this 'peter-pan-collar' stuff? What if DeAnna and I had come in here looking like clones of each other? Besides, I get the feeling that she probably really does wear dresses like that."

"She used to."

Beverly looked over at DeAnna and caught her eye. DeAnna looked down. Beverly was not sure if DeAnna recognized her or not.

Beverly had never been to a hearing or anything like this before. She listened with amazement as Steve and his lawyer launched a full-scale attack on DeAnna. First mentioned was the initial period of absence and lack of contact with the children. The attorney had several pictures of DeAnna modeling--all in the most revealing outfits--and pointed out the marked contrast in the modest dress she was wearing in court and the outfits in the pictures he had. Without mentioning specifics of any religion, Mr. Abbott successfully intimated that DeAnna had broken religious covenants, not specifying which one's, because to be specific in this case would be to do far less damage than to be vague. When DeAnna's attorney, who was not nearly as impressive as Mr. Robert Abbott, Steve's attorney, presented to the judge the information on DeAnna having quit her modeling job and that she was now working at World of Fabrics, Beverly was silently grateful. It was about time her attorney presented something in her behalf. Not that Beverly was on her side against Steve, but she just didn't believe that DeAnna deserved to be portrayed quite so villainously. As she listened to Steve, and she heard his mellifluous voice as he talked about struggling to keep the family together and trying to care for the needs of his little girls, she realized just what a smooth operator he was, how manipulative he could be. He and Robert Abbott had pounced on every scrap of evidence to portray DeAnna in a negative light, and the judge appeared to be falling for it. Steve's attorney next contended that DeAnna's job at World of Fabrics was a ploy fabricated for the sole purpose of appearing sweet and domestic and needy for the hearing. The judge was nodding his head. Steve was hoping it was true that Judge Rhinehart was as conservative as they had said he was. Those photos of DeAnna had been well worth the trouble taken to obtain them. Beverly then heard Mr. Abbott's description of her--tragically widowed at a young age, a devoted mother of a young son, loving and kind to Steve's daughters, living a life of celibacy, modest and virtuous to the extreme and stalwart in her religious convictions. It was to Beverly as unreal as their portrayal of DeAnna.

"They didn't even mention about my psychology degree that I'm working on. It would seem that might be considered by the judge. Steve would forget to mention that to his attorney. And did he have to say that about celibacy? Does he need to remind me? Does the judge really need to know that? Modest? Well, yes, but I will never and have never worn a peter pan collar. He makes me sound like some saint. Yes, I've coped with widowhood. Yes, I enjoy Davey now, but for many months I just went through the motions. I love the girls, but I don't know anything about raising little girls. I can't sew. I left the car lights on in a dark, nearly-abandoned parking lot, endangering my son. I made out with my dentist. I'm a real person. Couldn't my virtue be implied the same way DeAnna's lack of virtue was implied?" She quieted her thoughts.

Judge Rhinehart asked Beverly to come forward.

"You are engaged to be married to Mr. Winston?"

"Yes, I am."

"State your name for the record."

"Beverly Smithson Crandall."

"Mrs. Crandall, this hearing is to decide custody of the minor children, Monica, Erica, and Annalisa Winston."

"Yes, your honor."

"Will you please tell me about your relationship with the little girls."

"I met them several months ago after Steve and I started dating. They are beautiful little girls. At first I didn't know what to do with them. I have an active little boy, and they are very dainty and clean and sweet, and that took some getting used to. Because we are hoping--I mean planning--to become a family, Steve and I often go on what we call 'family dates' to the park or to a restaurant or a Disney movie. They seem to enjoy Davey, that's my son, and they have learned that they can come to me if they need something or if they hurt themselves, or if they want to talk." Beverly was trying hard to make a good impression. She could hear DeAnna crying softly. Of course she would be. Beverly was convincing the judge that she should be the mother of choice to DeAnna's children. She fought against her feelings of sympathy toward DeAnna. She was not saying anything that was not true. "I believe I love them--that I have the beginnings of those feelings of love that you have for your children, and I believe they have feelings of affection for me. They are excited about having Davey as a brother. They play together well. Sometimes he thinks they are silly and sometimes they don't understand his games, but it's fun for me to watch them play together and learn about each other. Monica is very smart and observant. Erica is very sensitive and sweet. Annalisa is a very loving little girl. She will climb up on my lap and give me a hug, just about every time I sit down. She's a sweetheart. They all are."

Then the judge threw her a curve ball. "Do you believe it's in the best interest of these children for Mr. Steve Winston to be awarded full custody?"

Steve's lawyer interjected. "If I may, your honor, I neglected to mention that Mrs. Crandall is studying at the University of Utah for a degree in psychology, which she has nearly completed."

"Thank you, Mr. Abbott. That does not make her an expert, but I'll allow that she might have additional insights as a result of her studies."

Beverly looked back at Steve. How could he look so cocky? Time after time she had given him her opinion on this subject. Somehow he expected that since they were in court, she would say what would be politically expedient instead of what she believed to be true. She swallowed. Once before Steve had gotten away. She couldn't let him get away again. He was her ticket out of the Single Adult program, of endless bad blind dates, of a fixer-upper house with no one around to fix it up, of celibacy.

She cleared her throat. "I believe that Steve is a good father to his girls, and I'll try my best to be a good stepmother, but I believe that the girls would benefit by having their mother involved in their lives. When Steve and I became engaged, I noticed later that day that Erica was very unhappy. I asked her what was wrong and she told me that she was glad that I was going to be her new mother, but she wanted to know if that meant she was never going to get to see her other mother again." Beverly had started, and the rest of the words flowed out of their own accord. "I believe that since DeAnna left her family, Steve has deliberately kept her from seeing the girls as a punishment for her leaving him, and I believe that he has not always been able to keep the best interests of the girls ahead of his feelings of anger and bitterness at DeAnna. I also believe that, whatever she has done, she loves her children. I was not around when this family fell apart, but I was at World of Fabrics a few weeks ago, and DeAnna waited on me. I didn't know who she was. She didn't know who I was. She helped me with my purchase, and told me proudly about how she had just been put in charge of the store display windows. In one of the display windows were Halloween costumes that she had made for the girls, knowing that she probably would not even get to see them wearing their outfits. At Easter she made dresses for the girls and I think she mailed them. She loves to sew, and she understands about it, and I don't believe this job she has was taken only for the benefit of appearances at this hearing. I believe that she has made mistakes, and I don't know all of the history behind her modeling and her current job, but I'm afraid I don't see her in entirely the same light as she has been portrayed before this court. And, in fact, I'm not quite as wonderful as they said, either. I believe she loves her children and should share in decisions concerning their upbringing. I believe that the children love her and miss her, and I don't believe it would be emotionally healthy for them to have her excluded from their lives." Beverly finished. "If Steve is given full custody, I believe that he will use it to do that as much as possible." She didn't dare turn around and face Steve. She knew that she could not just go back and sit next to him like everything was fine, but she did not expect what she did see when she turned around and met his eyes. She had seen that look--a look of hatred--only when he talked of DeAnna and what she had done. He narrowed his eyes and looked straight at her and right through her. Beverly took a seat several rows back. She didn't think she would ever forget the way Steve had just looked at her. She had done what she thought was right. She could not lie--not even for Steve. Now she would pay the price. She fingered the beautiful engagement ring. He would want it back. She removed it from her finger and clutched it in her hand. He would not forgive her. Steve was not into forgiveness. Would he let her say goodbye to the girls? What would she tell Davey? How would she close this chapter in her life?

Encouraged by Beverly's words in her behalf, DeAnna Matthews Winston told the judge of her mistakes, of her lack of judgment and her realization that she had been manipulated, and of her love for her children. She told of getting out of her modeling career and doing what she had wanted to do in the first place. As the story unraveled, Beverly was astonished. All of this might have been avoided if there had been communication and understanding between Steve and DeAnna about a part-time job at World of Fabrics. Now all that seemed possible was an uneasy truce at best and at worst, a lifetime of misunderstandings, manipulations, anger, bitterness and hate with three beautiful innocent little girls caught in the crossfire.

Beverly waited for Steve outside the courthouse.
"I'll find a way home. Here, I guess . . ." Beverly could not say any more. She reached out her hand and gave him back the engagement ring.
He fixed that same look on her. "Well, I guess we're even now."
"Even?"
"Thanks to you, the judge is probably going to award joint custody. So, you finally got back at me for dumping you in college, causing you to lose your scholarship."
"If that's what you think, Steve, you're further gone than I realized. You know, this may come as a shock to you, but everyone does not live for revenge. We could have been happy together, but you would not choose happiness, even when it was one of the choices. You chose anger and bitterness and hate and revenge." Beverly saw DeAnna coming out of the courthouse. "Talk to her, Steve. Try for once to understand and not to judge. Think about the girls. If you can't do it for yourself or for DeAnna, please do it for the girls."

Beverly felt much like she had in the first days after Dave's death, like she was just going through the motions of life. She hadn't even told anyone about the break-up. *"I just can't go through it all--the questions, the pity, the judgments. All this just when Thanksgiving is coming, so I can have double the reasons to crash. I guess it's time to plan our yearly escape trip. Other kids will have normal memories of Thanksgiving. My son will wonder what's going on, the first time he has a traditional Thanksgiving."* She lay down on the sofa and put a pillow over her head. *"What do I tell Davey? 'Remember the guy that I told you was going to be your new dad, well he never wants to see my face again.' This is exactly what I was afraid would happen. I'm messing up my son, and the girls--they will think I disappeared without a second glance, just like they believe their mother did. What a mess! And I can't think of anything I can do to make it better."*

Davey came into the room, carrying the latest creation he had built with his Lego blocks, setting it on the end table. He lifted up the pillow. "Mom, are you in there?"

"Davey, what are you doing?" she asked, awakening to the feeling of her son lifting up one of her eyelids..

"I'm just checking to see if your eyeballs are home."

"Gotta write that one down." She sat up. "Yes, they were still there last time I checked." He held up his creation. "Hey, that's pretty good." She switched gears. "So Davey, how would you like a trip to Disney World in Florida this year for Thanksgiving?"

CHAPTER THIRTY-FOUR
ANGEL MORONI PLAYS THE TRUMPET

Davey had been in kindergarten now for several months and seemed to be doing very well. He went for half a day in the afternoon. Beverly was taking afternoon classes at the University of Utah and trying not to think about Steve. She hung Davey's latest piece of artwork on the pantry door. The refrigerator door was already full.

"You're a really good artist, Davey."

"Miss Klingler lets me color when I'm done with my work."

Beverly fed him dinner, bathed him and put him to bed. When she headed off to her bedroom, she stopped and went into his room and looked at him sleeping there peacefully. *"I can't believe he's already in school."* She reflected back to his first day of kindergarten. She had approached it with mixed feelings. On the one hand, she'd had all the traditional feelings of a mother sending her first (and possibly last) child off to school--that he was no longer completely hers, that he was growing up. On the other hand, she had reflected on the fact that she would not be spending her days with Davey and the cast and crew of Sesame Street and could increase her hours at school herself. Besides, Davey had marched into the school room without so much as a backward glance, leaving Mom standing there, alone and forlorn. She had realized, again with mixed feelings, that she was disposable, so she had gone home and left him to the task at hand. She brushed the hair back from his forehead and gave him a quick kiss. "Goodnight, Davey. I love you."

Every day Davey came home with tales of new friends and pictures of his favorite Kindergarten characters--the "letter people." There was Mr. B., who was made of Bunches of Balloons, and Mrs. H. with the Horrible Hair. And thus, Beverly thought he was getting along just fine, until she got a call from Dr. Horowitz, the school psychologist for the district. Beverly silently noted, as she sat across from his desk in the office he was using that day, that Dr. Horowitz had Horrible Hair. Totally bald on top, he had compensated by letting the remaining fringe grow untamed, curly and bushy. He produced a crayon picture drawn by Davey. It was a picture of a mother, a father and a little boy.

"I understand, Mrs. Crandall, that Davey's father is, uh . . ." He searched for the right word. ". . . deceased."

"Yes, that's right," said Beverly.

"We are concerned because the children were supposed to draw a picture of their families, and Davey included his father in this picture."

Beverly studied the picture. "It's obvious to me that Davey was copying a family picture we have at home that has his father in it," said Beverly, sure that the explanation should take care of the psychologist's concerns.

"We are concerned that Davey know the difference between fantasy and reality."

"Dr. Horowitz, Davey brings home pictures of alphabet people made of Fancy Footballs and Peculiar Pancakes, and I don't run down here worried about him understanding the difference between fantasy and reality. If you're suggesting that Davey does not understand that his father is dead, I can assure you that he does. I don't see the harm in him drawing pictures of his father. I have told him stories about his father, and Dave is a real person to Davey, but I'll talk with him about this if it makes you feel better."

That evening Beverly sat with her little boy, and they discussed his picture of the family. "Davey, the people at school liked your picture of our family. They called me in to see it. It looks a lot like the one we have hanging on the wall. Is that what you were thinking about when you drew it?"

"Yup. Did I do good coloring?"

"You did great coloring! I think you're a very good artist." Beverly switched gears. "Let's talk about your daddy for a minute. You don't really remember him, do you? You know that you were just a little baby when he died."

"That's why I had to draw him from the picture instead of my 'remembery.' But Mom, how did he die? I know it was a accident, but you never told me how it happened."

Beverly had known that someday he would ask for more details. She had decided that when he asked would be the best time to tell him, but now that the time had come, she fumbled for the right words. She sent a quiet prayer heavenward to help her with the explanation. "There was a bad snowstorm, and your dad and his paramedics were helping to work on an accident. Somebody else's car went out of control on the road and it hit your dad. He was hurt very badly. They took him to the hospital and tried to help him get better, but sometimes when people are hurt really bad and the doctors can't make them better, Heavenly Father takes them to Heaven and makes them better there." It seemed to satisfy him, and Beverly felt good about it, too. He went on to another question.

"Mom, are there fun things to do in Heaven?"

"I'm sure there must be."

"What do you think my dad is doing?"

"I don't really know, honey. I know that your dad liked music and I know that there's music in Heaven."

Then Davey asked her about the picture, revealing that he was more aware of what was going on than Beverly realized. "Why didn't the teacher like my picture?"

"Who said she didn't like it?"

"She didn't hang it on the wall like she did with the other kids' pictures. She looked at it for a long time, and then she took it to the principal's office--where you go when you're in trouble."

"Your teacher didn't understand why you drew a picture of your dad in the picture since he's dead."

"Okay. I'll draw another one."

Two weeks later, Beverly was called back for another conference with Dr. Horowitz. This time he had on his desk a picture of a mother and son with a large angel flying overhead. The angel had a moustache and was playing a saxophone. Beverly was admiring how well Davey had drawn the saxophone. Dr. Horowitz furrowed his brow. He started by insinuating that all was not well.

"Mrs. Crandall, are there any men in your life?"

"What?"

"I mean, does Davey have any male role models in his life?"

"He has four uncles and two grandfathers."

"Davey is named after his father, isn't he?"

"Yes."

"He must feel that he has a lot to live up to."

"Perhaps, Dr. Horowitz, if we had known Dave was going to die, we might have named him Bob or Jim."

Dave stood nearby. *"Or Elvis Englebert."*

A thought occurred to her. *"Or Elvis Englebert."* She smiled. *"Where did that come from? I'd forgotten all about that."* She continued. "What do you suggest I do about that--from a psychological point of view--change his name?"

"There's no need to get defensive, Mrs. Crandall. We are somewhat concerned that Davey is--well, his teacher says that when the other little boys talk about their fathers, Davey talks about his father, too, sometimes in the present tense."

Dave beamed. *"Way to go, Davey!"*

"I assure you that Davey knows his father is dead. Did it ever occur to you that a little five-year-old boy does not fully understand past and present tense? Why are you so uncomfortable with him identifying with his father in ways that normal little boys do?"

"You tell him, Bev!"

"Because his father has--passed on. Do you talk about Mr. Crandall at home?"

"You bet she does. She's crazy about me."

"Of course I do. I've told Davey stories about his dad. I've shown him pictures. Why can't anybody understand? Davey was only a baby when his father died. I've tried to create a memory of his father for him. Is that so emotionally unhealthy? Have you spent any time with him? From where I sit, Davey has a much healthier attitude about life and death than you do!"

Dr. Horowitz bent his balding head over the kindergarten drawing. "Perhaps I *should* call him in."

"Do you mind if I go to his class and get him?" Beverly asked. "It's kind of scary for a child in Kindergarten to think he's being sent to the office. While I'm there, you *might* take note of his obvious artistic talent. Look at that saxaphone!"

Beverly returned with Davey. Dave waved from the doorway. *"Gotta go. I'm AWOL again."* They sat down and Dr. Horowitz began. "Tell me about this picture, Davey."

"Well, that's Mom and that's me and that's my dad. He's a angel. He died in a accident. He was helping fix a accident and then another car was going too fast. It swerved like this." He started making car noises and moving his hand around the table in illustration. "It started sliding in the snow and then it hit my dad." He crashed his car-hand into Dr. Horowitz's stack of books on the desk and made explosive car crash noises. "The car drove away but my dad was totalled," he said, matter-of-factly."

"Davey!" Beverly was chagrined. "That's not how I explained it to you!" *"I didn't even know he knew a word like 'totalled.'"* Davey was in school now, and under the influence of other little boys and Saturday morning cartoons, he had decided to make the explanation more interesting. Oh, for the days of Big Bird and Cookie Monster! Dr. Horowitz was taking copious notes.

Davey, unaware that he had just "totalled" his mother, answered the rest of Dr. Horowitz's questions.

"Tell me about this." He pointed to the saxophone.

"That's what instrument he plays."

"In Heaven or did he play it on earth?"

"Both. He played it on earth, and he didn't want to have to take lessons on some other instrument in Heaven, so he plays it there, too."

"Don't angels usually play harps," suggested Dr. Horowitz.

"Angel Moroni plays the trumpet," said Davey, in defense of his father's saxophone. Sensing that Dr. Horowitz was curious about their family situation, he continued. "I was engaged for a while to get a new dad, but my mom told the judge something about how Steve needed to learn to share the kids and then he didn't like her anymore." Beverly put her head in her hands. Davey continued. "He had an ex-wife and three ex-kids."

"Okay, Davey, you can go back to class now. I just need to talk to your mother a little more."

Beverly had recovered somewhat from Davey's explanation of the accident. She stood up.

"I know that you're concerned about Davey, and I know that explanation was dramatic and . . ." Beverly groped for the right words. "If Davey was not comfortable with the fact this his father is dead, he could not have told you about the accident and the saxophone equally as matter-of-factly. He has an imagination, just like most kids his age, but if you sort things out, I think you'll find that Davey is about as well-adjusted as any other five-year-old. I'm sorry if I lost my temper, but this is a sensitive subject to me."

"Let's talk about his relationship to his uncles and the grandfathers."

"I assure you, Dr. Horowitz, that there are men in Davey's life. He has floated his rubber duckie in his grandfather's bath water, so he could see that he was like other males. He has boy cousins that he plays with and there's a young fellow from our neighborhood who helped him build a tree house in our backyard. I don't see why his own father--or the memory of him--can't be one of the men in his life--even if it means that he draws pictures of angels playing unusual musical instruments. If he keeps getting called to the office every time he draws a picture, he's going to start wondering what's wrong with him. Then we (she used the term 'we' generously) will be creating a problem where none exists in the first place. The only thing that's 'wrong' with Davey is that he has a good imagination."

"Perhaps you're right," he admitted.

Beverly left the office, at least satisfied that a compromise had been reached. She was glad Davey hadn't told Dr. Horowitz about going into warp speed to get out of the way of a car or about the deliberate demise of the eggs in the road, not to mention the old man who was going to jump over their car. But it was not long before Beverly got another call.

"Mrs. Crandall, Dr. Horowitz would like to see you . . ."

CHAPTER THIRTY-FIVE
HOW FAR TO HEAVEN?

Davey pulled on his favorite pants and shirt. "No school today, Bud. It's a holiday. Do you know what Memorial Day is?"

"Is that the day you said we would go to the 'remembering place?'"

"Yes, go get in the car. We need to get some flowers for Daddy. What kind do you want? Do you have a favorite color?"

"I want to get him a balloon."

Beverly pulled into the parking lot and went into the little florist shop to pick up the flowers she had ordered. She was greeted by a sales clerk.

"Hello. I'm Virginia. May I help you?"

"Yes, I'm here to pick up some flowers. The name is Crandall."

Virginia reached behind her into the refrigerated case. "Here they are." She put the arrangement on the counter.

Beverly looked it over. "I'm sorry to be a bother, but I didn't order a vase. They are going to the cemetery. Maybe I forgot to make that clear."

"Not a problem. I'll just take them out and wrap them in some paper. Or I can put them in one of our disposable vases."

"That would be good. Yes, let's do that."

While Virginia transferred the flowers, Beverly picked up a heart-shaped mylar balloon on a stick that they could stick in the ground at the cemetery and showed it to Davey.

"Do you like this one?"

"No."

"How about this one?"

"No."

"Tweety Bird?"

"No."

"A good-luck clover?"

"No."

"A yellow smiley face?"

"No."

"All right. I'm just going to pick you up, and you reach the one you want, okay? We can't take all day trying to pick a balloon." Beverly was getting impatient. Davey started to cry.

"They don't have the right kind."

"Oh, for Heaven's sake, Davey, they must have twenty-five different designs here. I'll let you get whichever one you want--Happy Golden Wedding, Porky Pig-- just choose one."

"But it's not the right kind!"

"Well then, what kind do you want?"

"You know, the kind they fill up at Chuck E. Cheese and when you let go of the string, it goes to Heaven."

"Oh honey, I'm sorry I didn't understand." Beverly's impatience vanished. "Excuse me. It's Virginia, right? Could you fill us up two helium balloons please-- to go."

"We're sending them to my dad in Heaven," Davey proudly announced. Beverly looked away, careful not to meet the saleslady's eyes, not wanting to show her emotions. Virginia rang up the flowers. "No charge for the balloons."

"Thank you," Beverly said, this time meeting Virginia's eyes, despite the emotions showing in her own. "That's very nice of you." She saw the same emotions mirrored back.

"Don't mention it. I might send a balloon or two off to Heaven myself later today. I lost both my parents last year. Thanks for the idea."

"Oh, I'm sorry. Was it an accident?"

"No, Dad just couldn't go on without Mom. His health wasn't good and after Mom died, I guess he had more pulling him to the other side than there was to keep him here."

"That must have been a rough year."

"Yes, it was. It's still rough. I didn't know I would miss them so much. Every event that comes and goes reminds me that they are gone."

"I've decided that what grieving people need is a calendar with no holidays on it. Special events and holidays are the hardest, aren't they?"

"They were both so good at being supportive of my children, their activities and achievements. And my youngest won't even remember her grandparents."

"Better than not being able to remember your father." Beverly kept that thought to herself, realizing that this was not a time to one-up the grieving sales clerk. *"She just needs someone to listen, just like I needed people to listen. It's not much, but it's something I can do."*

"I'm thankful we had them spend last Christmas with us. At least we got some good pictures of them with all the children, so they'll have those to remember Grandma and Grandpa by." She wiped off the counter as she spoke. "I'm sorry. What am I doing, spilling my guts to a perfect stranger?"

"I don't mind," Beverly answered. *"Funny she didn't ask me about my loss, after what Davey said about taking the balloons to his dad. I was probably like that, too, right after losing Dave. I don't recall being aware of anyone's pain but my own. I was like an injured soldier on the battlefield crying out for painkiller. Now that my wounds have been tended to, I can look around and see that I'm surrounded by fields of other wounded people. Maybe now I can tend to someone besides myself."*

Virginia wiped her eyes. "You're sure I'm not holding you up?"

Beverly held up the flowers. "I've got a delivery to make, but he's not going anywhere." Beverly felt a tug on her pantleg.

"Mom, let's go! How come you have to talk so much?"

"Just a minute, Davey." She got down on his level. "This lady's mother and father both died last year and that's what we are talking about. We'll go soon."

"Are they gonna make you go live in the orphanage?" Davey questioned her.

Virginia laughed. "No, I think I'm safe from that." She spoke to Beverly. "Thanks. You've brightened my day. And your son made me laugh. I needed that. Thank you for listening."

"It gets easier. Someday the grief will lessen and the good memories will shine through."

"I hope so." Virginia came around to the other side of the counter. She reached out her arms and gave Beverly a hug. "Thanks again."

"Good luck. I hope you have a nice Memorial Day."

"You, too."

Beverly pulled the vase out of the ground at the base of the headstone. She arranged the flowers and poured in the water from the jar she had brought with her. She brushed off the stone and traced out his name with her finger. Nearby a little boy stood with two big balloons. "Davey, bring the balloons over here. We need to find an open space so they don't get caught in the tree branches. See, right over there is a good spot. I'll take the red one and you take the blue one." They walked across the road to the spot Beverly had pointed to. "Okay Davey, tell me when."

"Ready, set, go." They let go of the strings and watched as the two balloons rose heavenward. "Mom, how far to Heaven?"

"Too far, Davey, way too far. I think that when you can't see the balloons anymore, you know they made it to Heaven." They stood and watched as the balloons got smaller and smaller until they became little dots and faded from sight.

"There you go, Heavenly Father," said Davey.

"What did you call him?"

"Heavenly Father. That's what everybody calls him." Beverly hit herself in the forehead with the heal of her hand.

"Why didn't I see this one coming?" She took his hand and they walked back to Dave's grave. She sat down with Davey on her lap. "Davey, sometimes I try to explain things to you, and I don't do such a good job. Other things I guess I never have thought I needed to explain to you. Heavenly Father is who we pray to. He's Jesus's Father and the Father of all our spirits. He is God. Dave is your father in Heaven, because he was your father on earth and now he's in Heaven, but he's not the one they are talking about in church. He's not the one we pray to."

"It wasn't him who made our car start?"

"No, but I like to think he looks down on us sometimes to make sure we are okay, and maybe he's allowed to help us sometimes, but let's call him your 'dad in Heaven' so we don't get him confused with your Father in Heaven, okay?"

"Okay. Is this where my dad is buried?"

"Yes. I always called it 'the remembering place,' because I thought you were too little to understand about people being buried."

"Well, I know now, because I watched Ben bury a dead bird that he found. But Mom, when I die, make sure they bury me with my head above ground because I want to still be able to see what's going on."

Beverly laughed. "Davey, if all these people were buried with their heads above ground, I don't think I would come here very often." She rearranged the flowers again. "Is there anything else you'd like to know about death and dying while we are on the subject?"

"I think I know everything now. I hope my dad looked better than that bird Ben found."

"Davey! How do you come up with these things? The next thing I know, I'll be called in to Dr. Horowitz's office and there will be a picture of a cemetery with all the heads above ground."

"Hey, Mom, did you know that Dr. Horowitz is a not-married man? My teacher told us because her name is Mrs. Klingler and she said don't call her Miss Klingler because that's what you call a not-married lady. She said that men are always called 'Mister' if they are married or not married, like Mr. Stewart our principal is married, and Dr. Horowitz is Mister, too, but he's not married."

"Davey, I don't need your help finding me a husband."

"Well, you're not doing very good on your own."

"I'm doing just fine, thank you very much."

"I think Dr. Horowitz likes me to draw pictures so that he can talk to you. He thinks you're pretty."

"How would you know that?"

"Because he looks at you a lot."

Three days later, Dr. Horowitz called up Mrs. Crandall. In front of him was a picture--sort of a cross between an angel and a clown--an angel holding a bunch of balloons. Beverly delayed her appointment with him for a few days.

When Davey came home, he was in the hot seat. "Davey, did you draw a picture on purpose so that I would have to have a meeting with Dr. Horowitz?"

"Did you like it? It was a picture of my dad in Heaven with the balloons we sent him."

"I haven't seen it yet. And you didn't answer my question. Did you draw a picture on purpose so that I would have to have a meeting with Dr. Horowitz?"

He looked down. "I want a dad."

"I know you want a dad, Davey, but let's not get desperate." She pulled a photo album out of the bookcase. "Do you see this picture from my wedding to your dad? See how we are kissing in this picture and how we are looking at each other in this one? Someday I'll probably meet another man that I have those same kind of feelings for and then he will be your new dad, but getting you a dad is not like getting you a bike or a wagon. We can't just get any old one."

"I wouldn't want just any old bike, either, Mom."

"Okay, so you understand a little bit. I can't just go looking for a dad for you. I have to look for a husband for me. We have to look together, but I get first choice."

"That's not fair."

"It's more than fair, trust me. And it might take a long time. But hey, you have a mom that likes to do boy stuff, and you have two grandpas and some uncles that love you very much and that's just going to have to be good enough right now."

"Well, Mom," he said, resignedly, "if you're not going to get me a dad right away, how about a dog, at least?"

CHAPTER THIRTY-SIX
RUNNING THE GAUNTLET

Beverly was glad they had asked her to substitute in Primary. She could hide out without having to talk to anybody. It was old news that Beverly had given her engagement ring back to Steve, but only a couple of her close friends really understood why. The rest only knew what they saw. Beverly wondered how long it would take before people quit asking her about it. She'd already run the gauntlet through the foyer after church the previous Sunday. She remembered back.

"Beverly, whatever happened to that nice young man you used to bring to church?"

"Things just didn't work out."

"Now, Beverly, if that good-looking fellow wasn't good enough, who will be? You can't compare everyone to Dave."

Inside Beverly had fumed. *"I didn't compare him to Dave! Do you want me to list off Dave's five worst faults? I remember them, okay? I don't think he was perfect, but I do miss him, if that's all right with you. I don't go around holding Dave up as the gold standard by which I judge other men. You don't understand! You don't know! I don't want to have to explain every little thing to everyone."* Instead she had said politely, "There were a lot of things we both had to deal with. Things just didn't work out." She knew that most people inquired out of concern-- with, of course, the exception of Sister Cooper and her sidekick, Sister McAffee-- but it was still hard to explain. Sometimes she just wanted to stand up on a pew and tell everyone to mind their own business, to let it go. Beverly was sort of a cross between her mother--the gentle, understanding Naomi--and her outspoken Aunt Marlene. As a result, she had a habit of being gentle and kind until she'd reached her limit and then she spoke her mind.

Brother Higginbotham had insinuated that if she didn't marry again soon, Davey might have serious gender identification problems when he got older. She had pointed to her little boy, who had been twirling around and around the flagpole with his shirttail untucked and his shoes untied. "He looks to me like he knows he's a boy!"

She gathered her things and went in search of the Primary President to return the lesson manual. She was not having any luck finding a member of the Primary presidency. She headed down the hall to check the Primary room again. What she did find instead was Brother Higginbotham--again. She walked past him, but he followed her into the Primary room, which was empty.

"Since you're not engaged anymore, Beverly, there's this real sharp fellow I work with and I'd like to introduce . . ."

"No more blind dates, Brother Higginbotham. Not from you. Not from anybody."

"Well, then I hope you're going to be involved in the singles' program. I know it seems that sometimes there are not always a lot of people there that you would want to get involved with, but all it takes is one person to make a difference. If you would start going to those functions, then soon some sharp guy would say 'now there's a sharp gal,' and he would start attending, and then some other sharp gals would see him and they would say, 'now there's a sharp guy' and they would start attending. Soon there would be a whole bunch of sharp guys and sharp gals in the singles' program, and they could all marry each other, and then it could start all over."

"I lose more shoes this way." Beverly took off her black heels and handed them to Brother Higginbotham. "What do you know about starting over, Brother Higginbotham? Come see me when you've walked in my shoes."

Beverly walked out through the cultural hall in her stocking feet and out into the parking lot. Parked next to her car was a familiar maroon van. Toni Leigh was closing the door after she had loaded the last of her children. She turned and saw Beverly.

"I ran into Steve yesterday. I can't believe what you did to him, Beverly! What were you thinking? Do you think another catch like Steve Winston is ever going to come along? He's rich. He's handsome. He would have done anything for you, and in return, you stabbed him in the back. I told him that in the future if he ever needed a character witness, I would be glad to stand up for him and . . .'"

Beverly felt tears stinging her eyes. "Davey, get in the car."

"Look Toni, you, and everybody else, only know what you see. Only Steve and I know the ins and outs of our relationship, and obviously, he wasted no time filling everybody in on things from his point of view. You can borrow my shoes when Brother Higginbotham gets through with them."

"What?" Toni Leigh looked down and saw that Beverly was standing there in her nylons--shoeless.

"Really, Beverly," she chided. "That's not very ladylike."

"And I know how to pump gas and mow the lawn, too, and I don't faint when I break a fingernail!" With that, she got in her car and drove off. *What do they know, any of them? If they knew what a hard choice I had to make, maybe they would be patting me on the back for doing what I thought was right and putting aside my own feelings of what I wanted and doing what I thought was best for the girls. Do they think it was easy letting Steve go and having to spend the rest of my life going on blind dates--seeing what Brother Higginbotham's got hiding behind 'door number three?'"*

A quieting communication came to her. *"God does not judge by the outcome of a relationship but by your actions while you're in it."*

"That makes sense. I need to tell Jean that. There's not just a great big black mark if your marriage didn't work. Heavenly Father knows how hard you tried or did not try and what your actions were during the relationship and after, for that matter, and judges accordingly, not just that it didn't work. That's fair. Heavenly Father is fair."

CHAPTER THIRTY-SEVEN
CLOSING A CHAPTER

"Kelly, how do I know when I've *really* reached acceptance of Dave's death? I felt like I was doing so well, but then I had to go through this whole loss thing again with Steve and the girls. I never got to say goodbye to them. In many ways it was the same as getting the news about Dave's accident. I didn't know when I went into court that day that that would be the end of it all. When the anger and the pain surfaces, I sometimes feel like I've slid back down the mountain about three miles." Beverly went on. "I let the girls down. I don't know what Steve has told them about why I'm not around anymore. If past performance is any indication, it was not good. I let my son down. First I told him he was going to have a new dad, then I had to try to explain why the deal is off."

"Beverly, what I hear is that you have been trying to take care of everyone else. You worry about your son, you worry about Steve, about his girls, even about his ex-wife. What I want you to tell me is how *you* are."

"Well, okay, the stress of all this is getting to me."

"Last night out without Davey?"

"A couple of weeks ago, I think."

"Last physical check-up?"

"I'm fine."

"It's part of caring for yourself."

"I said I feel fine."

"You haven't had one lately, have you?" Kelly continued. "Last vacation?"

"Thanksgiving, as usual."

"Bought yourself a new outfit?"

"I bought a new purse."

"Beverly, this is the place where you can stop being strong. You can be vulnerable here. This is supposed to be help for you. Today we're not going to fix Steve or his family. That's his job. We're not going to talk about whether or not your son is okay with all this. He'll likely recover sooner and better than you will."

"Okay, I haven't been sleeping that well. Sometimes I wake up with headaches and realize I've been clenching my teeth most of the night, not a great relaxation technique. I'm all messed up. I don't know whether to miss Dave or Steve now. I'm tired of being alone." Beverly began to cry. "I don't want to have to start all over again. I know there were problems with Steve, but I knew what I had. Right now, it feels like I'll be alone the rest of my life. And I don't know if I'll ever stop being angry. I can mask it for everybody, but it's there. I'll probably end up being a lonely bitter old crone."

"What's behind the anger? What else is there that you can't express as easily?"

"Pain. That giant heartache that I thought was going away and now it's back."

"Why do you think that is?"

"That's easy. If I'm angry, I'm not vulnerable."

"Beverly, this is a place where you can be vulnerable. Let your pain talk to me for a few minutes. Close your eyes. Let go of your defenses. You don't need them right now. You're in a place where it's safe to share your pain."

Beverly sat quietly for a few moments and then she began to speak, barely audible. "Dave's gone. He's never coming back. He'll never be there to push his son in a swing or take him fishing or watch him grow up. He'll never see him go on a mission or get married. He'll never hold our grandchildren. He'll never come back for an evening and watch television or fix the lawn mower or make love to me. He's not coming back. I believe I'll see him again and be with him again, but I have to live the rest of my life without him. Steve's gone now, too. My future is back to being full of the unknown."

"Everyone's future is full of the unknown, Beverly, in some way."

"Yes, but they can take comfort in the future they *think* they have. I tried to start over, just like everybody told me to do, and what did I get from that but more heartache? I don't know if I can keep going."

"I think you're doing better than you give yourself credit for. Look at what you've already survived. This is hard, but it's not harder than losing Dave was."

"But I feel like I'm dealing with losing Steve on top of losing Dave."

"Then don't deal with them together. Try just to deal with the recent loss."

"I'm so tired of being sent back to 'square one.'"

"You're not at 'square one.' Everything you've been through and dealt with has not gone away. It has all brought you to where you are now, given you wisdom and experience and strength. You're at square 5,674. You may take a few moves backwards from time to time, but the experience you've gained and the things you've accomplished are still with you. You're experiencing some depression right now, which is very normal given the recent events of your life. Try measuring your life by majority rules. Are you up more than you're down? Are you happy more than you're sad? Are you positive and hopeful more often than you're negative and pessimistic? That way you don't beat yourself up for the negative emotions. Let's face it. They are there for everybody to some degree or another. You didn't get any closure in your relationship with Steve. Your last words to each other were unpleasant. You didn't get to see the girls."

Beverly sighed. "You know the more we use that word, the less I know what it means. I used to think closure meant the end of the pain, but my grand-mother had tender feelings about a child she lost until she died at 83. We all knew about Uncle Henry. Now I'm more inclined to think of what we call closure as a beginning, like the point of accepting a loss and beginning to deal with it. Parents who've had a child abducted talk about getting closure when they find out what happened to their child. We put a nice definitive word like "closure" on it like finding out that their child was brutally murdered and buried off somewhere in the woods is the end of their pain. It may be the end of their not knowing. It may be the end of their searching, but in truth, the losses we suffer become part of who we are and in some way, they are always with us."

"So do you think there's anything you can do to help you start to deal with the loss of your relationship with Steve and the girls?"

"Yes. I realize now that I need to see them, or at least try to see them."

Kelly got up and went to her filing cabinet. "Remember that study I told you I was going to do on the importance of the funeral and viewing as closure. Sorry. Nobody's come up with any better word. I'll let you know when they do. Anyway, I'm still working on it. I'm studying people who were actually able to have a viewing and some sort of a goodbye versus people who had a closed casket or missing or unidentifiable loved one and the way they handled grief from there. I'll give you a finished copy of it when it's done. I appreciate the input you gave me from your own situation. I don't have as many people participating as I would like, because it's hard to find them. I can't just start reading the obituaries. I have to wait for people to tell me about someone they know."

"Did you ever contact Dr. Evans?"

"No, I didn't. You know how I mentioned that these are supervised sessions, that a licensed counselor reviews my notes and tapes? Well, he told me that having a client refer people to me for my research creates a dual relationship with that client. For example, if I contacted Dr. Evans, he might inquire as to how I know you and my disclosing our counseling relationship would be a breach of confidence. I'm able to use the examples you have shared with me from your own life, though, and that has been a big help. Basically, I must maintain a certain professional distance and my counseling relationship with you precludes me involving you in referring people to me for my research. Likewise, it would be inappropriate for me to hire you to housesit or to offer to line you up with my single brother. I apologize for not already realizing that, but I'm still in my learning curve."

"I guess that's understandable. That makes two of us who have learned something new. So are you making progress on the research?"

"I do have a fair amount of people who are participating in the study. I find that people who have a terminally-ill loved one actually start the grieving process before the person dies. It's a very interesting subject. People don't know enough about how to grieve and the purpose it plays."

Beverly responded, "What gets me is when they refer to being there in your *'hour of need.'* Hey, if it only lasted an hour, I could deal with it. It's been nearly five years since Dave died, and I guess this is as good as it gets. I can usually talk about it matter-of-factly. I feel like I could probably handle a new relationship, if another one should come along, but I don't feel the need to find somebody to make the pain go away. I guess I'm doing okay. I've got some goals for the future. I've just about got my degree. So how do I tie up the loose ends with Steve? I didn't know how to explain that to Davey, either. There are a lot of things I don't know how to explain to Davey, but I can count on however I explain something to him, he makes it more interesting for the next person he tells. But back to Steve, there I was all through our relationship telling him to deal with things, and yet I'm not really sure I'm over losing Dave, either."

"There will always be ways that losing Dave will affect your life. Twenty years from now that same song on the radio may still bring a tear to your eye, Beverly. To take the pain out of death is to take the love out of life. There's never a time that you can say you are 'over' it in terms of it not affecting your life. You're dealing with it, facing it, as best you can."

"I've faced everything but the Thanksgiving turkey. I might have made it last year when Steve and I were planning to get married, but when we broke up, I went even further than usual. Florida is beautiful that time of year. Disney World and Epcot were great fun."

"Some things are like monsters under the bed. You know that when you turn on the light, they won't be there, but you have that few feet you have to go across the floor in the darkness to get to the light switch, so you stay in bed, afraid of the monsters. You have to turn on the light to make them go away. Do you remember what you told me about your friend from church that told you that the longer you waited to go home, the harder it would be? You went right home. You faced that. It was hard, but every time you came and went it became a little easier, because every time you face something that's hard to face, you take away a little of its power to cause you pain. Thanksgiving you didn't face, and now, by avoiding it every year, you have built it up into a great big monster that you're sure is going to bite your foot off if you get out of bed and run for the light switch. That monster is following you, and you just need to turn around and go 'bleeah' in its face and scare it right back. Nobody else can make it go away. A turkey can't hurt you. It can just make you remember. Maybe you need to sit down and remember when there's no turkey involved. Disassociate the turkey from the event. Take away it's power to cause you pain. Cook a turkey every week for three months if you have to, and if you can afford to. If you had gone to be with Steve's family for Thanksgiving, it might have been a perfect setting--all those distractions of new people to meet and talk to would have taken your mind off things. The setting would have been unfamiliar. You might have done just fine."

"Well, I *was* going to go until he got mad at me."

"Anger is often people's pain talking. It's hard, however, to be sympathetic to pain when it comes in the form of anger. We usually respond with more anger."

"I'll try to remember that. It's true. Anger *is* often pain in disguise."

"You'll land on your feet, Beverly. I know you will."

"Yeah, like a cat always lands on its feet, right? Sometimes I feel like a couple of punk kids dropped the cat out the third floor window and she landed on her feet, so then they go back down and say, 'Okay, let's try the tenth floor, this time.' The poor cat is going 'Meeowwwr' for nine stories to get into position." Beverly did her best imitation of a falling cat, flailing her arms around, clawing the air.

Kelly laughed. "Keep your sense of humor, and you'll get through."

"I guess when I lose that it will be time to bury *me*--head above ground, of course, so I can see what's going on."

"That's another thing that will get you through--your little boy. You've got to bring in some of those drawings you've been telling me about."

"Well, I do need a second opinion, to see if my child is 'deeply troubled' like Dr. Horowitz seems to think."

Beverly followed through on her decision to call Steve. The conversation was awkward at first. "Steve, I don't expect you not to still be mad at me, but I was wondering if maybe I could see the girls, take them to the park, talk to them. They need to know that I didn't just disappear off the face of the earth, especially after what happened with DeAnna leaving the way she did."

To her surprise, he was agreeable. "How about if we meet you at Sugarhouse Park by the pond at noon on Saturday?"

"Okay, I'll pack a picnic." Beverly hung up the phone. *"We?"* He was coming, too?

"Davey, we're going to the park to see Monica, Erica and Annalisa. Get your shoes on."

"Can Scampy come?"

"Yes, you can bring the dog."

She opened up the picnic basket and put the chocolate chip cookies inside. *"What was Steve going to say? How was he going to be?"* As she packed the sandwiches into the picnic basket, she imagined the scenario. The little girls would run to her and hug her around the legs. She would look down into their smiling faces. Davey would run to them from the swings carrying his new puppy and they would gather around him. Steve would be watching from afar, but slowly he would be drawn into the family circle. He would come to her with declarations of love.

"You helped me see the error of my ways. I hope you don't mind but I invited DeAnna to join us on this picnic today so that she would be able to see the girls and so that they would be able to see that I have no hard feelings and that we can all be one big happy family."

"I knew there was a reason I felt inspired to make an extra ham and cheese sandwich, Steve."

The phone rang and interrupted Beverly's daydream, right before the photographer from the church could get there to take their picture for a Family Home Evening Manual cover.

"Hello, Beverly." It was Dr. Evans.

"David, how are you? Hey, we were just on the way out. We're meeting Steve and his girls for a picnic in the park. Can I call you back later?"

"Oh, sure." His voice went flat. "I thought Jean said you had, you were . . . Never mind. I have tickets to the symphony tonight, and I thought of you. I know it's short notice, and you have plans and I'm holding you up. Goodbye."

She stood there for a moment with the phone in her hand. *"He sounded down. I'll have to call him back later and see if I can cheer him up."*

She loaded the boy, the puppy, the food and the Frisbee into the car and drove to the park. Steve was already there. She spotted the girls over at the playground. Davey and Scampy ran over to them. Beverly began to unfold the blanket and set out the food. Steve came over. "Need some help?"

She looked at him--tall, good-looking with that thick dark hair and those gorgeous blue eyes. She remembered back to when they had first met in their Family Home Evening group in college. So much time and so much history had transpired since then. "Sure. You can get out the paper plates and the sand-wiches." He sat down on the blanket but didn't move to get anything out of the picnic basket. Instead he reached into his pocket and pulled out her engagement ring. She caught her breath. He had come back! He still wanted to marry her! She was elated.

"Beverly, I want you to have this back. I've had a lot of time to think, and I can't let you get away twice in a lifetime. I was really mad at you, but you did what you thought you had to do. The judge scheduled another hearing, and he talked privately to the kids, wouldn't allow either of us to be there while he talked to them. He awarded joint custody, but the girls are living with me. He came down on me pretty hard, on both of us, actually."

"What did he say?"

"You remember how my attorney presented things about the girls having stability, being in the same school, to persuade him to let them stay with me?"

"Well, he told me that he was an army brat, that he had changed schools so often he had lost track of how many times, that he didn't want to hear me talking about giving the girls stability by not having them change schools or friends when we were giving them one of the worst kinds of instability children can have. He practically accused us of child abuse. He said that the kind of stability that counts is the stability that comes from having two parents that love and respect each other. He told us we had already failed at that endeavor and that the best we could do now is give them the stability of having two parents who were willing to put aside their personal differences and work together for the good of their children. He said that if we continued to demonstrate that we weren't willing to do that, he'd find some parents for them that were. He told DeAnna that children have an easier time growing up if their parents have already done it, that running off to become a model was fine if you were 22 and didn't have children to be responsible for. And he told her she might want to consider an Assertiveness Training class, something he certainly didn't need. Then he turned his charms back to me, told me that a marriage license was not a license to run roughshod over your wife, dressed me down a bit more about what he'd observed and picked up from her testimony."

"Wow! It sounds like even your KSL voice didn't work on this judge."

"There's more. He ordered us to take some counseling together and attend a series of parenting classes, something that is supposed to teach us how to work together for the good of the children. We've been to one of the classes already. They had a bunch of grown-ups come talk about the unkind things their parents did to each other after they divorced. It was a real eye-opener, especially to see the way it has affected them into adulthood. For the first time, I started to see what a jerk I have been. It wasn't easy to take. I've been a jerk to DeAnna and to you, but most of all, I've been a poor excuse for a parent to my daughters, all the while telling myself and everyone else that I was doing what was best for them. Basically, the judge said all the things you've been trying to tell me all along. We're still working out the details, but DeAnna is seeing the girls every other weekend and we switch off on holidays." He put his head down. "It's not as bad as I thought it would be. The girls seem happier. I should have listened to you. I want you back, Beverly."

The words that came from her mouth surprised her. "I'm not here today to try to get back together with you, Steve. The best time for a divorce is during the courtship. I'm here to close a chapter, to say goodbye to you and to the girls. It wouldn't work, Steve. If people are fighting as much as we were even before marriage, I hate to see what we would have done afterwards. I love you, Steve, and I care about you, but I just don't think we have the right ingredients for a successful marriage. I have baggage. You have baggage. We are very different in some important ways. We always seemed to have trouble communicating. Our relationship would be challenging under the best of circumstances, and we don't have the best of circumstances. We even had a fight the day we got engaged."

"You called it a discussion."

"That's because I didn't want to admit that we were having a fight. Steve, I hope you'll call me sometime and maybe we can get together and go to Chuckie Cheese on a family date. I want to be your friend. I just can't be your wife."

"That's the oldest line in the book. 'Let's just be friends.' People say that and then they never see each other again."

"I mean it. I mean the things I say, Steve. You found that out the hard way. You should know *that* about me by now, even if you don't know anything else."

"You want to be friends--like that depressed dentist that calls and cries on your shoulder?"

"Sure, why not? We've known each other a long time, you and I. Those are the best kind of friends. You can get free psychological advice, lengthy discourses on the subject of marriage, babysitting services. No laundry, though. Still, even without the laundry, it's a good deal, Steve." She set out the sandwiches. "People can love each other as friends even if they can't love each other as husband and wife. Dave was my friend long before he was my husband. There are too many husbands and wives in the world who aren't friends. We rushed into this relationship. Let's take a step backwards. Maybe you'll be more ready for a relationship after you've worked out some more of the details between you and DeAnna. I may still be around. I may not. Who knows? I'm just so glad to hear that you are going to work together for the girls. I love them, too, you know."

"And I love you."

"And a part of me will always love you, Steve."

Steve put the ring back in his pocket. "I'm not giving up. I'm going to hang onto this, in case you change . . ."

"Race you to the picnic," Davey said. Suddenly the blanket was awash with kids, a puppy, sandwiches, chips and spilled Kool-Aid.

"What happened to those three sweet, gentle little girls I used to know?" Beverly asked.

"I did," said Davey proudly.

Annalisa climbed onto Beverly's lap. "See what my mommy gave me?" She held up her hand to show off a pink plastic ring.

"That's very pretty, Annalisa, but not as pretty as you."

"Is it as pretty as me?" asked Monica.

"It's prettier than Davey, but not prettier than you." The girls giggled.

Davey picked up his dog. "Come on, Scampy. Come on, Steve. They're talking about stupid *girl* stuff. Let's go over to the swings and we'll have a man-to-man talk." Beverly watched them walk away together. Steve tousled Davey's hair.

Erica came over to Beverly. "Our mom said if we ever saw you again, we should tell you 'thanks.' I don't know for what." Beverly sat quietly for a moment getting her emotions under control.

"Well, you tell her she's welcome."

CHAPTER THIRTY-EIGHT
BEVERLY COOKS A TURKEY

Beverly stood over the frozen turkeys at the grocery store. She was talking to herself under her breath. "Okay, this is it. Which one of you is it going to be? I'm not going to be intimidated any longer." Dave was sitting in the frozen food display. *"Pick me! Pick me! Pick me!"* He moved around pretending to talk through the different turkeys. She picked up the smallest turkey she could find and put it in the cart. He followed her to the checkout. *"Okay, ignore me, Beverly. I'm dead, I know, but you could pay a little more attention now and then. You used to appreciate my sense of humor. Oh, well. I'm glad to see you're going to cook a turkey. And don't feel so bad about Steve. Your relationship had value, to you and to Steve. I know you feel that you have made very little progress in some ways, and you didn't get what you were hoping for, but there are things you've done and said that will ring true to Steve over the years, that are already starting to sink in. Those little girls have a relationship with their mother because of you. Why is it so hard for people to see the good they've done when they don't get the outcome they hoped for? Oh, you've stopped thinking about Steve for a minute. So, you're going to invite the dentist over for turkey. Go for it! I like him. You wonder if maybe you're going to marry him? What makes you think I know? One thing I can tell you—you should never have studied psychology. Now you're going to be a tool—you know, like it says in your patriarchal blessing, 'Many will be attracted to you and you'll have influence in their lives for good. You'll weather the storms of life and your life will be as a beacon light to others.' Unfortunately, that means you're going to have to hit a few more rocks before the boat comes in to port. You have to know where they all are, I guess, before you get to that beacon light part. I'm really sorry about that, Beverly. I wish I could make things easier for you, but easy is not one of HIS favorite words. You'll understand when you get here."*

As Beverly put the turkey on the counter, a warm feeling came over her and she felt like everything was going to be okay. *"I must be doing something right."*

She called Dr. Evans. "I'm cooking a turkey tomorrow. You want to come over?"

"Cooking a turkey, in July?"

"You're the only one I know who would understand."

"Oh right, Thanksgiving and all that."

"Are you coming?"

"Sure, what time?"

Beverly took Davey to Uncle Randall's earlier in the day while the turkey was cooking. He was going to have a sleepover with his cousins. When she went back into the house, she smelled the turkey cooking and managed to put other thoughts out of her head and concentrate on something else. She decided to use the nice dishes. This was a special occasion. David Evans paused at the door before he rang the bell. He could hear Beverly talking to herself. *"It's only a turkey. It's only a turkey."* He smiled and rang the bell.

Beverly invited him in. She had set a beautiful table for two.

"Where's Davey? Isn't he part of this celebration?"

"Oh, I arranged for him to spend the night with his cousins."

"Anything I can do to help?"

"No, have a seat. Dinner's almost ready. He sat down. He was a little confused. It looked like a romantic dinner for two, she had gotten rid of her son for the day . . . And yet when he had called her recently, she had been going out with Steve.

Midway through the meal, he decided to ask. "Beverly, now that you've explained to me your entire Thanksgiving history and your trips to Disneyland, Disney World and Yellowstone Park, can I ask you a personal question? Are you still getting married? Jean told me that you and Steve had broken up, but then when I called, I thought it sounded like you were back together again. I mean, this looks like a romantic dinner, and I don't want to assume anything if I'm just here to help you celebrate that you were able to cook a turkey, and as your dentist, to make sure that you brush and floss after your meal."

"No, I'm not getting married. It's a long story. Someday maybe I'll tell you all about it. I'm reasonably available. I've got a dog now, so a husband is optional."

"As long as you've got someone to bark at you."

"If you think this looks like a romantic dinner, I say, 'go for it.'"

After dinner, Beverly brought out dessert. "This is my own creation. I call it 'dental floss a la mode.'" David looked at the plate. Sure enough, there was a thin string of dental floss under the ice cream.

"You're a crazy woman."

"I know, but I cooked a turkey."

After they had finished their ice cream, Beverly began to clear the table.

David Evans stopped her. "Wait! Don't take my plate. I found the wishbone. You can't throw it away. Sit down."

"All right! Let's make a wish!" Beverly pulled on one side of the wishbone. David Evans pulled on the other. Nothing happened. They pulled harder but the wishbone would not break.

"I just realized something. It's supposed to sit and dry out, isn't it?"

"Yes, it doesn't matter how much you want to make a wish if the wishbone isn't ready."

"Sometimes you just have to wait until the time is right." He winked at her. "Beverly, will you save this wishbone for me and call me when it's ready?"

"Why don't *you* take it home and call *me* when it's ready, Dr. Evans."

"Knock off the 'Dr. Evans.' Call me David."

"Okay—David."

ABOUT THE AUTHOR

Susan grew up in Salt Lake City, Utah. As a member of The Church of Jesus Christ of Latter-day Saints, she is part of the Mormon community about which she writes. She has attended Utah State University and the University of Utah and also holds an honorary degree from the School of Hard Knocks.

She's a member of the American Association for Therapeutic Humor, the Hawaii Island Writers Association and the Society of Children's Bookwriters and Illustrators. A right-brain person, she always has several creative projects going simultaneously and on and off works at left-brain jobs to support her creative habits.

Widowed in her twenties, she followed the advice "write about what you know." She lives in Hawaii with her husband, Thom, a professor at the University of Hawaii-Hilo, also previously widowed. She has one son, one stepdaughter and four stepsons.

an excerpt from

BROTHERLY LOVE
(a prequel to Unfinished Business)

Steve hadn't planned on falling in love with his Family Home Evening sister, Beverly, while attending Utah State University. He was supposed to be waiting for his high school sweetheart to come home from her mission so they could get married. How could he tell her he was in love with someone else?

Steve cringed. He had forgotten to get a Christmas gift for DeAnna's parents, President and Sister Matthews. He had been too busy meeting Beverly's family and spending time with her. He was still feeling guilty for his little white lie to his parents--skiing in Salt Lake with some friends. "We did go skiing," he placated his conscience. He had sent DeAnna some Cache Valley Cheese--the Deluxe Assortment--and some "missionary appropriate" tapes of the Mormon Tabernacle Choir. What more did they want? So maybe it wasn't as personal a gift as he'd given her in the past, but . . . Mabel Matthews broke into his thoughts.

"Come downstairs, Steve. I was going to keep this a secret, but I just *have* to show you." She fluttered off down the stairs. Steve dutifully followed her down to the family room, which was almost completely covered by a queen-size quilt, still in the frames, laid out in all its splendor. In the middle of the quilt was the Logan Temple. It looked like Sister Matthews had pieced it together, painstakingly, brick by brick, every window, every turret. Steve knew nothing about quilting, but even he could see that this was a masterpiece and that hours upon hours of Sister Matthews' nervous energy had been spent on it. "Some of the sisters thought I should enter it in the church-wide quilting contest. I have to admit I was tempted, but I told them, 'It will be reward enough for me to see it on display at my daughter's wedding.'"

It was snowing when Steve returned home. He got a snow shovel and started to clear the walks. He threw the snow with greater gusto than usual, venting his frustration. His father pulled into the driveway. "Thanks son. It really piles up fast, doesn't it?"

"It's pretty deep, all right," said Steve. When he went in, his mother fixed him some hot chocolate and he sat down in front of the fireplace.

"Can I get you a quilt?"

Steve snarled. "No, I don't want a QUILT!!"

an excerpt from

PUSH ON

(part 3 in a series of 4)

Beverly is back, torn between two widowers—Dr. David Evans, the man she has been dating for two years, and the new man in her life, Bob Buchmiller.

Beverly and Bob walked out of the Delta Center with the rest of the crowd exiting from the hockey game. "Beverly. I like you a lot. I'd like to spend some time with you again tomorrow night, if y'all can fit me into your schedule."

"We *all* is right. I stood up another man to go out with you tonight."

"Does he know he's got competition?"

"He does now. He was real bummed out having to stay with a babysitter."

"Ya mean the little fella. I thought you meant the other guy you're dating. So what does he have to offer you that I don't have?"

"So Carolyn has filled you in on my life?"

"I'm gonna cut to the chase. Gotta head back to Texas soon. I like you." He reached out and took her arm and put it through his. "Let's face it, we're not kids. I know you're involved with someone else, and you're right, it's really none of my business. I just don't want to be doing any claim jumping."

"If I was committed to someone else in the way you're asking, I wouldn't be out with you tonight, would I?"

"That's all you're going to tell me?"

David Evans sat in his car on State Street waiting for the light to change. The symphony had been wonderful. He was on a date with a woman most men would give their eye teeth for, and all he could think of was coming up with a good excuse to take her home early and get the date over with. He was signaling to turn right, but there were too many people crossing in front of the car for him to be able to make the turn.

"I can't believe you let all those people go in front of you, David. What are you waiting for, an engraved invitation? Turn, already! Just nose out there and the people will get out of the way. *Oh, look!* Isn't that your little friend, Beverly? *Ooooh!* Look at that man on her arm!" Alexa leaned over and honked the horn. Beverly looked in the direction of the horn, and her face went white. It was David! The woman waved at her from the passenger seat—that obnoxious drop-dead gorgeous woman from the symphony guild. David turned the corner and was gone.

"Beverly, we can cross now. Are you all right? You seem a little distracted."

"I guess I might as well tell you. You were asking me about the man I've been dating, a horn honks, I look up, and it was him—and he was with *that woman.*"

"Well, good. Then he won't mind if I steal you away to Texas."

"Look Bob, you can't just rustle me up like some stray cow without a brand! This is not that simple. Nothing is ever simple. Why isn't anything ever simple?"

an excerpt from

ARE WE THERE YET?

(part 4 in a series of 4)

Beverly is now remarried and is adjusting to her new life and trying her hand at being a stepmother to Stephanie, 21, and Justin, 17.

"Well, Elder Shane Rainer, if you've got your heart set on this Stephanie you've got to have a plan. You can't go back home, the typical returned missionary looking to get married, acting all lovestruck—especially not with *this* girl. She's expecting that. You've got to turn the tables on her. All these years she's been your *friend* while you pined away for her. Give her a dose of her own medicine."

Shane pulled a swimsuit off the rack. "I've been needing a new swimsuit. How do you think this color will look next to my pasty-white-haven't-seen-the-sun-in-two-years skin? You going to that Young Adult party coming up at that waterslide place?"

"I might."

"Then bring your sunglasses. I've got to get out in the sun again sometime. You need a ride? I can fit quite a few people in the Explorer."

"So I've noticed. Have you been called as Ward Chauffeur or something? Maybe you and I could go alone, without a bunch of other kids—so I can hear about your mission. I *am* the one who wrote you letters and kept up with you."

"You're right. You've been such a great *friend*, Steph. We'll just let the rest of them find another way to the party."

"Steph, what's the matter?"

"You talked about your mission all the way there and all the way back."

"We needed to clear up the misconception of us out tracting from igloo to igloo by dog sled. I thought that's why you wanted to go together—to hear about my mission."

"So how did you like my new bathing suit? I bought it special for today."

"To tell you the truth, if you want my brotherly opinion, I thought it was a little bit skimpy for a nice Mormon girl."

"Well what if I *don't* want your stupid *brotherly opinion?*"

"You know how they say to sing hymns to ward off unclean thoughts? You had an entire male chorus going by the wave pool. I swear I heard them singing 'High on a Mountain Top' in harmony. Do you want a bunch of guys paying attention to you because of some sexy bathing suit and not even knowing what a sweet spirit you have? Has your dad seen that one? I'm surprised he let you out of the house."

"*Sweet spirit?* You called me a *sweet spirit!* That's it! No, my dad hasn't seen it! I bought it to get *your* attention, if you must know! What does it take? All you can talk about is your mission. All the way home—'Elder Kelsey this' and 'Elder Kelsey that!' Who is this Elder Kelsey anyway?"

"He's a genius."

an excerpt from

PACKING FOR HEAVEN

Life has been good to Toni Cirroni. She has a beautiful big family, the home of her dreams, they own a successful restaurant. Suddenly everything is changed with an illness that turns their lives and their finances upside-down. As Corina battles her illness, her mother fights a battle with her pride.

Weakened from her latest round of chemotherapy, Corina was not able to participate in serving food at the soup kitchen, but she had been so sad at the prospect of not going that they had found a way.

The soup kitchen was west of town, near Pioneer Park, near the freeway—not in a very nice area of town, but that was to be expected. Tastefully dressed, Toni stood out like the proverbial sore thumb against the backdrop of shabbily-dressed people at the shelter. Alex had mentioned to her that she might be a touch over-dressed for the occasion but she could not take the chance that the homeless would think she was one of them. He had changed, almost overnight, as if all the things that had mattered to him once no longer mattered. Sure, nothing could mean more than maintaining their daughter's health and getting her the treatment she needed, but Toni was hopeful that this could be accomplished without their entire lifestyle changing. She checked again on Corina, who was lying down on a camp cot in the corner. Thank you, Mom. I wish I could help. Toni went back to her spot in the food line, next to her husband.

"Alex, I'm not sure she should be here."

"You heard the doctors. If it lifts her spirits, it's good for her."

"How about my spirits?"

"You gotta lift those yourself." He scooped a large helping of mashed potatoes onto a waiting plate. "Spuds?" he asked the next fellow. The man brightened.

"Are you from Idaho? I'm from Idaho." Toni followed with a ladle of gravy. "Think of it this way," Alex said to her. "You didn't have to cook today. Look at the kids. They're enjoying themselves."

"Okay, I'll try to have fun." Toni grimaced.

"Mr. Dwyer was impressed that we were coming down here today."

"How about his son, the little corporate worm? Does he come down here and plop mashed potatoes onto plates?"

"He should!" Alex said enthusiastically.

"Why are you in such a good mood today?"

"It's Thanksgiving, and I'm thankful."

"For what? We're in financial distress. Our daughter may be dying. Why are you so confounded cheerful? What are you so thankful for?"

"I'm thankful for today, okay? I'm thankful that now, here and now, we are all together and doing something meaningful. Come on, Toni. We have a lot to be thankful for. It's all in your point of view. Is the glass half full or is the glass half empty?"

"Oh, the glass is full, all right. The question is--full of what?"

an excerpt from

HEAVEN HELP US!

*Karen Donaldson, the woman who can derail any lesson, comes into money,
livening things up in the ward and turning the bishop's life upside-down.*

"Now tonight Sister Potter is going to share some much-needed information for
our 'Homemakers' Hints' and then we will divide up for the classes and at 8:30
we'll go into the cultural hall for refreshments."

Sister Potter brandished a women's magazine. "I was reading an article that I
thought should be brought to the attention of the ladies of the ward, and Olive was
good enough to give me a couple of minutes. It's not healthful to eat raw eggs
because they can cause food poisoning. Any kind of uncooked batter with raw eggs
in it is not healthful—cake batters, cookie doughs—and Heaven knows how much
some children like to lick the bowl or the beaters and . . . "

Karen Donaldson spoke up. "And when all the kids are grown, you can have
the bowl and beaters all to yourself." A couple of sisters snickered.

Sister Potter continued. "I'm sure you've enjoyed that pleasure, Karen, now
that your children are older, but now that you understand that it's a dangerous
practice . . ."

Karen countered. "So is skydiving, but it's a risk some people are willin' to
take. Why did you know that at Smith's they stock Mrs. Field's Cookie Dough that
you can bake yourself, only a couple of times I've bought some and none of it even
got cooked."

Sister Potter pursed her lips. "It's not intended to be eaten raw. We should not
be promoting what could be a very dangerous, even life-threatening, practice,
Karen."

"Oh, I buy Mrs. Field's Cookies cooked, too. You bet! They're the best! But
there ain't nothin' so comfortin' when you're having a bad day as a good old chunk
of cookie dough. What about that ice cream that's got cookie dough in it? They
don't expect you to be fishin' 'em out and cookin' those little pieces of cookie
dough, do they? If it comes in ice cream, I don't rightly see how ya could. They
sell it that way, so it must be okay."

"The article is very clear that this is not something to trifle with."

Karen responded. "Oh yeah, there's lots of good stuff in those ladies' maga-
zines. Of course, I don't leave Good Housekeeping lying around my house, on
account of it looks a little hypocritical, being as how housework ain't exactly my
cup of cocoa, but it was in one of them I read about how if you want your toilet to be
cleaned without a lot of scrubbin' to just throw in a couple of those denture-cleanin'
tablets, so I bought some, and I'm tellin' ya, that works pretty good—got the old
porcelain shining just like Grandma's dentures, so you might be right about the
cookie dough, Sister Potter, but even if you are, it's a chance I'm willin' to take. In
fact, I think that's the way I want to go. I could die with a smile on my face, and all
I ask is that they bury me with a chocolate chip stuck in the corner of my mouth."

Sister Potter got off her final words, which she was unsure if anyone heard over the
laughter, and sat down, humiliated.

GROUP THERAPY

The story of several divorced ladies from the same stake, who have created an unofficial support group trying to survive the failure of their marriages.

"Okay, it's like this. We've been divorced now for almost two years. I've been out with a few other women, and, to be frank, none of them hold a candle to Maureen."

"So why did you leave her?"

"We just kind of grew apart over the years. Lately, I've come to realize that it was mostly my fault. I was always working, working out—doing something that excluded her. When she'd try to get me to spend time with her, I'd call her a nag. I wasn't the most sensitive husband around. But I've changed. I want her back, but she won't give me another chance, so I did something a little underhanded. I went on-line, because the kids told me she's been spending a lot of time on the computer talking to people who are interested in her hobbies. Anyway, I created this guy, his screen name is 'SKIUTAH77' and looked her up, pretending to be interested in cross-country skiing. I'm a downhill man, myself, but Maureen always wanted to go cross-country skiing."

"Did you ever take her?"

"Didn't you hear me? I said I was a downhill man. Anyway, over the last few months, I've been talking to her on-line, trying to find out what I can do to get her back. It took awhile—I had to get her to trust me—but she eventually started to open up to me about her marriage—our marriage—and things from her point of view. Because I wasn't me, I couldn't defend myself. I just had to be sympathetic and tell her how I couldn't believe any man would take her for granted. I've done such a good job of being sensitive, that she wants to meet me. We've been talking for about five months now. I've made a lot of progress. She really thinks I'm a sensitive nice guy. I told her I was about 6 feet tall with light brown hair, like you."

"Let me get this straight, you've spent five months lying to the woman to get her to trust you? Now you want to mix me up in it? I don't think so, Dan. This isn't like in high school when you hired me to write prom invitations for you."

"Yeah, maybe if you'd used some of that ability to get yourself some dates you wouldn't be over thirty and still single." Dan continued. "I've kept printouts of almost all of our e-mails so you can study up. Anyway, I need you to meet her, be 'SKIUTAH77' for a couple of dates and then tell her you're getting back together with an old girlfriend, basically dump her, but in a nice way, because you are a sensitive nice guy, after all."

"I am."

"That's the spirit! Then I'll come along behind, after you've dumped her, give her a shoulder to cry on, do all that sensitive stuff, and we're back together."

"No, I mean, I *am* a sensitive nice guy. And you're a selfish jerk, even more than you were in high school."

"Can you study up, pretend you like to go cross-country skiing?"

"I *do* like cross-country skiing."

"Even better! Then you'll do it?"